The Girls From Alcyone

by Cary Caffrey

This novel is a work of fiction created by the author. All characters, events and organizations portrayed in this novel are works of the author's imagination.

Cover art by Zoedev Studios
Published by Tealy Books, NB, Canada
All rights reserved.
ISBN: 978-1-105-33727-7

For Gisele, for all the reading and listening (and the listening, and the reading…). With thanks to Pete, Mickie, Flood, Tiffinie, Scott, Kelly, Michael, Bob, Andy and Stef. You all get a cookie.

Prologue
Planet Earth

March 2, 2339

The wet cloak hung heavy over Dr. Lisa Garrett's shoulders. The wide hood kept slipping low over her face so she had to keep lifting it to see where she was going. She cursed as her foot found another deep puddle. Though cumbersome and stifling, the cloak at least gave her some protection from the torrential rains that always fell on Earth these days.

She might have passed unnoticed through the narrow and crowded alley were it not for the three hired bodyguards who shadowed her. The men stayed close to her side studying all passersby, shooting warning looks at anyone who ventured near their ward. They kept their sidearms in plain sight, worn on clips at their hips in easy reach of their hands. There could be no mistaking their intent.

Lisa knew the streets of Earth were no place for a young man or woman to be walking alone, but she felt ridiculous with the hired thugs traipsing after her. She couldn't wait to get back to Alcyone and the Academy where she'd no longer need the service. As much as she detested Earth, she had insisted on coming. Her work for the Kimura Corporation, the small but prestigious mercenary company, was at a critical juncture and she couldn't trust anyone to negotiate the meeting on her behalf. She needed this girl too much.

Kimura hadn't wanted her to make the trip from Alcyone. On Earth, she'd be exposed to attacks from rival corporations—either from those who wished to steal her as an asset or kill her as a threat. While the dangers were real, she was probably at greater risk of becoming the victim of a simple random mugging.

The heavy steel gate of the habitat groaned opened for her as she approached; the security system having already logged her as an expected guest. Inside, the small lobby was decorated in typical Earth fashion—garbage and graffiti, and smelling faintly of urine. She frowned at the puddled floor, almost as wet as the street outside and fed by a perpetually dripping ceiling.

Lisa removed her hood. The constant humidity was doing a number on her hair. She ran her hands self-consciously through her damp chestnut curls. At twenty-five, she was much younger than usual for someone holding Ph.D.s in Neurology, Genetics and Biomechanics. Her soft, curved face and large hazel eyes belied a fiercely competitive nature and a sharp, analytical mind.

Lisa knocked on the armored door of the small, cube-shaped apartment while her bodyguards waited at a discreet distance. "What a shit-hole," she muttered to herself, looking around at the crumbling hallway.

As the door opened, a middle-aged couple greeted her, but Lisa's eyes were drawn to the young girl standing just behind her parents. She recognized Sigrid instantly. Nine years old, with long blond hair, she was very small for her age. The girl was just a tiny, timid thing, but she was perfect—a perfect physical specimen, an ideal, and a very rare, genetic match for her program.

Finding her had not been easy. It was only her access to Kimura's vast resources that had enabled her to locate the girl. Now she just needed to persuade the parents to let her take their child away, halfway across the galaxy. Probably for the rest of her life. At least the family's current financial predicament was no secret. It was hardly an uncommon problem, but such information could prove to be important—and something she could use.

"Mr. and Mrs. Novak," Lisa said, extending her hand. "I'm so very pleased to meet you."

Mrs. Novak took her hand nervously. "Dr. Garrett...yes. Sigrid, come say hello to the Doctor."

The woman urged her daughter forward. Lisa noticed that the woman pronounced the girl's name *Seegrid*, rather than *Zigrid*. She made a mental note.

"Call me Lisa." She bent low, extending her hand to the small girl who took it politely.

Mrs. Novak motioned her inside. "Come in—please."

They ushered Lisa into a tiny living room where she took the proffered chair, while the Novaks and their daughter settled on the small sofa facing her. The apartment was typical of the identical habitat units found in any city on Earth; small and cramped, but efficient. The modular structures could be stacked on top of one another as needed. The cramped confines might be called intimate by some—mostly by the corporations who sold them—but Lisa found them stifling.

"Lovely place," she observed.

"Oh, thank you so much. It's not much, of course..."

Lisa smoothed the pleats of her skirt. She knew how sensitive these meetings were, and how easily things could swing either way. Everything hinged on what she had to say next, and she chose her words carefully. "I can't tell you how happy I am that you agreed to this meeting, Mr. and Mrs. Novak. I know Kimura has already informed you they were considering Sigrid for the Academy—"

"It does sound exciting!" the woman blurted.

Lisa cocked an eyebrow, noting the woman's agitated state—or was it anticipation?

"I want you to know that Sigrid is very important to us," Lisa told them. "Many girls are considered for the program, but few are chosen. But in your daughter's case..." Lisa's eyes fell to the small girl sitting between her parents. "I'm very pleased to say that she does qualify. We would very much like to have Sigrid come and stay with us—if you'll allow it."

The parents breathed a relieved sigh, clutching each other's hands. Definitely a good sign—the family was clearly more desperate than she'd thought.

"We're so relieved—and so happy for Sigrid!" Mrs. Novak said. "She's looking forward to the Academy—I know it. There's...just one thing..."

Lisa braced for the question—the question that always came.

"We were just wondering...we're very grateful, of course—we know how reputable Kimura is, but this program...what exactly is it you're going to do to Sigrid?"

Lisa's answer was well-rehearsed, and she leaned forward with a warm smile. "Sigrid will receive the very best education and training from Kimura. I can promise you there's nothing like this program anywhere on Earth. You're very lucky, Mr. and Mrs. Novak. Sigrid is a very special girl. She's been blessed with a unique gift—one not found in millions of other girls."

"A gift?"

Lisa nodded and her smile widened. "Yes. And I will show her how to use that gift."

Before Mrs. Novak could enquire further, Lisa took a data-pad from her purse and unfolded it, nudging it across the coffee table to the Novaks. On it was displayed the contract with the very extravagant sum Kimura would forward to the Novaks' accounts. "I believe this will be more than adequate to take care of your entire family's financial...situation."

Discussing the finances always felt perverse to Lisa. Fortunately, Mr. Novak's eyes bulged at the amount displayed on the pad. He pressed his thumb to the screen eagerly.

Mrs. Novak made a show of at least pretending to read the contract before signing. "The program does sound intriguing. I'm sure if Mr. Novak wasn't...well, if Peter hadn't had such bad luck with the markets..."

Lisa grimaced. She never understood their need to explain their financial difficulties.

Mrs. Novak sniffed. "No one could have foreseen the downturn in commodities. Still, I'm certain we would have wanted Sigrid in the program, regardless. We always suspected she was gifted. Isn't that right, darling?"

Mrs. Novak nudged her husband whose eyes remained fixed on the money displayed on the pad. He nodded, grunting assent.

Lisa retrieved the pad and folded it back into her purse. "Of course."

"And with Sigrid's birth-debt..." Mrs. Novak wrung her hands together. "Well, you know..."

Lisa knew all too well. Birth-debts were the increasingly popular practice that allowed debt-ridden families to defer their burdens to their unborn children. Girls like Sigrid were often born into staggering seven-figure debts. For the Novaks, selling their daughter's life contract to Kimura would rid the family of generations of financial ruin. It would take Sigrid most of her life to work off that debt as an indentured laborer for Kimura.

"Yes, of course," Lisa said, with practiced sympathy. "A tremendous burden on a young girl." Lisa believed in her heart that Sigrid would be better off with her than with these people—better off on Alcyone than on this crowded, dirty and crime-infested planet. The only people left on Earth were the people who couldn't afford to leave.

She reached across the table and took the little girl's hand in her own. "You and I are going to have a tremendous adventure. Have you ever heard of Alcyone?" The girl shook her head. "It's a beautiful planet, and it's full of girls just like you." Lisa smiled as she watched the girl's eyes light up. The girls always responded well to that. "There will be fields and mountains and grass, and lots of other girls to play with. Would you like to come with me and meet them all? I'm sure they'll love you so much."

Sigrid nodded vigorously, but Lisa could feel how nervous she was as the girl's tiny hand tightened in her own.

"Come then."

She led the girl to the door. Her parents already had her bags packed.

Chapter 1
Kimura Academy for Girls

February 17, 2341

Sigrid felt herself being prodded awake. Peeling back the covers, she stifled a groan It couldn't possibly be morning—she'd only just closed her eyes. The darkness still lurked outside and the ceiling lights of the dormitory glared painfully bright. All around her the thirty-one other girls of the Kimura Academy were struggling to rise from their bunks, still exhausted and sore from the previous day's activities.

"Wake up, sleepyhead."

Shielding her eyes with a hand, Sigrid looked up at the eleven-year-old girl standing over her. Suko was already up and dressed, and tying her long black hair into a ponytail with a bright red strip of cloth.

Suko smiled down at Sigrid and reached out a hand to help her up. "Time to get up."

"No!" Sigrid pulled the blanket back up over her head. "Go away."

"Come on. You'll miss breakfast," Suko said, her thick Kiwi accent making breakfast sound more like *brickfist.*

"I don't care. I was dreaming." *Of sleep,* she realized.

Suko pulled at the blanket, but Sigrid held fast, curling up even tighter in the sheets. "You'll get in trouble—*again.*"

"Traitor!" Sigrid said, throwing her pillow at Suko.

Sigrid felt a pang of guilt for yelling at her friend. It wasn't Suko's fault—Suko was her best friend, but right now...right now, she just needed to rest. Just for a few more minutes...

Sigrid's whole body ached. Her muscles were stiff and twisted in painful knots. She felt positive they must be trying to kill her. They never let her sleep, at least never enough. Every minute of every day consisted of classes, lessons, and hours of brutal physical training. The physical training was the worst. The girls were drilled endlessly in calisthenics, and the martial arts classes seemed to center around Sigrid being punched repeatedly. Sigrid found herself completely intimidated—the other girls were so much bigger and stronger than her. She was rapidly becoming *exceptional* at being knocked down, always to the delight of the other girls.

Even stranger were her sessions with Dr. Garrett; sometimes they'd just talk; other times the doctor would poke and prod her with strange devices. Sigrid didn't understand what the weekly sessions were for, and Dr. Garrett would just say, "This is to make you better," and then she'd stick her with something again.

"UP!"

Without warning, the sheets were torn from her bed. Felix Rosa, her instructor, glared down at her, eyes narrowed in disapproval. He took care of all their training, watched over them at their studies, and dealt out punishment and discipline when needed; which was often the case, especially where Sigrid was concerned. As hard as she tried, she could never keep up or get anything right.

Decades of disciplined training had kept him so lean and hard-muscled that he appeared to be chiseled from stone. He wasn't always horrible. He was actually often pleasant and nice to her, but right now, she hated him.

"You slow the progress of the entire group, young one," he scolded. "Do you think everyone will appreciate two extra laps around the track in the rain today because of you?"

No; that would only mean more beatings from the other girls. Even as he spoke, they stood by their bunks, regarding her with raw contempt.

"Come on, it won't be so bad," Suko said. She reached out a hand and yanked Sigrid out of bed.

Sigrid was a little in awe of Suko. She had such an easy grasp of things. She excelled in all their classes, especially math where Sigrid felt completely hopeless, and she never seemed to tire or falter during the brutal physical activities that made up much of their days. She was tall for her age, at least three inches taller than Sigrid, and very pretty. And all the girls liked her—something Sigrid couldn't even dream of.

"Less talking, more attention," Rosa said, pointing to the spots at the foot of the bed where he expected the girls to be standing. "All of you, two minutes to dress, then outside."

Sigrid groaned and her shoulders slumped. It was the same instruction every morning. The girls would run ten full circuits of the academy field, return to the dormitory, bathe, dress and be ready for a modest breakfast before the hours of lessons began. Tardiness and lack of cleanliness were not tolerated and always punished.

Sigrid couldn't believe she'd ever been excited about attending the Academy. It had all sounded so incredible back then—a trip in space, new friends, an entire new planet to explore. Now, Sigrid only wanted to be home in her own bed, to see her mother and father again. But that wasn't going to happen. The Kimura Corporation owned her and it was her duty to serve them, doing their bidding until her family's debt was repaid in full. The next years of her life would be much the same: lessons, training, *beatings,* more running and more lessons.

Sigrid had barely finished tying her bootlaces, still struggling to pull up her pants, when Suko pulled her by the hand. With Sigrid firmly in tow, Suko trailed the other girls heading for the training grounds outside.

A blast of rain greeted Sigrid as she left the dorm. The wet wind sent a chill through her, jarring her awake as it whipped at her hair and face.

"Nice day for it," Suko kidded.

Sigrid snorted a laugh. As miserable as she felt, Suko was always able to lighten her mood, and side by side, the two girls started off on their morning run.

The rain threatened to turn to sleet, or even snow, in the late winter cold, making the muddy ground icy and slick. Sigrid's legs felt weak and her shoes skidded in the slush. She feared she might fall and muddy herself—that would be just great—but Suko steadied her.

The training area was in the center of a large courtyard, framed by the four main buildings that made up the Academy. The buildings were all two-story structures with tiled, pointed roofs, connected by a six-meter-high wall that wound its way around the entire perimeter. Outside the walls, the high, snowcapped peaks of the Northern Mountains loomed on all sides. There were no roads leading to the Academy; the only way in and out was by air.

Sigrid heard one of the instructors shout, "Move it, ladies," as she forced one tired foot in front of the other.

"Come on, you'll feel better after *brekkie*," Suko said, treating Sigrid to an encouraging smile.

The other girls lapped Sigrid—some more than once—as she hobbled along unsteadily. By the time she reached the dormitory she was soaked and frozen, her lips blue. The other girls were already bathed and eating—all except Suko, who stayed with her until she was washed and dressed.

She was late for breakfast, of course, and extra lessons were assigned to the entire class as punishment. Sigrid knew her *real punishment* would come later, delivered by the other girls. She didn't know what form it would take, but her classmates would make her pay, just as they always did. She could see them already sizing her up, figuring out how best to make their feelings known.

Her answer came that night. She had just finished brushing her teeth and was making her way back to her bed when one of the girls thrust out a foot to trip her. Another girl pushed her roughly from behind sending Sigrid tumbling to the floor, scattering her towel and toiletries. The other girls gathered in a crowd, laughing at her.

Sara stood over her. Her thin brown hair hung loose over her face, and she pulled it back behind her ears as she sneered at Sigrid. "Why is it that *you're* the slowest, but *we* always get punished?"

Sigrid knew there was no right answer—a sarcastic answer came to her lips, but she didn't have the courage to utter the words. Instead, Sigrid ignored her and began gathering up her dropped items. Sara kicked them away and pushed her back down.

"Come on. Get up," Sara said, challenging her.

Sigrid was too weary to fight back. The outcome seemed inevitable, Sara would pummel her, as she always did. Sigrid just wanted them to go away. She hated the school and she hated them. She wanted to go home. Her sudden burst of tears took her by surprise, only deepening her embarrassment and humiliation.

"Crybaby," Sara spat. She went to kick her again, but she suddenly found herself sprawling as Suko pushed her from behind.

Sara leapt to her feet and spun around, charging back, but Suko stepped forward, placing herself between Sigrid and the other girls. There was a warning tone in her voice when she said, "Leave her alone!"

"Why do you always stand up for her?"

Suko didn't answer; her fists were clenched and her chest rose and fell quickly. Someone tried to grab her arms, but she elbowed the girl in the stomach, then punched another of Sigrid's tormentors in the face. Blood flowed freely from the girl's broken nose as she ran away crying and cursing.

The other girls backed away, eyeing the trail of blood between the bunks. Suko gave them as menacing a look as her eleven-year-old body could muster. She helped Sigrid up from the ground and picked up the towel, soap and toothbrush from where they lay scattered.

"Thanks," Sigrid said. She was suddenly very aware of the tears on her face and she tried to wipe them away quickly, as if that would hide them.

"Bunch of fuckwits, all of them," Suko said as she led Sigrid back to her bed. "I don't know what their problem is."

"Me," Sigrid said with a little shrug.

Suko laughed and hugged her. "You have to fight back. She's just a bully. They all are."

"I know." Sigrid blew her nose loudly in her sleeve and sniffed. "But there are a lot of them."

"Yeah, but they'll always have to go through me."

Chapter 2
Bullies

From The Journal of Dr. Lisa Garrett

July 11, 2343

RE: Project Andraste
Dear Hitomi-san,
I write to you, even though I know, as always, that these letters won't get to you until after the fact.

I am pleased to report that all the girls are responding well to the Genetic Recombinant, with no signs of ill effects and no signs of rejection. Please inform Dr. Wolsey of that for me—I'm sure we'd both enjoy seeing the man eat a little crow for once. It seems clear now that we were correct in our selection of the subjects, all of whom show a similar genetic predisposition to the Recombinant. We have already monitored a tremendous increase in aptitude, intelligence, strength and reaction time. Felix seems to have his hands full. Thank you for that recommendation by the way. The man is a godsend and I'm not sure where I'd be without him.

We are still years away from introducing any of the bionics or the Control Module, but I'm pleased to say that the foundation is being laid.

I just wish you were here to see what we've accomplished. You deserve as much credit as anyone in this.

Yours truly,
Lisa

* * *

Sigrid felt completely self-conscious and was having trouble maintaining her focus. She couldn't stop thinking of the thirty girls, all watching her, waiting for her to fail. She really needed to focus more on the girl standing across the mat from her.

The girls sat in a large circle on the padded floor of the gymnasium. They were all dressed in the same *judogi*—the loose, belted coats and trousers—that Rosa had them wear for their martial arts classes. Rosa's belt was black, although the girls all wore belts of different colors and grades. Months of relentless training and instruction still found Sigrid stuck at yellow. Despite Suko's extra help and tutoring, Sigrid knew the other girls were leaving her behind.

Today they were studying an ancient form of Jujitsu, and it was Sigrid's turn on the mat. Her opponent was a much taller girl named Mei. Sigrid liked her well enough, although she'd like her a whole lot more if Mei would stop beating her with the wooden katana she held.

"This is Jujitsu, Ms. Novak, not arm-wrestling," Rosa chided. "You must use your opponent's force *against* her."

Sigrid frowned—he could say the same thing over and over, but it wasn't helping. Sigrid was unarmed while the other girl had a sword. She couldn't take her eyes off the thing, dreading yet another walloping.

"You must *draw* her into your sphere of defense."

Sigrid thought Mei was doing a pretty good job in her sphere... "But—"

"Again!" Rosa said, clapping his hands as he backed away from the center of the mat.

Sigrid failed to evade the first attack and paid for it with a bloodied lip. One of her teeth felt loose, as well. She touched the back of her hand to her swollen mouth and it came back red. Her opponent took some pleasure in this and gave her a menacing smile before launching another swing at Sigrid's face.

The speed of the attack took Sigrid by surprise—but she somehow managed to parry the thrust this time, lashing out with her own leg and kicking Mei in the sternum. Mei stumbled backward, but came rushing back at Sigrid with a wild over-the-shoulder chop. Sigrid sidestepped the swing and clamped down hard on Mei's wrist, twisting as hard as she could. The *bokken* fell to the ground.

Mei looked completely surprised. Clearly annoyed, the older girl grabbed at Sigrid's wrist, but Sigrid brought her hand, palm-up, twisting and thrusting down, breaking the grip before landing a solid blow to Mei's chin. Even Sigrid gasped, surprised at her own skillful execution of the move. *I'm winning!* she realized. Her heart beat faster; she'd never beaten anyone—ever!

Sigrid grabbed for the girl's collar and kicked hard at her ankles. She pushed with all her strength, determined to knock her down, but Mei was far bigger and stronger. Sigrid's clumsy attempt at brute force failed and Mei pushed her backwards, planting her foot hard in her stomach. The attack sent Sigrid tumbling onto her rear, winded.

Mei fell upon her instantly. Thoughts of a *victory* were quickly dashed as Sigrid tried desperately to block the fists that flew at her face. Mei landed several blows, bruising her further and bloodying her nose.

Then Suko surprised all of them. She leapt up and grabbed Mei by the collar, hauling her off Sigrid; who was now completely shocked as well as shaken—the girls were *never* to interfere with another match.

"Ms. Tansho!" Rosa bellowed. All the girls froze. "This is not your fight."

"But she was—"

"Ten laps around the compound."

After a quick, worried look to Sigrid, Suko bowed to Rosa and darted off to do her laps. The other girls grew quickly silent, fearful that Rosa might send them out to run more laps as well.

Rosa clapped his hands and gestured for the girls to continue. Sigrid couldn't believe what Suko had just done for her—she fretted her friend would get in terrible trouble. She was still watching Suko jog away when Mei charged and flattened her with a diving tackle. Mei seemed in no hurry to get off her, either, as she lay on top of her, crushing her chest.

"You have no focus, young one," Rosa barked. "Ten laps for you, so that you may think about your failure."

Sigrid groaned and tried to pull herself out from under the older girl who was making things as difficult as possible. She heard a pleased snicker from Sara.

Mercifully, Rosa also heard it. "And you may join her as well, Ms. Skarsden, since you find this so amusing. Ten laps—*go*!" Sara mouthed several curses, but stood and bowed to Rosa before slinking off to join Suko and Sigrid on their run of shame. "All of you—you *must* learn that when one of you falters, you all falter. Ten laps each."

The girls sat stunned for a moment.

Rosa clapped his hands so loudly it sounded like he'd fired a shot. "Go!"

The girls moved slowly to their feet, bowed and skulked off, none of them daring to groan or complain.

Sara caught up to Sigrid easily, and slowed, glaring at her. Sigrid saw the hate in her eyes; she knew Sara was plotting something particularly foul.

Sigrid didn't expect it to come so soon, though, as someone pushed her hard from behind. She almost caught her footing, but a loose rock was her undoing and she stumbled sideways. Sara clinched it by giving Sigrid an extra shove and she skidded hard to the ground, face first, skinning her knees and the palms of her hands. The cut on her lip reopened and she tasted blood and dirt.

As Sigrid lay there, she thought the ground felt oddly comfortable. If only she could just lie there for a moment. She rolled onto her back and found herself staring up at Suko; her head blocked out the sun, creating a halo around her black hair and ponytail.

"I don't think Sara likes me very much," Sigrid said, staring up at her friend.

Suko grabbed her hand and yanked her up. "*I* like you," she said, in such a way that made Sigrid smile. "And I thought you did great against Mei. You totally freaked her out with that wrist block."

Sigrid tested the looseness of her tooth with her tongue. "Yeah, well next time I'll watch out for the follow-through."

Sigrid was the last to finish her run—along with Suko, who ran beside her. She was just entering the dormitory to wash when Sara stepped out and blocked the doorway, standing on the steps with her arms folded before her. Two of her cronies stood behind her, making sure that neither Sigrid or Suko could get past.

"Ah, crap," Sigrid said.

Suko rolled her eyes. "Give it a rest, Sara. You'll make us all late."

"If we're late, it's her fault," Sara said. "I'm sick of this and I'm sick of you. Why they even wanted you here is beyond me."

It was beyond Sigrid too, but she wasn't about to tell Sara as much.

Sigrid could see that Sara was itching for a fight, eager to beat the tar out of her, but she was determined not to give her the satisfaction. Doing her best to ignore her, she started up the steps—only to be pushed back down by Sara. Sigrid tripped on the last step and fell onto her rear, hitting her tailbone. That brought a big laugh from the other girls.

Sara's lips curled into a sneer and she looked down at Sigrid. "You're never going to graduate, you know. You're going to be stuck here forever. You'll never work for Kimura. They're going to take back every penny they gave your family."

Sigrid looked at her skinned knees and hands, felt the loose tooth in her mouth. Every muscle in her body ached. Sara wasn't the only one who was fed up. She hated Sara, but more than that, she hated herself for being scared.

Something inside her snapped. Sigrid screamed and launched herself at Sara, grabbing her around the legs and throwing her from the steps. Sara fell hard onto her back and Sigrid was on top of her before she could recover, pounding her face and chest. There was no thought of technique in her attack; she clawed Sara's face and pulled at her hair, punching her over and over.

Sara's cronies ran forward, but Suko blocked their path, giving the two girls a warning look. Sara would have to finish this fight on her own.

Sara screamed with rage, finally managing to throw the smaller girl off her, but Sigrid regained her feet first, leaping and planting a hard kick into Sara's chest. Sara fell to the ground, but Sigrid didn't relent, kicking her where she lay—over and over again; in her kidneys, in her ribs and with several clouts to her backside. Even as two of the instructors pulled her off, Sigrid kicked and thrashed like a wild animal, out of control.

As Sigrid calmed, she saw that all the girls had gathered to watch. Rosa was there as well.

Sara looked up at her, beaten and bloodied; she'd have several spectacular bruises, Sigrid was sure. She knew she'd gone too far, but beating Sara had been wonderful. Whatever Rosa dished out to her as punishment would be worth it. She looked at Rosa now, waiting for the expected dressing down.

He studied her with a frown, his hands resting on his hips, but instead of the expected outburst, he grunted a simple, "Hmph," then turned and walked away. As Sigrid watched him leave, the instructors released their grips on her arms. Apparently, that was that.

With the disturbance over, the instructors ushered the girls back into the dormitory to shower and dress before supper. The girls were quiet for the most part, but Sigrid could hear the faint whispers and felt their eyes upon her.

She usually tried to avoid the showers when the other girls used them; they always teased her relentlessly about her body—they were so much more developed than she was—but today she didn't care. No one seemed to be in the mood to tease her, not after the drubbing she'd laid on Sara. She took an extra-long shower, taking care to wash the cuts on her hands and knees. Her face stung in a number of places, but the water felt wonderful on her sore muscles.

Suko joined her at the sink while she combed out her hair. "I'm proud of you."

Sigrid frowned. "For beating a defenseless girl on the ground?"

"Beat her?" Suko laughed. "You gave her a right bashing. She deserved it."

Sigrid winced. "Do you think she'll be mad?"

"Oh, she'll be *pissed*. But she'll think twice about coming back at you."

Sigrid hoped Suko was right. She felt a strange sense of guilt—not for the beating she'd laid on Sara, but the fact that she'd completely enjoyed it. She only hoped she wouldn't pay for it too harshly at a later date.

After dinner, they had a little time before *lights-out*. Suko lay on her bunk with another book; Sigrid sat next to her on the bed, holding the latest stack of letters she'd received from her mother.

Sigrid smiled as she felt the paper with her fingers. Her mother was *so* old-fashioned. But paper or electronic, *all* messages had to be uploaded to the supply ships that came twice a year. Once uploaded, they would be transported through the Warp Relays and downloaded when they reached their destination. It was a slow way to send messages, but infinitely speedier than radio transmissions that wouldn't arrive in her lifetime. And neither she nor her mother could afford the *Couriers*—the little unmanned drones that orbited the Warp Relays. That was the fastest way to communicate, but the *Couriers* were prohibitively expensive.

Sigrid unfolded her pad, thinking of what to write back.

"More letters?" Suko asked, looking up from her book. She seemed annoyed. "I don't know why you bother. They won't get them for a year."

Sigrid shrugged. "I miss them. It doesn't feel so bad this way."

"Yeah, but it's not like you're going to see them again."

Sigrid put down her pad. "What? Why do you say that?"

Suko turned on her stomach; a sour look came over her face. "What do you think's going to happen when you're finished here?"

"I..." Sigrid hadn't thought about it; at least she tried not to.

"What do you think they're training us for?"

"I know, but..." *But what?* "I just thought..." Sigrid felt flustered. Suko never spoke of her own family—she always avoided the subject—but Sigrid missed hers deeply. That her letter writing should anger Suko made no sense. "Well—I still *miss them!*" She turned back to her letter, frustrated and angry, but she couldn't think what to write anymore.

"I don't know why. Your parents sent you here—they sent you away. They sold you, Sigrid" Suko rolled onto her back, crossing her arms over her chest. "I hope I never see mine again. I *hate* them."

"Hate them! Suko, they're your family."

"Even when we leave here, I won't go back. I don't think they'd take me even if I did."

Sigrid felt too shocked to say anything—never seeing her family again? She couldn't even consider that. After all, there were lots of children serving indentured contracts; theirs just happened to be with a mercenary organization. As bad as things were, Sigrid knew there were far worse places that children were sent to. How often had her parents warned, '*Be good or it's off to the factories*'?

But Suko—how could Suko's family not take her back?

She was closer to Suko than she'd been to anyone. *If Suko wasn't here...*Sigrid shuddered at the thought. Her life at the Academy, torturous as it was, without Suko...

No. If Suko's family wouldn't have her then the answer was clear. "Then you'll just have to come and stay with me," Sigrid said, with a firm nod of her head. "We're family, now. We're...*sisters.*"

Suko looked up at her, staring at her, studying her. Finally, her gaze softened as the anger drained from her face. She smiled and moved closer, leaning her head on Sigrid's shoulder. "Sisters...I think I like that."

Sigrid did, too.

* * *

August 16, 2343

Sigrid continued to wait for the inevitable reprisal from Sara, but as much as the girl kept staring daggers at her, she kept her distance and they both settled back into a routine of studies and exercises. Without Sara's prompting, none of the other girls seemed interested in bothering Sigrid either, and she began to let herself relax for the first time.

Today, though, Sigrid and the rest of the girls were escorted out to the newly-constructed firing range for their course in Advanced Weapons training. The *old* weapons caused her enough trouble; Sigrid wasn't quite sure how she'd deal with these new ones.

She did like her new instructor though. Chesna Dubnov was cut from much the same mold as Rosa; she stood tall, with a lean, athletic figure, and sported an impressive scar over her eye.

Sigrid could only wonder why the woman had chosen to keep it, given it was easy enough to fix. Still, it did add a certain mystique, enhancing the woman's already lethal qualities.

An assortment of weapons had been brought up from the armory and mounted on racks behind them. The racks were stocked with everything from recoilless handguns, eSMGs and knives, to the larger, more powerful weapons, some modern and some ancient. Arquebuses, crossbows, plasma-rifles, EMP grenades; the collection seemed part museum, part arsenal. Despite the *exotic* selection, Chesna decided to start the girls off with the standard issue 18 mm Marine sidearm. Sixteen of the girls were lined up at the front facing a series of targets down range—some as much a hundred meters distant. The large recoilless pistols were dreadfully loud, and Sigrid covered her ears as she watched the other girls practice, dreading her own turn soon to come.

"You're supposed to *hit* the targets, ladies," Chesna scolded as she paced back and forth through the ranks of the girls. "All right! That's enough." The girls stopped firing and the range fell silent again. Chesna scanned the monitors in front of her; she made a show of shaking her head in disgust. "Forty-eight percent accuracy...and that's the best score."

Khepri clapped her hands, but stopped when Chesna glared at her.

"That wasn't a compliment," she said and sighed, resting her hands on the broad weapons holster at her hip. "I don't mind saying that I expected a lot more of you girls. All right—next group, you're up. I expect you to double that score."

Sigrid stepped forward, taking the weapon from the girl in front of her. She checked the chamber before slapping a new clip into the handle, as Chesna had shown them.

Hesitantly at first, the girls began firing at the targets. Sara cursed in the stall next to Sigrid; she glared at the target, then regarded the weapon in her hand skeptically. "I think it's broke," she said.

"Keep firing, Ms. Skarsden—and don't blame the weapon."

Chesna stopped by Sigrid next. "Are you waiting for a formal invitation, Ms. Novak?"

"No, ma'am."

"Then I suggest you get to it—this is a timed exercise."

Sigrid swallowed and hefted the heavy pistol; she needed both hands to hold it steady. Dreading the scolding she was sure to get, Sigrid held her breath, aimed, and squeezed the trigger.

Sigrid's jaw dropped—she'd actually hit the target, square between the *man's* eyes. She realized, then, that Chesna was still standing behind her.

"Think you can do that again?"

Sigrid looked back at her with her mouth still open. She wasn't sure what to say, so instead turned back to the target. With the weapon grasped tightly in her small hands, she fired again, three quick shots, all perfectly grouped, splintering the wood around the previous hole she'd made.

"Very good, Ms. Novak." Chesna pointed further downrange at the more distant targets at seventy-five and a hundred meters. "Now those."

"Those?" Sigrid asked; she didn't see how she could possibly, but Chesna gave her shoulder a squeeze.

This time, Sigrid held the pistol in her right hand. With her body turned sideways to the target, she raised the weapon, aiming down the length of her outstretched arm. Squeezing her left eye shut, she fired two shots, and only two shots, yet scored a hit on both targets—although she barely winged the more distant of the two. It seemed enough to satisfy Chesna though, and she patted Sigrid's shoulder.

Beside her, Sara cursed again; she still hadn't managed a single hit.

"You should watch this one, Ms. Skarsden. You could learn something."

Sigrid stiffened as Sara's eyes narrowed and stared at her. She felt herself flush.

Chesna seemed unaware, though. With her hand still on Sigrid's shoulder, she leaned closer, speaking low in Sigrid's ear. "Although I can't say much for your technique. Both hands on the weapon next time."

"Yes, ma'am."

Chesna grinned, satisfied, and led Sigrid back to the racks of weapons. "See anything you like?"

Sigrid looked to the weapons mounted before her; her hand played over a longbow that was easily taller than her. The long-barreled sniper rifle also caught her attention. Her eyes glazed over.

"Uh—all of them!"

* * *

Sigrid slept deeply and happily that night. After so many months of struggling with her studies, she realized that she'd finally found something she was good at. The swords she trained with always felt unwieldy, and despite her efforts in the hand-to-hand exercises, her failures were becoming legendary; the other girls had such longer reaches than she did. But now she knew—*she could shoot anything*.

After dinner she'd yammered Suko's ear off before bedtime, babbling on about all the types of weapons and how she'd hit every one of Chesna's targets. Of course, Suko had been there and seen the whole thing, but she let her friend prattle on, smiling at her excitement.

"That's great, Seeg," Suko said, feeling genuinely happy for her; but her eyelids were heavy and she yawned. "Now, you *hafta* let me sleep! I'm knackered." Suko laughed and hit her with her pillow.

Sigrid didn't think she could sleep, but exhaustion from the day's constant activities took hold and she passed out before she knew it, snoring soundly.

She wasn't sure how long she'd been asleep when the strange, muffled sounds woke her. Her eyes struggled to focus in the dark; she could barely make out the shape of several girls by Suko's bunk. She sat up, fully awake—two sets of strong hands grabbed her arms and two more girls grabbed her legs, tossing the sheets aside and tearing her from her bed before she knew what was happening.

Sigrid screamed. Four girls covered Suko with a blanket, pinning her to her bunk. "Suko!" she cried out, but someone clamped a hand over her mouth. Kicking and screaming, she was dragged into the showers at the far end of the dormitory. She bit down hard on the hand covering her mouth—the girl yelped and pulled it away. Sigrid called out again, more frantically, "*Suko!*"

As much as she struggled, it was no use; the girls dragged her down, sitting on her arms and her legs. Sara knelt behind her head, staring down at her with a menacing, satisfied grin. "Hold her," she said.

Sara stuffed a small wash cloth roughly into Sigrid's mouth, then used a rag to tie a gag around her head and neck, cinching it tight. It knotted in Sigrid's hair, and she cried out a muffled scream, but Sara just laughed. "Thought I'd forgot about you, you little bitch?"

Sigrid felt their hands reaching for her underwear and her shirt, and she screamed, terrified—just a smothered, gargled sound through the rags. She got a leg free and managed a good kick to one of the girls' faces, clawing at another, but there were too many of them and they pinned her back to the cold floor.

Sara leaned over her, staring at her, and Sigrid felt herself flush, humiliated and scared. Her heart pounded as another girl approached with a length of rope and handed it to Sara. She tried to pull away, but the girls held her fast as Sara quickly bound her, winding the thin twine around Sigrid's wrists and ankles.

The ropes tore at the skin on her wrists, but Sigrid didn't cry out; she knew it would just spur the girls on. Laughing at her, they dragged her into the showers and tied her to a length of pipe.

Sigrid flinched as Sara leaned close to her. "Don't worry. We're just going to give you a little shower." Sara nodded to one of the other girls who turned the faucet full-on cold.

The blast of icy water hit Sigrid hard, and the girls laughed with glee, watching her struggle as she pulled at the ropes, trying to free herself. Two more girls turned on the adjoining showers, directing even more water onto her, ensuring she got a good dousing. Sigrid breathed water through her nose and choked, almost gagging on the cloth stuffed into her mouth.

"Sleep tight, bitch." Sara's hand rested on the light switch as she looked her up and down. Sigrid turned her body away from her, as if to shield herself from the girl's stare, but it only made Sara laugh. Then, with a satisfied sneer, Sara flipped off the lights, leaving Sigrid alone and shivering in the dark.

Sigrid yanked on the ropes, but the thin twine only dug deeper into her wrists. Worse, the knots seemed to slip and bind tighter as the ropes got wet. As hard as she pulled, there was no escape. Within minutes her fingers and hands were numb and pruned—the water was so cold it hurt. She cried out and stamped her feet on the tiles, begging desperately, but of course, no one came back to free her.

Where was Suko? She worried now what they were doing to her. If they hurt her, when she got out she was going to...to...what? Kill them? Beat them up? There were more of them and they were bigger. What could she do against all of them? *Nothing.* Bound, as she was, and shaking horribly from the cold, despair filled her; Sigrid couldn't hold back the tears that came, and she wept.

She cursed herself—cursed herself for crying and for being a fool. To think she'd actually imagined the bullying was behind her. Her shoulders ached, her hands were numb and her wrists felt like they were on fire. She was freezing. Sigrid could no longer move her fingers. She strained to arch her back, stretching, to relieve her wrists, but the girls had done a thorough job. The gag in her mouth was soaked through and Sigrid choked again on the ice-cold water and her own tears.

She had no idea how long the girls left her there, and when the bathroom lights finally flicked on she was too exhausted look up. Suko ran to her and shut off the water. She tore the gag from her face and covered her with all the towels she could grab from the laundry. Sigrid shook uncontrollably as Suko held them around her, rubbing her shoulders furiously.

"It's okay," Suko whispered.

She saw that Suko's right eye was swollen and her lip was cut. Her arms were bruised where the girls had grabbed her and held her down. "*F-Fuckers...*" Sigrid managed through her chattering.

"Don't worry about me. I took care of them." Suko pulled at the knots with her fingernails and her teeth, but it was no use—the knots were stuck tight, the thin twine had shrunk in the cold water. "Don't go anywhere," she said with a wink.

"I'll w-wait h-here," Sigrid said, somehow managing a smile.

Suko returned, carrying a butterfly knife, clearly stolen from the gym.

"W-we're not supposed to have those—Rosa will k-kill you if he finds that!" Sigrid said, suddenly worried Suko would get in trouble.

"I thought it might come in handy," Suko said as she sawed at the twine, taking care not to cut Sigrid.

Finally freed, the pain Sigrid felt in her hands became overwhelming as the blood surged back into them; she clung to Suko, shivering, and wept openly.

"I'm sorry," Sigrid, said, embarrassed at her outburst. "I'm acting like a child."

Suko scoffed. "They're the children—bloody animals. Don't worry, they'll get their comeuppance."

Suko half-carried her back to her bed, putting her own blanket over her as well. Sigrid couldn't stop shivering, nor would she let go of Suko's hand. Suko crawled in next to her, huddling close. She placed the knife next to her under the pillow. "Tomorrow I'm teaching you *little red fist*," she said, referring to one of Rosa's favorite Kung Fu moves.

Sigrid laughed, but her shivering turned it into a series of choking coughs. She somehow managed a smile, though. She was safe now.

* * *

Sara felt something on her face, a pressure, and she awoke with a start. Something was on her chest. No, *someone* was on her chest. She looked up and realized that Sigrid was on her bunk. The tiny girl was kneeling on her arms. Something flashed in the dark—the little bitch had a knife.

Sara's eyes bulged wide as she saw the knife come toward her face and Sigrid pressed the blade to her cheek.

"If you *ever* touch Suko again..." Sigrid hissed. There was a chill in her voice, but her hand was calm and steady where it held the knife to her.

Sara did her best to sound defiant. "What? You're going to cut me?" Both girls were breathing hard, their eyes fixed fiercely on each other. "You don't have the guts."

Sigrid's wrist flicked out and Sara felt the blade nick the soft skin under her eye. She screamed and shoved as hard as she could, sending Sigrid tumbling off the bed.

"You little bitch!"

The lights came on, and they all saw Sara standing there—blood oozing from between her fingers where she clutched her hand to her face. "You *bitch!*"

"Next time it'll be your eye," Sigrid blurted. She instantly regretted it; she couldn't quite believe she'd said it. But it was done.

Sara ran out, screaming in rage, leaving Sigrid sitting on her rear holding Suko's knife in her hand, traces of blood on the small blade.

Suko rushed to Sigrid's side, grabbing up the knife. "Oh, my God—are you okay?"

Sigrid nodded, still a little stunned, not quite believing herself what she'd done. But Sara deserved it, and Sigrid wasn't going to let her bully her or hurt Suko again.

Chapter 3
Survivor

Felix Rosa stood at the large picture window in Dr. Garrett's office. Outside, the girls worked at their exercises. One of his instructors worked with a group wielding Naginatas, the long Japanese bladed-staffs, while another group of girls ran a short obstacle course.

Dr. Lisa Garrett sat at her desk looking over Rosa's report on the girls' *activities* from the night before. Things had almost gotten out of hand. No. Things *had*, and now she had to figure out what to do. Her goals may have been purely scientific when she'd started the program, but the reality remained that she was responsible for raising thirty-two teenage girls—thirty-two *genetically enhanced* teenage girls, whom Kimura was currently training in some very deadly arts.

Lisa rubbed tiredly at her temples. "You must wish sometimes I'd supplied you with a group of boys."

Rosa dismissed the suggestion. "Actually, I find them remarkably focused. They apply themselves to all their tasks with a great deal of veracity, and they demonstrate a tremendous aptitude and willingness for learning. They are dedicated and hard-working. Frankly, I've found the experience most satisfying."

Lisa sighed. "Just think, if we were at *Stage Four* I might be able to program out bad behavior."

Rosa chuckled. "You might want to consider starting at that stage with the next lot."

Lisa sat back in her chair, examining the report on her pad. "In my old school, we would have expelled the lot of them. Unfortunately, we don't have that luxury." She needed all the girls—they were too rare a commodity. "But we can't have them killing each other either..."

"If this were a military academy, I might consider corporal punishment."

Lisa considered that briefly before dismissing it outright. "We'll hold off on the *lashings* for the moment."

"Do you want me to cancel their survival training?"

"No, that's fine. It might be good to get them all out of here for a while. A change of pace might be just what we need right now."

Rosa nodded. "I'll make the arrangements."

As he headed for the door, Lisa stopped him. "One thing, Felix...Novak—the little one..."

The grin that came over Rosa's face was all the answer Lisa really needed. "She's an interesting one. She doesn't have the easiest time of it, not quite so big or fast as the others, but...she never quits."

Lisa smiled. "Good."

* * *

August 17, 2343

Sigrid and Suko stood together and watched as three *Kingfisher* transports zoomed out of the summer sky toward them. One at a time, they came in low, hovering briefly before coming to rest side-by-side in the center of the compound. The whine of their four dual-mounted thrusters only fed the girls' anticipation. Today's trip would be their first outside the Academy walls since they'd been brought there over four years before.

For a group of girls who had grown up in the crowded and dirty streets of Earth, Alcyone presented a completely alien environment; one of lush trees, mountains and flowing rivers. It was nothing like any of them were used to. The planet was sparsely populated, with only a few mining and manufacturing centers. The total population didn't even top one million. The fact that today they'd get to ride in the *Kingfishers* presented a new attraction and Sigrid couldn't wait.

The flight didn't disappoint either. The pilots were more than happy to show off. They seemed to make an extra effort in climbing steeply and pulling up hard at the last moment as they cleared the last of the towering peaks that surrounded the Academy. Sigrid's heart was in her throat, and she held tight to Suko's hand as they swooped down, skimming a few feet above the ground, as they dived into the river-valley beyond.

The short flight was over all too quickly, and the transports deposited the girls in a clearing by a river that widened into a large pool. The girls took to it instantly, running screaming and splashing into the cool green water. A few of the instructors tried to get the girls out and back in parade rest, but Rosa let them go. He'd brought them here to blow off some steam—best to let them get to it.

Sigrid loved to swim, but swimming was prohibitively expensive back home. Eager to dive in, she couldn't get her boots and shorts off fast enough. She grabbed Suko by the hand. "Come on!"

Suko held fast, digging in her heels. She'd never been to a swimming pool, let alone seen a river. "Wait. What if there's...*things* in it?"

"Things? What *things*? There are probably fish—"

"I—I can't swim."

Sigrid was surprised—she'd never seen Suko frightened of anything. She pulled her hand again, but more gently this time. "It's easy. I'll show you. It's okay."

Keeping one apprehensive eye on the water, Suko pulled off her boots and shorts and let Sigrid lead her in. The day was warm, it had to be at least thirty-two degrees, but the water felt like ice on her ankles, and she squealed, hopping from foot to foot. "No way—it's bloody freezing!"

"Come on, you big weenie." Sigrid wasn't having any of it and she pulled Suko deeper into the river.

When the water got up to her thighs, Suko screamed, flapping her arms. "You're crazy!" But Sigrid kept walking backwards, dragging her in. The river deepened quickly and Sigrid began treading water—Suko was doing her best to keep her toes on the rocks as the water lapped at her chin. When the ground disappeared from under her, she panicked and thrashed and swallowed a mouthful of water, but Sigrid didn't let go. She swam backwards calmly, holding both of Suko's hands, guiding her along. Suko kicked and splashed wildly with her feet, but Sigrid barely seemed to move her legs at all.

"I love it! Isn't it great?" Sigrid declared with delight.

"Gr-*b-b*-great," Suko managed, spitting up more water.

"See! It's easy."

Sigrid let go of Suko's hands, but Suko began to sink instantly and she kicked out, grabbing onto Sigrid. "Don't…!"

"It's all right. I got you."

Back in Sigrid's arms, Suko relaxed and let herself be guided along. The water felt lovely against her skin, even if a bit cool.

A half hour later, things were much more calm and quiet at the riverside. Most of the girls lay sunning themselves on the rocky beach. Rosa and the other instructors were relaxing up on a big rock where they could keep an eye on all of them.

Suko had long given up on the concept of swimming as recreation by the time Sigrid pulled herself out of the water.

"That was soooo good," she said as she flopped down, wet, beside Suko. Sigrid shook out her hair, playfully spraying Suko in the process.

Suko squealed in protest. "No! It's cold."

"Landlubber," Sigrid teased.

Suko lifted up the elastic of her briefs and frowned. "And I got sand in my underpants."

The sudden low rumble of engines drew their attention and they both looked up in time to see another of the fast-moving *Kingfishers* crest the treetops on the hillside, zooming low to land in the clearing just downriver. All the girls stood up and craned their necks to see what was going on.

"I guess it's time to go," Suko said. She took Sigrid's hand as they walked down to find out what the fuss was about. As they got closer they could see the crew offloading supply cases from the transport.

"Is that food, sir?" the redheaded girl named Leta asked.

Rosa grinned. "In a manner of speaking, Ms. Halliday."

Sigrid had always thought Leta beautiful. She was tall for a girl, with large, deep-green eyes and a face framed by a thick mane of heavy red curls. She also seemed to be developing at an alarming rate—alarming to Sigrid, anyway, who could only dream of such curves.

Sigrid was close enough to see that the supply crates contained rope, saws, axes, some long-bladed machetes and shorter knives. *Not exactly food,* she thought.

Rosa began handing out the tools, studying the girls around him. "You all looked like you were enjoying yourselves so much, I thought you might like to stay for a while. We had considered leaving you here on your own without any of this. I had complete confidence that you'd all be just fine, but since this is your first outing we thought we'd cheat a little and give you some tools to make your stay here a little more comfortable."

"Stay, sir? Here?" Leta asked.

"You don't like this spot, Ms. Halliday?"

Leta didn't answer; she stood blinking at him, twirling a stray curl around her long fingers.

"We'll be back to see how you're all making out in a few days." His gazed hardened, focusing on some of the girls individually—Sara and Sigrid in particular—as he spoke. "I trust you'll all do well to take care of yourselves. Look to each other—and trust in your training." He stepped up into the transport. "I expect to find you all in good health when I return."

Like the other girls, Sigrid was too stunned to say anything; there were hundreds of questions in her head, but none made it to her lips. And then, the transports were gone, lifting off and speeding away over the hillside. Silence returned to the clearing, with only the sounds of the river behind them and the wind passing through the thick standing of trees.

"What do we eat?" one of the girls asked.

None of the girls answered. They all knew what Sigrid knew. This was a test. They'd all taken their survival courses, but that had been classroom training, just theory in books, but this—this was designed to test them for real in the wilderness.

Mei took charge. She was the oldest, by a month, and everyone liked her so there were no objections. She divided up the tools and sent the girls off in groups to begin searching for edible plants and berries, and firewood for cooking.

"What about shelter?" Suko asked. "If we're going to be here for a while…"

"Food first," Mei said. "Then we'll figure out some kind of shelter."

Mei put Sigrid in a group to find food—something a little more substantial than berries. She shooed Sigrid off, with the simple instruction: "Go kill something."

The river seemed like the simplest option. It was teeming with large fish. Sigrid knitted her brows in concentration as she fashioned a spear, using one of her leather bootlaces to lash her knife to the end of a strong, thin branch. With Suko splashing behind her, she set off to one of the shallower areas to spear some dinner. It turned out they did a much better job of frightening the fish, but once they stopped splashing about and managed to remain still for a few minutes Sigrid speared her first.

"I got one!" she exclaimed. She raised the silver fish on the makeshift spear to show everyone, but it promptly wriggled off the blade and splashed back into the water. Suko dived after it, only remembering after the fact that she couldn't swim. She splashed about frantically until Sigrid came to her *rescue* in the four-foot deep pool.

Realizing she could stand, Suko gave her a sheepish look. "You *saved* me!" She laughed, and kissed Sigrid hard on the cheek. "My hero."

Sigrid pushed her head under. Suko found this highly amusing and splashed back, but the other girls nearby berated them for losing the fish. Sigrid was more careful with the next one, making sure to grab it and give it a good whack on the rocks.

An hour later, despite the afternoon heat, their feet were so cold, and their teeth chattering so hard, that they were forced to give up the hunt.

"Well, we bagged seven," Suko said, counting their catch. "Hopefully the other girls are having better luck."

Shivering on the bank, they pulled their socks and boots on. Not wanting to dispense with the spear just yet, Sigrid split her other bootlace in half so that she could tie both boots up halfway. They flopped a bit, but not so much that she couldn't walk.

There was a fire going and one of the girls had caught a rabbit. Lei-Fei made a show of skinning the unfortunate creature, doing a good job of grossing out most of the girls. Only three other girls had caught any fish, but the woods were laden with leafy greens and berries, so they all managed to eat enough to feel pleasantly full.

Suko patted her stomach. "Too bad Rosa didn't leave us a *pottle*—we could've made some chips. That would've been choice."

"I have no idea what you just said," Sigrid said—she still struggled with Suko's *kiwi-isms*. They both laughed.

As she relaxed by the fire with Suko, her belly full of fish she'd caught herself, and with none of the earthly noises of traffic and people shouting, Sigrid couldn't remember ever having a better time.

Mei roused them all up. "We still need some shelter, people. Let's get to it."

Some of the girls were already off in the woods looking for branches and tree boughs to start building lean-tos. Sigrid and Suko headed off to join them. Suko had one of the axes and was just beginning to work on a small tree that looked good for a support beam when she heard a rustling and a scream a short-ways off. The two girls froze, listening, and then heard it again—a squeal, and then someone cursing.

"That sounds like Khepri," Suko said. "Come on."

The undergrowth was thick and the earth soft, forcing the girls to scramble and claw their way through the dense forest. They found the dark-haired Persian girl sitting with her back up against a tree. She was hurt and holding her leg. Sigrid saw the three long gashes down the side of her calf—she'd been *clawed.* Blood seeped through her fingers and down her leg.

She looked up at them, slightly dazed, as they approached. "Hi, guys." She sounded more embarrassed than distressed.

Sigrid knelt by her side and pried the girl's hand away from the wound. More blood oozed out. The cuts were long, but not deep. "I don't think you'll need stitches. I think it looks worse than it is. It's all the blood."

Sigrid took off her shirt and tore it into several strips to bandage Khepri's leg.

Khepri grimaced. *"Blech..."*

"What happened?" Suko asked.

Khepri pointed off into the woods. "Big! It was bigger than me. One of those *deer-thingies.*"

Sigrid knew she meant the elk-like animals that roamed the forests here; smaller than elk on earth, but with an impressive array of razor sharp antlers.

Khepri laughed, embarrassed. "Silly, really. We just startled it—it charged—just kind of ran over me. I think it was more scared of us than we were of it."

Sigrid tied off her makeshift bandages. They'd have to figure something else out for her when they got her back to the camp, but the pressure was already slowing the bleeding.

"Sara ran off after it," Khepri said. "She got it with her spear."

Suko's face darkened in anger. "She left you here?"

Khepri shrugged. "Well, Sara…you know."

"Which way did she go?" Sigrid asked.

Khepri pointed deeper into the forest further up the hill.

"You'll be okay here for a bit?"

"Feel better already."

"You're going after her?" Suko asked, surprised.

Sigrid shrugged. "I want to see the animal. We'll be right back—just a few minutes."

"I'll be here," Khepri said and shooed them off.

It wasn't difficult to find Sara; they just followed the trail of broken branches, trampled undergrowth—and blood—until they found her, crouched behind a rotting, fallen tree trunk.

Sara waved them down, signaling for silence as they approached. Sigrid peered over the thick, green moss that covered the trunk. She caught a glimpse of the wounded, furry creature as it limped off ahead of them, disappearing into the thick underbrush with Sara's own makeshift spear sticking from its furry rump.

"I got it good," Sara said. "Let's go."

She led them out and the girls followed, moving with a swift, soundless grace. They tracked the wounded animal up a steep hill and along a narrow, muddy trail. Far below, they could hear the river rushing by, rumbling and growing in volume as the canyon they skirted narrowed and deepened.

The trail led out onto a rocky outcropping on the side of a cliff. Water rippled freely down the rock-face making the ledge slick and their footing precarious. Sigrid slipped, stumbling and teetering on the edge, but Suko caught her with a steadying hand, easing her back against the cliff wall.

"Thanks," Sigrid said. She gulped as she looked down. They could all see the steep pitch that ended in a sheer drop plunging deep into the canyon as the river roared its way over the swirling rapids—the sound was deafening.

"My pleasure," Suko said, relaxing her grip once she saw Sigrid was safe.

The trail they were on came to an abrupt end, revealing a gap in the rocks that led into a cave. The three girls looked at one another, not sure what to do.

"Do we go in?" Suko asked.

As an answer, Sara immediately made her way inside. She'd taken two steps when they all heard a low, bawling moan—then the *elk* thrust its head out of its hiding place. Sara was completely startled and jumped back, her foot slipping on the rock. She teetered briefly on the cliff edge, her arms flailing. Suko grabbed for her, catching her hand, but Sara's momentum was already carrying her over and she only ended-up pulling Suko with her as the two girls tumbled backward down the steep slope.

Sigrid had a brief glimpse of the animal tearing away down the path, but her eyes were glued in horror as she watched Suko tumble helplessly down over the loose mud and rock. Suko lost her grip on Sara. She managed to slow herself, spreading her arms and legs out as she descended face first. Sara fell backwards, doing several spectacular somersaults.

For a terrifying instant, Sigrid thought they'd both go careening over the precipice ahead of them, but Suko came to a skidding halt a few meters from the edge. Sara was saved as well, but only because she slammed into a tree—Sigrid heard the *smack* as Sara's head hit the trunk.

Without a thought for her own safety, Sigrid scrambled down the slope as fast as she could, skidding, sliding, grabbing onto the branches that lashed at her legs and face. Gripping a tree-branch with one hand, she reached out and grabbed Suko's ankle.

"I got you!" Sigrid hauled her away from the edge, grabbing onto her belt and hefting her back to her feet. Suko's shirt was torn and she had several scrapes on her nose and face.

"Thanks." Suko said; she had to shout over the din of the thundering river below.

Getting to Sara proved more difficult. Sara sat with her back to the tree at the very edge of the cliff. She looked dazed. Sigrid could see the blood trickling from both of her ears.

Grasping hands with Sigrid, Suko reached out to Sara, but she was too far away. "I can't reach her!"

Inching *very* carefully, Sigrid crouched as low as she could, grabbing onto one of the many roots that stuck out of the loose earth. It seemed secure enough, and she eased her weight onto it, but when Suko leaned forward, it gave way, uprooting itself a good two feet, sending both of them skidding closer to the edge. It held though, if just barely. Sigrid caught her breath.

Suko turned back to her, her eyes wide.

"Sorry," Sigrid said—Suko gulped and nodded.

Suko reached down again, stretching out—her fingers still inches away from Sara. "You need to reach up!"

Sara looked up at her, struggling to focus. "I hurt my head." She laughed, then, looking at Sigrid, her eyes narrowed. "I don't like you very much."

Sigrid rolled her eyes. "Really? Now?"

"Take my hand!" Suko ordered.

Still groggy, Sara looked down and saw the drop and the rocky riverbed below. Suddenly panicked, she flailed, reaching for Suko's outstretched arm, pulling hard, and scrambling to her feet, but the loose earth gave way and her feet slid out from under her, dangling over the cliff's edge.

Sara clung desperately to Suko's hand. "Don't let me fall…"

For a sickening moment, Sigrid felt Sara's weight pull all three of them downwards, threatening to drag them all over the edge; the river now loomed fully in Sigrid's view, some thirty meters below. Sara looked at her, desperation in her eyes, fighting to keep her grip as much as she fought to stay conscious. She scrambled madly for footing, but found none.

Sara's thrashing wasn't helping any and the tree root Sigrid clung to tore free. Suko stared in horror, helpless. "Sigrid!" she called out, but there was nothing she could do.

Sigrid dug her heels into the earth, but Sara's weight pulled them forward. Gravity reared its ugly head, and Sigrid's vision filled with the sharp rocks of the riverbed. They were going over.

In an act of desperation, Sigrid surged forward, grabbing Suko around the waist, pushing with all her strength and leaping as far as she could out over the cliff. Suko screamed, and Sigrid thought she might have screamed along with her, as the two girls fell headlong into the canyon below.

For a terrible moment, all Sigrid saw were the rocks rushing up to meet them, but her desperate push had been just enough, and the two girls landed, not on the rocks, but in a deep, swirling pool at the side of the river. They hit the water hard and plunged deep below the surface. Sigrid felt the strong current swirling them about, pulling them even deeper until her feet found rock, and the river swept them both along on the bottom.

Sigrid's grip on Suko never faltered. She pushed off the bottom, kicking and swimming as hard as she could. The pull of the river tugged at them, trying to drag them back down, but Sigrid fought it, finally breaking the surface.

The sound was deafening, and the surge of the whitewater completely disorienting. Suko thrashed in her arms and they both fought for air, swallowing large gulps of the water that crashed over their faces. Sigrid lost her hold of Suko as they both went over a huge, sweeping rapid, and for a terrifying, heartbreaking moment, she feared Suko had gone under. But Suko emerged a few meters away downstream, reaching out to her, kicking hard with her feet to stay above the water.

Sigrid swam to her and got an arm back around her. The river widened here, still strong and fast, but Sigrid was able to float along, holding Suko up and keeping her head well above the spray. They drifted along, letting the current carry them. The walls of the canyon were steep, stretching high up above them on all sides. Sigrid scanned the banks for a safe spot, finally kicking toward a flat mossy rock to the side. Exhausted and dazed, they dragged themselves out.

Suko coughed up a considerable amount of water and collapsed on her stomach, panting. "You're one crazy girl, Seeg. But you saved my life." Suko rolled over and took in their surroundings, deep in the river canyon. "I think."

Even Sigrid had to chuckle. They were safe, they were alive, but where were they?

Suko sat up, suddenly. "Where's Sara?"

Sigrid shook her head. "I don't know. I didn't see her."

Both girls were shivering and they huddled together, holding each other. "You're bleeding!" Suko said.

Sigrid hadn't even realized; she'd lost her boots and socks, and somewhere along the way she'd cut her foot. The gash ran from the ball of her foot to her heel, bleeding bright crimson and leaving a widening trail that spread out over the wet rock on which they sat. "*Uhgch...*" she said, sickened by the sight.

Suko took the knife from her belt clip and cut a long strip off the bottom of her shirt. She wrapped Sigrid's foot as best she could, tying the wet bandage tight.

"Can you walk?" Suko asked.

Sigrid looked at the vertical cliffs of the canyon that surrounded them. "I don't think that's an issue here." Across the river, about fifty meters away, was the other bank. The cliffs seemed to drop much lower on that side.

Suko followed her gaze. "We're not going back into *that*."

Sigrid saw the fear on her face, but she couldn't see any other way out. "The camp's on that side. We've got to get across." Sigrid waded into the shallows, wincing as her injured foot touched the freezing water. She turned back to Suko and held out her hand. "Come on. It'll be okay."

Suko took a step away from the river.

Sigrid's voice softened. "Do you trust me?"

Suko's eyes were fixed fearfully on the water, but when she took Sigrid's hand, she nodded. "Yes."

"All right." Sigrid guided Suko slowly into the water until it was swirling around their hips. "Just relax and think *floaty* thoughts." She turned Suko so her back was half-facing her and wrapped her left arm around Suko's waist. "Okay, now just lean onto my hip—like you're sitting—lift your feet."

"Oh—kay..." Suko lifted her feet, and immediately began to thrash her arms in the water to steady herself.

Sigrid tightened her grip. "Just sit back—don't try to swim—relax your arms."

Suko forced herself to relax, and found that she was indeed floating—well, *sitting* on Sigrid's hip. Sigrid pushed off and began side-stroking across the river.

Sigrid could feel Suko tense up as they moved deeper into the river, but she didn't fight her. Sigrid tried not to think of the sound of more rapids and falls further ahead, and concentrated instead on the shoreline in front of her, still so far away. The current was dragging them downstream, faster than she'd expected.

The cliffs dropped lower and lower—the rush of the rapids ahead became ever deafening. Sigrid snagged a rocky outcropping, but the swim had left her too weak to climb up. Suko had to hoist her up onto the edge of the bank. Cold and exhausted, they lay panting on the muddy ground, shivering and clinging to each other.

"How far away from camp do you think we are?" Suko asked.

"I don't know, but it's that way," Sigrid said, pointing upstream. Getting back on her feet took some effort. With the cut on her foot and having no boots, Sigrid had to lean heavily on Suko. "This sucks."

They'd walked for perhaps an hour when Sigrid needed to stop. Both her feet were raw and her injured foot throbbed like merry hell. Sigrid still didn't know how much further they'd need to go. It was well into the evening and the sun had nearly set; it would be dark very soon.

Suko helped Sigrid sit down, leaning her back against one of the wide redwood trees and carefully unwrapping the sodden dressing on her foot. She tore off another strip from the bottom of her T-shirt, wadding it and applying pressure, using another strip to tie it in place.

"You need to stop bleeding," Suko said. "I'm running out of shirt."

"You? What about me? I gave mine to Khepri." Sigrid said, looking down at her bare midriff; all she wore now were her shorts and athletic bra. They both laughed.

"We shouldn't walk anymore," Suko said, sitting next to Sigrid.

The temperature was starting to drop and Sigrid shivered. "I just need a break."

Suko put an arm around her and pulled her close.

Sigrid was exhausted and felt herself relax into Suko's arms, resting her head on her shoulder. "Much better. Let's just stay here for a bit." Her eyelids felt heavy, and Suko's body felt warm against her. *I'll just close my eyes for a second,* she thought.

She realized she'd fallen asleep only when she awoke much later, cold and shivering. She felt a surge of panic when she realized Suko was gone. It was completely dark—she couldn't see her anywhere. "*Suko...!*" Her voice croaked; her throat felt raw and sore.

She heard a rustling in the brush behind her, and footsteps. "I'm here!" Suko called to her, rushing back. "Sorry—I had to pee." Suko slid back next to her. Both girls were freezing, and their arms wrapped around each other, hugging for whatever warmth they could get. "We can't stay here—we'll freeze."

Sigrid nodded and tried to rise, but she couldn't put any weight on her foot.

"And you can't walk," Suko said, looking at her with concern. "Come on—hop on." Suko bent her back lower, offering it to Sigrid. "I'll piggyback you."

"You can't carry me all that way."

"We don't even know how far it is. We might almost be there." Sigrid looked doubtful. "Come on, Seeg. We can't stay here."

Sigrid surrendered to her friend's logic and climbed on her back. It was the first time she'd been grateful for her small size. Except for a few stumbles in the dark, Suko was able to carry her with little trouble. Both girls had remarkable night-vision, and thanks to their enhanced strength Suko was able to keep a consistent pace, even up some of the steeper pitches. They both knew that if they followed the river long enough they'd eventually reach the camp.

Sigrid's arms and thighs throbbed where she clung to Suko's back, but she dared not complain—not with Suko doing such a valiant job carrying her. Still, she could feel Suko's legs growing more unsteady beneath her, and her gait was beginning to falter.

"We should rest," Sigrid said.

No further prompting needed, Suko collapsed, and both girls tumbled to the ground.

"Good idea," Suko said, exhausted and panting. She lay on her back, staring up. "I am *so* hungry."

As if on cue, Sigrid's stomach produced a loud growl, making both girls laugh. "Me too." They were both shivering again and held on to each other.

"I'm just glad you're here," Suko said.

"*Me?*" Sigrid said, through chattering teeth. "I'd rather be back in camp around a fire, thank you very much."

"I'm serious. If I have to be stuck out here with someone, I'm…well, I'm just glad it's you."

Sigrid raised her head up, looking at Suko—Suko, who always protected her and stood up for her. Suko who was always there for her. "I'm glad you're here too," she said, then kissed Suko softly on the lips. Suko kissed her back, holding her hand tightly before resting her head on Sigrid's shoulder.

When Sigrid awoke, the sun was just cresting the tops of the hills to the east; she felt Suko stirring at her side. Both girls were numb and sore—the blood on Sigrid's bandaged foot looked black, but at least it wasn't bleeding anymore.

"*Shit a brick…*" Suko said, sitting up.

"What?"

"Stupid, stupid, stupid…"

"*What?*"

Suko pointed at the hillside by the river bank, and Sigrid recognized it immediately; she could just make out the edge of the clearing where they'd set camp, perhaps less than a half kilometer distant—and *behind* them.

"We walked right by it," Suko said. Her look of disgust turned to a smirk and she laughed.

"Crap," Sigrid said.

Suko helped her up; Sigrid still couldn't walk, and she let Suko carry her the rest of the way back to the encampment. When the other girls saw them, they came running forward shouting their names—obviously worried and glad to see they were okay. Two girls whisked Sigrid off Suko's back and carried her the rest of the way.

While Mei cleaned and put a proper dressing on Sigrid's foot, Sigrid told the girls what happened. Sara hadn't come back; Sigrid did her best to describe where they'd fallen from the cliff. She hadn't seen Sara fall, but after the incident that she described, no one was hopeful. Mei sent two groups of girls to search for her, but no trace of Sara was found.

"We'll keep looking," Mei said. "If she's out there we'll find her."

Few girls shared her optimism—they definitely feared the worst.

Sigrid noticed a few of Sara's cronies eyeing her suspiciously. "Do…do they think I *killed* her?" Sigrid whispered to Suko when they were alone.

Suko shook her head slowly. "I—I don't know…"

The other girls had managed to finish the shelter, which comprised little more than a small makeshift lean-to, barely big enough to fit all of them. The next night was still cool, but much more pleasant, spent under cover and warmed by the presence of the others—and Suko, who kept her arms wrapped tightly around her.

"I can't breathe!" Sigrid said. They both giggled when Suko held her tighter still. Sigrid didn't really mind; she was warm and felt safe in Suko's arms.

After another full day of rest, Sigrid's foot had healed enough to walk and she joined Suko and some of the other girls in a hunt. Already growing tired of fish, the girls were determined to catch something more substantial. It took a great deal of time and patience, but six of them eventually tracked and cornered one of the *elk*. It was Sigrid who managed to spear it, landing the killing blow. Slaughtering the beast was a hopeless and bloody disaster, leaving many of the girls green. But when it was done, Sigrid was presented with the first cuts, cooked over the roaring bonfire. The girls teased her playfully, referring to her as, *'Our Great Provider'*. Sigrid found it both ridiculous and delightful.

When the transports arrived ten days later, Rosa was greeted by the sight of thirty-one ragged and bleary-eyed girls, who seemed far from pleased with him. He was impressed by the size and fortification of their shelters, even more so when he'd been presented with the trophy of the *elk* antlers. But when told that Sara was missing his face took on a grim, solemn look. He acknowledged the news with a simple, curt nod. Two *Kingfishers*, and more transports from the school, were dispatched to look for her, but days and nights of exhaustive searching failed to turn anything up. There was no trace of her. Sara was gone.

Once the shelters had been dismantled and the area cleaned, the girls piled back into the remaining transports for the trip back to the school. The sight of the Academy had a strange effect on Sigrid after her days in the wilds. The thought of her soft, dry bed, and warm food served to her by the attending staff didn't excite her, as much as it felt ostentatious and unnecessary. How had she ever thought of this place as *austere?* The school was a virtual resort, her dormitory a palace.

It was good to be back though, and she lay in her bunk that night thinking of the nights spent in the wilds with the girls, with Suko. It was the first night in a week where she hadn't had Suko's protective arms wrapped around her; she couldn't help but miss them, and she tossed restlessly for an interminable amount of time, unable to sleep despite her exhaustion.

Chapter 4
Proposition

May 3, 2346

The smoky air hung heavy in the dim light of The Prancing Beagle—one of the more popular watering holes of *Vincenze Station* in orbit above Crucis Prime. Major Karl Tarsus took another long gulp from his glass of ale, wiping his mouth with the back of his sleeve as he studied his companion. He didn't know the man's name, but that wasn't surprising; most of his clients preferred a degree of discretion. He'd worked for *Smith*—as he'd dubbed the man—on a number of occasions. Always the usual things: interdictions, search and seizures and the inevitable saber-rattling when the occasion called for it; but it was smalltime stuff.

Smalltime suited the major just fine. He wasn't an ambitious man. As long as he could maintain his small fleet of four ships and keep his levies paid to the Mercenary Guild, that was just fine. But what *Smith* proposed was so outlandish that, when the man proposed it, he'd spewed his last mouthful of ale across the small table, drenching the man's lapel and jacket sleeve.

"You want *me* to go after Kimura?" Tarsus asked. "You want me to attack one of the oldest private Mercenary organizations in the entire Federation." Tarsus could hold back no longer and he burst into uproarious laughter. *Smith* stared back at him, unblinking, while he used a handkerchief to clean the drops of ale from his jacket. "I'm sorry, but I think you've got the wrong man. We're a small operation. We have four ships—*when* they're all functioning. Kimura…well, let's just say they have a lot more."

Smith pressed his thin lips together, clearly struggling with his patience. "We're not asking you to attack the entire Kimura Military, Mr. Tarsus—"

"Major," Tarsus corrected him.

Smith gave him a dry look. "Major. I don't even want you to attack them at all. All we want is for you go to Alcyone—"

"Yes, yes—you want us to grab a bunch of schoolgirls off a Kimura Base. I know, Mr...." Tarsus waited once more for *Smith* to offer up his name, but of course the man said nothing so he continued, "I assume you don't have a permit for this operation, either." Tarsus knew he didn't. By law, any military action, mercenary or otherwise, needed to be sanctioned by the CTF, otherwise known as the Council for Trade and Finance, the governing body of the Federation of Commercial Enterprises.

"No, Mr. Tarsus. We have no permit."

"Then I'm afraid there's nothing we can do for you. If my outfit gets caught operating without a permit...I'd lose my guild standing. Not to mention the retaliation from Kimura."

"Spare me the negotiation tactics, Mr. Tarsus. You have no compunction against unsanctioned operations. We're quite familiar with your organization—which is why we came to you." *Smith* leaned forward. "Tell me, Mr. Tarsus, are your guild levies in good standing?"

Of course, they weren't. Tarsus took a long pull on his ale.

"Your accounts are well in arrears, Mr. Tarsus. You'll lose your guild standing soon enough, and I don't see any other clients lining up to pay you the kind of sum I've just offered. Shall we dispense with the negotiation tactics, and cut to brass tacks?"

Tarsus waved him off. "I'd still be a fool to go up against Kimura. I have no ego in these matters. I know my organization's limits...and this is beyond ours."

"Thirty-two girls, six-point-two million dollars a head—surely that should be enough for you to take on any extra help you might need."

Tarsus mulled it over and took another pull on his ale, emptying the glass. $6.2 million was an extremely generous amount. There was obviously more to the job than *Smith* was letting on, but that wasn't surprising. He signaled the waitress over, ordered another and allowed himself a moment to appreciate the girl—all long legs and hips. *Smith* had a point and he knew it.

"Very well," Tarsus conceded, and grumbled, "I suppose we both knew I'd say yes the moment you sat down."

"Perhaps even before, Mr. Tarsus." *Smith* rose to his feet. "I'll transmit the particulars to your ship."

Tarsus waved his hand dismissively again. "Yes, yes—I'll have my man call your man…"

Smith turned on his heels and departed. Only when Tarsus was sure the man had left the bar and no one else was paying attention to him did he call over his second in command. Lt. Commander Selene Tseng slid into the booth across from him. He looked admiringly at his 'second'. Her jet black hair curved in a flattering fashion around her strong face. Her tall, thin figure belied a raw energy he'd seen unleashed on unsuspecting attackers on many occasions. She was the most skilled pilot he'd ever encountered in his long career, and her steely, ice-cold nerves at the helm had delivered him from many a scrape over the years.

She was his protégé, even though she didn't know it. At twenty-seven, Tarsus worried she might be too young to be taken seriously in command of a ship of her own. But her time would come, and soon. He already relied on her a great deal. He could trust her, and that was why she was the only member of his organization that he'd ever brought with him when meeting *Smith*.

"Did you get him?" Tarsus asked.

Selene held up a small recording device. "Right here, Major."

Tarsus nodded, satisfied. "I think it's time we learned the identity of our benefactor, don't you?"

Chapter 5
Upgrades

From The Journal of Dr. Lisa Garrett

September 14, 2346

RE: Project Andraste
Dear Hitomi-san,
I'm very pleased to report that we've reached the next milestone in the project. Today, we began the process of implanting the girls with the Primary Control Module. It shouldn't take more than a day or two to complete the procedure on all of them. This will be the foundation for the Artificial Neural Network that we discussed so many times.

I've decided to implant an Optical Module as well, along with a small test program—something Felix has suggested. I feel this will be a good benchmark for some of the other bionics and modifications we hope to introduce in the coming years.

It will take many months to monitor the effects, but early data suggests a 100% success rate—no signs of rejection or mutation.

As for the Genetic Modifications, the girls all show the same improvements in all aspects of their biology. It will be years more before we can consider adding any of the high-level programming, but we should be able to start working with basic bionics in short order. As per your recommendation, we'll stick with proven technology: optical implants, communication modules, etc., before introducing some of the more radical designs.

I wish very much that you could be here. Your expertise in nanotechnology would be most welcome and of great help.

Yours truly,

Lisa

Chapter 6
War Games

November 17, 2346

"Gear up!" Chesna bellowed.

Sigrid grabbed the eSMG, checking the chamber and safety before strapping the gun to her back. The Markov XP 18 mm clipped to the holster at her hip, while the long bowie knife fitted neatly in the sheath in her tall boots. All of the girls had similar load-outs.

"That's right. You're all magnificent bitches," Chesna said, appraisingly, as she inspected their ranks.

Sigrid felt *magnificent*. Chesna had trained them hard for months. Each girl was now a crack shot, and they could field-strip any of their weapons in a matter of seconds. But it was more than that, more than just the training, and Sigrid knew it. Dr. Garrett's treatments...

Sigrid ran her finger over the small access port of the Primary Control Module—or PCM—tucked behind her ear above her hairline. The skin around the small, two-millimeter-wide port was still raw and red where a small section of hair had been shaved from her head. But this was the only evidence of the surgery she'd recently undergone. Sigrid was still getting used to the idea of having a computer network wired into her head, and she couldn't stop touching the small opening.

The sun had already set behind the mountains and darkness was setting in fast. There would be no moon tonight—Rosa had chosen this night in particular to test their new upgrades. Dr. Garrett had implanted all of them with an optical implant. It gave the girls several different viewing options: infra red and night-vision. They could even see the chemical composition of the objects in their surroundings. Their genetically-enhanced vision already afforded them superior sight, but with the new optics they could see as clearly as in the light of day—albeit in a slightly hazy monochrome grey. It was jarring at first, but Sigrid had adapted to it quickly.

Across the compound, eight of the little T-48 VTOL transports sat parked in a row, waiting for the girls assembled in the field before them. The *Starlings* were small atmospheric flying craft, distinguished by their counter-rotating propellers mounted on each side of the fuselage. They were noisy and cramped, with barely enough room for four passengers in the rear compartment. The *Starlings* usually sported two 44 mm cannons mounted on each side, but those had been removed for the moment.

Sigrid caught the gleam in Suko's eyes as she surveyed the ships. "Where do you think we're headed?"

"As long as we get to fly, I don't care," Suko said.

The girls had been divided into eight fire-teams. Leta and Khepri joined Sigrid and Suko to complete their group. They gathered in front of Rosa and Chesna for the mission briefing.

Suko tossed a large, long-barreled sniper rifle to Sigrid. "Don't forget this."

Sigrid gripped the rifle, letting her hands play over its cool, smooth surface. It was surprisingly light and fitted well in her diminutive hands. Sigrid knew she was the smallest of the group, and certainly not the toughest or best fighter, but she was a dead-shot with anything that had a trigger.

The rifle spoke to her—literally. When Sigrid touched the weapon it scanned her implant for her preferences, automatically making adjustments to take into account her height, weight, grip-pressure and reach. It was engineered with much the same nanotechnology that the girls now shared, although on a much more primitive level.

After checking the chamber, Sigrid aimed down the sight, caressing the under-barrel.

"I think it's *love*," Leta teased, and even Sigrid laughed at this.

"All right, girls. Listen up!" Rosa shouted. The girls became instantly silent. "Ms. Dubnov and I have something a little special prepared for you today—a little game we want you to play." He slapped the side of the 3'x3' cargo container he was sitting on. "This is a Mark Four military transport container. We've dropped four of these out there, about 150 kilometers from here. Your objective is to find and locate just *one* of these. There are two ways to win this scenario: one—locate the container, defend the target and await extraction; two—eliminate the other teams, preventing them from securing the target. I look forward to seeing which course of action wins out. Just so you're all properly motivated, winning teams will ride back in the transports; losing teams will enjoy a nice long walk back through the forest. It's lovely this time of year, though, so I'm sure you'll all enjoy yourselves, win or lose. Questions?"

A girl raised her hand, hesitantly. "Uh, how do we find the containers, sir?"

"I'm glad you asked that. Each target carries a tracking device. We've granted all of you network access to the Nav-Sats in orbit. Data will be displayed to you via the optical implant that Dr. Garrett has seen fit to equip you with. Next question?" Rosa scanned the girls, but no one else raised their hand.

"You may be wondering about the ordnance options," Chesna said. "For the duration of this exercise, you'll all be using shock-rounds."

The shock-rounds were non-lethal paper projectiles capable of delivering a jolt of electricity in the 300 kV range. Every girl there had endured being blasted with the little *stunners*; Sigrid rubbed reflexively at the spot on her rear thinking about it.

"Now, unless all you ladies want to be walking back," Rosa said, "I suggest you get underway before the other teams find their cargo first. Transport assignments are uploaded to your PCMs."

The girls didn't need any more prompting. They rose to their feet instantly, grabbing up their gear.

"*Rattle your dags*, ladies. Let's move it!" Suko shouted, and, as one, the girls leapt forward, charging for their transport.

* * *

The compact T-48 had just enough room on the four jump-seats for Sigrid, Suko, Khepri and Leta. There were no doors on the craft and the girls all sat sideways, facing out for a better view. Sigrid rested her foot on the mounting-step, her hand clutching the handrail on the roof. The rush of air was invigorating as they crested the treetops and climbed quickly, high up and over the row of jagged mountains before them.

Their *Starling* pitched down sharply once it passed the last of the peaks, skimming dangerously close to the rocky cliffs. The night was black as pitch. Sigrid had only a vague sense of the rocky outcroppings dashing by, little more than a few feet away from her—a testament to the pilot's skill and daring. Sigrid flipped her optics to the new night-setting and her surroundings swam quickly into focus. She took a moment to adjust the sharpness until everything felt natural.

The pilot accelerated, shedding altitude quickly, sweeping down low over a grassy plain. Sigrid waited for her ears to pop after the distinct change in pressure, but her new systems made the transition smooth. The ground gave way abruptly as they came to an escarpment. Down below, stretching out for hundreds of hectares, lay a dense green jungle. The nose of the *Starling* dipped again as the pilot took them lower still. What Sigrid thought to be the ground turned out to be the heavy canopy of the jungle forest—it looked thick enough to build a house on, and topped out at nearly a hundred meters above the jungle floor.

The pilot signaled they were landing as they sliced through the trees towards a small clearing. Sigrid linked her PCM to the Nav-Sats, their location was displayed clearly in her HUD. The flight had taken them 147.24 kilometers from the school, but they were still nine kilometers away from the nearest cargo drop. Sigrid tapped the pilot on the shoulder. "Can you take us closer?"

The pilot frowned in response and jerked his thumb, signaling an emphatic, *'out!'*.

"Worth a shot," Leta said.

The four girls hopped out and the *Starling* zoomed off as soon as they'd cleared the props. Sigrid looked around. Thick-trunked redwoods towered over them. The ground was mossy and soft and thick with leaves. Even at night the humidity was stifling. It was all so different from the mild climate they were used to. Within minutes their clothes were damp and clinging to them.

Suko grabbed her bowie knife and cut the legs off her trousers. "Much better," she said and sighed.

"And fashionable," Sigrid teased. The long pants were uncomfortably hot so she quickly followed Suko's example, slashing off the legs of her own pants—Leta and Khepri did the same.

"I just hope there aren't any brambles," Leta said.

Suko realized she hadn't considered the underbrush. "Oh…"

"Oh, crap," Khepri said, wondering if she could reattach the pant legs.

Leta surveyed their surroundings. "Which way do we go?"

All the girls keyed their PCMs to summon up the information. Two of the containers were over twenty kilometers distant with the other two located closer at twelve and nine kilometers, respectively. They ruled out the closest target—it rested on the other side of a rather imposing mountain. The other one might be further, but they'd have a clear run to it .

"All right," Suko said. "We'll go for that one—looks like we head east about five klicks to that river, then we can just head north along the ridge."

"Sounds like a plan," Leta said.

They took off toward the river, running impossibly fast for average teenagers—though they were hardly average girls. Thanks to their genetically modified bodies, most of the girls could cover a kilometer in less than two minutes. The undergrowth wasn't very thick, but they encountered numerous fallen trees that needed to be hurdled over or crawled under. This slowed their progress, but only slightly. Sigrid did her best to keep abreast of the pace. If anyone other than Suko had been leading, they'd have left her behind long ago, but Suko stayed by her side, jogging easily.

"Want me to carry that for a bit?" Suko asked, pointing to the sniper rifle Sigrid was forced to lug along.

Sigrid shook her head, concentrating on breathing and not stumbling. "Figures they'd give me all the extra stuff to carry," she said, managing a brave smile.

"You're doing great."

After all of Dr. Garrett's work on her, Sigrid had hoped her days of trailing the other girls were over, but of course they'd all received the same enhancements. As fast as she had become, she was still slower than the rest of the girls.

As they reached the river bank, Suko stopped suddenly, dropping to a knee. "Hold up!" Suko looked around quickly, scanning the area. "What the…?"

"What is it?" Sigrid asked.

"I could have sworn…I'm sure I picked up something up on the scan. It just blipped—but it's gone."

"Can you replay it?" Khepri asked.

Suko scanned the data, playing it back and transmitting it to the other girls through their implants. Sure enough, they all saw it, just a brief blip picked up from the Nav-Sats, and then it was gone.

Sigrid gasped. "What was *that?*"

"It looked like something flying by," Suko said, "but then I lost it,"

Leta craned her neck, looking skywards. "Probably just one of the transports."

Suko narrowed her eyes. "Maybe—I don't know. Let's just be careful. I don't feel like getting *zapped*."

Khepri looked uneasily at the dark forest and the river before them. "Let's get moving. I don't feel like walking back, either." She began to wade out into the river. It was about twenty meters wide, and shallow. The dark, murky-brown water was barely moving.

"*Gah…!*" Khepri said, as she moved further out in the water.

"What?" Sigrid asked.

She turned back with a disgusted look on her face. "It's all *swampy*—muddy. I keep sinking."

Sigrid nudged Suko and grinned. "Well, at least I don't have to carry you across."

Suko gave her a swat on her rear.

The other three girls waded in. It was slow going—Sigrid's feet kept getting sucked down into the clinging mud. She fell over and had a horrible feeling as her hand got sucked down as well. Suko grabbed her belt and yanked her up. "Now, who's carrying who?"

Sigrid gave her a sly look. "Shouldn't that be, *whom*?"

Suko swatted her again.

Three of the girls made it across, but Khepri had stopped just short of the bank, still up to her knees in the murky water.

"What is it?" Suko asked.

Khepri crinkled her nose in disgust. "I lost my boot in the mud!"

"We'll come help," Suko offered.

"I'll find it!" Khepri said, clearly irritated over the missing footwear. Losing a boot would *not* be good, given the distance they still had to travel. "What the..." Khepri said, standing up straight.

"What is it?" Sigrid asked.

"Something just—*Gahh!*" Khepri screamed, leaping back out of the water—closely followed by the biggest snake Sigrid thought could ever exist. The other girls screamed in unison as Khepri fell back on her rear in the mud.

Sigrid had no idea how long the creature was but it looked at least twenty centimeters thick at its middle. It was the same murky-brown color as the mud by the shoreline and had no eyes in its round, bulbous head. The girls drew their pistols, but before they could fire off a shot, the snake slid back into the dark water, disappearing below the swirling surface.

Sigrid's heartbeat pounded in her ears. Nobody moved; they were all still aiming at the spot where the serpent had vanished just a moment before.

Khepri finally broke the silence. "Found it!" She held up the muddy boot in her left hand. They all burst into laughter—they also moved well away from the edge of the water.

"I hope we don't have to go back this way," Leta said.

Suko nodded. "Well, let's make sure *we're* not the ones walking back. Come on. We need to find that crate."

According to the map, their best route was up a steep, slippery hill. Scrambling up the nine-hundred meter slope took far longer than any of them liked. Sigrid worried they wouldn't get there in time—and that she was the one slowing them down. At the top of the hill, they were relieved to find that the forest gave way to a grassy clearing, sweeping down into another valley.

Suko pointed north. "Straight that way. Another nine-point-three kilometers. If we follow that ridge, it should be somewhere near the base of that hill."

Sigrid unhooked the sniper rifle from its harness and sighted down the scope to the spot. The forest was tangled and dense there. She adjusted the scope, zooming in to 40x, then again to 80x; the stabilizer in the stock kept the weapon perfectly steady. Gradually, Sigrid pulled back, scanning along the ridge-line.

"Shit," she said. She spotted something—something moving. She sighted again and focused on the team of four girls ahead of them moving along the ridge toward *their* target. "Dammit!"

"What?" Suko and Leta asked both at once.

"There's another team up ahead," Sigrid told them, without taking her eye from the scope. The other three girls crouched low, instinctively. "I think they're going for our cargo."

"Shoot 'em!" Khepri urged.

"I can't! The stun-round's only good for eighty meters."

Suko was already taking off after them. "Come on!"

Khepri threw her arms up in the air. "Wait! They're too far ahead."

Suko turned back, smiling excitedly. "Yeah, but they still have to wait and hold for extraction. They might get there first—but we can still win. We can do this!"

Leta grinned. "Then, we better get moving."

Spurred on, the four girls tore down the grassy slope, running much faster now, clearing the distance with superhuman speed. They stopped twice for Sigrid to scan ahead with her sniper scope, but there was no sign of the team ahead of them. When they got within five hundred meters of the target they slowed, moving much more cautiously; each girl held an eSMG in her hand as they spread out into the tangle of the forest. They knew the other team would be waiting somewhere up ahead.

Sigrid's heart was racing in her chest as she scanned the thick undergrowth around her. She was so intent on scanning ahead and on her flanks that she didn't see the half-buried log in front of her, and she tripped, sprawling forward in the dirt. She banged her knee, and her weapon fell from her hand.

It was also what saved her. Just as she fell, Sigrid heard the telltale *whoop-whoop* of two shock-rounds whipping by over her head and smacking into the tree beside her. Leta wasn't as lucky and she was struck; Sigrid watched her fall, twitching onto the forest floor about twenty meters away.

Sigrid rolled behind a tree without thinking, ducking as two more shots whizzed by her ear, crackling through the air. She looked around frantically. She couldn't see Suko or Khepri. A wave of panic swept over her. Had they run off or had they also been shot? Her heart hammered out a frantic rhythm in her chest—she couldn't find the eSMG she'd dropped! *She didn't want to lose.*

She heard the crack of a twig and footsteps coming closer—heavy footsteps. Too heavy and clumsy to belong to any of the girls.

Sigrid forced herself to calm down and concentrate. Pulling her sidearm from its clip at her hip, she rolled out from behind the tree. The man in the strange olive-green uniform almost tripped over her as he ran by.

Sigrid rolled onto her back, leveling her sidearm at him. There was a frozen moment where the two of them simply stared at each other, both surprised by each other's presence. The man snarled; it was enough to snap Sigrid out of her shock, and she fired three shock-rounds into his chest.

Nothing happened. "Shit." The man was wearing body armor. The paper stunners were useless.

Startled at first, the man regained his composure and stared down at the teenage girl lying prone before him. He laughed as he leveled his huge pistol at Sigrid's face.

But Sigrid was lightning fast in response. Her genetically modified reflexes took over and she scissored her legs and flipped up onto her feet before he knew what was happening. He fired, but the blast was late. She stepped in close and grabbed hard at his wrist, twisting it forcefully.

The man grunted in pain and surprise and dropped the gun. Angry, he swung his fist at her head. Sigrid was glad to be so short at that moment; she barely had to duck, and she brought her knee up hard into the man's crotch, following through with as much force as her five-foot-tall body could muster.

Groaning loudly, he sank to his knees.

Gouging, biting, hair-pulling...hitting below the belt. Rosa had drilled it into them. There was no such thing as a fair fight. All vulnerabilities must be exploited.

Suko and Khepri ran up; Khepri gaped at the man "What the fuck...?"

"He's wearing body armor," Sigrid said. Khepri raised her pistol and shot him pointblank in the face.

"*Garr...sonofa...*" He snarled, flailing and twitching violently before passing out.

"Holy shit!" Suko said.

"Who the hell's that?" Khepri asked. She nudged him with her foot, making sure he was unconscious, before tying him with a set of plastic binders.

Suko picked up his assault rifle. "And what's he doing with this?" She pulled out the magazine—it was full of *shockers*, similar to the type the girls were using.

"Do you think it's part of the exercise?" Khepri asked.

Suko shrugged. "I suppose. Hey—where's Leta?"

"Leta!" Sigrid leapt to her feet. She'd totally forgotten her. She darted off toward the place where Leta had been shot, barely taking three steps before tripping over the damned log again. "Mother fu—" Sigrid looked down. She'd been mistaken. The obstruction wasn't a log. It was the body of one of the girls.

"Jia..." Sigrid turned her over, brushing her dark hair out of her face. Her eyes were open and glassy. Sigrid could see that she was dead—stabbed in her chest and abdomen.

Suko dropped to her knees beside her. "Oh my God..."

Khepri shook her head in disbelief. "What the fuck?"

All three went instantly into defense mode, scanning the area carefully.

"Let's find Leta," Sigrid said, and they moved off with due caution.

When they found Leta, she was struggling to sit up.

"Owie..." she moaned, rubbing the tender spot on her chest where the charge had hit. The stun-round was still stuck to her so Sigrid pulled it off, unhooking the little barbs carefully. Leta was still a little woozy and so the girls had to steady her. She pulled open her shirt looking at the angry welt on her breast. "Bloody well hit me in the *boob*." She giggled.

Khepri cocked an eyebrow and muttered, "...not like it's hard to *miss*..."

Suko elbowed Khepri firmly in the side, forcing a grunt from her. "*What?*"

60

Leta shook her head to clear the fog. "Anyway, I'm okay. What happened?"

The girls told her of the man, how he'd attacked Sigrid, and about Jia, and how they'd found her stabbed to death.

"This is *insane,*" Leta said. "This can't be part of the exercise. They wouldn't kill us..." A doubting look spread over her face. "Would they?"

"Fuck it. I'm calling for Evac," Suko said. They'd forfeit the exercise, and there would be hell to pay, but none of them were worried about that anymore.

Suko keyed her communications implant—another element of their new bionics. Her eyes shot open in surprise. "I—can't get through! Something's jamming me."

Sigrid felt a heavy knot form in her gut. "If someone's jamming our signal..."

"Someone doesn't want us to get out of here," Leta said.

Khepri shuddered. "What do we do? Do we go back?"

Suko shook her head. "No way. What if there's more of these guys—what if they go after the others? We have to go after them."

Khepri's jaw dropped. "Go after them! With what? Shock-rounds? We don't even know how many there are."

"Fuck it," Leta said. "Let's kill 'em all."

"How? *Where!*" Khepri protested.

Suko gave her a firm, but calming look. "If someone's jamming us—if someone's really after us, then they'll go for the cargo beacon. If they're not, then Jia's team should be there. Either way, that's our target. We have to at least check it out."

"Fuck, ya," Leta said.

"Wait," Sigrid said. "What if this is one of Rosa's tricks...?"

"Then *I'll* kill him," Suko said drily.

There was nothing more to be said. The girls gathered their gear and headed to the target drop.

A dense thicket lay between them and their target. The four girls approached the area cautiously using all the tricks Rosa had taught them. They advanced quickly and in silence, flitting from cover to cover, little more than shadowy blurs in the dark woods. Not a twig was broken, or a leaf disturbed. All the time, they watched their flanks, scanning ahead with their thermal and chemical optics for anyone hiding in the underbrush.

At the bottom of the hill, just as Suko had predicted, they found the container—guarded by five men in the same green uniforms. Like the first man they'd encountered, they all wore light body armor and bulky night-vision goggles. All of the men carried assault rifles.

"Shit," Leta said.

Suko looked at Sigrid. "Any sign of Jia's team?"

Sigrid pulled out the sniper rifle and scanned. She shook her head. "Just these guys."

"What are we going to *do?*" Khepri asked.

A familiar, determined look came over Suko's face. "We take these guys out."

"With what?" Khepri looked at her weapon in disgust. "They gave us bloody toys."

Leta growled, "You know Rosa's training. We don't need weapons. We can take these assholes."

Sigrid continued to scan the men through her scope. "I can get one easy. Maybe two before they know something's up."

Suko's eyes were still fixed on the scene before them. "Well...the others won't likely stand around waiting to be shot. We'll need to get close."

Leta's face lit up. "Ooh! I have an idea." She started pulling off her shorts and shirt. "Rosa's always going on about *misdirection*, right..." In a matter of seconds she had stripped herself down to her underwear.

All the girls had gone through a rather healthy growth spurt thanks to their modifications and enhancements, but the process provided an added effect on Leta and her more obvious womanly attributes. Leta untied her hair to release the tight ponytail she kept and shook out her voluminous curls. They cascaded over her shoulders and down the curve of her bare back, reaching down to the narrow tuck of her waist. At nearly six feet, the term *statuesque* hardly did Leta justice. Her full, curving hips gave way to a pair of long and *stemmy* legs; the simple bra she wore labored to contain her shapely breasts. Sigrid felt positively like a child in comparison.

Suko grinned. "This is your plan?"

Leta wasn't done yet. With a wink to Suko, she took out her bowie knife and slashed a large gash in her hand.

Suko held up a hand, trying to block the ghastly sight. "*Gah!*...what are you doing?"

Leta let the blood pool into the palm of her hand before rubbing it over her face and chest. She grabbed up handfuls of muddy earth from the ground, slathering the muck all over her arms, face and stomach. "Do my back," she said.

Picking up on the plan, the girls joined in, with Leta adding even more blood from her injured hand. The effect was ghoulish.

"One last thing," Leta said. The girls watched as Leta contorted her face, her mouth curving down. She seemed to heave and convulse a little before the tears came as she made herself cry. "There—that should do it," she said, pouring forth an impressive stream tears.

"Dear God..." Suko said, torn between horror and amusement.

"This'll distract them!" Leta said. "A little...*misdirection*. Just like in our training. Wait for me to get close, then move in."

Sigrid grabbed Leta by the arm. "Are you crazy? They'll kill you."

"I don't think so. Look, they tried to stun me the first time—*and* you. Besides," she said, "you guys got my back."

"Yeah, but they *killed* Jia..."

"Just be ready to move in."

Still very uncertain, Sigrid let go of Leta's hand, and the girls headed toward their target and the group of men guarding it. Suko moved to the right in a flanking maneuver, while Khepri slunk around to the left side. Sigrid found a spot where she could cover them all with her sniper rifle. When the other girls were set, Leta strode forward, putting on quite a show; she thrashed through the thicket in the darkness, sobbing and making quite a racket.

Through her scope, Sigrid watched as the men's attention shifted. She could hear Leta calling out to them, "Help—help me, please!" Three of the men moved cautiously toward her, but the others kept watch on their flanks. When Leta crashed into the clearing—a sobbing, half-naked, bloody mess—the other men couldn't help but turn to stare at her.

As Leta collapsed on the ground, crying, the men hurried to the beautiful girl in distress. The men on the perimeter also began to head over to witness the drama.

Sigrid had one of them in her sights; she saw the pale flash of his exposed neck and squeezed the trigger. He stood up, stock straight, convulsing as the little slug unleashed its charge of electricity. Before he hit the ground, Sigrid aimed at the man on his left and fired, hitting him in the back of the thigh. The man went down in a heap.

The men on the perimeter were completely focused on the chaos in the middle of the clearing when Suko and Khepri rushed silently out from behind them. Both girls fired their eSMGs. Suko hit her target in the unprotected area by the man's rear, but Khepri missed. She was still rushing at the man when he turned, leveled his assault rifle and blasted her. Khepri screamed and fell—unconscious or dead, Sigrid didn't know.

Sigrid fired again; the shot glanced off the man's armor, but it was enough to distract him. Suko jumped on him from behind, tackling him to the ground.

Leta was unarmed and had to improvise. She leapt on the back of the only man still standing. Her legs wrapped around his waist as she held his neck, clamped in the crook of her elbow, while her free arm provided extra leverage. She looked like a wild animal, bloody and filthy, and with her red hair flailing madly about as she clung to the man's back. He clawed at her, stumbling, trying to throw her off, but she kept her grip, even as he fell over backward, landing hard on top of her, until he finally went limp.

Sigrid turned the scope back on Suko. She was pinned down, wrestling the last of the men. Both of them had their hands on his assault rifle, grappling for possession. Sigrid aimed, looking for an exposed spot; she couldn't let anything happen to Suko...

She heard, more than felt, the *thwack* of the stun charge as it hit her in the rear. There was no pain; that would come after the effects of the stun wore off. The rifle fell from her hands and she slumped to the mossy earth, face down in the mud. Her head swam and she kept losing focus, but she didn't lose consciousness. Her genetically modified body could handle the effects much better than the men. She experienced a moment of terrible panic when she tried to breathe and choked back a mouthful of dirt, but someone grabbed her from behind and flipped her over. She spat out mud and a twig, and concentrated on breathing through her nose.

She struggled to focus on the man sitting on her chest. He clutched the collar of her shirt, gathering it in his fists, pulling her face close to his. His mouth hung open as he scanned her from behind the bulky night-vision goggles. His breath smelled foul and felt hot on her cheek.

He tapped the communicator clipped on his ear. "I got one!" he shouted, clearly happy with himself. He waited a moment and tapped the transmitter again. "Stevens…Martinez…?" He waited again, scanning the woods around him. "Son of a…" Tearing the goggles from his face, he drew a long, black ceramic-bladed knife and held it to her neck. "…*bitch*."

He cuffed her across her chin with the side of his fist. It hurt like hell. Then Sigrid realized, yes—*it hurt*. The *shocker* had a paralytic effect, but it was wearing off remarkably fast. She wiggled a finger—she could move. Slowly, she reached down to her hip and unclipped her pistol, but her fingers were still clumsy and the man heard the movement.

"Bitch!" he said again and grabbed the gun away from her, tossing it aside.

He was still watching the gun fall when Sigrid pulled the knife from her belt. She slashed at him, cutting him in a wide gash across his arm. He grabbed her wrist and kneeled on both her arms.

"Fuck!" He looked at the blood flowing from the cut. "What the fuck are you girls on?" He held the tip of his own knife under her chin. "I'm not supposed to hurt you, unless you resist." He drew the tip of the knife down along her neck to the collar of her T-shirt. He lifted up the shirt collar with the tip of the blade, slitting the fabric. "I think we're past that…"

Sigrid felt her pulse quicken as he drew the knife down her chest. He made a quick upward slash and more of the light fabric parted. He smiled. Sigrid tried to lift her legs; she wanted to grab his neck in a scissor hold, but was still weak from the effects of the stun.

He struck her hard with the back of his hand—the knife grazed her cheek and cut her. "I told you to keep still!" Sigrid tried to kick him again, only to be punched hard and repeatedly. She felt blood dripping from her nose as her vision became fuzzy. When he punched her again she almost blacked out.

"Get your hands off her, *fucker!*" Suko's scream rang through the trees like a war cry.

Sigrid saw only a blur as Suko dived over her and onto the man. She tackled him high, slamming hard into his neck. They both rolled over in the mud in a wild and grappling heap. The man still had his knife, but Suko had hers as well. She parried his swipe easily and brought her own blade down hard, twisting it as she plunged it deep into his chest. His body twitched in a last, violent spasm, spitting up blood as his life leaked away.

With the fight over, Suko ran, stumbling, back to Sigrid. "Seeg!" she called out, pulling her close and hugging her hard. Sigrid lay limp in her arms as Suko wiped the mud and blood from her face. "Sigrid!" Deeply concerned, she checked her friend's condition. Sigrid's eye was swollen and her nose was a bloody mess. "Tell me you're okay!" she cried, trying to shake the life back into her.

"*Ow*...not so hard!" Sigrid said in mock protest. "I'm okay—just feel a bit...woozy, is all."

Leta arrived at the scene, panting for breath. She knelt beside Suko, wrapped her muddy arms around Sigrid's neck and hugged her almost as vigorously as Suko had. "Thank God you're okay." She looked over at the limp form of the young man and saw Suko's blade sticking out of his chest. "You...*killed* him."

Suko wiped her sudden tears away with a dirt-streaked fist. "I thought—I thought he was going to kill Sigrid."

Sigrid thought she may be right.

"Why would Rosa do this?" Leta demanded, tears flooding her own eyes. "Who *are these guys?*"

None of the girls could answer that one.

"Let's get to the beacon," Sigrid said. "Let's get the hell out of here."

The others nodded and they made their way back down the slope to the cargo container; Sigrid leaned heavily on the two girls. The body of the other man Suko had killed lay on the ground where he'd bled out from the gash in his neck, but the others were gone. The stun charges were only effective for a short time and the other men had escaped.

Leta looked around frantically. "Where's Khepri?"

They all scanned the woods, holding their weapons ready, but there was no sign of the men or their friend.

"They must have taken her," Suko said.

"Fuck it," Sigrid said. She slapped the homing beacon on top of the container that would send a signal to their transport to come pick them up. Nothing happened. Sigrid activated her implant and scanned the transponder. It was armed, but not transmitting. "Dammit!"

"Jamming...?" Leta asked.

Suko huffed. "Well, this is going right *down the gurgler.*"

"For once, I think I actually know what you mean." Sigrid tried accessing her com-link again. Nothing. A horrible thought occurred to her. "Do you think there are more of them? Do...do you think they're going after all the girls?"

Leta stomped her feet in the mud. "What the fuck is going on?"

Suko hushed her with a hand. "Quiet!"

Sigrid also heard it—the sound of a transport coming toward them.

The three girls moved quickly into the cover of the surrounding trees. The transport was on them fast. Sigrid could see it was a large craft—not the T-48s they'd flown in on. Neither was this one painted in the red and black colors of Kimura, but rather a dark-olive-drab, and with no markings on it.

It hovered above them; its four heavy thrusters blasted up fragments of dust and dirt and rock, forcing the three girls to shield their eyes. It hung there for what felt like an eternity before spinning horizontally on its axis, scanning the area with two floodlights suspended from its belly. Sigrid almost cried out as her optics were overloaded by the blinding, bright lights. She quickly dialed down the implant before opening her eyes again. She got a good look at the pilot in the cockpit. He wore the same dark-green uniform, but he wasn't anyone she recognized. Two more crew members manned the hulking chain-guns mounted on each side.

They had to have spotted them. Sigrid quickly calculated how she'd react, where she'd move, if the thing opened fire. But then a blast from its thrusters pushed it up and over the crest of the hill and out of sight.

"What the hell was that?" Leta said.

"Wait, look!" Suko pointed off in the direction the transport had gone. They could all hear its thrusters powering down as it came to rest beyond the copse of trees that concealed them, landing less than a kilometer away.

"Come on!" Sigrid said. They took off as fast as they could through the trees, and within a minute they saw the transport sitting in a small clearing near a rocky creek. Suko raised her fist, signaling the others to stop. She dropped to her knee. Leta and Sigrid instantly followed suit, taking cover in the brush.

Down below, just ahead of them, were another group of men gathered around the transport. Her heart sank when she saw four of the other girls lying face down in the dirt. Khepri was definitely one of them, and so was Mei, and possibly Lei-Fei. There was no way to tell whether the girls were alive or dead, but Sigrid and Suko and Leta all shared an unspoken resolve—they would not let the men escape with their friends.

Suko signaled Leta to flank around to the right. Leta nodded, disappearing quickly into the woods.

"Sigrid, I want you stay here, just like last time. We'll wait for you to take the first one out."

"No!" Sigrid said, grabbing Suko's arm. She didn't want Suko to leave her again. But when she looked again at the fallen girls she knew it was the only way. "Okay—I'll be okay."

Suko squeezed her shoulder and headed off.

Sigrid un-holstered the sniper rifle. The men were hurrying to load the girls into the transport. At least they were alive—*she hoped.* She couldn't let the transport take off, but her weapon was useless against the craft.

She heard the boom of the thrusters powering up; she couldn't wait any longer. Sigrid fired her first shot, hitting one of the men in the face—not the most effective spot for the stun-round, but it gave her a certain satisfaction. She aimed at the next man and fired. He fell hard, lying twitching in the dirt. She heard the shouts and ducked back down as the men opened fire—*real* bullets this time. She cursed. If only she had some actual lethal ammunition. One explosive round could take out the lot of them.

Sigrid heard more firing, this time from Suko and Leta shooting from their flanking positions. They each fired quick, efficient bursts and all their shots hit home. The pitch of the transport engines increased to a whistling howl. She couldn't let it take off, not with the girls still inside. Before she knew what she was doing, she was off and running down the hill towards it, covering the seventy meters in less than eight-seconds.

The large craft was already lifting away from the ground. She dived, grabbing onto one of the landing struts. Suko darted after her, barely managing to get a hand onto the tail gear at the back. Sigrid quickly hauled herself up into the belly of the craft. The two crew in the gunnery pods looked up, startled. Strapped into the pods, they were completely helpless. Sigrid showed them no mercy. She threw her bowie knife, burying it in the chest of one, before smashing the butt of her rifle in the face of the other.

She almost failed to react in time as the pilot fired back at her with his sidearm, but it was a wild, desperate shot, which she dodged easily. She was already off balance when he threw the controls hard over, banking the craft so steeply Sigrid almost tumbled out of the open port.

Sigrid clawed her way the three steps to the open cockpit. When the pilot reached back to fire at her again she was ready. She grabbed his wrist, and without even bothering to disarm him, she twisted his arm around and fired three times into his chest. The pilot slumped forward on the stick and the transport nosed sharply down, hurtling toward the ground not far below.

She made a mad grab for the control stick and heaved it back. The thrusters screamed in protest, and the transport bucked, leveling out moments before impact.

Sigrid slid into the co-pilot seat and throttled down. Her actions were greeted by an abrupt and eerie silence—she'd somehow managed to kill the engines—the huge transporter dropped the last fifteen feet and crashed to the ground. The four captured girls looked up at her blearily from the back of the compartment where they'd been piled, still bound, still suffering under the effects of the *stunners*. But they were alive.

And then Sigrid remembered—*where was Suko?* She hadn't made it into the transport.

"Suko!"

Sigrid leapt from the craft and landed running, frantically searching for her friend. She found her lying in the little creek bed, sprawled on her back, motionless. Sigrid ran to her, splashing through the shallow water, calling out to her.

Suko sat up wearily, probing her back with her fingers. "Ow…I think my bum's puckeroo."

Sigrid was so relieved to find her in one piece. She threw her arms around her, hugging her tightly. "Thank God you're okay."

"How are the others?"

"They're alive. Okay, I think."

Sigrid helped her to her feet, and the two hobbled back to the transport. Leta was already there, cutting the binders off the girls. They all looked okay, although a little groggy.

"What the hell's going on?" Mei asked. "Sigrid, you—killed those guys…"

"They killed Jia," Suko said—she still couldn't believe it herself.

"*What?*" Mei looked completely shocked.

"They were going to take you—or kill you! I don't know!"

Leta hauled the body of the pilot out of the cockpit, depositing it unceremoniously on the ground outside. One of the crewmen from the weapons pods was alive, but unconscious. The girls worked quickly to bind him, securing him in the back of the hold. Leta took the empty pilot's seat. She studied the controls; her fingers flitted over the various switches and gauges until the thrusters reignited. She turned to the girls behind her. "You guys might want to strap yourselves in."

"You're not going to fly this thing…" Suko said.

Leta shrugged. "I mean, how hard can it be?"

The other girls scrambled for the empty seats. Mei and Lei-Fei were already clambering into the empty weapons pods.

"This is insane!" Sigrid said—but she too was giddy at the idea of flying the commandeered craft.

Leta looked back over her shoulder; satisfied that the girls were all seated and strapped in, she hauled back on the stick—and the engines promptly died. "What the…?"

Sigrid climbed into the co-pilot's seat next to her; she'd had a few moments of experience flying the beast. "I think you have to press the thingy," she said, pointing at the main-thruster control switch. Leta hit it and the engines growled in response.

"Are we *sure* this is a good idea?" Mei asked again.

"We have to try," Suko said. "We have to save the others."

Leta got off to an *adventurous* start, but the robust craft shrugged off her brush with the surrounding treetops. The flight was erratic, if not a little hair-raising, eliciting the occasional scream from the passengers. The more the transport pitched and bucked, the more the girls shouted suggestions on how Leta might steady the craft.

"Shut up! I'm flying!" Leta barked back at them. "And you can quit that bloody squealing, too."

Sigrid took command of their navigation, guiding Leta to the other drop zones. At each point, they found a group of girls waiting patiently—most without a care in the world—simply wondering why their communications were down. But several of the teams had encountered similar groups of soldiers. Mercifully, Jia had been the only casualty. By the time they had picked up the final group of girls, Leta was doing a superb job at the controls.

"This thing flies itself," she said. "No—*literally*. Once I figured out I could just punch in the coordinates..."

Just before dawn, the Academy came into view. Sigrid noticed the smoke rising from the compound from more than a kilometer away. As they got closer, she could see that one of the supply sheds had been reduced to a smoking ruin. Some of the staff were still working to put out a fire that raged through the roof of the main building. The attackers hadn't only targeted them, but the entire Academy as well. *What the hell was going on?*

The staff hurried to the transport ship as Leta brought it in for a shaky landing. Dr. Garrett was the first to reach the steps, followed closely by Rosa and Chesna. Both instructors were now armed, and pointing their weapons at the transport—as were most of the staff. Some of the instructors were marching off a group of the green-clad soldiers; prisoners, no doubt.

The portal of the craft opened and they lowered their weapons as they saw a rather mud-caked Leta smiling down at them.

"Report!" Rosa demanded.

Leta couldn't hide the pride that shone through her eyes. "Just doing some flying, sir."

Sigrid rolled something green and heavy through the open door. It landed on the hard earth with a thud and an audible *grunt*—it was the crewman they'd captured. "Thought you might like another prisoner to question, sir."

Rosa erupted in laughter.

Sigrid, Suko and Leta jumped down from the belly of the craft, all of them shouting at Rosa simultaneously, eagerly telling him about the men they'd encountered in the woods, how they'd been attacked…and how Jia was found murdered.

Rosa waved them all quiet. "I'll debrief you all later. I want you all to report to the infirmary. We'll talk, but only after they've looked you over."

With groans of disappointment, the girls headed toward the main complex, while two of Rosa's staff hauled their prisoner away.

Once everything was quiet, Rosa turned to Chesna. "You recognize this?" he asked, looking at the stolen transport ship. It was an ancient Rollins Corp Lancer-Class low-orbital drop ship, specifically adapted to ferry troops to and from orbit.

She scoffed at the sorry-looking craft. "There's only one Mercenary Group I know that flies one of these rust-buckets."

"Tarsus." Rosa shook his head. "Karl, what have you gotten yourself into now."

Chapter 7
Battle Ready

January 5, 2348

Sigrid showered quickly that morning. She barely stopped long enough by the basin to brush her teeth and give her hair a quick comb. All the girls were in a hurry—the shuttles would be landing soon and no one wanted to miss such a spectacle.

Suko was dressed in a slim-fitting long-sleeved shirt and capris. She waited by Sigrid's bunk, with both hands on her hips, glaring at Sigrid and tapping her foot impatiently. "Hurry up!"

"I am!" Sigrid protested. She took off the damp towel she wore, taking time to fold it neatly over the rod at the end of her bunk—untidiness was always dealt with harshly at the Academy; if things weren't stowed or folded properly there'd be hell to pay. Suko looked on as Sigrid stood before her cubby, tapping a finger on her chin as she considered what to wear.

Suko sighed. "I already put them out for you." She pointed to the chosen clothes on the bed.

"You're *dressing* me now?"

"I just know how long you take to dress."

Sigrid held up the one-piece brown leotard Suko had chosen. "But I like the *blue* one."

"Then wear *that one*—or go naked. I don't care. Let's *go!*"

Sigrid pulled on the outfit. It was made of a thin fabric that stretched and fitted snugly. Despite the winter weather, a light windbreaker was all she needed to keep herself warm. The girls were becoming increasingly adaptable to all but extreme swings in temperature. Around her waist, she fastened the weapons belt with its two low-slung holsters strapped to her thighs. The two modified Markov PM6 sidearms she always carried clipped into the holstered brackets exactly at the point where her hands hung.

The girls were always armed now, ever since the attack over a year ago. Rosa had insisted on it as policy.

Suko rolled her eyes. "You and your...*guns*."

The pistols were modified versions, specifically designed with the girls' new bionics in mind. Each pistol featured built-in scopes that linked directly to her PCM, and were capable of targeting whatever she looked at. She could also instantly select from a variety of *smart* ammunition of the lethal and non-lethal varieties.

Sigrid pulled the two pistols out and gave them a quick twirl before depositing them back in their clips. "They're my babies," she said, rather pleased with herself. "Besides, it's not like you're not packing." She reached under Suko's shirt and dug around, pulling out one of the balisong butterfly knives she kept tucked in her trousers.

"This? Why, this is just a simple, practical tool." Suko took the little folding knife and flipped it open with a practiced flourish before handing it back to Sigrid, who tucked it back in Suko's pants. "Now," Suko said, "get your boots on or we'll miss it all."

Sigrid had barely pulled on her boots when Suko grabbed her hand and hurried her outside. Little had changed in their morning routine since they'd first met.

A light flurry of snow fell from the overcast sky. The peaked roofs of the Academy were already covered with a thick, white crystalline blanket. The ground was muddy and slick where the plows had worked to clear the training area. The Academy grounds had changed quite a bit during the past year. Outside the walls, several temporary structures had been erected to house the company of eighty-five Mercenary Marines who had been commissioned by the Kimura Corporation to guard the girls from further attack. Kimura had initially considered the remote location on Alcyone sufficient to keep Dr. Garrett's research—and their investment—safe, but the attack had demonstrated how vulnerable they were.

Sigrid and Suko walked hand-in-hand through the crowds that now occupied the training grounds. Stacks of the giant hundred-meter-long intermodal cargo containers took up much of the northern corner of the grounds. Even more stacks lay outside.

The girls had to step carefully to avoid the traffic as work crews busied themselves offloading and organizing the supplies that always seemed to be arriving these days. Sigrid knew that Dr. Garrett hated all the mess and chaos, but most of the equipment in the compound would be moved into the new annex in the near future.

The Kimura Corporation was impressed with the girls progress and had tripled their investment in Dr. Garrett's operation. A brand new annex for the Academy had been built higher up in the mountains and was three-times the size of the existing facility. Soon, the girls would move there, and a new group of students would take their place in their existing dormitory.

The girls had grown accustomed to their isolation on Alcyone—having so many people around felt quite strange. Stranger still were the looks they got from the cargo handlers, who had a tendency to stop and stare. The Marines exercised a bit more self-discipline, but Sigrid could still feel their eyes on them as she walked by, hand-in-hand with Suko. Having grown up in isolation with nothing to compare themselves to, the girls didn't realize they looked little like normal school girls. Years of harsh training had fashioned them into a lean and lethal bunch; all the girls carried themselves with a certain predatory grace. The modifications Dr. Garrett had provided had enhanced virtually every aspect of their biology, giving a healthy extra push where nature left off.

For years, Sigrid had fretted as she watched the other girls develop ahead of her. She'd been self-conscious about her own body, often wondering if she'd ever catch up. Her growth-spurt had kicked in late; and while she'd been disappointed when her height peaked at five-foot one—*and a half*, she insisted—at least the rest of her had filled out nicely. She was finally starting to feel like a young woman instead of the adolescent schoolgirl she'd felt like for so long.

One of the cargo-workers, a young man in his twenties, fell into step beside them.

"Hello, Sigrid," he said; he hadn't bothered to acknowledge Suko. "Where you headed?"

Sigrid greeted him with a polite smile. "They gave us the morning off. We're going up to watch the landings."

"Lucky you. I'd go, but we're pretty backed-up here. Too bad about the clouds though. You're not going to see much."

"Better than more of Rosa's exercises."

"Yeah—I've seen that stuff…" He glanced over his shoulder at the crew working behind him. "Look, I gotta get back before my supervisor has a fit. But I was wondering…maybe we could meet later—after my shift…?"

"Okay." Sigrid nodded and watched him trot off.

She turned to walk back toward the gates—and bumped straight into Suko. Suko tightened her grip on Sigrid's hand.

"*Ow…*"

"Who was that?" Suko asked, drily.

"That's, uh, Matthew—"

"Matthew." Suko seemed unimpressed. "I think he looks dodgy."

Sigrid felt oddly flustered. "No, he's…he's nice, actually."

"I didn't realize you were hanging out with the *workies* now."

"We weren't *hanging out*. We were just…" Confused, Sigrid looked at Suko. Suko's chest was rising and falling quickly and her jaw was slightly clenched. Sigrid felt the tightness of Suko's hand around her own and the intensity of her gaze.

Sigrid stepped closer, taking Suko's other hand. "Suko, he's just a boy—*he's nobody.*"

Suko's eyes softened and she opened her mouth, as if to say something, but they were interrupted by Leta who ran up to join them.

"What are you doing down *here?* You're going to miss the whole thing!"

She slipped between the two girls, linking both their arms in her own. She looked spectacular, as always. Her damp, red curls hung loosely over her shoulders and down her back, sparkling with flecks of thawing snow. The light sleeveless shirt she wore clung to her, showing off her toned arms and strong shoulders.

A sudden *boom* overhead made all three girls look up.

"Come on!" Sigrid called, towing them along and increasing their pace to a run. The sound was the sonic boom of a shuttle entering the atmosphere high above. The three girls ran out through the Academy gates and up the slope to join the other girls who had gathered to watch the shuttles coming in. They got there just in time and clambered up onto a snowy ledge where they'd have an unobstructed view.

Sigrid raised her hands toward the heavy, overcast sky. "I can't see a thing!"

"You're not using your *head*," Suko said, snickering. She tapped Sigrid on her forehead.

Sigrid sighed and silently cursed herself. She activated her optical implant and scanned skyward; the heavy thermal signatures from the shuttle's massive thrusters were clear to see as it blasted down through the clouds. Scanning the electrical signatures provided an even more dazzling sight. The ground shook beneath them as the throaty roar of the re-entry boosters grew louder and louder. Sigrid quickly ramped down the frequency in her audio modules to avoid being overwhelmed by the noise.

They all cried out when the shuttle burst through the clouds, close above their heads at two-hundred feet. The skeletal craft comprised a tangled framework of thrusters connected by a long supporting structure. It looked surprisingly delicate. Sigrid wondered how it could possibly support the massive hundred-meter-long transport container it carried in its cradle.

The shuttle's sixteen thrusters flared brilliantly as it descended on the Academy grounds. The Cargo-Handlers hardly gave the thing a second glance as they continued with their duties; even though the leviathan craft looked as if it were about to crush everyone beneath it. With a loud, clanking thud of metal on metal, the shuttle deposited the container expertly on the growing stack in the middle of the compound. After pausing to disconnect its burden, the pilots maneuvered the craft swiftly to the side, hooking onto one of the empty containers. The thrusters flared and roared again as the shuttle climbed quickly back into the thick cover of the clouds. The whole operation had taken less than a minute.

The girls hooted and clapped in appreciation.

Over the next two hours, seven more shuttles arrived to deliver the remainder of the cargo from the freighter parked in orbit. Even more impressive, at least to Sigrid, was the busy fleet of smaller transports that emptied the containers and whisked off the supplies to their final destination in the new annex.

"I can't believe this is all for us," Suko said.

"And for the new girls, I suppose," Sigrid said.

It was odd to imagine that a new group of younger girls would soon be moving in to take their place, stranger still to think they would be leaving soon to move to the new annex. She'd have her own room there, in the much larger facility, something all the girls were looking forward to, but Sigrid still felt a certain anxiety about being uprooted.

And a darker anxiety was lurking even deeper within her. They were about to begin the final phase of their enhancements, and their time at the Academy would soon be over.

Soon, they would be leaving Alcyone.

Chapter 8
Annex

From The Journal of Dr. Lisa Garrett

February 21, 2348

RE: Project Andraste
Dear Hitomi-san,
I've been spending much of my time at the new annex getting things prepared for the final phase of our work. It's hard to believe so much time has gone by, but I couldn't be more pleased with the results.

Our greatest challenge has been to keep an accurate chart of the girls' progress. We had hoped to see improvements, physically anyway, in the range of twenty-five to forty percent, but the evidence suggests something more in the realm of 135% greater than normal. We've created quite the batch of young Olympians here. Their endurance and ability to adapt to climactic extremes has been most impressive.

Tomorrow we'll bring the girls to the new facility where we'll begin the final phase of the their modifications. I'll finally be able to integrate the systems and initiate the final sequence. It's time to hook it all up and turn it on, *so to speak. We've dubbed the procedure 'Activation.' It seems to sum it up fairly well.*

The new Master Control Program has been tested and retested, and I'm satisfied that the subjects are ready to have it uploaded to their Primary Control Modules. If this works as we expect, all their modifications will coalesce into a fully-functioning Artificial Neural Network, allowing them to operate at maximum capacity.

We anticipate improvements in their ability to process sensory data by an order of magnitude as their own biological receptors integrate with the bionic Sensory Modules. I would imagine that this will be much like the blind suddenly being given the gift of sight, except that this will involve all their senses at once. It should prove to be a somewhat profound experience for them, and we will record their transformation for complete analysis.

We've received the data-packet you've supplied us—the Tactical Operations Database, I believe you called it. Once the Control Program is activated, we'll upload this packet to the girls' PCMs for field testing.

I know what Dr. Wolsey would be saying right now, but I'm sure you'll agree that we're long past the fail-safe point. There's no turning, back.

All that remains is to turn it on.

Yours truly,
Lisa

* * *

Three *Kingfisher* transports took off from the compound carrying the thirty girls and their instructors. The heavy overcast skies hung as low and gloomy as Sigrid's spirits. The Academy was almost back to normal, finally freed from the clutter of giant containers and crews. The only visible change was the temporary barracks that housed the Mercenary Force; the majority of the mercenaries would stay at the Academy to guard the new girls, while a platoon would accompany the senior girls to the 'Annex', as it had been aptly named.

They weren't going far; the Annex was only fifteen kilometers distant, but much of that was straight up. As the transports burst through the cloud bank, Sigrid caught her first glimpse of the new facility. The mountains here were a series of sheer, vertical cliffs; the Annex was literally carved directly into the side of the tallest peak. The Kimura engineers had spent the last few months blasting and tunneling to create the facility. Five stories of terraces and windows were visible from the exterior; Sigrid could see people moving about on several of them—staff members and workers who had gathered to watch the approach of the transports.

There was no visible landing platform though, and the transports climbed even higher, up and over to the far side of the hollowed-out mountain. They landed on a platform built atop the wide glacier at the base of the peak. The ice was smooth and as firm as concrete, and held the heavy structure easily.

The glacier shone brilliantly, reflecting the dazzling midday sunlight. As the girls exited the transports, their enhanced eyes adjusted easily to the blinding light. Lacking such modifications, the instructors had to wear dark goggles. They also wore heavy coats to protect them from the wind that ripped across the ice.

Sigrid gasped as she stood before the large portal the engineers had cut into the rock. Twenty-five meters high and more than a hundred wide, it was large enough to allow entrance and storage for the transports and trucks that would service the facility. Icy flecks of snow, whipped by the fierce, gusting winds, struck Sigrid's bare arms and stuck in her hair.

Suko placed Sigrid's discarded coat over her friends shoulders and dropped Sigrid's duffel at her feet. "I think you forgot something," she said, pointing at the bag.

Sigrid was still staring at the maw ahead of them; she felt as though it would swallow her.

"Come on—it'll be okay," Suko said, wrapping an arm around her. Sigrid picked up the duffel and let Suko lead her by the hand to their new home.

Inside, the hallways were all of polished stone, hollowed out from the mountain above them, with some sections constructed with shaped permacrete. The idea of living in a series of tunneled-out warrens had seemed depressing. Sigrid had imagined her new home to be cramped and claustrophobic, but the high corridors and spacious common areas—with large windows and terraces—filled her with a sense of awe. She'd never seen a place like it.

Their guide led them up two levels to the living area where they'd be quartered. Each girl was presented with her own room, something most of them had never had. Only the richest families, most of whom lived in Earth's cordoned-off enclaves, could dream of having rooms to themselves.

Sigrid dumped her duffel on her bunk and looked at her new home. The walls were of the same grey, polished stone as the hallways outside, but the room wasn't drab at all. The rock had a sparkle to it that caught and reflected the light from the overhead lamps. Her bed was larger than the one she'd had in the dormitory, and she had her own desk. There were no closets, but a small armoire sat in the corner, along with a number of hooks for hanging jackets and clothes.

"Looks just like my room," Suko quipped.

Sigrid jumped; she hadn't heard her friend come in. Suko put her arms around Sigrid's waist, resting her chin on her shoulder.

"Could be worse," Sigrid reasoned. She was starting to think the Annex might not be so bad.

"I have a surprise for you." Suko put her lips next to Sigrid's ear and whispered, "There's a swimming pool."

* * *

Sigrid sat alone in her room, a little overwhelmed by how quiet it was. Nine years of being surrounded by more than thirty girls had not prepared her for the emptiness of the sudden solitude she was experiencing. There had been no work for the girls that day. They'd spent their time exploring every inch of the Annex, though they'd all been assured that tomorrow would be all work. If she didn't get to sleep soon, she'd pay for it in spades in the morning.

Sigrid undressed. She tossed her shirt and bra in the laundry and folded her pants neatly on a hanger before she climbed into bed. Normally, sleep came as soon as her head touched the pillow. Rosa and his staff always did a good job of making sure the girls were exhausted. Sigrid tossed and turned for a further ten minutes before casting her blanket off and staring wide-eyed at the stone ceiling.

"Fuck..."

The door to her room glided open almost silently. She grabbed up the discarded blanket and covered herself quickly. But it was just Suko. She poked her head in cautiously and entered the room once she knew Sigrid was awake, closing the door behind her.

"I couldn't sleep," Suko said. Her long black hair flowed down around her shoulders, shimmering in the dim light. She wore only the small T-shirt and briefs she normally would for bed. Sigrid moved over to make room as Suko slid onto the bed next to her.

"I can't sleep, either," Sigrid said. "I don't think I'm used to all this quiet." What she didn't say was how strange it felt not having Suko next to her.

"I know." Suko stared up at the ceiling. "I was just thinking about tomorrow."

"Me too. I keep wondering what it will be like."

Suko frowned. "Dr. Garrett said we'd be *better* after the *final phase*. But it's not like I feel sick."

Sigrid crinkled her nose in a frown. "I don't think I like the sound of being *Activated*. What does that even mean?"

"And, better? Better than what? You'd think it'd kill her to explain something for once. They never tell us anything."

"That would make too much sense—nothing they do here seems to make *any* sense." Sigrid leaned her head on the pillow next to Suko, touching the tips of Suko's fingers with her own. "And then, I guess they'll send us away."

"I was *trying* not to think about that." Suko poked her playfully.

"Sorry." Sigrid chuckled softly. "When they do, I hope they send us to Crucis—maybe they'll send us to the Naval Academy. That's what Chesna thinks. That might not be so bad. Maybe we'll all go." *As long as we go together*—she didn't have to say it.

Neither of them spoke for a while, both were lost in thought. Sigrid didn't know what the next day would bring, but for the moment, Suko was next to her and that was all that mattered. She began to feel she might finally get some sleep and succumbed to the softness of the mattress...

Suko leaned on her elbow. "Well, I should get back—I just wanted to..." She was looking down at Sigrid, her hair hanging loose over her face, brushing against Sigrid's. "I just wanted to see how you were doing."

Suko made it halfway to the door before Sigrid stopped her. "Wait. Stay. I don't think I'll be able to sleep in here by myself."

Suko's relief was accompanied with a smile. "Me too. I mean...if it's all right...unless you think we'll get in trouble."

"Come. There's room." Sigrid lifted the blanket and patted the mattress beside her.

Suko stared down at her; she paused, looking almost shy for a moment, but then she pulled off her T-shirt and slipped in next to her.

Sigrid flinched as their bodies met under the covers. She laughed. "You're *cold*."

Suko laughed back. "You're *warm*."

Sigrid covered them both with the blanket and wrapped her arms around Suko, pulling her closer. This was much better than being alone in her empty room. They lay there facing each other, eyes open. Suko brushed the loose hair from Sigrid's face, tucking it gently back behind her ear, stroking the soft hair of her neck with her fingers. Sigrid breathed deeply and felt her eyelids grow heavy. She was almost asleep when she felt Suko's lips touching hers; kissing her softly, Suko whispered, "Goodnight."

There wasn't much room in the small bed. Suko was perched slightly on one elbow, her other arm rested between them, which Sigrid could feel pressed up against her. Suko still felt cold so she pulled her closer, sharing the warmth of her body. As she moved, she felt Suko's hand slip between her thighs; her fingers were ice-cold and she shivered at the touch. The two girls stared at each other, eyes wide open, barely breathing.

"Goodnight," Sigrid whispered back, finally returning the kiss. She let her lips linger there, not pulling away. Her mouth parted slightly and she felt the tip of Suko's tongue flick over her lips, then a kiss on the tip of her chin and the soft spot on her neck. When her lips found Suko's a second time, her mouth surrendered to the open intensity as she felt Suko's tongue dart deeper into her mouth.

Sigrid slowly lifted her leg, freeing Suko's hand, but Suko didn't pull away or withdraw it. Slowly, nervously, Suko inched her hand higher, pausing as the tips of her fingers brushed the seam of Sigrid's underwear.

A wave of delight mingled with terror swept over Sigrid, and her heart pounded, sending butterflies coursing through her body. Both girls froze, stared at each other. And then Suko kissed her again, tracing her fingers over the soft material of her briefs. Sigrid's whole body trembled under the delicate touch. She pushed up against her, and, *finally,* she thought, Suko reached into her underwear, touching her very softly with the tips of her fingers.

Sigrid took in a sharp breath as she felt Suko's fingers slip inside her. She wrapped her knee around Suko's waist, squeezing her gently.

Suko stopped; she looked at her anxiously and withdrew her hand. "Are you okay?"

Sigrid nodded vigorously and whispered, "Yeah—more than okay."

Sigrid reached down and quickly pulled off her underwear before redirecting Suko's hand. She covered Suko's hand with her own, guiding her with her own fingers. As Suko began to caress her with more urgency, Sigrid felt the warmth blooming within her, a tingling that stretched from her spine to her toes. Her arms coiled around Suko's neck—she kissed her deeply, pressing her body hard against her. Sigrid moaned softly and shuddered as her orgasm surged quickly into a rushing, sweeping climax. She flopped down into the mattress, fighting to steady the excitement in her breaths.

It took a moment for her head to clear. She was still grappling with what had just happened—she hadn't realized anything could feel so wonderful, so intense, so sweet. She wanted more.

Sigrid sat up and nudged Suko onto her back. She kneeled over her, tucking her hair back behind her ears. She felt the softness of Suko's skin beneath her hands, the curve of her breasts. Suko shivered as Sigrid drew her hands slowly down the length of her stomach, pausing just below her belly-button. Suko raised her hips to help Sigrid as she pulled her underwear off. She kissed the tips of Suko's knees, her lips traced a line up the inside of her leg; her cheek brushed against the soft warmth of Suko's thigh. She kissed her lightly, first with her lips then her tongue, until Suko responded in ecstasy, shuddering softly against her.

As they gathered their senses and breath, Sigrid became very aware of Suko staring at her. Suko beamed brightly, her eyes twinkling like never before.

"What?" Sigrid asked; suddenly feeling quite self-conscious. Blushing, she held the edge of the blanket over her.

Suko laughed. "What do you *think?*"

Sigrid blushed hotter still. "Oh…right."

Still flush with excitement, Sigrid lay back down next to Suko, pulling the blanket over both of them. They shivered, as if suddenly cold, then held each other close.

"*Now*—I think I'll be able to sleep!" Sigrid said, snuggling fully into a much warmer Suko.

"You…you don't suppose anyone *heard*, do you?"

Sigrid looked around and pounded the hard stone wall with the back of her fist. "I think we're safe."

They kissed again—a brief struggle with the blanket ensued as they fought playfully to get the blasted thing to cover their toes. Within minutes, they were both snoring soundly.

* * *

February 22, 2348

Suko had been gone all morning; she'd been called to the Treatment Room to be *Activated*, as they called it, leaving Sigrid to pace the lengths of her tiny quarters while she waited for her own name to be called. There was no schedule because the doctors were not entirely sure how long the procedure would take, but that only fueled Sigrid's anxiety toward the whole affair.

Finally, her turn came. An orderly showed up at her door and led her to the Treatment Center. Dr. Garrett greeted her and waved Sigrid to a padded chair surrounded by an array of terminals and displays.

Dr. Garrett smiled warmly. "Hello, Sigrid. How are you feeling today?"

Sigrid was too nervous to answer, but Dr. Garrett, focused on preparing the procedure, didn't seem to notice. She brought the data-uplink module over to hook up to Sigrid, who flinched and pulled away.

"It's all right, Sigrid. This won't hurt."

"I know, ma'am, but…" She swallowed. "What *will* it be like?"

86

Dr. Garrett considered the question before answering. "The clinical term might be, a *heightened situational awareness.*" Sigrid heard a pronounced *click* as Dr. Garrett slipped the data-uplink into her access port. Dr. Garrett smiled. "You're going to feel *great.*"

Sigrid gulped.

"Now, I'm going to put you out for just a moment," Dr. Garrett said. "Can you count back for me?"

Still not quite convinced, Sigrid nodded and began her practiced count backward from ten. She remembered getting as far as seven this time, and then nothing. As with her other treatments, it felt as if only a moment had passed when she blinked her eyes open. Doctor Garrett was leaning over her, looking at her expectantly.

"How do you feel?" she asked.

"I feel..." Sigrid was about to say *fine*, but she suddenly became acutely aware that something was very, *very* different.

She felt a rush—a surge of sensation, a hyperawareness of...everything; smells, noise, the touch of the fabric on her skin...color...she could *smell* color. When Sigrid looked at Dr. Garrett, she could feel the woman's heart beating. The sound was deafening. Her PCM fed streams of data to her, displayed in her HUD: pulse, heart-rate, respiration, perspiration. She could even smell the woman's breakfast on her: orange juice, coffee, two slices of rye toast—and something else...

"You had *sex*," Sigrid said. Then looking at Dr. Mitchell, she said. "With *him.*"

Sigrid giggled, but the laughter shook her violently inside. She could feel the blood moving through her veins—and count the corpuscles. Her skin, her hair; everything *crawled.* She could see her entire self; not as a whole, but as every individual composite. Heart, pancreas, brain, bionics; even the billions of nanomites that scurried through her system. She could identify each one individually. "Hello, little robots," she said and laughed, as if tipsy with sensation.

Her attention was drawn to the two orderlies in the corner; the men fingered their stun batons, eyeing her suspiciously. They registered as *minimal threat.* One of them leaned on his left foot, as if wondering if he should attempt to restrain the girl. Sigrid had already calculated seven ways she could take him down and incapacitate him if he tried as much.

The walls had been recently painted; the stench of its solvent filled her lungs. Worse were the acrid aromas of sterilizers and cleaners, all mixing into a toxic stew, along with Dr. Mitchell's cologne. Sigrid threw up what felt like an endless gushing stream. In slow motion, she watched as particles burst from her mouth; she found herself analyzing the content of each particle as the memories of her breakfast came flooding back.

Dr. Garrett was holding her by the shoulders, shaking her. Sigrid could see that she was talking, but the words hadn't yet left her mouth. The Doctor's stress levels had elevated dramatically. Sigrid didn't know why this was so—she felt fine. In fact, she felt so good, she thought she'd go tell Suko.

In a flash, Sigrid was at the door of the treatment room. This seemed to increase the general state of agitation in everyone around her. Two of the technicians lunged to grab her. Much too slow. She tripped one and knocked the other on the head, causing them both to fall into a heap. She burst through the door and into the hallway. Four security officers were rushing toward the Treatment Room—*toward her*. Sigrid didn't know what they wanted, but they clearly had something on their mind. She braced to strike before they could bring her down.

Then came a stabbing sensation in her buttock. She spun and saw Dr. Garrett holding an empty syringe. She felt the cold lorazepam enter her bloodstream. Sigrid wondered why she'd done that. As she pondered the question, she felt the nanomite swarms coursing through her system, already working their magic to break down the drug and nullify its effects.

Sigrid laughed. She couldn't remember ever feeling so good. She was about tell Dr. Garrett how wonderful it all was, when one of the security guards hit her with a shock-round. What a curious sensation. "Hey!" Sigrid protested.

"Sigrid!" Dr. Garrett grabbed her shoulders, shaking her. "Sigrid! Can you hear me?"

Sigrid's ears were buzzing and her rear smarted from where the guard had zapped her, but, yes, she could hear her now.

"*Ow*," she said.

She felt the euphoria recede, her control flowing back. Her senses were still being bombarded from every which way, but she could make sense of things now. It was a question of focus—she just needed to *focus*.

As her vision cleared, she became aware of everyone gathered around her, staring at her. The ties on the back of her hospital gown had come loose during the melee. She reached around to hold the gown closed.

"Are you...okay?" Dr. Garrett asked.

Sigrid thought, and nodded, "Yes." She took a few careful breaths, feeling the air rush through her lungs before blowing it out in a long exhale; it sounded like a gale-force wind in her head. "Is that...normal?"

Dr. Garrett didn't need to answer; Sigrid could read the woman's body-language and biochemistry easily enough; the way she gripped Sigrid by the shoulders told her this certainly wasn't normal.

"Your reaction was rather...extreme." Dr. Garrett said finally. Her eyes were darting all over Sigrid, as if worried Sigrid might freak out again. "How do you feel?"

How did she feel? *Like some giant, ravenous, predator-cat that's just been rolled in catnip, is how I feel!* Sigrid thought, but she couldn't tell the doctor that—could she?

"May I go to lunch now, please?"

"Ah...I'd like to do some tests first."

Sigrid hoped the tests wouldn't take very long.

* * *

The tests took far longer than Sigrid liked, but once Dr. Garrett was satisfied that Sigrid had adapted to the treatment adequately, she released her from the hospital ward. Sigrid walked back to her room slowly and carefully. If she didn't concentrate, she became quickly overwhelmed by the sounds of her own footsteps reverberating in the halls. It was worse when she passed through a group of people—breathing, sweating, talking, hormones raging. There was a growing hunger lurking in her, and it practically growled.

Suko wasn't in her room when she looked so she went back to her own, closing the door quickly behind her. The silence proved too much and she found herself calculating the volume of blood distributed by each heartbeat—she wondered if she could manipulate the flow and the rhythm? Yes, she could.

She needed to find Suko. The memory of their night together—stored in perfect detail in her PCM—came rushing back. Sigrid fell back against the wall, closed her eyes; she could still feel Suko next to her, the touch of her hands.

Gah—she had to get out of there.

She decided to change into the long-sleeved, one-piece suit that had become their new uniform. The jet black fabric was emblazoned with the red Kimura logo and had a zippered front culminating in a stylish high-collar. Tall lace-up boots and her twin Markov pistols completed the outfit.

She finally found Suko sitting in the cafeteria with Leta; both had lunch trays in front of them, although neither plate looked touched. Suko's eyes shot up to meet her gaze as she entered and walked quickly over to the table. Sigrid's pulse quickened and her temperature rose; Suko's closeness filled her with a rush of excitement. She found herself involuntarily scanning Suko; her pulse and adrenals were elevated too. It was obvious that both girls had received their treatment, and their senses were firing on all cylinders as they regarded each other with the same hungry intensity. All of Sigrid's skin tingled; she reached out a hand, half expecting sparks to leap from Suko's skin to the tips of her fingers.

"Oh, get a room, you two," Leta said.

Sigrid tried her best to look innocent, but felt her face flushing hot. "What? What do you mean?"

Leta laughed; a few of the other girls were looking over and grinning too. "You think we can't sense it? It's written all over the two of you."

Suko chuckled. "I guess there's not much we're going to be able to keep from each other."

Apparently not, Sigrid thought, somewhat chagrined.

Sigrid tried to keep appearances by taking a lunch tray, but she couldn't eat either. She tried a spoonful of her soup, but found herself lost, calculating the volume and ratio of the various ingredients. And Suko kept looking at her. It was very distracting.

Suko had dipped the tip of her finger in her water, running it over the rim of her glass in slow circles; her foot gently grazed against Sigrid's leg, sliding up the length of her calf. She swallowed, and wet her lips with the tip of her tongue—

"Oh, dear *God*," Leta said.

Suko shot her a guilty look. "Sorry."

As casually as they could, Sigrid and Suko walked out of the cafeteria. Suko's room was closer and they slipped quickly inside, grabbing for the zippers of each other's jumpsuits before the door had even closed. Suko threw Sigrid onto the bed and dived on top of her. As much as last night's tryst had been cautious and tender, this afternoon's adventure was purely carnal, enhanced further still by their newly modified sensory-receptors.

They had no idea how much time had passed when they collapsed, side by side, on the bed.

"Rock walls or not, I *know* someone heard that," Suko said.

Sigrid laughed. "I guess this is what she meant."

"What?"

"Dr. Garrett. She said we'd experience a *heightened situational awareness*."

Suko chuckled. "Definitely. That has to be it."

Chapter 9
Graduation

February 23, 2348

A few of the girls were still having difficulty dealing with the effects of *Activation*, so Dr. Garrett had prescribed a period of rest for those still feeling *overwhelmed*.

The period of respite left Sigrid free to spend all her time with Suko. Each minute alone seemed a chance for Sigrid to explore every inch of Suko's soft, warm skin. Suko teased her, saying that she was *mapping* her, charting her like one of Rosa's bloody survey exercises. Sigrid was indeed on a mission, loosing herself in each of Suko's eager embraces.

For the next four days they only left her room at mealtimes and for their daily consultation with Dr. Garrett. Sigrid had been mortified when Dr. Garrett cautioned her not to *overly stimulate* herself. Dr. Garrett hadn't said it outright, but Sigrid figured out the staff was monitoring the girls' activities—*all of the time*—collecting data for analysis from their telemetry sent to the main servers.

Sigrid and Suko had both been a little embarrassed to learn they were being so closely monitored, but there was nothing they could do.

After not seeing them for days, Leta decided to drag the lovers from their nest and take them on an outing. The new girls had just arrived at the Academy and she proposed a trip down to meet them. She'd finagled one of the *Starlings* from the motor pool. Sigrid and Suko jumped at the chance to accompany her.

As they entered the hangar, Sigrid noted that Leta was making a point of sticking to the shadows, peering around corners, beckoning them to follow when no one was looking.

Sigrid frowned. "I thought you said you had permission."

Leta gave a sheepish shrug. "Well...they didn't say, *no*."

"Good point," Suko said, as they piled into one of the parked *Starlings*. Leta's hands flew over the controls with a practiced precision as she executed the startup routine. "Since when can you fly one of *these*?"

The thrusters roared to life, blasting the ground outside with a gush of wind.

Leta smiled. "Since now. I found the manuals in the Tactical Database." She pointed out the various operations. "Thrust, lift, pitch...piece of cake. Check it out."

Sigrid accessed the database stored in her PCM and instantly found the files, along with more files on basic flight characteristics. "*Ooo*, sweet!" she said, impulsively reaching over Leta's shoulder and grabbing the stick—she yanked it back. The *Starling* shot up into the air, narrowly missing the hangar roof before buzzing low over a row of parked transports and scattering their astonished ground-crews.

"Hey!" Leta protested, wresting control from Sigrid. "You'll get us grounded."

"Sorry—I couldn't resist."

"Well, get your own."

Sigrid sat back in her seat with a guilty grin. "Okay...I'll be good."

Leta rolled her eyes and gunned the thrusters. The T-48 shot through the open hangar doors and into the morning sunlight. Sigrid wasn't sure if Leta was showing off or just trying to figure out the controls, but she put the *Starling* through a startling series of aerobatics—Sigrid fumbled quickly to fasten her seat and shoulder-belts.

"Scaredy-cat." Leta stuck out her tongue as she put the *Starling* into a half-roll. She pulled out over the peak that hid the Annex, then zoomed low, skimming the surface of mountainside. "I think I'm getting the hang of this," she said, going inverted again.

Sigrid gulped as she stared *up* at the ground now above her head.

Leta's final maneuver brought them low over the Academy as she buzzed a group of Marines on a training run. As they flew by,

Sigrid caught a glimpse of the new group of girls assembling in the center compound.

She pointed. "Look!"

Leta hauled back, coming hard about, then circled above them. The new girls began pointing up, some even waved. Leta zoomed back over the Marine compound before performing a spine-crushing landing in the airfield just outside the Academy walls.

A heavyset man wearing sergeant stripes stormed out of the hangar, ready to rip a new asshole for the pilot who had clearly lost his mind. He stopped short of the craft, staying clear of the props as they wound down. Sigrid saw the redness on his face, the veins bulging in his neck. It didn't require genetically modified sensory receptors to see the man was furious and looking for a pound of flesh. She almost suggested that Leta take off again and flee back to the Annex.

Hesitantly, Sigrid climbed out from her jump seat and stepped down onto the muddy ground. The still-spinning props whipped her long blond hair over her back and shoulders. She pulled a loose strand from her face as she met the man's glare.

All his bluster vanished in an instant and his jaw dropped as his eyes slowly traced the length of Sigrid's body. Her formfitting uniform and knee-high military boots complemented the curve of her feminine hips, accentuated by the pistols strapped to each of her shapely thighs. Even as short as she was, Sigrid cut a striking figure, though she'd never been leered at so openly before. The instructors had always been professional and paternal, but this man looked at her with a craving, a hunger. The veins in his neck no longer bulged, but his face remained flushed red. When Suko and Leta came up beside her, Sigrid felt his pulse quicken as he took in the three women.

Dear God—he's becoming sexually aroused. She looked at her two friends—they'd also picked up on it.

"Something we can help you with, Sergeant?" Leta asked, with a hand on her hip.

The sergeant must have realized he was gawking. He closed his mouth and straightened himself. "Ah…next time, make sure you radio for clearance." He gave a dismissive wave and stormed off. The girls were out of his chain of command anyway.

The three of them stifled a laugh and headed toward the school, eager to see the new crop of students. They found the new recruits in the courtyard—forty-two girls between nine and eleven-years-old—gathered around Rosa. They listened as he gave the girls their induction speech, similar to the one he'd made to them so many years ago, telling the new group what instruction they would receive and what Kimura would expect of them.

It aroused a poignant feeling in Sigrid. Had it really been nine years since she'd come here and sat on that ground, listened to that lecture? Leaving Earth, her family, all her years of training; it was still so confusing. Perhaps more so now. She would be leaving soon, they all would be—leaving to begin their work as Mercenaries, working to repay their family debts that the Kimura Corporation had purchased.

Whatever would happen to her out there? And what of Suko?

Many of the new girls had seen them approach, their attention drawn away from Rosa and his lecture.

Rosa looked up sharply at the interruption, but rather than send the trio away, he invited them to come closer. The younger girls froze in awe, perhaps from some inherent connection, or maybe because the three older girls in black, with weapons slung at their sides, painted such an impressive and deadly picture.

Rosa's face relaxed into a slight grin. "Ladies—perhaps you would like to come and meet your new sisters."

The three girls approached the group, stepping into their midst. The little girls gathered close, reaching out to touch them and say hello. Sigrid was amazed. They all seemed so young. She couldn't help but wonder if they would have an easier time of it than she did. Would they be bullied as well? Would they be beaten?

Rosa surprised the gate-crashers by asking them to join the new girls in the dining area. As they took lunch with the new arrivals, the three shared stories of their experiences, passing on whatever advice they could to the young girls. Some of them were still frightened and homesick, but the older girls' presence seemed to calm them.

Finally, it was time for the younger ones to continue their lessons, so the three girls took their leave. The visit made Sigrid feel strangely sad and homesick herself, but not for Earth and her family. She was missing this place *here*, and she dreaded having to leave it again. A dark foreboding came over her accompanied by a pain in her gut she'd not felt for some time. The return flight to the Annex didn't lighten her mood any, either.

When they arrived back at the wide hangar entrance atop the glacier, Sigrid's heart sank one notch lower. Blocking the entrance was a parked transport ship. Painted in the black and red colors of the Kimura Corporation, the transport was far too large to enter the hangar and lay on station outside.

Sigrid heard an order over her comlink; she was to proceed immediately to Dr. Garrett's office. Suko and Leta received the same order. All three looked to one another, anxiety etched on their faces.

"Who do you think it is?" Leta asked.

Sigrid stared up at the ship. It was definitely an interstellar-job. When her eyes passed over the registry numbers painted on its side, her optic module fed the information automatically into her database and the ship's ID popped up in her HUD. It was registered as the *Agatsuma*, out of Kappa Aquarii. Home of Kimura Corporation.

Sigrid felt a cold shiver course through her. "They've come for us."

* * *

Two Mercenary Marines stood guard outside Dr. Garrett's office—the first sign that something was up. A young corporal retrieved Sigrid's pistols, along with the two knives she kept in her boots. Sigrid would have felt less naked if they had asked her to remove her clothes.

Most of the other girls were already gathered in the reception area; Sigrid observed as one by one the girls were called inside while the other girls waited for their own turn in silence.

Sigrid was the ninth to be called. Dr. Garrett did not greet her as she came in. Dr. Garrett always had a friendly word for Sigrid, ever since the very first time they'd met at her parents' apartment on Earth. The fact that she said nothing set alarm bells ringing in Sigrid's head. Sigrid swallowed hard.

Seated behind the polished stainless steel desk was Shinji Kimura, Deputy CEO of the Kimura Corporation. She'd never met the man before, but her optics scanned him, displaying his ID from her database. Shinji did not appear much older than Dr. Garrett, although she knew his age to be forty-two. His face was sharp and angular, and his eyes were narrow and a dark shade of brown. He sat stock still, facing her with a blank stare. She could tell he was studying her. He may not have had her bionic optics, but she could see things registering in his eyes, calculating, collating.

Two men with equally humorless dispositions stood to either side of him. No one had said anything as either greeting or introduction. Sigrid wasn't sure if they were waiting for her to speak. An uncomfortable minute passed. She decided to bow in greeting; she would at least be polite.

Sigrid was in mid-bow when she saw the man on Shinji's left shift his weight on his right knee. The motion was subtle and swift, but the threat registered instantly in her PCM; the motion was calculated, the solution presented to her. This was the *Master Control Program* at work. Not controlling her actions, but feeding her vital information and sending her systems into action, reacting to her instinctively.

Even before the *shuriken* left his hand, Sigrid was already moving. Her optics registered and tracked the weapon, her PCM calculated the velocity and trajectory of the small but deadly *Ninja Star*. Sigrid reached up, slapping both hands together as she caught the razor sharp throwing knife between her palms, eight centimeters from her face. She'd already anticipated her next action; her weight was already shifted forward, and she hurled the *shuriken* with all the deadly force she could muster back at her assailant. The knife hit him squarely in the chest and the man keeled over, face first, dead by the time he hit the floor with a sickening thud.

The man to Shinji's right drew his sidearm. *Too slow.* Anticipating the first shot, Sigrid sidestepped, and rolled under the trajectory of the next one before he'd even fired. She came to her feet in front of him and swiftly kicked up, sending the man's pistol flying upward before bringing her heel down hard on his neck. The force of the blow sent the man crashing down. Sigrid was on him, ready to strike, calculating different ways she might deliver the next blow: *lethal, paralyzing, maiming...?*

"Stop!"

Sigrid froze. Shinji Kimura stood placidly, holding out his hand to her. She was still in combat-mode, not quite certain what had transpired, but the man's body language read calm, his pulse and respiration even and measured. He carried no weapons and seemed to present no threat—even though his goons had just tried to kill her.

Sigrid looked to Dr. Garrett for direction. The woman gave her only the slightest of nods. Not knowing what else to do, Sigrid took the Deputy CEO's outstretched hand.

"Very good, Ms. Novak. *Most* impressive."

Sigrid stumbled slightly backwards. "This was a...test?"

"Of course."

"Your test is trying to *kill* me?" *Had he done this with all the girls?* Sigrid couldn't believe it. "What—what if you'd killed me?"

"Then, you would have failed. If you can't dodge a simple knife, you would be of little use to us."

Sigrid felt her blood rise. "And the other girls? Did they...*pass?*"

"Most," he said. He sat back down in the chair by the desk. "But only *you* attacked, Ms. Novak. Your solution was...most unique. While your fellow students all chose evasion, you chose to attack. Where others chose defense, you chose aggression, and with deadly force." He turned to Dr. Garrett and said, "You may tell the other girls to leave, Dr. Garrett." His eyes fell again to Sigrid.

"Pack your things, Ms. Novak. You will accompany us to Aquarii, immediately."

* * *

February 23, 2348

"You're going!" Suko cried. "Now?" She was clinging to the back of Sigrid's uniform, clutching at the fabric. Sigrid was doing

98

her best to pack her duffel—trying her best not to look Suko in the face. She couldn't bear it.

She leaned down to pick up her meager belongings; a picture of her parents, the stacks of letters from her mother, and the small, stuffed rabbit she'd managed to keep with her all these years.

"You can't go! Not after..." Suko wrapped her arms around her from behind and pulled her away from the duffel and her packing.

Sigrid hugged Suko's arms even tighter around her. "It's not like I want to."

Suko's eyes were raw and red with emotion. "Tell them to take me!"

"I did—I asked. He's only taking me."

"It doesn't make any sense—just because you killed one of his men...?"

"I know!"

Suko's eyes darkened and her body tensed. "Tell them I'll meet with them—I'll kill the other guy. I'll kill him."

"I wish you could."

Suko sniffed. "What's going to happen to the rest of us?"

"He said...Mr. Kimura just said I'm to go to Aquarii. He said they're going to present me to the Board of Directors for evaluation. Then...they'll decide what happens with the rest of you." Sigrid groaned. "Of all the girls, why pick me?"

Sigrid felt dizzy and sick. She leaned heavily against Suko, who stroked her hair and shoulders. Everything was happening so fast. If only she could stay. But it was already time to go.

They were waiting for her.

It took all her force of will to free herself from Suko's embrace. She didn't look back. She couldn't. Sigrid grabbed her duffel and strode toward the door.

Suko darted past her and backed up against the door, blocking Sigrid's way. "You're *not* walking out on me like that." Suko was crying. "You *can't.*"

Sigrid threw her bag to the ground. "It's not like I have a choice, Suko. Don't make this harder than it is."

"Well, I'm not going to make it easy. I'm not letting them take you. I won't." Suko grabbed Sigrid by the shoulders, her eyes were wide and desperate. "Sigrid, let's get out of here. Let's leave."

"Leave? Suko…?" *What Suko was saying—it was impossible.* "But, Kimura…they'll never allow…"

"We can try. Sigrid—don't go. Come with me."

Sigrid's heart beat faster. *Could they really run away?* For a brief moment she allowed herself to contemplate Suko's outlandish proposal. But her heart sank just as quickly. It was impossible.

"Suko, it's crazy. Kimura would track us. We'd never get off the planet."

"You don't know that!"

"Suko…" Sigrid slumped on her bunk, holding her head in her hands. "You're just making things worse." How could she leave? The answer was simple: she couldn't. They wouldn't let her. Even if she did, even if by some miracle she and Suko managed to escape, her family would be *ruined.*

Sigrid rubbed hard at her temples. Her head throbbed as a wave of nausea washed over her. Suko sat next to her. She sobbed as she leaned her head against Sigrid's shoulder and pulled her close. Sigrid wanted to stay more than anything, but how could she? The decision had already been made long ago. Kimura owned her and her family. They would take her away and there was nothing she could do.

"I'm—I'm sorry, Suko."

For a moment, Suko just stared back, her face a mixture of hurt and confusion. Suko wiped her nose with her arm. "Then, you're…you're really going?"

"What choice do I have?"

Suko looked down, staring at her feet. "I would never leave you."

"That's not fair! What you're asking me…it would destroy my family."

"The *family* that sent you here."

Sigrid heard the anger in Suko's voice—anger at her, or Suko's own family, she wasn't sure. She put her hand on Suko's arm. "Suko, I know how you feel about your family—"

"And I know how you feel about *yours.*" Suko pulled away from her hand so abruptly that Sigrid gasped. Suko's eyes were redder still, and her nose was running freely. "But I guess you don't know how I feel about you."

The words stabbed at Sigrid, but this time it was Suko who couldn't look at her. Sigrid reached for her, crying, but Suko turned away, shrugged off her touch and ran for the door.

"Suko…!"

Suko darted out into the hall, bumping into two Mercenary soldiers coming the other way.

"Suko! Wait!" Sigrid was up and running after her, but the two Marines at the door blocked her way.

"Time to go, Ms. Novak," one of them said, holding up his hand.

Sigrid staggered back and fell onto her bunk. It was too late. Sigrid knew she'd never see Suko again. She lay back on the bed, staring up at the ceiling, unable to move. Moving would mean leaving, and leaving would mean that this was real, and not just some terrible nightmare.

Finally one of the soldiers cleared his throat. Sigrid looked up. They were both staring down at her as she lay on the bed.

"What," Sigrid said. It was not even a question. She didn't care. Nothing mattered anymore. Suko was gone.

Chapter 10
Agatsuma

February 23, 2348

The journey to the waiting transport ship felt like the walk of death to Sigrid. None of the girls in the halls looked up at her as she passed by them, shadowed by her mercenary escort. There was no one to meet Sigrid or see her off as she boarded the *Agatsuma*. The two mercenaries deposited her at the bottom of the staircase that reached up into the belly of the ship. As Sigrid entered, the stairs retracted behind her, sealing her in; sealing her fate, she reflected.

She was vaguely aware of the ship's thrusters firing as the Corvette lifted off. The inertial-dampers shielded the crew from the crushing g-forces as the ship blasted its way skyward. By the time a single crewman arrived to escort her down the narrow corridors to her quarters, the *Agatsuma* had already cleared the atmosphere and broken orbit. Sigrid was instructed to wait until called for. She hardly heard the crewman—so lost was she in her own bleak thoughts.

She'd held herself together so far, but as the door to her quarters closed behind her, the despair cascaded over her. More alone than she'd ever felt in her life, she collapsed on the bunk, buried her face in the pillow, and wept. She still couldn't believe Suko was gone. How could she face the rest of her life without her?

And Suko's words still stung her. *"You don't know how I feel about you,"* she'd said.

Didn't she? Without Suko, Sigrid felt she would have perished long ago. Suko had always been there for her. Suko had protected and cared for her. When they were together, she felt whole and complete. Without her, all she felt was deep despair.

The realization hit her like a brick. She loved Suko. More than that. She was *in love* with her. *And I never told her,* Sigrid thought, horrified. She groaned and held her head in her hands. Sigrid felt sick. What had she done...

Sigrid couldn't decide what was worse; the thought of Suko hating her, or the thought of never seeing her again. If only she could apologize, if only she could tell Suko she loved her. But she couldn't turn back time. With every second, the *Agatsuma* was accelerating away from Alcyone and away from Suko.

Suddenly angry, furious at herself and at Kimura, Sigrid grabbed the small clock from the little bedside table and hurled it at the door. Only then did she see the young woman standing there; the ensign ducked and squealed as the clock sailed past her and smashed into the bulkhead behind.

Cautiously, the ensign poked her head back in the doorway. She held her hand to her chest. "Oh my—are you all right?"

Sigrid tried to answer, but was overcome by tears again.

"Oh, my poor dear," the girl said, rushing to Sigrid's side. She gathered Sigrid into her arms, holding her close and rocking her. "Whatever's the matter?"

Sigrid's body shook as she succumbed to her grief. She had no idea who the girl was, yet she clung to her, pressing her face to her chest. The ensign stroked her hair, hushing her gently.

In time, Sigrid's trembling subsided. She frowned, suddenly embarrassed at her emotional outburst. "I'm sorry." She wiped at her eyes with the heels of her hands.

"That's quite all right."

Sigrid saw her clearly for the first time. She looked about twenty. Her long, curly black hair was tied in an elaborate series of knots and braids, tucked neatly behind her head—not a strand out of place. The smooth, dark brown skin of her face framed a pair of large brown eyes and a pronounced, dimpled chin. Her full lips were painted red, her cheeks artificially flushed; even her eyes were enhanced by the elaborate colors and lines of her makeup.

Sigrid noted the girl was an ensign in Kimura's naval forces. Her finely tailored uniform looked sharp enough to cut paper. Sigrid released herself from the embrace almost apologetically. She'd left a smear on the girl's lapel.

"Are you...all right?"

What could Sigrid say? *I've just left the woman I'm in love with*... Did people say such things to people they'd just met?

"I'm fine," Sigrid said. She wiped her nose and gave a big sniff.

The young ensign handed Sigrid a tissue and shifted herself on the bunk, facing Sigrid. She held out her hand. "I'm Ensign McTeer, and I'll be your Orientations Officer. Are you...sure you're all right?"

She wasn't, but Sigrid nodded and wiped at her eyes again. "Sorry. Call me Sigrid." Sigrid said, emphasizing the *seeg*—everyone got her name wrong at first.

"Very well. Then you must call me Karen," the girl said in such a friendly fashion that Sigrid felt some of her tension ease; she even managed a small smile. "You're not technically in my chain of command," Karen continued, "so I suppose there's no need for us to use titles—although, I would advise you to address most of the officers by their rank until they say otherwise. I'm not sure if the Captain would appreciate you calling him *Steve* just yet." Karen winked.

Sigrid heard herself laugh. "No, I don't suppose he would."

Karen rose and retrieved the two bags she'd dropped: a small, square case and a long garment bag, which she hung on a hook behind Sigrid's door. "I suppose you're probably wondering about all this..."

Sigrid nodded again.

"Well, to start, I guess I'm here to help prepare you for arrival and for your...*presentation* to Kimura."

"Presentation?"

Karen smiled. "Mr. Kimura—the man you met, was concerned that your years at the Academy might have left you a little...rough around the edges—his words, not mine. He's asked me to..." Karen looked a little embarrassed,"...*smooth* things out, I suppose."

Karen stood and held out her hands to Sigrid, prompting her to stand. Sigrid did so, a little uncertainly. There was a full length mirror on the back of the closet door. Karen positioned Sigrid in front of it and stood behind her.

"Now, this *outfit*—" she said, examining Sigrid's coverall somewhat distastefully, "—might be fine for skulking around in the dark on some clandestine task. You might even wear it around the ship if you like, but for most functions I'd normally recommend something more formal. Unfortunately, we don't have a tailor or quartermaster on board. I brought a few things of my own. I hope that's all right?"

Ensign McTeer unzipped the garment bag and took out two outfits still on their hangers. The first was a formal ship's uniform; Karen held it in front of herself and studied Sigrid with a frown. "No—this won't do. I'm afraid it will be quite big on you." Karen was, indeed, several inches taller than Sigrid, but then, so was everyone, Sigrid reasoned. Karen put the uniform back in the bag and held out a dress this time; it was made of a deep, shimmering blue fabric, with patterns of color that shifted in the differing aspects of light. "I think something like this might be more appropriate for dining with the Captain tonight."

Sigrid regarded it a little skeptically. She'd never seen such an elaborate garment. All the clothes she'd worn at the Academy were more of the utilitarian sort, function over form.

Karen nudged her, offering the dress. "Here—I know you'll be a knockout in it."

Sigrid knew forty-eight ways to knock someone out, but none of them involved wearing a dress. She stripped off her jumpsuit and stepped almost cautiously into the dress; she wasn't even sure which was the front or back, but Karen helped her by guiding it on.

"I was worried it might be a bit long, but I think it's okay," Karen said.

Long? The thing barely came halfway down her thigh! On Karen, it must have been daringly short. She began to pull her combat boots back on.

Karen stopped her. "I think *these'll* work better," she suggested, pulling several different pairs of shoes from the bag. "I wasn't sure of your size so I had some of the girls lend me their favorites. Hopefully, we can find something that fits."

Karen dropped several pairs of slippers and high-heeled shoes in front of Sigrid, but her small feet swam in most of them. The only pair that fitted properly were platform soled boots that zipped up just past her ankle. The heels were preposterously high. They looked ridiculous and impractical, but when Sigrid stood up she found herself looking *down* at Karen.

After a few careful steps, she discovered she could move around in the boots more easily than she'd first imagined.

"I love them!"

Karen chuckled. "Lieutenant Meres will be happy to hear that." With a hand on each shoulder, Karen guided Sigrid to the chair at the table. "Now, for the rest," she declared as she opened a case on the table, revealing an assortment of makeup, lipsticks and brushes.

The makeup kit held a small mirror which Karen placed in front of her. When Sigrid looked in the mirror, she covered her mouth, horrified. Her face was puffy, with eyes bloodshot and red from crying. She looked terrible! Fortunately, Karen was a master-artist. A cool, soothing cream reduced the puffiness and a touch of rouge brought color back to her cheeks. When the ensign was done, a completely different Sigrid stared back from the looking-glass.

"Goodness…" Sigrid said, admiring Karen's masterful work. She wished Suko were there now; she couldn't help but wonder what she'd think if she saw her like this. Would she laugh? *Would she like it?* Lost in thought, she barely noticed as Karen brushed out her hair and completed her outfit with a series of sparkling bracelets.

Karen examined her *creation*. She seemed quite satisfied with her work and gave Sigrid a wink. "There. Totally sexy."

Sexy? Sigrid thought. *Me?*

Leta was sexy. The girl was all long legs and breasts, and with that mane of flaming red hair, Leta oozed sex-appeal. Suko was exotic and beautiful, long and slender. But Sigrid, on the other hand…her own face had always seemed rather plain, her nose too big, her blond hair limp and dull. But when she looked at herself now—she had changed so much in the past year.

Was it the clothes? The shoes? Was she really sexy too?

"All done," Karen said. "Now, I think there's just enough time for a tour of the ship before dinner."

Sigrid didn't think she could eat, though the idea of getting out of her tiny quarters suited her just fine. The distraction from her misery would be welcome. But she didn't feel quite dressed yet. She rifled through her duffel to complete her outfit in the way she knew best. A pair of throwing knives slipped easily into each of her boots, with one down the front of her bra for good measure, and she *never* went anywhere without the twin Markov's strapped to her hips.

Karen groaned as Sigrid fastened the heavy holster around the dress. She reached out a hand to stop her. "That's…not quite the look I think we're going for." Karen reached into the case she'd brought and handed Sigrid a small pistol in a tiny holster with a single leg-strap. "They told me you girls never go unarmed, so I brought this."

Sigrid pulled the weapon out. It was nothing more than a small hideout pistol; the power-pack only held enough charge for a few shots, but it seemed lethal enough.

"Thanks," Sigrid said; she still wasn't sure where to put it.

"Pardon the reach," Karen said as she fastened the small holster to Sigrid's thigh, high enough to be concealed by the hem of her dress.

Sigrid let the ensign lead her through the narrow corridors. The craft she'd traveled on as a child had been one of the large commercial ships. The *Agatsuma* was a sleek Corvette—a predator in comparison. This was a military vessel. The crew compliment of forty-two belied the lethality of the small ship, which bristled from stem to stern with armaments.

The few crew members she passed wore the sharp, black and red naval uniforms of Kimura; all looked immaculately groomed and professional, very different from the rough-looking Marines she'd grown used to at the school. Sigrid took note of the mess-areas and the small gymnasium where a handful of crew were working out, but of special interest to her was the Tactical Operations Center. The Weapons Control room led out into a long corridor that spanned the length of the ship, giving access to Torpedo Control and a bank of weapons pods. All the pods were manned and ready; Sigrid sensed that all the crew were intent on something. There was a great deal of chatter.

"What's going on?" Sigrid asked.

"Don't worry," Karen said, "it's just a drill. Lately—with all the *nonsense* going on—Captain Maalouf has been drilling the crew around the clock. I suppose he feels it's best to be prepared."

Prepared for what? Sigrid wondered. She wasn't sure what Karen meant by 'nonsense' either, but she made a note of inquiry. Right now she was far more interested in watching the crew in the nearest weapons pod. The pod controlled one of the four quad-mounted rail guns mounted on the exterior of the ship. Sigrid knew from her lessons that the combination of mass and inertia was far more effective against targets in space than laser weapons, or even torpedoes, which could be defeated easily with countermeasures. Hurling a handful of pebbles across space at .65 *c* could rip apart a starship just as easily as a nuclear detonation. Of course, they didn't really use *pebbles*. The gunnery officers could select from a number of lethal projectiles. The preferred ordnance were the tiny *shredder-rounds*. Equipped with proximity fuses, the rounds would break into thousands of tiny fragments as they closed to within striking distance of their target. Any rounds not passing through the target would detonate, causing further carnage. The only drawback of the weapon was that it had to be manually aimed and fired.

Sigrid wondered what it would be like to fire something with that much power, but there was no opportunity to dally. It was nearly time for her appointment with the Captain. They were running a bit late so Karen hurried her along. As they ran through the corridors, heading quickly for the Captain's Mess, Sigrid noticed several of the crew giving her appraising looks as she hurried past in her short, flowing, blue dress.

Sigrid and Karen burst through the double doors, startling the two officers already in attendance. The mess room itself was just big enough to accommodate the small dining table. First Officer, Commander Tapert and Chief Engineer Romi, were there waiting for the Captain and their new *VIP* guest. Sigrid felt a moment of panic when she realized that Ensign McTeer wasn't staying for dinner; she held onto her hand.

"Don't worry—you'll be fine," Karen reassured her.

Sigrid looked to her, worriedly.

"We'll take good care of her, Ensign," Commander Tapert said, smiling at Sigrid. Chief Romi greeted her in turn, taking time to shake her hand.

As friendly as they appeared, Sigrid still felt them eyeing her, as if she were a curiosity. She remained aloof, feeling very self-conscious.

"I'll check in on you later." Karen gave her a kiss on the cheek, patted her on the shoulder and departed as the doors opened to admit the captain and Shinji Kimura.

Captain Maalouf smiled warmly and greeted Sigrid, extending his hand. The captain was a short man of dark complexion, with what Sigrid found to be a charming and pleasant demeanor.

He invited Sigrid to take the seat next to him, with Kimura on the right. "Ms. Novak—it's an honor and a pleasure to finally meet you. You've become quite the curiosity on board."

"Me, sir?"

"Oh, yes. We've all heard about your lineage and training—well, at least what isn't classified, which isn't very much." The captain looked from Sigrid to Shinji Kimura. "From the little I've heard, you must be commended, Mr. Kimura. The program sounds most impressive."

"I'm afraid I can't take any credit for that, Captain. The Academy is strictly my mother's domain."

The captain turned back to her. "Do you mind if I inquire as to your specialization?"

Sigrid raised her eyebrows. *Murder? Espionage?* She wasn't quite sure what she was permitted to say.

Shinji Kimura answered for her. "Ms. Novak is trained as a highly versatile operative, Captain. In fact, I'd be surprised if she couldn't assume any post on your ship."

"Is that so?" the Captain remarked, studying Sigrid with even more interest; Sigrid felt herself shrink lower in her chair. "Then we're lucky to have you aboard, Ms. Novak."

The Mess Attendant came in, filling water glasses, offering wine and other spirits. Sigrid was relieved to see their attention shift away from her.

"Red or white, miss?" the attendant asked her.

Sigrid had no idea, having never tasted wine, so she simply nodded. "Yes, please."

Watching her closely, the Captain chuckled as he signaled the steward to bring forth their meals.

The selection of entrees turned out to be impressive; a far cry from the simple fare Sigrid was used to at the Academy. There were roasted meats, whole fish, trays of exotic vegetables and fruits. Sigrid stared at the plate that was presented to her—she was far too distraught to eat, her stomach still twisted in a tight knot.

Captain Maalouf noticed her pushing the roasted zucchini across her plate. "Is it not to your liking, Ms. Novak? Can we bring you something else?"

Sigrid flushed as she noticed the other men looking at her. "No—no. It smells wonderful. It's just..." *She couldn't tell them...couldn't tell the captain.* "I think I'm having trouble adjusting—to the gravity." It was a lie; one the captain easily recognized, but he nodded.

"Your first mission," he grunted. "I understand. It's been a while, but I do remember what it was like—fresh out of the Academy. Don't worry. You'll make the adjustment."

Sigrid nodded politely and returned to her food. A nibble at a carrot was about all she could manage, but she put on a brave face. It was easy to sit in silence, listening as the officers discussed the itinerary of the journey. It would take 6.7 days at maximum acceleration to reach the Warp Relay that lay just outside the boundary of the solar system. Sigrid noted the grumbling of the officers as they discussed the surcharges and fees charged by Daedalus Corporation—the company that controlled the network of Warp Relays that allowed travel between the different systems in the Federation.

The captain told them there was no other traffic scheduled in or out of the system, yet he remained cautious. They would be at their most vulnerable during this portion of the voyage. As they closed on the Relay, they also ranged further from Alcyone and any help that they might get from ships stationed there. Skirmishes with *Independents* were becoming alarmingly frequent, and Daedalus was not famous for warning of incoming traffic changes or of ships traveling through their system of relays.

Shinji tilted his head at these revelations. "So you don't trust Daedalus?"

Captain Maalouf chewed his last forkful of steak and swallowed before answering. "I trust no one—least of all Daedalus. They maintain their neutrality, but that doesn't mean they'll do us any favors by announcing changes to the relay traffic. They never do. But with all the trouble with the *Independents*, we'll maintain alert status until we reach Aquarii."

"I'm surprised, Captain. I didn't think the *Independents* had anything that could threaten a ship like this."

"A few years ago, perhaps, but recently...well, someone's been selling to them."

"*Independents*, sir?" Sigrid asked. "Who are they?"

The captain smiled. "Nothing to worry about, my dear."

"They're not really *anyone*," Shinji explained. "They're mostly companies that have separated themselves from the Federated Corporations. Some have even gone so far as to attempt to form governments on the planets they control. Of course, they've all been abysmal failures. Captain Maalouf is correct—they're of no concern."

"Still, the Council will have its hands full, what with all the secessions. Almost makes me miss the old days when the CTF could actually maintain order. Nothing but a toothless tiger now."

Sigrid knew from her schooling that the Council for Trade and Finance was responsible for maintaining order in the Federation, but it had never been disclosed that they lacked the ability to maintain control. If that were the case then she'd need to update her database.

"Who controls the Federation now, sir?"

They all stopped eating and regarded her with amusement. Captain Maalouf laughed out loud. Sigrid flushed at her apparent gaffe. "An excellent question, my dear. The Council maintains—well, *claims*—authority, but the Federation has grown...too many planets, too fast."

"My mother, the Lady Hitomi, calls it a *Market Correction*," Shinji said with a snicker.

"With so much more territory, so much trade," the captain continued, "and so many more companies working the systems, the Council hires companies like ours to plug the gaps in their patrols. But those *gaps* are growing."

"The attack on the Academy, for instance," Shinji offered. "That would have been unheard of just a few years ago."

"In the past, *no* mercenary company would take a contract against another. Guild law forbade it, and for obvious reasons. The results would be chaotic—not to mention the tariffs and fines. But greed, it seems, often wins out against logic. The CTF is stretched thin, the Mercenary Guild fractured. We used to pass by ships from other companies without a care in the world. Now, skirmishes are commonplace occurrences. I'm quite positive you and your girls from the Academy will have all the work you can handle."

* * *

After dinner, Sigrid was escorted to her quarters. She didn't know what to do with herself. She unfastened the dress and unpacked the rest of her things, trying to get herself set up, but the more she tried to make the modest quarters comfortable the more the room felt oppressive and stifling. She sat on the bed and hugged her pillow, trying to quell the pangs of loneliness that twisted at the knot in her stomach, but the pain only got worse. If only Suko were there. If only she could be with her just a little longer...

Sigrid groaned. It hadn't even been a day; how would she survive a week?

"Gah!"

Sigrid stood up abruptly and zipped the dress back up, fastening it behind her neck. She couldn't confine herself to quarters—*she'd go mad!* She checked the door, half-expecting it to be locked, but it slid open for her. Sigrid stiffened, startled at the sight of the crewman standing guard outside her door.

"Ma'am," he said with a nod.

"Am I allowed...out?"

"Of course, ma'am."

That was a surprise. She'd expected him to send her back inside; instead, he accompanied her as she started off down the corridor. *Guard or escort?* She still wasn't sure.

Sigrid had no idea where she was going; she only knew she had to go somewhere—do *something*. The tiny observation lounge provided a moment of distraction, but she needed something more—something more physical. She found just the thing when she reached the small gym. Though late in the evening, the ship ran twenty-four-seven and the gym was crowded with crewmen and officers exercising.

As Sigrid walked into the locker room to change, she caught sight of Ensign Karen McTeer dressed in a towel and heading toward the showers.

"Oh, hello, Sigrid. How was dinner?"

"Odd."

Karen caught her frown. "I hope they weren't too cruel."

"Cruel? Oh—no! They were fine. I just…well, there's a lot I don't understand, I suppose."

"Well, that's what I'm here for. Are you on your way in or out?" she asked, pointing back to the gym.

"In—I thought I could use a workout."

Karen's eyes widened; Sigrid was, by far, the fittest person she'd ever seen.

"I just need to work off some steam," Sigrid explained.

"Well, I'm just on my way to the mess to meet some friends. We'd love to have you—if you like—if you're not busy, that is…"

Sigrid considered the offer; she really didn't want to be alone at the moment, and Karen was so friendly… "Yes, that would be lovely, thank you."

Karen's face lit up; she squeezed Sigrid's arm. "Perfect. Hang on, I'll be right out."

Sigrid watched Karen retreat to the showers. After a few minutes, a fresh-looking Karen returned and led her quickly to the mess.

Karen's companions were already there with a table waiting. Karen introduced the young man as Lieutenant Christian Lopez. He rose and took Sigrid's hand in greeting; his easy smile was warm and friendly, despite his slightly rough look. He towered above Sigrid; his large hand made her own seem small as a child's. The other girl was introduced as Ensign Melissa Greenway. Unlike Karen and Lieutenant Lopez, Melissa greeted Sigrid with evident apprehension.

Karen elbowed her in the side. "*Melissa...*"

Ensign Greenway blushed. "Sorry."

"She's clearly been listening to the latest batch of rumors," Karen explained.

Christian gave her a wink. "The way people are talking about you, they'll expect you to be eight feet tall."

Sigrid was shocked. "Me! What did I do?"

Karen gave her a sympathetic look. "They're all just a little...curious. It's nothing."

"Well, you have to understand," Christian explained, "we were taken off assignment to come ferry you to Aquarii—that's a lot of ship for one little girl—sorry...young lady. And then we hear about the Academy. That gets people talking."

"I've already *told* them not to ask you anything," Karen said, patting her hand and glaring a warning at her two friends.

Christian grinned. "Of course, that just means we get to keep making up our own versions. Don't worry. In mine, you breathe fire."

"*Christian...really!*" Karen chided, swatting him on the shoulder. But it was all rather lighthearted and Sigrid felt her mood lifting as she followed the easy banter they all shared.

"Who wants a drink?" Christian asked. "I could use a drink."

"Ooh—me!" Karen said. "I want something tall—with an umbrella."

"One girly-drink, comin' up. Sigrid?"

"Water's fine, thanks," Sigrid said.

"Water? Nah-uh. I'll get you something good."

"I'll take a lemonade," Melissa said.

"Hard," Christian said, with a leer; Melissa rolled her eyes.

"Ladies..." Christian bowed respectfully before heading off to the dispenser to fetch their drinks.

He was back in a flash, with something tall and orange for Karen—with an umbrella—a vodka and lemonade for Melissa and two tall pints of something dark and foamy for himself and Sigrid.

"Cheers," he said, raising his glass.

"Cheers," Karen said, mimicking him. Sigrid joined them and they all clinked their glasses together.

Sigrid had never had beer before; the dark liquid teemed with delicious-looking bubbles that wriggled down from the creamy head of foam. Despite its deep, dark color, Sigrid found the taste light and smooth. She quaffed the pint of ale back like a seasoned veteran.

She felt a tingling sensation in her extremities as the alcohol worked its way into her bloodstream. Her head felt light. The bubbles reacted in her stomach, causing her to burp loudly. Karen laughed. But within moments, the nano-swarms in her system surged forward, working to process the alcohol. The tingling quickly abated.

Christian looked at her expectantly. "Well?"

Sigrid considered the beverage. It was like nothing she'd ever had before. It was flavorful and very refreshing. She smacked her lips, still experiencing the taste. "Good!" Sigrid said, giving a thumbs up.

"A girl after my own heart." Christian raised his glass to her and took a large mouthful.

Sigrid offered to get the next round. As she waited in line for the dispenser a man standing behind her bumped into her. She didn't think much of it, but then he bumped into her again, harder this time. She turned to see what was going on and saw a young crewman leering down at her.

"You're *new,*" he said.

Sigrid looked him up and down, warily. "Yes—I just came on board at Alcyone." She turned away—it was her turn at the dispenser.

"You're *her!* You're one of those girls."

"I suppose." Sigrid could tell that he was already drunk, and so were his companions. The three of them stood snickering behind her. She heard one of them make a comment about her rear—it didn't make her feel flattered at all. She flushed red. As she placed two more pints of ale on her tray, he bumped her again, making her spill both glasses.

"Whoops!" he said, barking out a drunken laugh.

Sigrid retrieved the toppled glasses and gathered some towels to clean up the mess.

"Lemme help." He leaned over her, pushing her up against the dispenser, then put his hand over her own as she tried to mop up the spill. "Well, aren't you a little one."

Sigrid wasn't sure what the regulations were concerning her aboard the ship, but she knew a bully when she saw one and she'd just about had her fill of him. Sigrid pushed him back—not hard enough to hurt him, though sufficient to make it clear he'd overstepped.

"Easy…!" he said, holding his hands up. "I was just trying to help."

Christian, who'd been watching the altercation grow, had seen quite enough. He hastened over and lodged himself between Sigrid and the crewman, placing a warning hand on the man's shoulder. "I think you've had enough, crewman. Why don't you boys go sleep it off."

The crewman swatted Christian's hand away and stepped closer to the Lieutenant. "I'm off duty."

"You're also out of line."

"Sorry—*sir*."

Christian didn't see the sucker-punch coming, but Sigrid did—her hand moved up so fast it shocked both men. They stared as Sigrid held the crewman's fist in her own hand, centimeters in front of Christian's face. The startled crewman tried to pull his hand away, but it might as well have been locked in a steel vice. Sigrid tightened her grip and twisted and watched the man sink to his knees, his face contorted with a mixture of shock and pain. They all heard the sharp crack as she broke his arm at the wrist. He howled in pain.

Sigrid glared down at him. "I've had a *very* long day."

"You broke my fucking arm!"

Sigrid calmly turned back to the dispenser, refilled the pint glasses and got two more drinks for Karen and Melissa. Behind her, two crewman quietly set about hauling the injured man off to the Medical Ward. Sigrid was given a wide berth as she made her way back to the table.

"Well," she said, handing out the drinks. "Where were we?"

Karen tried her best to stifle a laugh. "Oh my God!"

Christian returned to join them. He took a long pull from his pint, before looking seriously at the three girls. "I could've taken him, you know."

Karen and Melissa erupted into laughter and raised their glasses to Sigrid.

Melissa frowned. "Do you think he'll press charges?"

"Charges!" Christian cried, losing some ale in the process. "I put *him* on report."

"Good for you," Karen said.

Despite the near fisticuffs, Sigrid enjoyed the rest of her evening immensely. The camaraderie went a long way toward easing some of the loneliness she felt, but she still couldn't sleep that night. She spent most of it tossing and turning, uncertain of her future, uncertain about herself, and missing Suko terribly.

* * *

March 1, 2348

They were almost at the Warp Relay when Sigrid heard the call come through her comlink. Karen was waiting for her in the forward observation lounge so Sigrid joined her there. It took several minutes to find her because most of the off-duty crew had gathered there and were crammed into the small lounge near the forward viewport.

"I thought you might like to see this before we drop," Karen said, gesturing to the wide window in front of her.

Sigrid leaned forward and peered at the spectacle. She'd seen pictures of the Warp Relays, but never one for real. The sight took her breath away; especially seeing it charged up as it was, ready for the *Agatsuma* to drop through its portal into warp-space. The Alcyone Relay was small compared to some in other systems, but it was still over 400 meters in diameter. The latticed, ring-like structure looked fragile and delicate; orange and white sparks danced back and forth between the lattices. The entire structure glowed with an intense blue light, hinting at its immense and latent power.

"Look, they're orienting it," Karen said, pointing.

Sigrid watched as the relay spun on its axis; she knew this was the result of the *Agatsuma's* navigator feeding coordinates to the relay-system, aiming the device at their destination of Aquarii. Now, it was just a matter of dropping through the portal at the appropriate angle and velocity, where they'd appear, instantaneously, at their destination.

"I always come here to watch before a jump," Karen said.

"It's beautiful."

"Have you ever seen a drop before?"

Sigrid shook her head.

"You're going to *love* this."

The *Agatsuma* accelerated toward the Relay and it glowed brighter still as their proximity and velocity increased. She felt several subtle bumps in the floor as the ship continued to make minor shifts in its angle of approach.

Karen placed her hand on her stomach. "Oh—I hate when they do that. That always makes me nervous."

"What do you mean?"

"They're adjusting the approach angle—if the navigator gets that wrong, by even the tiniest fraction, we could pop out on the other side of Alpha Centauri, or who knows where."

"Don't tell me that now!"

But Karen laughed, easing Sigrid's sudden anxiety. "Oh, don't worry. It's all preprogrammed. There hasn't been a warp malfunction in years." Karen pointed ahead. "Here we go."

Sigrid found herself reaching out and holding the ensign's hand as the Relay loomed closer, all at once filling the entire viewport. Sigrid heard the telltale hum, growing ever-louder as the ship's hull resonated with the powerful energy field. She shielded her eyes from the brilliant flash; Karen's hand tightened in her own. The stars seemed to grow, becoming bloated, quickly expanding, coalescing with one another until all were merged into one. For a long while, everything that was became white. And then, like snow falling, the white melted away, scattering, coalescing again into individual stars that shimmered in the darkness as they took shape.

"Not bad, huh," Karen said.

Sigrid could only nod in agreement.

* * *

Captain Maalouf sat in his command chair in the crowded CIC. He looked down in quiet annoyance at the flashing red alarm on the panel of the console before him. Four hundred and eighty-seven drops, and that light had always been green, but now it flashed a red warning.

"Report!" he barked at the Tactical Officer.

Lieutenant Christian Lopez swung into his own seat; his hands danced over the panel in front of him. His eyes widened slightly. "Sir—we have a contact off the port bow," he said, tying in his monitor to the main screen at the front of the bridge so the captain could take a look. A small ship, just a fifth the size of the *Agatsuma*, lay waiting for them some 25,000 kilometers distant. "It registers as the *Morrigan*, a small scout-class vessel attached to the Dalair Military Group."

"Helm—evasive action," the captain barked. "I want some distance between us and that ship."

"Aye, Captain," the Helmsman said.

"Dalair?" the XO asked, looking to the captain. "What the hell are they doing out here? This is a Kimura controlled system."

"Hail them," the captain ordered. His face was fixed in a scowl as he tried to figure out the scenario. The *Agatsuma* outgunned the tiny scout-ship five to one. Attacking them didn't make sense. "Let's see what they want."

Before the Communications Officer could respond, they all heard three loud bangs, reverberating on the hull. Maalouf looked up in alarm.

"Captain, we hit something!" Lopez shouted; he continued to scan the incoming data.

"Missiles?" Tapert asked.

Lopez shook his head. "No, we weren't *hit*, we hit something. Captain..." Lopez brought the new data up on the screen, "...we've been mined!"

The image of the *Morrigan* was replaced by a remote view of the exterior of the *Agatsuma*. They all saw the black, cylindrical object, about three meters long and half a meter thick, attached to the hull of the Corvette.

"Shit," Captain Maalouf, muttered under his breath. "All stop." He turned again to his Communications Officer, who stood frozen, staring at the image of the deadly explosive device attached to their ship. "Well, Ensign, let's get 'em on the blower and see what they want."

The young ensign shook herself out of her funk and set to the task. "They're hailing *us*, sir."

"Well—*put them on.*" Maalouf shook his head. *Rookies*.

The forward view screen switched to the image of the *Morrigan*'s bridge. Centered on the screen was a very large man. He looked to be shoehorned into the command chair where he sat. Realizing that he was connected, he leaned forward in his chair, his face becoming serious and intent. "This is Captain Gregory Oslov of the *DSS Morrigan*. By order of the CTF and the Federation of Commercial Enterprises, I hereby order you to stand down and surrender your cargo. Failure to comply will result in sanctions and fines—amounts to be set by CTF."

Captain Maalouf chuckled. "*Sanctions?* And what of the limpet mine attached to the hull of my ship?"

Captain Oslov looked up at him from below a raised eyebrow. "Incentive."

"I'm not aware of the CTF permitting the use of mines near a relay point, Captain. Are you sure this is a sanctioned operation."

Captain Oslov shrugged. "You may, of course, take any grievances to the Council—"

"Should I survive this encounter…" Another shrug was all the response Oslov was willing to give. "You say this is by order of the CTF—I don't suppose you're willing to let us wait for verification of your permit for seizure?"

"A formal request for authentication is, of course, your right, but we *will* take possession of your cargo."

"Or you'll blow us to bits."

"I'm glad we understand each other, Captain Maalouf."

Maalouf shifted in his chair. "Not quite, Captain—this *cargo*…there seems to be a misunderstanding. We carry no *cargo*."

"You're carrying an illegal weapon, Captain. We want the girl."

Chapter 11
Hostile Takeover

Captain Maalouf handed the data-pad to Kimura's Deputy CEO. On it was a copy of the permit for seizure of the *cargo*.

"This is ridiculous," Shinji said, tossing the pad back across the table in the captain's ready-room. "It's a fake."

The captain nodded. "There's no way to be sure, but I would tend to agree."

"Have you transmitted a copy of this to my mother?"

"Yes, but the transmission won't get to Aquarii for hours; we'll have to wait just as long to receive a reply."

Shinji sighed tiredly. "And how long has the *esteemed* captain given us to comply?"

"Twenty minutes. That gives us another twelve minutes to either respond—or come up with a plan."

"And there's nothing you can do about the mine?"

"We've analyzed it. Any tampering will result in our demise, I have no doubt. Even our scans seem to make it twitchy."

"And our forces on Aquarii?"

"We've monitored several ships heading this way, but any help is days away—which explains Oslov's desire for a hasty resolution."

Shinji pounded his fist on the table. "I don't believe it. Someone's already tried to take the girls once. This is just a trick to get us to hand her over."

Captain Maalouf studied his passenger closely. Although he was in command, he knew that Shinji could still override any action he might take. He chose his words carefully. "I believe you, but it doesn't change the fact that we have a high-explosive limpet mine attached to our hull. Any action we take will result in the destruction of this ship. You may refuse to hand her over, sir, but my first responsibility is to this ship—"

"Your first responsibility is to *me*," Shinji spat.

The captain sat back, his hands open. He'd said his piece, but the rest was up to Kimura. Unless…he had a thought. "If you'll forgive me, sir, we might be missing the obvious…"

Shinji looked at him impatiently. "Continue."

Captain Maalouf straightened himself. "You've told me very little about our…*passenger*, but from what I've seen…"

"Yes, yes—go on!"

"Perhaps we *should* hand her over."

* * *

Captain Maalouf entered the bridge of the Corvette, followed closely by Shinji Kimura and his XO. "Did you contact Ms. Novak?" he asked the Communications Officer.

"She's on her way, sir."

"Good." The captain dropped wearily into his chair. "Time?" he asked his XO.

"Three minutes, Captain."

"Hail the *Morrigan*. Let's see how Oslov wants to handle this."

The officer keyed her console. In an instant, Oslov's large face filled the forward viewing screen. "Cutting it close, Captain."

Maalouf shrugged. "Exploring all possibilities."

"Of course."

"We'll meet your demands, but I want assurances. The codes to that little Christmas present you've attached to my ship would be a good start."

Oslov shook his head. "Afraid I can't do that, Captain. Your ship outguns mine five to one. We'll wait until we're well away, and then we'll send you the codes."

Captain Maalouf spread out his hands. "And what exactly is stopping you from blowing us to bits, even if we do hand the girl over to you?"

Oslov leaned his large frame forward. "Absolutely nothing."

Maalouf sat back, and exhaled loudly. "I see your point. Very well, we'll extend our docking ring and wait for you to come alongside."

Oslov chuckled. "Not going to happen, Captain. You'll not come anywhere near my ship, not with that mine attached to your hull."

Damn—but it had been worth a shot, Maalouf reasoned.

"You'll transfer your Cargo by EVA."

Maalouf's eyes widened in surprise. "You want her to EVA over twenty-five thousand kilometers? I don't think so."

"What I want is for you to send her out in an EVA suit, and then back off ten thousand klicks. We'll move in as you back away, then pick her up. Once the transfer is complete, I'll transmit you the deactivation codes."

Maalouf considered the proposal. It was as he would have done. Docking with the *Agatsuma* would be a foolish mistake, allowing his crew to board the smaller craft, possibly even blowing them to bits while cradled together. This way Oslov would keep his ship at a safe distance, allowing him to activate the mine if he sensed any duplicity on Maalouf's part.

"Very well, Captain. She'll be on her way in a moment."

The captain signaled an end to the transmission and Oslov's image winked out. Commander Tapert, who'd observed the exchange, leaned over. "He's no fool—so far."

"Let's just hope our *cargo* is everything they seem to think she is."

* * *

Sigrid stood by the airlock, stripped of everything but her underwear. Her clothes, weapons, even the earrings Ensign McTeer had given her had been taken from her, as ordered by the captain of the *Morrigan*. Shinji Kimura and Ensign McTeer stood by observing as two EVA technicians helped her into the bulky pressure suit and adjusted the boots around her feet and ankles. Sigrid noted the distress on Karen's face as she looked worriedly at her new friend.

"Is this really necessary?" Ensign McTeer asked, frowning at Sigrid's state of undress. She was protectively trying shield Sigrid with her discarded clothes but was just getting in the way.

"Those were our instructions, ma'am. She's not allowed to take *anything* with her. The instructions were quite specific."

"I'm very sorry about this, Ms. Novak," Shinji said. "I'd intended to present you to my mother before anything like this happened. We hoped to complete your training on Aquarii before asking you to undertake any field operations. It appears your first *mission* is coming just a bit sooner than anticipated."

Sigrid pulled the pressure suit up over her waist, hooking her arms into the shoulders before zipping it up over her chest. "Don't worry, sir. I'll manage." The words echoed strangely brave in her ears. But wasn't this like just another exercise? Rosa loved to concoct elaborate scenarios when training the girls. Sigrid wondered what he would think of this one with all its caveats.

Shinji and Ensign McTeer briefed her as much as they could. She knew the ship was in peril, and the lives of everyone on board depended on her. The captain had little choice but to surrender her to the *Morrigan*. Failure to do so would result in the destruction of the *Agatsuma*. If they were lucky, once they had Sigrid on board, the captain of the *Morrigan* would transmit the deactivation codes. *If* they were lucky...

But Captain Maalouf was concerned that Oslov had no intention of deactivating the mine. If the permit was indeed a fake, if Dalair was acting in violation of Guild Law, then eliminating the *Agatsuma* and its ship full of witnesses would make sense. They needed Sigrid, but the rest of the crew was only a liability. It would be imprudent to gamble on Oslov's sense of honor allowing them to live. The captain was emphatic; Sigrid would have to take the small Scout Vessel and *persuade* Oslov to release both herself and the *Agatsuma*—all without blowing them to bits while doing so. It was desperate, ludicrous even, but there seemed to be no other option.

One of the techs held up the suit's controller, pointing at the array of buttons. "This looks a little tricky at first, but it's really a cinch."

Sigrid donned the helmet and linked the suit's control system to her PCM. "It's okay." She tapped the suit's helmet and winked. "I got it all in my head."

"Looks a bit big, don't you think?" Karen said, eyeing the bulky suit, which was clearly intended for someone larger.

The tech frowned. "It's the smallest we got. It's all sealed and secured, though." He nodded to Sigrid. "You'll be fine."

Sigrid had already checked the suit's seals and knew everything was in the green. She gave the thumbs-up signal and stepped into the airlock.

Karen leaned forward, raising her voice, unnecessarily. "Remember—I've uploaded the *Morrigan's* schematics to your PCM. You should be able to deactivate the mine from either the bridge or the auxiliary systems in the engineering section." She stepped back out of the way, just as the lock-door slid shut behind her.

Sigrid listened to the sound of the air cycling out. It grew ominously quiet; her own breathing inside the suit's helmet was all she could hear now. She turned in time to see the outer door opening. Sigrid had never seen such a sight. She couldn't believe there were so many stars. Even on Alcyone, where there were no city lights to dampen the view, nothing had compared with this. There was little time to appreciate the view though, so Sigrid refocused on her task.

It was an odd-feeling to step out of the airlock and into space. It was difficult to believe she wasn't going to find herself tumbling down away from the ship, but as she pushed away, she floated freely in the vacuum.

Sigrid had never experienced weightlessness, but her enhanced physiology, her reengineered genetics, even her bionic systems, adjusted in unison; she had no difficulty orienting herself and she felt no sense of vertigo. The *Morrigan* was marked in her HUD and she could already see it moving closer while the *Agatsuma* zipped quickly away behind her. Using the thruster-pack, she oriented herself to face the small scout ship moving toward her. It was bearing down on her fast—very fast. Sigrid reached for the thruster controls, ready to blast out of the smaller ship's path, but then it slowed as it maneuvered in close to her.

It was a sleek-little ship, perhaps fifty meters in length, with a long, pointed nose. Its massive stern thrusters made up much of its bulk. She caught a glimpse of its forward viewport and bridge before the craft spun sideways and positioned itself beside her. A small airlock door slid silently open. She jetted toward it, then entered carefully, making sure her feet were positioned properly as the ship's gravity took hold of her. She monitored the atmosphere cycling in—there was something wrong with the oxygen content.

Gas.

They were gassing the compartment.

A deep voice boomed loudly in her helmet. "Welcome aboard. Please remove your helmet and suit."

* * *

Crewman James Skinner pulled the breather down over his face and hefted the riot gun they'd given him. Four other crewmen and the ship's XO stood next to him. All wore breathers, but the others were only armed with stun pistols. He couldn't understand what all the hype was about. He'd handled several prisoner transfers before, all perfectly—if he said so himself—and with far fewer precautions than they were taking now. What a load of fuss for just one little girl. He had to laugh. Pussies…

And the riot gun was a bit extreme. It fired an electrically charged net that would pin and pacify anyone unlucky enough to get hit with the thing. But why even bother with it; they'd already gassed the airlock. The girl would pass-out when she removed her EVA gear. If she refused they could always blast her back out into space, although killing her would lose them the bounty and all of their bonuses.

That wasn't going to happen.

The XO looked through the small window in the airlock door, staring down at Sigrid's unconscious body. "She's out," he said, signaling to the crewman by the airlock to open it up.

All the men stood ready, weapons raised as the door slid open. Seeing the girl sprawled out on the floor of the airlock, Crewman Skinner lowered his riot gun. *What was the big deal?*

The XO signaled the medic forward. He bent, checking Sigrid, first her pulse and then both her eyes, lifting each eyelid. He nodded to the XO. "Totally out, sir."

"Pump her."

"Don't need to—she's gone."

XO Keller considered, then dismissed his medic's advice. "Do it."

The medic shrugged, took a small syringe from his waist pouch and stabbed Sigrid's thigh.

Only then did the XO lower his own weapon. "All right, let's take her to the brig." He checked his wrist monitor—the environmental systems had pumped the last of the gas out. He pulled the breather off his face and took a deep breath. He hated wearing those things.

The quinuclidinyl-benzilate they'd dosed her with left Sigrid feeling quite nauseous, especially when the medic had followed it up with the sedative. He'd given her enough to put a horse out for a day. Sigrid did her best not to retch and kept her breathing low while the billions of nanomites scattered to combat all the drugs they'd pumped into her. Sigrid's bionics worked to keep her pulse low and steady, leaving little reason for them to suspect she wasn't completely down for the count.

Either Keller was paranoid, or just overly cautious, because he had another crewman tie her wrists with a set of plastic binders.

Great; just what she needed.

They were taking her to the brig. She knew from the schematics loaded into her PCM that their route would take her in the vicinity of the Engineering section, one deck below.

The crewmen charged with handling her had a bit of a time passing her down the ladder to the lower deck. One crewman held her hands, lowering her down to two more crewmen below, who gathered her up in their arms. Even with her eyes closed, her sensory modules picked up the men's reactions as they handled her nearly naked body. She hadn't anticipated this as affording a *distraction*, but the young men seemed to be concentrating far more on her rear than the task at hand.

While they carried her, Sigrid took stock of the crew's location on the small ship. Five crewmen had accompanied her down toward the brig, and four more manned the engineering section. That only left three, presumably on the bridge.

They were approaching the brig. Sigrid knew she couldn't let them lock her inside. If she were lucky, the captain of the *Morrigan* had already transmitted the deactivation codes for the mine, but Sigrid had to assume it was still live. The auxiliary control center was only ten meters down the corridor from her current position.

Now was the time.

Sigrid slitted open her eyes. Two crewmen gripped her arms on both sides; the one on her right held a riot gun; he also had several gas grenades clipped to his belt. Perfect. She held back a smile.

Sigrid bent her knees and sprang to her feet. She hooked her trussed-up wrists over the first man's head, spun him around and threw him into the body of the other man who'd held her a moment before. Both crashed heavily into the wall. It was a simple matter to relieve the crewman of his riot gun; she snapped it out of his hands as he fell, off-balance.

Three crew charged at her from the direction of the engineering section and she fired, watching the net spread out as it pinned the crewmen to the bulkhead. They spasmed—quite satisfyingly, Sigrid thought. She winced at their cries as the power-pack discharged its potent dose of electricity.

Her sensors registered a warning. Sigrid ducked and rolled under the stun-charge that whizzed past her head. In one fluid motion, she liberated two of the gas grenades from the felled crewman, pulled the pins and rolled one down each direction of the corridor. Only the XO had time to get his breather back on his face, but in his haste he dropped his stun pistol. Sigrid stepped in next to him and yanked the mask off his face; he took one panicked, short breath and slumped to the grated, metal floor.

Sigrid tossed the breather aside. The nanomites in her system could probably handle the gas, but she was still feeling nauseous from the earlier gassing, so she held her breath. She could hold it for six minutes easily enough. She relieved an unconscious crewmen of his knife, cut herself free from the binders and massaged her chafed wrists. The brief skirmish had lasted just under sixteen-seconds. She scanned and detected no alarms. Good. Sigrid did a quick count; all five of her escort were down, along with three of the engineers; she realized there was one remaining and cursed.

She peeked into the cramped Engineering Room, but there was no sign of him. That meant he was either on the bridge or her information was wrong. The Auxiliary Controls were in front of her. She moved to the console, where her PCM searched and found the correct network access, linking her directly to the ship's systems. A number of security protocols tried to block her access as she worked her way through the firewalls. *Suko would be better at this*, she thought. *Suko was always better at decryption.*

It took longer than she'd have preferred, a little less than a minute, but she finally managed to break through the security and found the deactivation codes for the mine. She breathed a deep sigh as she confirmed they hadn't tried to detonate it yet. Her efforts had so far gone unnoticed on the bridge, but that would change shortly.

Sigrid stifled a giggle as she fed a worm-hack into the control systems—this was a little mischief Suko had shown her. It was fast-acting and, if it worked, would keep any of the command crew from doing anything until she could gain full control of the ship.

* * *

Captain Gregory Oslov leaned forward in his chair and peered over the shoulder of the helmsman in front of him. The bridge on the scout ship was so small he could see the consoles of most of the crew. He'd gotten into the habit of looking at theirs rather than his own master-console in the arm of this chair. He was a control freak, and he knew it.

He checked the chronometer again. His XO had reported that they'd captured the girl and were on the way to the brig, but that report was two minutes old. Oslov wasn't about to relax until she was safely locked away. He didn't know much about the *package*, only that she was to be regarded as extremely dangerous. She'd been given the highest threat-rating by their commandant.

He was distracted for a moment by the flashing light on his communications panel. The *Agatsuma* was hailing him again, eager for the deactivation codes, no doubt.

"Not just yet, my friends," Oslov muttered, tapping his fingers on the arm of his chair. *Not until she's safely stowed and secured.*

He checked the time again. It had been too long. Oslov wasn't quite panicking, but the hairs on the back of his neck bristled. His

XO should have reported by now. He banged the com with the back of his fist, opening a channel.

"Keller—report!" He waited. Silence. *Fuck.* "Chen. Hiller!" Only the squelch and rasp of static answered back. The helmsman turned around in her chair and shot him a worried look. Oslov stared down at the small console attached to the arm of his chair. One light blinked like a beacon—the switch that would send the activation command to the mine he'd laid for the *Agatsuma*. Could he really do it? Could he blow up an entire crew of fellow Mercenaries? Would it make any difference?

He looked up at the helmsman. "What's the position of the *Agatsuma*?"

"No change, sir. Still just sitting there, ten thousand klicks out."

"All right. Lock us down until we can figure out what's going on. No one gets in here, you hear me?"

The young officer worked furiously at her controls, then a bewildered expression spread over her face.

"What is it?"

"I'm not sure, sir—everything checks out, but...nothing's working. I don't...I have no control!"

"Mother..." Oslov jumped to his feet and banged his head, *yet again*, on the low ceiling. He drew his sidearm and moved quickly to the door. Too late—it slid open. Captain Oslov was too seasoned a professional to be surprised or shocked at the sight of the small, nearly naked girl in front of him. He didn't want to hurt her; he wasn't a violent man, but orders were orders, and he didn't hesitate in his duty. He fired his weapon, point blank.

The speed at which she moved didn't seem possible. She became a flickering blur before his eyes. His slug pierced the air where she'd just been standing and exploded against the bulkhead down the corridor. Oslov's mouth fell open and his hand went slack. This time, he did hesitate. He stared wildly at her as she leveled the riot gun at him. The blast knocked him backward, sending him tumbling over the back of his captain's chair and pinning him up against the helm and navigation's consoles. He felt the surge of electricity judder his system; his eyes rolled back in his head, but not before he saw the girl leap over him; he heard a sickening thud and his helmsman's screams, then everything went black.

* * *

Sigrid pushed the unconscious body of the helmsman from her chair onto the floor, taking a moment to relieve the woman of her uniform jacket. She hit a switch on the control panel, deactivating her worm program and restoring control to the bridge. She took care to ensure that the auxiliary controls remained locked out; she still had to worry about the missing crewman, probably hiding somewhere on board.

Mercifully, the ship was small and she soon found him, snoring soundly in his quarters. He'd somehow slept through the entire action. Sigrid snorted at the comedy of it as she sealed him into his quarters before returning to the bridge. The *Agatsuma* was out of range of her implanted comlink so she used the *Morrigan's* transmitter and thumbed the channel open. The loud sound of cheering from the *Agatsuma's* bridge crew was a welcome assault to her ears. She put the image up on the forward viewer and smiled at the relieved countenance of the captain and the crew behind him.

"Well done, Ms. Novak. Is the ship secure?"

"Yes, sir. I've gained control of the bridge and I've locked out control through the rest of the ship. The crew is incapacitated. I've also deactivated the mine—I think you'll find it's quite harmless now."

The captain nodded acknowledgment. "Very well. Stay where you are—keep the bridge. We'll come alongside and send a boarding party aboard. I...don't know how you did it. We can't thank you enough. I'm sure there's a hefty commendation bonus in this for you."

Bonus? Sigrid hadn't considered that, but of course, this was the life of a Mercenary.

She acknowledged the compliment with a slight bow. "Thank you, Captain."

"Stand by. We'll be alongside in a moment."

The viewer winked-off and Sigrid was alone again, apart from the untidy heap of unconscious bridge officers. Something on

Captain Oslov's body caught her eye. He still held his sidearm in his limp hand—a matching one lay holstered on his left side. Sigrid picked it up. She always found the allure of such weapons compelling, ever since the day she'd discovered what a crack shot she was. The captain's pistols were unlike anything she'd held before. Slightly larger than the Markovs, these were a unique, custom-design. There was nothing like them in her database. They were pearl-handled and fit the palm of her hand perfectly, even better than her Markovs. Longer, heavier and fashioned from polished tungsten, they fired a variety of simple, high-powered ballistic rounds. They were lethal, brutal and utterly lovely.

Trophies perhaps? That's what Mercenaries did, right? She wondered if she'd be allowed to keep them, even as she removed the captain's holsters and fastened the belt around her own waist.

As she looked around the ship, another idea occurred to Sigrid.

Chapter 12
Mercenary

March 2, 2348

"You *what?*" Captain Maalouf demanded.

Standing before him in his ready-room, dressed in her Academy outfit, Sigrid raised her posture, hands clasped behind her back. She had scoured Kimura's database, and also asked the advice of Karen and Lieutenant Lopez. She was determined not to back down.

"Yes, sir." Her reply came measured and steady. "I claim the *Morrigan* as bounty."

Captain Maalouf leaned back in his chair and studied the small yet clearly determined girl in front of him. "You know that after a victory it is customary for the attacking ship to claim salvageable vessels as *prize*. Honoring your demands would mean the entire crew would have to forfeit their bonus—not to mention Kimura's own claims. The *Agatsuma* is still a Kimura vessel and they'll be expecting to charge a tax on the operation as well."

Sigrid had already studied the complex bonus structure thoroughly. On the face of it, the *Agatsuma* and the entire Kimura corporation appeared to have a legitimate claim on the spoils.

Unless Sigrid could make her case.

She felt a wave of doubt, but steeled herself and blurted out what she'd been rehearsing in her head all morning. "Begging your pardon, sir, no disrespect intended, but…well, you surrendered to the captain of the *Morrigan*. *You* surrendered, sir. As such, I was operating on my own. And…" Sigrid swallowed, "I claim the *Morrigan* as *spoils of war* under article 487, section 6C of the Mercenary Act."

Captain Maalouf scowled at her. "Article..." His hand moved over the console on his desk, as if to verify the quoted article, then he fixed her with a stony stare. "You know we had no choice in surrendering—that *was* part of the plan."

"Yes, sir. I realize that you were left with few choices. But still, you *did* technically surrender, sir." Sigrid coughed to clear her dry throat, as much as fill the silence.

The captain's eyes narrowed. "I could refuse..."

"And I would request arbitration."

Her words drew a wry smile from Maalouf. "This won't make you popular with the crew—they'll be expecting a bonus in this matter."

Sigrid breathed a sigh. *Was he really giving in?* "I'll still need to hire a crew to bring the ship in, Captain. Or have the *Agatsuma* tow the *Morrigan* to Aquarii. Either way, the crew and the ship would be rewarded for the task."

"You've given this much thought, I see."

"Yes, sir."

The captain laughed with more warmth this time. He nodded and leaned forward. "Very well, Ms. Novak. I concede. You may claim the *Morrigan*. I propose towing the ship the rest of the way—I believe you'll find the standard towing fees more reasonable than hiring a crew."

"Thank you, sir, but I'd prefer to crew the ship." Sigrid pulled out her data-pad from behind her back and placed it on the desk. "Here's a list of the personnel I require for the operation."

Captain Maalouf couldn't help but grin at Sigrid's determination. He leaned back in his chair and chuckled before rising and extending his hand. "Very well, Ms. Novak. And congratulations on a job well done."

* * *

March 3, 2348

Sigrid was once again grateful for her diminutive stature. As she stood behind the command chair on the cramped bridge of the *Morrigan* her head almost touched the ceiling. The other crew members had to stoop as they entered the crowded cockpit.

The door to the bridge slid open. Lieutenant Lopez came breezing in and banged his head smartly on the low ceiling. "*Mother...*"

Sigrid and Karen winced in unison.

"Glad you could make it, Lieutenant," Sigrid said, with a wink to Karen. "Think you can handle bringing the ship in-system?"

He nodded, then rubbed the sore spot on his forehead before taking his position at the helm. "You *know* I'm just a Tac-Officer. I've never piloted anything like this."

"Yes, but you're certified. I've checked your record." She also knew Captain Maalouf would be reluctant to release his more skilled bridge officers. Christian was certified, and she was grateful to have him on board—and to have his company.

Karen cleared her throat. "The *Agatsuma* is signaling they're ready to get underway."

Ensign Karen McTeer was still assigned to her personally, as her Orientations Officer and Sigrid had employed her as Communications Officer.

"Good. Let them know we're also set to go. We'll follow them in at ten thousand kilometers aft."

"Aye, sir—I mean, ma'am." Karen chuckled.

Sigrid peered through the side viewport and watched as the thrusters of the larger craft at their side flared brilliantly. The Corvette slid by them, slowly, then accelerated at an incredible rate before disappearing a few moments later. Sigrid frowned at the command chair in front of her—somehow, she didn't feel right sitting in it so she stood alongside it with her hand on the backrest.

"Ma'am?" Christian asked. They all seemed to be looking at her, waiting.

"Let's go to Aquarii."

* * *

March 8, 2348

For just over six days, both ships thundered through space, moving ever deeper into the heart of the Aquarii system. At the halfway point, they flipped 180° about, decelerating the rest of the way toward the small blue-green planet that was Aquarii II. The *Morrigan* could have easily covered the distance in half the time, but Sigrid chose to follow the larger ship in. She was in no hurry to get to Aquarii and passed the time by exploring every inch of the small scout vessel. It was lightly armed compared to the *Agatsuma*, with only two forward torpedo tubes and two rail-turrets, mounted dorsally and ventrally. Spanning less than fifty meters, the *Morrigan* was small, but fast and highly agile.

Much of her time was spent with Ensign McTeer. In light of the recent attack, Sigrid insisted the ensign should brief her on the political and economic climate of the Federation, rather than worry about what Sigrid was doing—or not doing—with her hair. Sigrid was surprised to learn how the Trade Federation had grown to cover twenty-four planets, with seven more already being explored for mining and resource extraction. When she'd been a girl, there had only been colonies in twelve systems. Much of the information was already included in her database, but Karen had a knack of explaining the complex nuances of the Federation's political structure in an illuminating way. Sigrid would never have thought to claim the *Morrigan* as a spoil of war, were it not for the ensign's tutoring.

On the bridge, Christian frowned at his controls. "I know you say I'm checked out on these things, but I hope you won't think less of me if I let the automated systems take us down."

Sigrid laughed. "Not at all. Take us in, Lieutenant Lopez."

"Aye, ma'am."

The nose of the *Morrigan* dipped down and the sight of Aquarii filled the forward viewport. Sigrid spied Aquarii's most unique and spectacular geological feature, *The Slash*, a wide and winding inland sea that divided Aquarii's two largest land masses, carving its way from ocean to ocean.

They pierced the atmosphere at 25,000 kph. After the smooth ride through the system, the sudden buffeting was a noisy, uncomfortable contrast. The inertial dampening systems handled much of the turbulence but Sigrid found herself clinging hard to the back of the command chair as the small ship bumped and jittered through re-entry.

The automated systems flew them low over the lush green and blue hills of Aquarii. Though more populated than Alcyone, it was still a natural paradise compared to the permacrete-covered landscapes of Earth. Sigrid marveled at the colors; she had never seen blue trees before.

The forests gave way to more industrialized areas as they came in over Aetos City, the largest city on Aquarii, populated by well over a million people. The Kimura enclave was a sprawling campus located in the heart of the city. They skimmed down over a wide airfield lined with a variety of ships, passing two hulking destroyers perched on the edge of the tarmac. At over 400 meters in length, these were the largest ships capable of planetary landings. Any larger warships and transports had to remain in orbit around Aquarii.

The autopilot brought them down on their designated pad close to the complex. Christian went quickly through the shutdown sequence to the whines and the wailings of the thrusters powering down. "You have arrived at your destination," he said with a leer. "Please enjoy your stay."

"Well done, Mr. Lopez," she teased. They both knew the ship's systems had handled the entire approach and landing.

They gathered in the lower airlock; Sigrid hit the release and the outer door swung open and down. A blast of warm, humid air washed over her. Sigrid gasped. But it wasn't the sudden change in atmosphere that startled her. There, at the base of the stairs, sitting in a wheelchair and surrounded by a platoon of security officers, was none other than the Lady Hitomi Kimura, CEO and head of the Kimura Corporation.

Clad in an elaborate gown of black silk, she smiled at Sigrid from behind a pair of dark glasses. Two security officers helped her to stand. Even with mechanical braces fastened to her legs, she leaned heavily on an ornately carved cane made of lacquered cherry-wood. She stood tall, much taller than Sigrid. Her thick, long, raven-black hair was tied back, held by a set of gilded kogai and kushi. Several long strands hung delicately down the sides of her face. Even at sixty-two, and hampered as she was by the disease that had taken the use of her legs, the Lady Hitomi exuded a powerful, captivating persona.

Sigrid approached her, followed gingerly by her own crew, who were clearly surprised at the entourage before them. Lady Hitomi took two unsteady steps toward Sigrid, who bowed deeply. She lifted Sigrid's chin with the tip of her finger, removed her dark glasses and regarded Sigrid with a smile.

"Welcome home, Sigrid," Hitomi said, pronouncing her name perfectly.

The Lady Hitomi pulled back a loose strand of hair that blew across her face. She tilted her head, shielding her eyes from the sun. As she did, Sigrid caught a glimpse—she wasn't sure at first—but then she saw it again as the breeze whipped the Lady's hair from her face; a small, two millimeter-wide slot. Hitomi Kimura had a PCM access port tucked hidden away behind her ear, just as Sigrid did. Just as the girls from Alcyone did. Hitomi was like them.

Sigrid stifled a gasp and concentrated on standing to attention. "Milady," was all she could say as she bowed again. She found it difficult to look the woman in the eye.

Hitomi Kimura waved her hand dismissively. "*Please* don't use that ridiculous title. It's a silly custom invented by the local inhabitants—they gave me such a grand title simply because I head the largest of the companies here. But it's a small planet and I suppose they imagine it adds something to the local color."

Sigrid knew there was *much* more to it than that. The commercial empire that the Lady Kimura had built was responsible for the entire thriving economy on Aquarii, but she knew better than to argue with the woman. "Yes, Mistress."

"That will do in a pinch, but you may call me 'Hitomi-san'...at least when we're alone."

"Yes, Mistress," Sigrid said, resisting an urge to curtsey.

Hitomi turned her attention to the ship behind Sigrid. Her smile widened. "A fine ship. Captain Maalouf tells me you've claimed it as bounty. You don't waste any time, do you?"

Sigrid felt herself flush. "My claim is based on existing regulations, Mistress. I only—"

"Not at all. You're well within your rights. I merely meant to express how impressed I was—that you took the ship single-handedly, *and* without casualties...that you took such bold action. The Captain was a little...disappointed at losing such a prize, but he'll get over it. Tell me, do you wish to auction it? I'm prepared to offer you a fair price. Our fleet could always use a fine vessel such as this."

Sigrid took a deep breath. Selling the ship to Kimura would go a long way to paying off her family's debt, taking years off her contract. It made logical, rational sense. And keeping it certainly wasn't an option; she could never afford the moorage fees.

But somehow, Sigrid couldn't bear to part with it. She couldn't explain it—*she couldn't afford it*—but she wanted it.

There was one more option.

"I propose a leasing contract, Mistress."

"Terms?" Hitomi asked, with an interested smirk.

Sigrid pulled her pad out from her pocket, unfolded it, and handed it to Lady Hitomi for inspection.

Hitomi read quickly in silence. Sigrid held her breath.

She had prepared a leasing agreement that would allow her to maintain title to the vessel. The ship would be released for use in the Kimura fleet, who would handle maintenance costs while paying Sigrid a usage fee. A set bonus would be paid should it be used in combat, more if the vessel proved worthy or claimed victory over another.

"I wasn't aware they taught business at the Academy, Sigrid."

"No, Mistress."

"Impressive." Hitomi looked over to Ensign McTeer. "You helped her with this?"

Karen bowed before speaking. "No, Milady. I only instructed her in the guild laws. Sigrid—Ms. Novak prepared the contract herself."

"Very well. Your terms are agreeable." She pressed her thumb to Sigrid's contract and handed her the pad. She stood, scrutinizing Sigrid for a long minute—Sigrid shifted on her feet, feeling quite self-conscious, though maintained her stance at full attention. Finally, Hitomi smiled again. "I hope this won't be the end of your surprises, young one."

"No, Mistress."

"Now, if you will forgive me..." She eased herself carefully into the wheelchair. "This is more exercise than I have had in a long while. You will join me for dinner, of course."

"Thank you, Mistress."

Her attendant began to wheel her away, but she stopped him. "Oh, Ensign McTeer will find you some quarters. Let me know if they are to your satisfaction." She signaled, and the man resumed pushing her along.

Sigrid's crew had watched the whole scene, transfixed.

Lieutenant Lopez broke the silence. "Holy crap! Do you know who that was?"

Karen stifled a laugh. "Close your mouth. You'll catch flies." She linked arms with Sigrid. "I told you we were traveling with a VIP."

"I know, but..."

A waiting ground-car took Sigrid and her crew to the main habitat of the Kimura Enclave. Sigrid parted with them there, saying her goodbyes, sad to see them go. Karen escorted Sigrid to her new quarters.

"Is all this for me?" Sigrid gaped at the suite, which was large enough to accommodate *all* the girls from Alcyone.

Karen nodded, warmed by the sight of Sigrid exploring the multileveled unit, turning on lights and inspecting the closets and appliances. One wall was filled entirely with a large viewing monitor. Curious, Sigrid interfaced with it and found that she could access thousands of entertainment programs. She hadn't seen *TV* since childhood. Sigrid paused her *channel* flipping and stopped on a film. The screen became inhabited with the three-dimensional image of a man and a woman, both completely naked. The man, tall and spectacularly muscled, gathered the woman into his arms and kissed her with a passion that made Sigrid blush. He whispered her name, *Sofia, Sofia*, and groped her naked breasts. The woman, Sofia, apparently, swooned and moaned with pleasure.

Sigrid sank back into the sofa, transfixed at the images in front of her.

"*Gah*—I hate that movie," Karen said as she walked past, exploring the suite. "Trust me, that's the best part."

Embarrassed, Sigrid flipped the monitor off. *It was a very good part.* She looked back at the blank monitor—she had a strange urge to sit and watch more.

"Here you go!" Karen trilled from the other room. Sigrid followed her in to see what was up. Karen was standing before a wide, walk-in closet that was easily bigger than the quarters she'd had at the Annex on Alcyone. It was filled with clothes—formal military uniforms, combat suits, business wear and dresses and dresses.

"Holy..." Sigrid said, running her hands along the racks.

"Check these out."

Karen held up several boots for Sigrid to see. They were more like the tall-military boots Sigrid was used to wearing, but these were equipped with high-heels.

"They must have read my report," Karen said.

"You told them *I'm short?*"

Karen snorted a laugh. "They asked me if I knew what you liked. I told them you *loved* the shoes I lent you—and, here you go." Karen pulled one of the formal uniforms off the rack. "Ooh! You *have* to try this on."

The uniform consisted of a pair of slacks and a jacket, black with red trim. The outfit was tailored perfectly for her; the pants were tight and zipped at her ankles, but she found she could still move with perfect ease.

Karen opened a drawer, eyes wide as she held up a bra for inspection. "Fancy." This one was trimmed with a lacy fabric and looked quite delicate. Sigrid quickly slipped it on. It felt soft and comfortable, not nearly as practical or as the functional underwear she was used to, but it was pretty and she couldn't help but like the way it looked—*and made her look.* Even the jacket seemed tailored to highlight her femininity, darting in at her sides and under her breasts, accentuating her curves in a provocative fashion.

Sigrid fastened the high-collar and marveled at the fine tailoring of the uniform. She looked almost as sharp as Ensign McTeer. Sigrid pulled on one of the new pairs of boots; they zippered up the sides, with laces that tied all the way up to her knee. Her pants tucked neatly into them without any folds or bulges. When Sigrid stood, she was pleased to find that she stood as tall as the ensign before her.

As always, Sigrid completed her outfit by arming herself; she chose the two pearl-handled pistols she'd liberated from Captain Oslov.

Ensign McTeer gave a long, low whistle as she admired Sigrid in her formal outfit.

Sigrid laughed affectionately. "What's this?" she asked; her uniform bore no rank insignia like Karen's, but there was a small rectangular emblem stitched into the chest, just above the breast pocket.

Karen leaned closer and examined it. "Campaign ribbon. The Captain must have reported your action against the *Morrigan*. I've never seen them issue one so fast, though. They've certainly got their eye on you."

Sigrid wasn't sure whether that was a good thing or a bad thing.

* * *

March 9, 2348

The boardroom of the Kimura Corporation stood high atop the central tower of the mercenary enclave. It was a grand, circular room, windowed on all sides, revealing a spectacular view of Enclave and Aetos City. The only means of access was a spiral staircase, leading up from a lounge and reception area one floor below.

The Lady Hitomi Kimura despised having to meet with the Board. She found the bureaucracy tiresome and would love nothing more than to dispense with the lot of them—probably about as much as they'd like to get rid of her. But worse was that she couldn't negotiate the awkward spiral staircase on her own. Being carried up the winding flight of stairs was humiliation beyond reason and served to remind all members of her weakness.

And then there was her CFO, her main detractor and general pain in the ass, Markus Emerson. Markus was well into his fifties; the Kimura CFO was devilishly handsome. Hitomi couldn't look at him without rebuking herself. She'd made a fatal mistake long ago and let the man get close to her. Though it was all in the past, it remained a thorn in both their sides.

Her security man was ready with her wheelchair at the top of the staircase, but today she refused it. Today she took the seven faltering steps to the head of the conference table—helped along by Sigrid. Hitomi marveled at how easily the girl held her up with an arm around her waist, the other on her elbow.

Two of her men rushed forward with a chair. She waved it away. Today she would stand. It was a small gesture, but she needed to remind her board that she was still in charge, still the CEO of one of the oldest mercenary clans in the Federation.

Hitomi turned to face Sigrid, who remained at her flank, hands clasped behind her back. She felt a great sense of pride as she took in the young woman. Smartly decked out in her formal-dress uniform, Sigrid appeared professional and lethal, despite her small stature and young age. An impressive sight, to be sure. Hitomi wanted the Board to get a good look at her today; she could already see the people before her studying Sigrid closely.

Lady Hitomi tapped her cane to the floor and the room fell silent.

"Thank you all for coming. I've called this meeting to deal with a rather startling development. We've kept the matter classified until now, but I've decided it's time to inform you all."

Hitomi gave them a moment, watching as her directors sat up a little straighter; their bored attitudes vanished instantly, to be replaced by concerned curiosity.

"Seven days ago, inbound from the Aquarii Relay, the *Agatsuma* was attacked. I shouldn't need to point out the significance of this to any of you. A Kimura ship, in Kimura-controlled space, attacked. This was no *random encounter*, either. The ship was intercepted by the *DSS Morrigan* claiming permit for seizure of a cargo of illegal weapons. This is the second attack directed specifically against Kimura and *Project Andraste*. I don't want any of you to confuse this with the recent skirmishes we've been having with the *Independents* either. This was a directed attack with a specific target in mind." Hitomi's eyes fell briefly on Sigrid. "However, I am pleased to report that the attack was a complete failure."

Markus nodded. "Captain Maalouf is an experienced line officer, a proven combat specialist."

Hitomi gave her CFO a stern look. "Your *proven specialist* surrendered his ship and cargo without firing a shot. I'll have you all know that the *Morrigan* was taken, single-handedly, by this young woman. Unarmed and left on her own, she quickly overcame the enemy, while an entire Corvette-full of our most highly trained officers and crew was forced to surrender…"

"Yes, yes. We're all familiar with the girl's abilities."

Hitomi doubted that very much, but she let Markus continue.

"You say the *Morrigan* had a permit for seizure? If this is true, it's most disturbing news."

Hitomi nodded. "Indeed, but we can't verify the authenticity of the document at this point; not until we receive confirmation from the Council Authority. Personally, I find it hard to believe that the Council would act against us in this way. Their purpose is to facilitate free-trade between the Corporations, not to interfere. It goes against everything they stand for."

"Does it?" Markus asked. "Isn't this exactly what they tried to do with Daedalus?"

Hitomi felt a knot in her gut; the same thought had crossed her mind.

When Daedalus Corp had first revealed the technology for the Warp Relays, the Council had tried to appropriate the technology in the name of the Federation, 'for the betterment of the humankind'. But everyone knew it was just an attempt to control an important new technology, possibly the most significant development ever.

The Council had argued that no one company should control such an important technology, but Daedalus had refused to surrender control. Scars from the conflict could still be seen all over the Earth and in the Orbital Colonies. As a means of truce, Daedalus had sworn neutrality, and for the last forty years an uneasy peace had existed. Humanity had expanded through the galaxy and many, many corporations had grown rich beyond avarice. None more so than Daedalus.

Again, Hitomi nodded. "As insane as it might sound, we must entertain the thought that the Federation Council has designs on *Andraste*."

Shinji had been sitting quietly next to his mother, but this was too much. "That's impossible! The Council would never dare. They have no direct jurisdiction over us. On what grounds could they possibly justify such an attack?"

"Do they need justification?" came the disturbing question from Dannette Kirsch, one of Kimura's principal shareholders. "If they really wanted to appropriate the girls, would we be in a position to oppose them? Are we even certain this wasn't just a ruse on the part of Dalair Military?"

"No, we're not sure of anything at this point," Hitomi said. "Captain Oslov maintains that the permit is legitimate, and the directive came from the CTF. I have no reason to believe the man, but I can't imagine why he'd wish to implicate the Council in this fiasco."

"This might actually make some strange kind of sense," a young man offered from down the table. "We've been monitoring the chatter between ships coming in-system. It's not just the one girl—there's talk of bounties on all the girls."

Hitomi shook her head wearily. "That anyone should even know of *any* of them—of *Andraste*—illustrates that we suffer a security breach in this organization. The ship that attacked the *Agatsuma* knew our flight schedule. They should never have been allowed to lie in wait for our forces like that."

Admiral Simpson swallowed and looked meekly up at the CEO. "My apologies, Lady Hitomi. We've since positioned several ships around the relay. That breach won't happen again."

"I should hope not, Admiral. I also propose we take extra steps to guard the facility on Alcyone. With your approval, I'd like to send the Third Destroyer squadron to Alcyone immediately."

Markus glared at her. "Are you mad? Our naval forces are already committed under contract. And now you'd have us expend even *more* resources? This project has been nothing but a drain on this company for more than a decade. And what has it brought us? Nothing—except that we've been financially hamstrung. The ranks of our creditors grow, while our list of allies grows thin. It's time to cut our losses. This entire project is a disaster and will surely bring ruin to the Corporation."

Hitomi studied the CFO, not bothering to hide her contempt. "Are you really willing to resign our assets based on the com-chatter of bored freighter captains? This girl—Sigrid..." Hitomi turned to her, relaxing her tone, "...represents decades of research. She, and all the girls, represent a potential boon for this company, not to mention a massive leap forward in human evolution. This is just the start—"

"What they represent, is a liability," Markus cut in. "The resources we've used—that you've personally reallocated—the staggering debt we've incurred... We are in no position to refuse the will of the Council, let alone fight a war against the entire Federation."

Murmurs of opinion echoed around the room, mostly in agreement with his statement.

Hitomi raised her hands for silence. "I think we're getting ahead of ourselves. We still don't know the Council's intentions."

"Then what do you propose?" Shinji asked.

"I see only one course of action. I will go to Earth and address the Council. I've already logged the petition with the local Federation Envoy."

"You?" Markus asked, staring at the braces on her legs. "In your condition?"

"I still have *some* pull with the Council."

"There was a time when Kimura had a *seat* on the Council," Markus said, unable to resist pointing out that which they all knew so well.

Hitomi conceded the point. Her father and grandfather had held a seat on the Council for Trade and Finance, but that was before Daedalus, before humankind had reached out into the cosmos. It was no secret that the Board blamed her for the loss of the position and the influence that it had once given their company.

"I also have twenty-one contract requests for the girls and more coming in." She tapped the data-pad in front of her, activating the wall monitor at the end of the room. "I propose that we accept these contracts now. On Alcyone, the girls will remain an easy target. Under contract, they will at least be dispersed, as well as come under the protection of the companies they serve."

Markus sat back down; she could see him trying to concoct some other argument, but Hitomi had planned her maneuvers carefully. There was little he could say against her at this point.

Hitomi flashed up the fee details on the screen. "Plus, the contracts are for extremely generous amounts. That should keep the shareholders off your backs, at least through the next quarter."

Hitomi scanned the board members; they were all busy perusing the contract offers. She could see the gleam in their eyes at the generous service fees being offered. Money always smoothed everything over.

"Shall we put it to a vote?" she proposed.

* * *

March 23, 2348

Sigrid emerged from her bathroom, fresh from a shower. She took a moment to wrap her hair in a towel before slipping into a soft, white robe. The last two weeks had been the strangest of her life. Ever since the meeting with the Board, Sigrid had found herself being paraded around for the Kimura officers and section-heads, the Admiralty, even the Corps of Engineers, all of whom were eager to meet her and put her combat training to a test. Sigrid was beginning to feel like a prized calf at auction—and not in a good way.

But there was no time to worry about that. Sigrid had a much more urgent matter to attend to. She flopped down on her bed. Lying on her stomach, she unfolded her pad and scanned through the letters she'd composed to Suko. She'd written at least one letter a day since she'd left the Academy. Writing them was about the only thing that made her time alone bearable. Ever since her arrival on Aquarii she'd been waiting for the opportunity to send them out. Tomorrow, two transports were leaving, on their way to Alcyone to pick up the new girls. The transports would take her letters, and Sigrid could finally tell Suko what she was so desperate to say.

At first Sigrid had been excited at the prospect, but as she flipped through the letters they suddenly felt horribly inadequate.

Sigrid pressed *delete* on her pad, throwing everything out, and hastily composed a brand new one.

Dearest Suko,

By now you know that more transports are coming to take more of you away. I don't know who they will take or where any of you might be headed. I can only hope that somehow your path will take you here, back to me, even if it's only for a short time.

When they came for me that day, I felt as if I had died. I am so sorry, Suko. You were right. I should never have left you—regardless of the consequences. I don't even care if anyone reads this or if saying this gets me in more trouble.

You said I didn't know how you felt about me. You were right—at least in that I hadn't stopped to consider your feelings. I love you, Suko. I can only hope that you love me too.

When they brought me here I didn't think I'd ever see you again. I convinced myself I was leaving for the right reasons. I now know that this was wrong.

And I promise—I will find my way back to you.
Somehow.

Yours always,
Sigrid

Sigrid paused briefly to consider what her superiors might think of the letter. They'd read it of course, screening it for security reasons. It was potentially treasonous, but she didn't care. As long as the letter got to Suko.

She was actually more nervous about what they might think of the two pictures she'd attached. One was of Sigrid standing before the *Morrigan*, dressed in her new formal uniform and boots, *trophy* pistols slung at her side. The other was of a more intimate nature. With Karen's help, not to mention her prodding and urging, Sigrid had composed a rather daring picture of herself, lying on her bed, dressed in a set of particularly delicate and lacy underwear she'd found in one of her drawers. Sigrid had been thoroughly embarrassed to consider taking the shot, let alone propose it, but Karen had immediately embraced the idea, convinced that Suko would *love* it.

Sigrid hoped so. She blushed just thinking about it. But as she lay back on her bed she was also delighted at the realization that Suko would see it. *As long as she doesn't laugh!* she thought. No, Suko wouldn't laugh.

Sigrid hit the transmit tab on her pad. There...it was done, sent; no going back now.

She imagined Suko reading it, lying in her own bed, looking at the picture. Would Suko forgive her? Did she still love her? She had to. Sigrid couldn't bear to consider anything else.

In all of her daydreams she and Suko were together again, reunited. So why not live out the dream? She already had a ship. Might she really take it and steal her way back to Suko? Could they get away?

Unfortunately, the romantic notion was riddled with flaws. Were she to attempt such a scheme, her tiny ship would be tracked and followed. And she had no means of paying the exorbitant fees charged by Daedalus for travel through the Relay System. Still, the fantasy brought with it the flicker of a smile to her lips.

As long as Suko didn't laugh or think her foolish for sending the risqué picture. As long as Suko still loved her.

Her door chimed. Sigrid sat up with a start and quickly gathered her robe back around her. It was late in the evening and she hadn't been expecting anyone.

"Come," she said as she moved into the living area of her suite. The door slid open. Sitting in her wheelchair at the door was none other than the Lady Hitomi. Sigrid poked her head out into the hall, expecting to see the Lady's security entourage, but the hallway was empty.

"Aren't you going to invite me in?" Hitomi asked.

"Yes—yes. Please!" Sigrid moved out of the way, painfully aware of the state of her suite. The place was littered with clothes, beverage containers and food wrappers. Sigrid scurried about, doing her best to tidy quickly, hoping to hide how she'd somehow become a slob in a matter of days.

She glanced up to find the Lady Hitomi giving her an amused look. "Sit, sit," she said, waving Sigrid to the seat next to her. "You can clean later—you *will* clean later, I hope."

"Yes, Mistress," Sigrid said, her cheeks burning with shame.

"*Hitomi-san,* when we're alone."

"Yes, Mis—Hitomi-san."

Without preamble, Hitomi held a pad out to her. Sigrid scanned the information, curious, though a bit confused. Lady Hitomi was tendering her first contract offer, a highly lucrative, if not unusual contract offer. And it was from Lady Hitomi herself.

"Sign here," Hitomi said, indicating where Sigrid needed to place her thumb. Sigrid did as she was told. Hitomi tabbed a new contract on the screen. "And here…"

"But, Hitomi-san…" Sigrid found the second contract more confusing than the first.

"I want to hire you and your ship. I want you to take me to Earth. There's a personal services clause in there as well; you'll be responsible for my security and well being."

"Me?"

Hitomi waved her hand. "It's nothing—a standard clause. Think nothing of it."

Sigrid might be just-off-the-ship, but she knew how unusual this was. A woman of Hitomi's importance should only travel on a well-protected and armed vessel, a Destroyer, if not a frigate or Cruiser; she was too important to the organization and to Aquarii. It made even less sense to give Sigrid a private contract; she was already bound to the Corporation. The Lady Hitomi could simply pack her up and order her along for a fraction of the cost.

Sigrid continued to stare at the contract in disbelief. This was not at all what she'd expected.

"The first contract grants you special dispensation to operate as an *Independent.* The second is for your ship," Hitomi added as explanation.

"Hitomi-san…why me?"

"Whether you like it or not, you, my dear, are in the *eye of the storm.* This business with Tarsus and now Dalair, possibly even the Federation Council itself…if they really are in league with each other, then we must know. If not, then the Council, as well as the Mercenary Guild, must be informed. And…I can't think of anyone else I'd rather spend time with, or feel safer with on this voyage."

Sigrid didn't know what to say.

"Now, I suggest you get some rest. You have a busy day ahead. You'll need your ship and crew prepared for departure tomorrow."

* * *

March 28, 2348

Sigrid stood on the tarmac next to her ship with Ensign McTeer at her side. The night sky brooded thick with inky-black clouds. The scheduled rain was beginning to fall, controlled by the slew of weather satellites orbiting the blue-green planet. The weather system wouldn't interfere with the launch of her ship but it made the ground crews less enthusiastic about their preparations for departure. They were busy fueling the fifty meter-long vessel, loading food-stores, checking weapon-systems and loading ordnance.

Her crew was already on board; she'd hired a number of specialists from a list of available officers and crew. She'd also requested, and was granted, further use of both Lieutenant Lopez and Ensign Melissa Greenway.

Sigrid heard a signal over her comlink; Christian's voice sounded, tinny, in her head. *"Your passengers have arrived."*

"Thank you, Lieutenant."

Sigrid watched as a long string of black Kimura ground-cars approached at speed. The sleek-looking vehicles hovered inches off the tarmac, pulling smartly up in a neat row before the *Morrigan*. Fifteen security personnel swarmed out of the vehicles, formed a perimeter and scanned the vicinity. Only when they were sure the area was secure did they open the door to the last car. Resplendent in a long gown of red silk, Lady Hitomi Kimura allowed her staff to help her from the car and into the waiting wheelchair before escorting her toward the base of the waiting ship.

"Permission to come aboard?"

Sigrid bowed deeply. "Of course, Mistress." She gestured behind her to the elevator that she had commissioned the engineers to construct for Hitomi's ease of access.

Hitomi smiled at Sigrid's thoughtfulness and bowed graciously in return. "I think it's time we get underway, don't you?"

Sigrid nodded excitedly. She was returning to deep space, but this time as Mercenary, a freelance Mercenary, and with her own ship and crew. "Right away, Mistress."

Hitomi joined her on the bridge to observe the liftoff. She seemed eager to have as good a view as Sigrid—who still didn't feel comfortable in the command chair. She offered it to Hitomi who declined with a small wave of her hand.

"I'm quite fine right here, my dear," she said, patting the arm of her wheelchair.

The traffic controller signaled their departure clearance.

Sigrid took a deep breath. "Take us up, Mr. Lopez."

"Yes, Captain—I mean, ma'am." He turned and gave her a meek smile. "Sorry...habit."

Sigrid felt the floor move slightly before the dampening system kicked in as the *Morrigan* lifted off its landing struts. The ground swung away abruptly as the ship sat back on its rear thrusters. The sky loomed dark above them as rain peppered the glass of the forward viewport. The roaring surge of the thrusters fired and the ship leapt upwards, passing quickly through the low, overhanging clouds. Even through the insulated bulkheads the sound was close to deafening, a testament to the raw power coursing beneath them.

In a moment, they were through the thunderheads. The sky above was crisp and bright; Sigrid could see two of Aquarii's five moons glowing richly above them, casting a silvery sheen over the clouds beneath. The vibrations eased as they cleared the atmosphere and quickly left Aquarii behind them.

"Take us to the Relay, Lieutenant," Sigrid said. "Maximum thrust."

"Aye, ma'am."

"Send a request to the Relay Monitor. Course: Earth, Sol System."

Hitomi leaned forward with her hand raised. "Um...Not just yet."

"Mistress?" Sigrid asked.

"I'd like us to make a little side-trip," she said, with a glint of mischief in her eyes. "Take us to Crucis Prime."

Chapter 13
Letters

April 7, 2348

Suko didn't hear the door chime. She had her head tilted back, submerged under the warm stream of water that splashed over her head and shoulders. She'd had a particularly long day; those little girls were running her ragged, especially now that they were receiving regular treatments of the genetic recombinant from Dr. Garrett. They were already growing in strength and speed. Suko couldn't believe how much energy they had—and how hard she had to work them to tire them out.

She had to laugh; when she'd accepted the job as instructor for the new group at the Academy, she'd somehow assumed that it would be her task to run *them* into shape. She'd had no idea what a handful she'd undertaken. She suddenly found herself with a new appreciation for her old instructors. Had she and the other girls really been such hard work?

Suko finally became aware of the pounding on her door and the chime ringing. She turned the water off and stumbled out of the shower, her wet feet slipping on the tiles.

"Come," she said, only then remembering to grab a towel and wrap it around herself as the door slid open. Leta stood there; positively bursting with excitement.

"Didn't you hear them?"

"Hear what—when?"

Leta pointed up. "The shuttles. They came. Suko, they...brought you something." Leta held out a pad to Suko. "I thought you should have it right away. It's a letter."

Suko felt her heart quicken as she took the pad from Leta. She was almost afraid to look, but there, blinking on the screen, was a letter from Sigrid. Suko looked from the letter to Leta. "Did you read…"

Leta's eyes widened in mortification. "What? No! *I'd never…*"

"No, of course not. Sorry." Suko frowned at the pad, she was almost afraid to open it.

"Well, go on!"

Suko looked to the pad then to Leta, hesitantly. Finally, she backed away from the door. "Well, you might as well come in."

Leta smiled gratefully and sat next to Suko on the large, comfortable chair in her modest quarters. Suko caressed the tab; she eyed Leta suspiciously as she angled the pad away from her.

"I won't peep—promise," the feisty redhead assured her .

Suko thumbed the tab and opened the letter, reading it slowly and carefully. She read the letter three times. Only after the third did she realize her tears were flowing and that Leta was holding her.

"How could I do that?" Suko asked. "How could I have done that to her?" she said as Leta rocked her gently in her arms. "I blamed her for leaving. I never even told her—I never even said goodbye. I just left her."

Leta did her best to comfort her. She wiped her tears with the edge of her sleeve and kissed her softly on her cheek. "I'm sure she didn't mean what she wrote. She was probably just angry."

Suko looked up between sob's. "Angry? What do you mean?"

"Did she find someone else? Is that what happened?" Leta frowned. "She met someone, didn't she?"

Suko pulled away from her. "What? *No!*"

"I just—I thought…" Confused, Leta tried to grab the pad from Suko. "Wait…what did she say?"

Suko pulled the pad away defensively. "She said…she said she loves me."

"*Loves you!*" Leta clapped a hand to her chest in relief.

"She said she's going to try to come back to me." Suko's tears had finally abated and she brightened at her own words. "She *Loves* me, Leta." Suko laughed.

Leta snatched the pad away from Suko and read the letter quickly. "Oh my God! Suko…" Leta swatted her hard on her arm. "You had me thinking she *left* you. Dear *God*—I thought you just got a *Dear John* letter." Leta continued to swat her on the arm and shoulder. "Silly girl. She's not *mad at you*. She's mad *for* you."

Suko laughed as she wiped at her eyes and blew her nose.

"Oh...my..." Leta handed the pad back to Suko quickly. "I don't think I was supposed to see that."

Suko took it; there was a picture of Sigrid standing before a ship. Suko thought she looked magnificent in her smart uniform. She also looked taller; Suko realized she'd adopted high-heeled-boots. "I can't believe it! She has *her own ship*."

Leta looked embarrassed. "Um...no, not that picture; the other one." Leta reached over and flipped the image to the second photo she'd seen just a moment before.

Suko's jaw dropped open, and she sat back in the chair, staring at the evocative photo Sigrid had attached. "*Wow...*"

"I *know!*" Leta leaned over her shoulder to admire the photo. "Perhaps I should leave you two alone."

Suko didn't answer. She was immersed in the picture. Leta laughed as she let herself out.

* * *

Two Kimura transports stood on station atop the shimmering glacier, ready to take twenty-one girls to their new assignments. Snow had fallen during the night and the wind whipped the light dusting of powder across the ice. Suko stood by the wide landing platforms, saying her goodbyes to each of the girls as they boarded the waiting ships. She was sad to see them go—well, most of them. The years of being at odds with some of the girls over their bullying had left some permanent scars.

Suko had been offered two contracts, but she'd chosen to stay at the Academy as an instructor. She was far from eager to head off into space on some perceived adventure. She felt no love for Kimura, but she did want to stay with the new girls. There was something about them; it wasn't that she wanted to *protect* them as such, but there was a bond there; a bond that wasn't rational or logical, but she felt it nonetheless.

This was where she wanted to be. If Sigrid wanted to find her, she would look here first, and so Suko would bide her time at the Academy.

Leta dropped her duffel at her side, lifted Suko in her arms, and gave her a tremendous hug, expelling all the air from her lungs.

"*Gah*—careful! The...*ribs*..." Suko gasped as Leta released her grip.

"I'm going to miss you, Suko."

"I can't believe they're sending you to the Naval Academy on Crucis," Suko said, with a little envy. Kimura had assigned Leta and six other girls to the Mercenary Naval Academy; there, the girls would go into officers' training to learn ships' systems and tactics. It was a much sought after position.

"I know, it's unreal," Leta said.

Suko could see how happy she was. Leta loved to fly. Then suddenly, the smile faded from her face. She touched Suko's cheek with her hand, wiping away a stray tear with her thumb. "She loves you, Suko. She'll come back."

"Or I'll go find her."

Leta glanced around quickly, but there was no one in earshot. She gave Suko a cautionary frown. "Don't do anything foolish. This...you don't just *leave* a job like this. They won't let you."

"I know. I'll be careful." Suko registered the obvious concern on Leta's face. She smiled and swatted her on her rear. "I said I'll be *careful*. Now get—go to your ship. They're waiting for you."

Sure enough, they could hear the thrusters of the transports firing up behind them. The Academy girls shared their parting moments: some with other girls; others said polite goodbyes to their instructors; and then there were the fond farewells to the Mercenary boys who'd captured their affections.

Leta kissed Suko hard on the lips and gave her one last rib-cracking hug. "See you 'round, Suko." Tears welled in her eyes as she snatched up her duffel and headed to the ship. Suko didn't leave until all the girls were on board and the transports had blasted their way up into the morning sunlight and out of sight.

Seven other girls stood nearby staring up at the heavens.

* * *

April 8, 2348

Crucis Prime was a small red rock that traced a distant orbit around the binary stars of Alpha Crucis. Unlike the other planets in the Federation, Crucis had no habitable atmosphere. What it did have was a vast treasure-trove of resources. Rich in minerals and energy, Crucis had quickly become one of the more vital and active trading hubs in Federation Space.

Vincenze Station had grown in magnitude over the years. A few decades earlier it had been little more than a floating tin can in space, serving as a docking hub for the mining and engineering crews who descended to strip the planet clean of everything it had to offer. Over time, different companies had arrived, adding more modules to the station as they were needed. There had never been any formal plans for the station's expansion, thus it resembled a random nightmare of twisted metal and modular construction.

"Ugly," Sigrid remarked, as she viewed the station from her position on the bridge.

The Lady Hitomi snickered behind her. "Any word on docking clearance?"

"None yet, Milady," Christian told her. "They're asking us to hold. They say it might be a few days before they can accommodate us."

"No doubt," Sigrid said. In front of them, spread out in the space, were fifty-six ships. Most were small, but there were several large warships: destroyers, cruisers, even several hulking battleships and troop carriers, all flying different Mercenary banners. The surrounding space was so crowded with ships and shuttles it seemed a miracle to Sigrid that they weren't all smashing into one another.

Hitomi scowled at the floating chaos in front of her. "Put me on. I want to speak to the Dock Controller."

"Yes, Milady," Karen said, and in a moment the forward monitor filled with the image of a tired and haggard-looking old gentleman. The collar of his uniform was pulled loose; he didn't look as if he'd shaved in days. Dark circles ringed his eyes.

"I *told* you I'd get to you as soon as we could. We've got a tremendous amount of traffic to deal—"

"This is the Lady Kimura Hitomi. We're requesting immediate priority clearance for docking. I trust that you can find your way to accommodating our small ship. I'm sure there must be someone willing to give up a spot. They will be compensated for their inconvenience, of course."

Sigrid stifled a laugh as the jaw on the Controller's face dropped. "Milady—of course, of course." His hands flitted over his console, his eyes frantically scanned the data in front of him. "We can accommodate you directly—no compensation required. I'll send the coordinates right away. Rooms for you and your crew will be prepared immediately."

"I thank you, but that won't be necessary. We won't be staying long." She signaled to Ensign McTeer and terminated the call. "Nice to know I still have *some* pull here. Now, let's go see what's going on. You have the coordinates yet?" she asked the navigator.

"Yes, ma'am," Ensign Greenway said from her station. "Docking bay thirty-seven."

"Take us in, Mr. Lopez," Sigrid said.

"Aye, ma'am."

Christian set to his task. Sigrid sensed the rise in his adrenalin. He'd need to take the ship in manually, maneuvering carefully between the waiting ships, all the while dodging the shuttles and service vehicles that crisscrossed their path.

He cleared his throat. "Sure you don't want to hire a docking pilot for this?"

"You'll be fine, Lieutenant." She gave what she hoped was a reassuring pat to his shoulder, and stepped back to let him concentrate on his task.

Christian pushed the thrusters forward, moving the ship faster through the traffic. Sigrid held her breath, watching—he sweated with the effort of juggling the unfamiliar controls—but she noted that the Lady Hitomi remained perfectly calm during the whole process. Despite a near miss or two, Christian's only gaffe was on his first attempt at aligning the ship with the station's docking ring; he missed it by a full meter. The sound of metal scraping against metal reverberated the length of ship.

"Sorry," he said, wincing.

Sigrid couldn't help but wince too. That would cost her. On his second attempt, all the lights flicked to green on the panel before her; they were docked.

"You have the ship, Mr. Lopez." Turning to Hitomi, she gestured to the door behind them. "Milady..."

"After you."

Sigrid led them out onto the docking platform. It was a wide ring that circled the entire station. Built in sections and sealed off from the station and the individual berths, the docking ring was lined almost entirely with glass, affording a spectacular view of the station and surrounding space.

Hitomi wheeled herself out behind Sigrid, flanked by four of her security contingent. Sigrid was surprised to see the Station Administrator himself come out to the platform to greet them. One of the dock workers stepped forward to scan the identification chip Sigrid wore pinned to her collar, but the dock-master slapped the man's hand away.

"That won't be necessary." He scurried past them both, hurrying to the Lady Hitomi's side. "Milady, it is both a pleasure and an honor to have you with us again. You should have announced your intentions—we could have prepared—"

"I was hoping to avoid a fuss, but there is something you can do for me."

"Anything, Milady..."

Hitomi handed a pad to him. "There are some people I was hoping to meet with. If you could track them down for me, that would save us a great deal of time and trouble."

"Of course. Right away." He handed the pad to his assistant behind him. "If you'll come this way, we can take care of this immediately."

* * *

The Station Administrator could only find one of the people on Lady Hitomi's list: Lt. Commander Selene Tseng, ex-Senior Officer of the Tarsus Mercenary Group. She was still in residence on the station. As a senior member of the disbanded group, she'd been saddled with much of the blame for the blundered operation against Kimura on Alcyone. Consequently, she'd been virtually blacklisted, and no other company had deemed to hire her. Doing so would have been considered a major affront to both Kimura and the Mercenary Guild itself.

They tracked her down in one of the many dockside pubs that were favored spots on *Vincenze*. These were the places where most of the freighter captains conducted business—even some of the mercenary leaders could be found here. Sigrid scanned her, confirming her identification in her database. Selene wore a casual jacket and pants, with the high, buckled boots common aboard ships. She wore no rank insignia or any mercenary colors, but then, the Guild had seen to strip her of her rank and status when the Tarsus Group had been disbanded.

Seeing them approach, Selene made to rise from her seat in the corner booth, but Sigrid slid quickly into the seat next to her. Selene had little choice but to sit back down. She reached for the pistol at her side, only to find an empty holster. She gasped. The weapon was gone.

Sigrid held the pistol out for her, handle first.

"Ah, Ms. Tseng," Hitomi said pleasantly as she joined them. "Just the woman I was looking for. I was hoping we might have a word."

Selene eyed Sigrid warily, but she took the proffered weapon and slipped it back into the holster at her side. She sighed resignedly. "Well, I suppose it was just a matter of time," she said, reaching for her steaming mug of black coffee. "What can I do for you ladies?"

The Lady Hitomi leaned forward, as calm and pleasant as always; there was no attempt at intimidation, although the four security personnel nearby served that purpose adequately.

"We want to know who hired Tarsus. We want to know who sent you after our girls—and why."

Selene blew on her coffee and took a careful sip. "I have no idea."

As Selene spoke, Sigrid's sensory modules took note of her reactions. Her pulse was slightly elevated, and there was the briefest spike in her blood pressure.

"She's lying, Mistress," Sigrid said.

Selene's eyes shot to Sigrid.

"And lies can have consequences," Hitomi said, softly.

Selene considered the young girl at her side—how she glared at her with such intensity. She shrugged and put her coffee on the table. "I don't suppose there's any harm in it now. It was a man.

He hired us to take the girls. He was willing to pay...*a lot.* I only ever saw him once. Karl worked for him on a number of occasions. He had money, and Karl needed the work. I never got his name."

"And you never inquired as to his identity?"

"Of course. Karl asked him every time they met. He was, however, not forthcoming in the matter."

"Of course."

"She's *still* lying," Sigrid said, rising with indignation. Hitomi placed a cautioning hand on Sigrid's, and eased her back into her chair. "At least, she's not telling you everything, Mistress."

Selene studied Sigrid closely, and nodded. "Fair enough—I tried to scan him once, but..."

Hitomi raised an eyebrow, waiting. "But...?"

Lt. Commander Tseng reached into her pocket and pulled out a small data chip. Hitomi snapped her fingers and one of her security men came forward to hand her a pad. Hitomi unfolded it and placed the chip on top of the screen to download the data. Displayed there was an image of a man sitting in a booth similar to the one they were in now. The image was crystal clear, showing everything in perfect detail—except for the man; he was totally blurred and pixilated.

"He must have been wearing a *jammer*," Selene offered.

"Expensive," Hitomi said. "I guess he really didn't want you to know."

Sigrid had heard of the devices; the *jammers* could scramble any electronic attempt at scanning the individual who wore the device. *Jammers* were very rare, *very* illegal, and very, very expensive.

Selene took another sip from her coffee. "Sorry I wasted your time."

"Not at all. We will, of course, compensate you for your time." She slid the pad across to Selene; Sigrid took note of the generous sum that Hitomi was offering her. Selene barely acknowledged the amount, but reached forward and pressed her thumb to the pad.

"One last question," Lady Hitomi said. "Major Tarsus—have you heard from the man recently? We'd love to talk to him, for obvious reasons."

Sigrid watched Selene open her mouth to answer; she felt the woman's pulse quicken, but then Selene paused and looked directly at Sigrid. "About two months ago, he was headed for Eridani looking to get something together, but I haven't heard since."

"Lying," Sigrid said.

Selene sighed. "All right, I did hear from him. He took a job working freight with an *Independent*—"

"Lying."

Selene sloshed her coffee down hard on the table. "Stop that! I am not lying."

"You're totally lying—she's lying."

"All right!" Selene frowned, then glared at Sigrid. "We were supposed to meet on Bellatrix a month ago, but he never showed. I made some inquiries. There were men looking for him. Not surprising—the Major has made a few enemies over the years. I don't think it's much of a stretch to think that someone may have wanted to see harm to him. Frankly, I assumed you were the ones after him."

"Where? Where did he go?" Hitomi asked.

"Gliese. At least, that's what I heard."

"And you didn't go after him?"

Selene shifted uncomfortably in her seat. "I couldn't afford the transport. I've been stuck here since Alcyone."

Sigrid nodded satisfied. "True."

"That's a nice trick," Selene said. "That thing you do—walking lie detector."

"She's a girl of many talents," Hitomi said.

"No doubt…"

Hitomi smiled. "It is a simple thing to monitor pulse, blood pressure, subtle changes in the dryness of the mouth and skin…"

Selene continued to eye Sigrid warily. "But she never touched me. How can you…?"

Sigrid was about to answer, but Hitomi stopped her, answering instead. "We girls have to have some secrets."

"We heard stories about you girls," Selene said. "After the operation went south…they said you were dangerous—some kind of experiment. They said you were a threat to the Federation."

"*Dangerous?* My, how people talk."

Selene took another drink from her mug. "I'm just saying, that's what I heard."

"And you believed it?"

Selene laughed, spewing out a mouthful of coffee. "Of course not. Men will always feel threatened by anything they can't dominate. And a pretty woman who can kick their ass…why, that might be the biggest threat of all."

"Interesting observation."

"So tell me, is it true—what they can do?"

"Difficult to say when I don't know what it is that you mean," Hitomi answered, innocently.

"I know what ship you came in on. It wasn't long ago that the *Morrigan* was registered to Dalair. One minute Oslov's heading off to collect on some bounty; the next thing I know, here comes the *Morrigan,* returning not under the Dalair banner—not even the Kimura—but as an Independent, and registered to a seventeen-year-old girl."

"I'm eighteen!" Sigrid said, indignantly.

"I heard about what you did. I heard how you took that ship."

Hitomi looked at Selene. "And just how is it that you came by this information?"

"I still have friends. There's a lot I hear, and there's a lot they'll tell a girl on her own in a bar here after a few drinks."

"And just what is this information going to cost us?" Hitomi asked. "There's no need to play us, Ms. Tseng. As I said before, I'm more than willing to compensate you."

"It's not money I need—well, that too. I need a job."

This time, it was the Lady Hitomi who showed surprise. "A job? You would work for us, even after—"

"That was just a contract. It was nothing personal. I told Tarsus he was biting the wrong leg on that one. There's been a lot of gossip about Kimura and those girls of yours—even with all the trouble brewing with the *Independents.* I want in. I want to see what all the fuss is about."

"And this would have nothing to do with the rumor about the bounty…"

"Oh, the rumor's real," Selene said. "But I don't care about that. You have a ship and I'm the best pilot there is."

Hitomi raised her eyebrows at the declaration. "Best pilot not under contract?"

"*The* best."

"It's her ship, Ms. Tseng," Hitomi said, pointing to Sigrid. "I think she's the one you need to impress."

Selene sat back and looked directly at Sigrid, clasping hands behind head and kicking her legs out under the table. She exuded a cocky confidence—every inch a hotshot pilot.

Sigrid scanned the woman very carefully. Her words had been bold, but she could sense no attempt at deception. The woman was supremely confident of her skills, and prepared to back up her boast. Sigrid wondered how Christian would feel if she replaced him at the helm—probably relieved.

"Very well, I accept your offer. I'll prepare a contract."

Selene smiled. "Standard rates should suffice."

Sigrid held her hand out to seal the deal. "Welcome aboard, Ms. Tseng."

* * *

After parting with Selene, Sigrid escorted the Lady Hitomi to her next appointment with the Mercenary Guild. Sigrid was surprised to see that the Guild resembled a private club rather than the stuffy offices of a bureaucrat. The Condottiere had already been notified of the Lady's arrival and was expecting her. She greeted Hitomi and her entourage warmly in the Guild lounge.

"Marylyn!" Lady Hitomi smiled broadly.

"Hitomi, how wonderful," The older woman said, rushing to Hitomi's side and taking her hand while also noting Sigrid at her side. "Is this...?"

"Yes, this is Sigrid Novak. Sigrid, Meet Marylyn Lawther, Condottiere of all the Mercenary clans."

"Milady," Sigrid said, with a deep curtsy.

"Oh, now! None of that here, my dear. We're all good friends. Now, come, let me look at you."

The woman took Sigrid by her shoulders and gave her a quick and appraising once-over before escorting them all to a set of comfortable chairs. Sigrid noted the lovely tea service set out on the low table near their seats, and there was an actual *real* fire roaring in the brick fireplace!

"Please tell me you're here for a while," Marylyn said to Hitomi. "I do so miss our talks."

"I'm afraid we'll be leaving momentarily. I just wanted to stop by and let you know—"

"If it's about that dreadful business with Dalair—we've heard all about it. It's all the chatter these days. Don't you worry, Hitomi-san, the Guild Heads have already agreed to convene. Dalair will be dealt with most harshly. This business of clans taking contracts against each other must stop. Things have long been out of hand. It's absolute barbarism."

Hitomi sighed. "It pleases me to hear that, but I'm afraid there's more."

The revelation made Marylyn pause her pouring of tea for a moment. "Not more nonsense, I hope."

"Of a different sort. There's a chance the Council may be involved in this."

"The Council? What business is it of the Council to get involved with Mercenary affairs? That just won't do."

"I agree. I'm on my way to a hearing on Earth—I just wanted you to know. But Council or not, if someone is taking out contracts on *any* of the clans—"

"They must be crushed... Sugar?"

"Please, one spoon."

"Now, do tell me all about these girls of yours," Marylyn said excitedly.

Sigrid found herself quite taken with the very charming, yet commanding, Marylyn Lawther, and after what turned out to be a most enjoyable hour, Hitomi announced it was time for them to depart.

Marylyn cautioned them about the bounty on Sigrid, but Lady Hitomi was confident they would be safe on the station. *Vincenze Station* had always been a haven for Mercenaries. It was highly unlikely for an *Independent* group to get aboard with the intention of hostile action without facing the wrath of close to a million angry Mercenaries.

They made one stop on the way back. Lady Hitomi caught Sigrid spying a weapons shop on the promenade. The store was little more than a pawnshop for out-of-work soldiers looking to score some credits, but Sigrid was drawn into its metallic charm. She found one item she couldn't resist. Sitting in what looked like an old umbrella stand, rusted and covered in dirt and dust, Sigrid discovered an old Katana. Despite the neglect, she could tell the blade was of the finest workmanship, its handle was modestly decorated and bound in black leather, with most of its gold inlay worn away. The shopkeeper had been happy to get rid of the relic, so Sigrid picked it up for a song.

Sigrid wasn't as skilled with blades as the other Academy girls, but she knew Suko would love it. She'd deliver it to her somehow.

Hitomi watched with interest as the girl paid for the obscure item. Sigrid wrapped it carefully in a cloth the proprietor had given her before tucking the long two-handed blade in her belt.

"It suits you," Hitomi said.

Sigrid glanced at the blade, a little embarrassed. "Oh it's not for me."

"No? Who then?"

Sigrid wasn't sure if she should tell her, or what the older woman would think if she told her about Suko. Sigrid was growing fond of the Lady, but she had to remember that the woman *was Kimura*; this was the organization responsible for taking her from Suko.

"It's for a friend," she said at last.

"I'm sure she'll love it."

They made it back to the docking ring without incident. Sigrid was pleased to find Selene already waiting for them. She'd changed into a one-piece ship's suit, much like Sigrid's, though Selene's sported a wide lapel, folded outward and cut low. She wore a lightweight, black pilot's jacket and the high-buckled boots from earlier, along with a large sidearm, holstered at her hip. Dark pilots' glasses covered her green eyes. The smallest suitcase Sigrid had ever seen sat on the ground next to her.

Selene was not alone, either. Standing next to her was a young man—he couldn't have been more than 20. He wore a baggy ship suit, his blond hair cut short.

"This is Rodney," Selene said. "He's the best mechanic in this quadrant. Trust me."

Sigrid studied the boy. "I'm afraid we're already crewed with engineers."

"Those Academy-types? They'll do in a pinch, but our Rodney here..." She patted the young man's shoulders. "He's got a gift. I've never seen anything like it."

"Forgive me, but you look a little young, Rodney," Hitomi said. "Where did you graduate?"

"Graduate, ma'am?" Rodney scratched his head.

Selene laughed. "Rodney didn't exactly do well at the Academy."

"It's not what you think," Rodney said awkwardly. "It's just that...well, I grew up on ships. Classrooms..."

Hitomi smiled. "You didn't think much of the instructors..."

Rodney frowned. "We didn't exactly get along."

"I understand completely. Have you ever worked on one of these?"

Rodney looked over his shoulder out the viewport to the *Morrigan.* "PS 16c falcon-class patrol ship. Manufactured by Diego Systems: fourteen years old, by the look of it, progressive, fusion-core reactionless drive engines—piece of cake—140 metric ton cargo capacity, dual-mounted rail-gun system with two forward-mounted quad-torpedo launchers, crew compliment of twelve. But, no—never touched one."

Sigrid grinned. "Very well. Welcome aboard. Ensign McTeer will see that you're both quartered."

"I'm sure whatever you have will be adequate," Selene said. "As you can see...we travel light."

After getting settled in, Sigrid took Selene and Rodney on a tour of the ship and introduced them to the crew. Some were surprised at the hiring of the ex-Tarsus officer; others seemed to be relieved to have an experienced helmsman aboard.

She was completely amazed at how familiar Rodney and Selene were with the systems of the small Scout, and it was Rodney, not Sigrid, who ended up conducting the tour, with Selene pointing out some of the more peculiar elements. Sigrid might have been able to tie into the ship's systems directly with her PCM, but it was Selene who *understood* those systems, and how best to use them, especially in combat situations. Sigrid was feeling better and better about the hiring. Rodney was particularly eager to make several modifications to the engines to *soup* them up, but the Chief Engineer was outraged at the suggestion. Sigrid hastily declined the offer, hoping to defuse the situation.

"Ready to get underway," Christian said as the two women entered the bridge. Christian had already vacated the helm and Selene now filled the seat, looking every bit the ship's pilot.

"Let me know when we've received clearance from the Dock Master," Sigrid said.

"Confirmed," Karen said from her station.

"Very well. Take us out, Ms. Tseng."

"Aye, ma'am."

Sigrid watched as Selene deftly moved the ship away from the docks, spinning it quickly on its axis and blasting away. Christian had sweated their approach, not exceeding 10,000 kph through the traffic, but Selene handled the small ship masterfully, knifing easily through the crowded corridor of waiting ships and service traffic at well over 42,000 kph.

Christian nodded in admiration. "Nicely done."

"Thanks."

"We're clear of traffic and free to maneuver," Ensign Greenway said.

"Take us to the Relay, best possible speed," Sigrid said.

"Destination, ma'am?" Melissa asked.

Sigrid smiled. "Earth."

Chapter 14
Ninja

April 15, 2348

As the *Morrigan* entered Earth's orbit, Sigrid could only stare, openmouthed, at the scene before her. Crucis had seemed crowded with the fifty-six ships that surrounded the station, but it was nothing compared to the clutter she saw before her. Thousands of ships lay between her and the blue planet below, with hundreds more already docked at the many orbital stations and docking platforms.

It was far too congested for them to gain clearance to bring the *Morrigan* down. They were forced to park in orbit and take the São Paulo Elevator, known affectionately as the *Lift*, down to the planet's surface. Sigrid and Karen accompanied the Lady Hitomi and her security contingent while her crew remained in orbit on the *Morrigan*. Once on Earth, it was only a short trip on the TGV to Buenos Aires, home of the Council for Trade and Finance.

Hitomi's security argued against her taking such a vulnerable mode of transportation, but the Lady insisted and sat beside Sigrid on the short train ride, marveling at the sights of the old planet as the TGV whipped along, suspended below the elevated rail system.

Aquarii and Alcyone were beautiful and largely pristine; there was nothing to compare with the diverse architecture of the urban sprawl before them. Grey smog hung heavy, mixing in with the mist and clouds that enshrouded everything. There was no end to the strings of modular habitats and towering permacrete structures that thrust their way up into the clouds. Hitomi pointed out the more important landmarks, remarking that many of the buildings lay empty; most people of any sort of means had long since left for new opportunities off-planet. All that remained were the tens of billions of working poor, and the very, very rich elite.

There were no stops between São Paulo and Buenos Aires, so they were all a little unnerved when the TGV shuddered to an abrupt halt. Sigrid peered through the window as the train rocked gently back and forth, suspended below the rails some fifty meters above the ground.

"What happened?" Sigrid asked. "Why aren't we moving?"

Hitomi didn't know either, but she stopped a steward as he passed by.

"Terrorists," the steward informed them, making *tisking* noises. "It seems they're causing trouble with the tracks again."

"Terrorists!" Sigrid said, alarmed.

The steward gave her a reassuring, if condescending, smile. "Shameful. But don't you worry yourselves. We're quite used to it now. It should only be a short delay." He continued on down the car, happily reassuring the other passengers.

"Terrorists?" Sigrid said again, still not quite believing it.

A man in the seat next to her leaned over and patted her knee. "Happens all the time now. A lot of fuss and bother, if you ask me."

Sigrid looked down on the hand that still lingered on her knee. She jerked her leg away and gave him a sharp look. The man returned quickly to his reading; Sigrid noticed Hitomi's amused expression and smiled.

Just as the steward promised, they were underway in moments. The TGV slowed again as it passed by the area where the trouble had been and Sigrid leaned forward, catching a glimpse of the damage of the surrounding area. Several of the shanty-like structures had been flattened in the bomb blast, yet the track was perfectly intact.

"I guess we got lucky," Sigrid said. *If the bomb had hit the tracks...*

"Yes...*lucky,*" Hitomi said.

Ten minutes later they were off the train in Buenos Aires. The Lady Hitomi's entourage was quite a sight; mostly because of the Lady herself, resplendent as always in her long, richly patterned gown of deep green and gold, complete with full headdress.

Wherever they went, people stopped to look. Sigrid had the feeling she was traveling with royalty, and in a sense, she was.

"We should arrange transportation, Milady," her head of security said, scanning the crowded streets.

"Nonsense. The hotel is only four blocks from here. It's a beautiful day and I would like Sigrid and the young ensign to enjoy the sights. I'm sure Sigrid is quite capable of taking care of me. Isn't that right, dear?"

"Uh..."

"There. You have it."

The man opened his mouth in protest, "Milady..."

Hitomi wasn't having any of it. "You four go ahead and meet us there. Take care of the luggage. We'll be along shortly."

To give him credit, her chief of security argued valiantly for several minutes, but there was no swaying Lady Hitomi's mind on the matter, and the four men eventually took a cab to the hotel.

"They're quite professional, but they do need to lighten up now and then," Hitomi said. "They're simply no fun."

Hitomi motored along in her wheelchair with Sigrid and Karen trailing behind her. "Come, girls; there's something here I think you'll like."

This part of Buenos Aires wasn't that much different from the ghetto in Geneva where Sigrid had grown up. Sullen, weary-looking people filled the streets, mulling about the open markets, combing through the bleak offerings of the merchants. The flesh traders were the most aggressive, attempting to ply their trade on Sigrid and even Hitomi herself—presenting the women with some rather graphic offerings.

Sigrid looked at the girls and boys, some young and frightened, some older and weary, beaten down. She knew she could have easily been sold into such a life, just like many girls in her financial predicament.

"Here!" Hitomi exclaimed, leading the girls into a crowded little shack, glowing with the warm lights from paper lanterns. The air was thick with steam and the wonderful smells of broth and cooking vegetables. "Phong! My good man, you look positively ghastly."

Old Phong ran out from behind his counter to greet Hitomi. Sigrid thought he *did* look ghastly, what with his scruffy hair, spotted withered hands and awesomely blackened teeth. But his face lit up at the sight of Hitomi and the girls. Cooing and chattering, he ushered them into his establishment and seated them in pride of place by his counter.

Sigrid looked around the little soup kitchen. The place wasn't without its charm—as long as she didn't examine the layers of grease and dirt on the floors and walls too closely.

Hitomi seemed to love it though, especially when the three of them were presented with steaming bowls of delicious-smelling soup. Sigrid marveled at the presentation; the vegetables and meat were cut and layered with such precision and care. The whole time, Hitomi chatted spiritedly with Phong in Vietnamese. Sigrid was surprised that her Mistress was so fluent, then completely astonished to discover that she could understand them perfectly once her PCM executed the programmed language files.

Sigrid's jaw dropped when she saw the tip Hitomi left for the man—*he could probably close for the month.*

"I simply adore his cuisine," Lady Hitomi intoned. "I always make a point of stopping here."

Sigrid liked it too, and so did Karen, who finished everything, even all the broth.

When they arrived at the Hotel Astrid, it seemed the entire staff was out to greet them, red carpet and all. The hotel manager welcomed Hitomi personally, extending his gratitude for her continued patronage. Lady Hitomi was the epitome of graciousness; as tired as the Lady was, she didn't refuse his offer of hospitality as he escorted her to the private VIP lounge for refreshments. Sigrid had never imagined such variety of foods and drinks even existed. Despite having just filled up on Phong's outstanding soup, she couldn't keep herself from sampling all the fare available, stopping only when she realized how tight her belt had become.

Sigrid groaned, the last morsel of cheesecake perched on her fork, raised halfway to her lips.

"Careful!" Karen cautioned. "You look a little green."

Sigrid steeled herself to the task and swallowed the last bite. "My mother always said, never let anything go to waste."

Karen chuckled. "Yes, and I'm sure that starving people everywhere appreciate your efforts."

The festive mood was spoiled when another group of people entered the lounge; Hitomi took instant notice. Sigrid saw a darkness descend over the Lady's face.

"Randal Gillings," Hitomi said, wheeling herself in his direction; she didn't even bother feigning politeness. "I thought this was a private lounge."

"If you'll forgive me, Lady Hitomi. I thought it best that I should meet you here."

Sigrid scanned him warily, standing with her arms folded in front of her. His name was Randal Gillings, chairman of the Council for Trade and Finance and CEO of Coran Industries, the single largest conglomerate in the Federation—short of Daedalus Corp. In his seventies, Gillings had the look of a man who had grown well accustomed to getting his own way. Sigrid instantly found him arrogant and unlikable.

Hitomi noticed the sour look on her Sigrid's face; her own expression was similar as she turned to Gillings. "What's on your mind, Randy?" Hitomi said. "The hearing isn't until tomorrow."

"That's what I came here to talk to you about. There will be no hearing."

The statement caught Hitomi off-guard. She stared at him for a moment. "I see."

"I'm sorry you've come all this way," he said.

Sigrid didn't think he sounded sorry at all.

"Aren't you even the least bit curious to see the information I've brought for the Council?"

"I think you'll be far more interested in the information I have for you, Hitomi."

Hitomi frowned. "Out with it, Randy, what's on your mind?"

"All the talk coming through the Relays these days seems to be about you—and not in a good way. There have been…allegations. We find this business of *Project Andraste* quite disturbing." He looked directly at Sigrid, somewhat distastefully. "*Human genetic manipulation?* Abducting children? These are grave charges, Madam Kimura."

"And *who* exactly has made these charges?"

"Do you deny them?"

"I see neither the need to confirm nor deny anything. Kimura is not in the habit of discussing any of its projects."

"Well, whether you like it or not, those projects *are* being discussed. Charges have been brought to the Council, petitions have been made."

Hitomi laughed.

"I would not make light of this, Lady Hitomi. I can delay the matter somewhat, but in time, the Council will be forced to make a ruling on this matter. I'm sure you would not wish to see the girls taken from you."

"Taken? On what grounds?"

"It is the Council's responsibility to investigate any suspect technology—especially when dealing with something that may pose a threat to the security of the Federation."

"A threat to the Federation...?" Hitomi laughed again. "Come now, Randy. I'm not sure who you've been listening to—"

"Don't play games with me, Hitomi," Gillings said, a sternness had crept into his voice. "I didn't have to come here—I'm warning you as a favor. Seriously, how did you think people would react...with gratitude? These girls don't just pose a threat to your...*rivals*, they threaten society itself. And the fact that you've only done this to girls. When people—"

"Sorry, but men are *not* compatible."

"—*When people* see what you've done...these girls of yours...people will see them as nothing more than an abomination. I don't think that will make you very popular with the general public."

"Well, I suppose I'm just *lucky* to have you here to watch over me." Hitomi didn't attempt to veil the sarcasm in her voice. "Your concern is most gracious, Randal, but hardly necessary. Now come, you can't expect me to believe you came all this way to give me a polite warning. You're after something. What is it you want? Tell me, and be done with it."

Gillings grunted. "Very well. The Council has been discussing your case at great length. And for some time. It's been clear for decades that we made a mistake with Daedalus. We should have never permitted them to create a monopoly with the Warp Relays. It's only prudent we monitor any new developments."

"Like *Andraste.*"

"I shouldn't even be telling you this—"

"Somehow, I have the feeling you're about to anyway."

"The Council is prepared to make you an offer. We are prepared to take over the project from you—from Kimura. We are willing to purchase the contracts of all the girls. In fact, we're even happy to take you on as a consultant."

Hitomi laughed long and hard. "Oh, Randy, you are a caution." Wiping her eyes, she looked to Sigrid. "You hear that, dear? How would you like to go work for the Council?"

Sigrid still stood with her arms folded across her chest. "No thank you, ma'am."

"There, you see, Randy—your first refusal. I would get used to that."

"Don't be so sure, Hitomi. You haven't seen the compensation package we are offering. Are you certain your Board will be as willing to deny us?"

Hitomi's face hardened. "The *Board* will do as I instruct."

"We'll see soon enough. I wasn't going to mention this, but I suppose it hardly matters now. Eight days ago we dispatched a courier to Aquarii. Your Board should have the offer by now. It will be interesting to see how they respond."

Hitomi flushed red and tried to rise from her chair. "How dare you. You knew I was coming here—"

"Not at all. A fortunate coincidence, Hitomi. Nothing more."

"And is it also a coincidence that you know so much about a project that was classified until quite recently?"

Gillings shrugged. "You may wish to conduct an internal security audit when you return."

"The Council has no business interfering with the affairs of a free corporation. The Council was formed to serve at *our* discretion, not its own."

"And we will serve you now. It's a fair offer, Hitomi. Your finances are a matter of record. We know of the attacks you've already endured. How long before you lose everything? And for what? Take the offer."

"Don't do me any favors, Randal."

Gillings raised his hands and backed away slowly. "I've said what I came to—more than I had to. You have our offer. I advise you take it. It may not be there tomorrow. Good day, Milady."

Hitomi looked angrily at him. "This isn't some experiment, Randal. This is evolution. These girls are unique. Their genetic structure is like no other. You can't deny them…" Hitomi looked down, closing her mouth, biting her tongue.

Gillings studied her for a moment, turned and left.

Sigrid watched him leave from Hitomi's side.

"Damn…" Hitomi said, muttering more curses under her breath.

"Mistress, what's wrong?"

"I let the bastard get to me. I fear I may have said too much."

"He seemed to know a great deal already."

"Indeed, but I should have never said anything about your genetics." Hitomi grew silent, lost in thought. "He was right about one thing…we have a spy in our midst."

* * *

With the party thoroughly spoiled, Sigrid and Lady Hitomi retreated to their rooms. Sigrid said a quick goodnight to Ensign McTeer before reporting directly to Lady Hitomi in her suite. The Lady had her tea service laid out and poured two steaming cups. She handed one to Sigrid.

"What did you think of our man, Chairman Gillings?" Hitomi asked.

"I thought he was a miserable old man who could use a good punch."

Hitomi snorted, almost choking on the tea. "Not too far off. But how about what he said?"

Sigrid thought for a moment. "I don't feel like an abomination, Milady."

"Good, because you're not. But circumstances, it seems, are conspiring against us, and rather quickly. I fear much of this is my fault."

"Yours, Mistress?"

"Long before the first attack on Alcyone, I demanded more protection for you and your sisters. But the Board denied me at every step."

"But—they sent the company of soldiers—"

Hitomi barked a laugh. "That? Hardly adequate for guarding a cargo of wheat. Sigrid, I know you don't believe it, but you're far more important than you can possibly imagine, and not just to Kimura—or to *me*..." Hitomi took a sip from her cup. "I know it's hard for you to understand, but you represent a threat to them. A shift in power. They fear you."

Sigrid laughed. "That doesn't sound like me, Mistress. No one at the Academy worried about fighting me."

"You are far too modest, my dear. They have good reason to be afraid of you, even if you don't believe it. But Gillings...he knows far too much. I would love to know where he's been getting his information." She looked up at Sigrid; there was a bright spark in her eye. "How would you like to pay a visit to the Council offices tonight?"

Sigrid checked her internal chronometer, it didn't seem likely that the offices would be open at that hour.

Hitomi placed her purse on her lap. "Do you know why my son picked you? Do you know why he brought you to me?"

Sigrid remembered the test very well, and with some distaste. "Because I killed that man. He said I passed his test."

"He brought you because I asked him to. I picked you, Sigrid."

"You? But he said...the test...?"

"Oh, he tested you—and I've scolded him about that."

"But...why?"

Lady Hitomi reached into the purse on her lap and took out a data-module, holding it out for her. "I have a present for you."

Sigrid took it in her hand.

"This is something I've developed on my own. No one knows about it, not even Dr. Garrett. This is a secret I've kept for nearly twenty years. You're the first person I've ever shown it to, Sigrid."

Sigrid examined the module; she could feel her own heart beat faster. She had no idea as to its contents, but there was something about the way Lady Hitomi looked at her and the small module nestling in her hand.

"What is it?"

"Tell me, you've studied history—you know of the myth of the ancient Ninjas?"

"Yes, Mistress."

"*We're alone*, Sigrid…"

Sigrid blushed. "Yes, *Hitomi-san*. If we're speaking of the myths, rather than history, it was said that they could disappear, make themselves invisible, disguise themselves as their adversaries, vanish in puffs of smoke."

Hitomi smiled. "And what if I were to tell you that it was all true?"

* * *

The one-piece uniform that the Lady Hitomi had provided for Sigrid was made out of a thin, but incredibly strong fabric. It was light, hugged her figure snugly and moved as she did. Superficially, it might have resembled a variation of the standard Kimura Uniform, but the material was laced with a unique, highly conductive nano-fiber. Everything she wore, everything from the high boots to the new holsters that held her pistols, even the harness that held the katana strapped to her back, all were made of the same material, all stitched with the same fibers.

The nano-fibers allowed the suit to become a pure extension of herself. She could interface with it just as she could any of her other bionic implants. The cloth had a highly unique feature: Sigrid could control the color of the material, shifting both the color and pattern to match anything in the environment around her, creating a perfect camouflage. And, for very short periods of time, Sigrid could adjust the opacity of the material, rendering it virtually invisible.

She tested the feature now, holding her arm up against the wall behind her. The material reflected the pattern and texture of the wall perfectly. Intrigued, she pressed her whole body up against it and watched as the cloth perfectly mirrored the textures and hues.

"Sweet," Sigrid said.

A broad smile spread across Hitomi's face. "Now, move away from the wall."

Sigrid did as instructed. It was difficult; she had to concentrate, but she was able to maintain the translucent effect of the suit. She wasn't quite invisible, she could still see the outline of her body, but if someone wasn't looking directly at her they wouldn't notice she was there. Her exposed hands and face looked odd though, they remained quite visible, as if they were suspended in the air. Sigrid waved her hands about and laughed.

"Now—the rest," Hitomi said.

Sigrid reached deep within herself. The Lady Hitomi had loaded the program from the data-module she'd shown her. This was her secret. Now it was time to test the *old program*. Sigrid accessed the algorithms; they were long and complex, and she combed through the hundreds of terabytes of data.

Controlling the transition took even more effort than it had to alter the suit, but Sigrid initiated the program.

Instantly, she shrouded.

Just like with the suit, Sigrid was able to alter the light reflecting on her own skin; still not quite invisible, a shimmering, translucent outline of her body remained.

Pleased, Hitomi clasped her hands together. "Marvelous."

Sigrid felt suddenly warm and dizzy and stumbled backward; her clothes reverted to their normal colors of black and red. She leaned over with her hands on her knees, reeling from the wave of nausea. "Whoa…"

"You must be cautious. Shrouding draws power from your own body's energy reserve. You can only maintain the effect for a short time."

"Yes, Hitomi-san," Sigrid said, taking a moment to recover. Hitomi handed her a glass of water, which Sigrid drank deeply.

Hitomi took Sigrid's hands in hers. "How do you feel? Do you detect any ill-effects?"

Sigrid ran a quick diagnostic of her body and functions. Despite a slight feeling of fatigue, she felt perfectly fine. "No, Hitomi-san. Just a little tired."

"Very well, but use these programs sparingly, at least until we're positive there are no side-effects. I don't want you hurting yourself."

"No, Hitomi-san," Sigrid said; she found herself surprised at the genuine concern the older woman seemed to have for her.

Hitomi looked at the wall chronometer; it was nearing two in the morning. "We don't have much time. I suggest you get underway."

* * *

Sigrid pushed the ceiling tile aside and poked her head down into the dark corridor of the CTF Tower. Her long blond hair was bound in a tight braid and hung down below her head, swinging back and forth in a pendulum-like fashion. The soft soles of her boots barely made a sound as she dropped to the polished, marble floor below. Sigrid had armed herself more heavily than she'd ever done in the past. Her belt was lined with the little throwing knives she liked, as well as a selection of blackout bombs, smoke-grenades, flashbangs and frags. She reached back and touched the hilt of the katana—her gift to Suko. Having the gift with her was like carrying a little piece of Suko; it may have been foolish, but it brought her comfort.

Her objective was on the 222nd floor, near the top of the CTF tower. The Council's main server was located there as well; it was not connected to any network so the only way to hack into it was by direct link. Sigrid would need to make her way there now, hack into the system and get out, all without being seen.

Sigrid called up the building schematics on her HUD and studied the possible routes. The stairs seemed safest, but she was running out of time; it was already 3:36 and Hitomi had warned that by 5 a.m. it would not be unusual for staff to start filtering back in to prepare for the working day ahead. Sigrid called for an elevator and waited in the shadows while it made its way down. It arrived without incident and the doors slid open. The elevator was empty, but Sigrid detected several monitoring devices so she engaged her shroud before entering. She pressed the button for 223rd floor, just above the offices; there was a viewing terrace located there that she'd chosen as her point of insertion.

Sigrid climbed through the ceiling hatch onto the roof of the elevator. Only when the hatch was closed did she allow the shroud to fade; she breathed a sigh as she felt her system recover. Holding the effect drained all her focus and energy.

There were little grips on the side and roof of the elevator—most likely for the service personnel—and Sigrid clung to them as the elevator shot upward at an alarming rate. She looked up to see the top of the tower grow ever closer as floor after floor shot by. If she hadn't been holding on, she might very well have been propelled into the air when the lift came to an abrupt halt on the 178th floor. She heard two people board the elevator beneath her, a man and a woman. They were muttering complaints about the elevator going up when they needed to go down, but they didn't seem suspicious so Sigrid relaxed a little.

It only took a second for the elevator to traverse the next few levels. Sigrid jumped off and clung to the wall of the shaft. She'd only just found footing when the elevator dropped away beneath her; Sigrid had a peculiar feeling in the pit of her stomach as she watched it disappear like a stone into the darkness, leaving her clinging to the rail of the vertical shaft some 740.271 meters up. She did her best not to think of the abyss that gaped beneath her. Whether she fell 50 or 700 meters made little difference.

The door was just below her so Sigrid scrambled carefully down to it. The walls of the shaft weren't exactly built for climbing and there were few handholds, but Sigrid negotiated her way down. Prying the door open was easy enough, and she was glad to find the floor she'd chosen unoccupied.

With her camouflage set to a dark, charcoal grey, Sigrid blended perfectly into the shadows as she made her way out to the terrace above the Council offices. At the upper levels, the tower was built in a pyramid-like fashion, and there was another terrace on the office-level just beneath her. Sigrid slipped up and over the high protective barrier—designed to prevent people from leaning out over the edge, no doubt—and dropped down to the lower level. The doors were locked and electronically sealed, but no match for the Lady Hitomi's excellent decryption algorithms.

Sigrid was in.

Quickly and quietly, Sigrid made her way down the hallway to the server room. She saw a guard there, walking by, making his rounds. He seemed oblivious to her, so she let him pass, before commencing the task of breaking into the server room.

The security here was much more complex. It took Sigrid almost a full minute to break through the locks on the great door, and it didn't get any easier once she was inside. The room was armed with motion and heat-sensors, audio sensors, even chemical and bacteria sensors, and cameras positioned at all angles.

Sigrid searched and found what she was looking for. The Security Node was located in a service panel in an alcove just inside the server room; she'd still need to get to that without being detected. She shrouded herself, again becoming virtually invisible—just a shimmering, translucent outline of a woman. Concentrating even harder, Sigrid lowered her body temperature by several degrees; she could only hope it was enough to shield her from the heat sensors. If it wasn't…well, she'd know soon enough.

Her optical implants picked up the location of the biological sensors. Sigrid selected four of the silicone gel-caps from the pouch at her waist and fixed them to the tiny palm-sized launcher she carried. Four quick shots took care of the sensors, coating them in a thin layer of silicone. After that, it was a reasonably simple matter to avoid the infrared beams by stepping lively as she moved toward the security panel. She couldn't deactivate the security completely—that would set off a series of alarms—but Sigrid put the system into a temporary diagnostic loop. It wouldn't last long, but she only needed a few more minutes. With the security systems temporarily deactivated, Sigrid de-shrouded. The effort had been particularly draining this time, especially after having to alter her core temperature; she didn't want to be doing that again any time soon, she decided.

Now, for the server.

Sigrid was surprised to find the security so light, and she gained access quite easily. *They probably never thought anyone would get this far*, she thought as the monitor lit up in front of her. Sigrid slipped a blank data-module into the access port on the side of the unit. Hitomi's *wish list* was extensive; she was to find and retrieve *all* files pertaining to the *Andraste* project.

It didn't take long to find the first, and one seemed to lead to another and then another. Sigrid was finding hundreds of communiqués, all of them voicing either outrage or concern over what they perceived as 'Hitomi's army of genetic monsters' and what it would mean if they didn't move to control them, and soon.

The loop in the security system would not last much longer and there were more files to download. The powerful processors implanted within her enabled her to scan through the thousands of terabytes of information rapidly. The files pertaining to the

Council's financial accounts took up most of the room on the four data modules she'd brought—especially since there seemed to be *two* sets of accounts. Sigrid chuckled; she knew Hitomi would find these of great interest.

Sigrid filled all four data-modules, then cursed; there was still more. Her own PCM could accommodate some of the information, but there was too much. She was about to extract herself from the system when she spotted the anomaly. One communiqué—she'd almost missed it. It wasn't logged as all the other messages were. Someone had even tried to delete it, but they hadn't been quite thorough enough. No. That wasn't correct. Someone had tried to *repair* it.

There was no ID tag and the message was nearly completely corrupted. Much of it didn't make sense; names, dates, payment schedules. Two names stood out instantly: *Alcyone. Dalair.* But it was the third name that stopped her cold. Tansho.

Suko...

It was Suko's last name, but there was nothing more. There was no signature, and she couldn't make out the recipient either, but she downloaded it quickly to her PCM. With luck, Hitomi could analyze it later.

It was time to go.

Sigrid exited the server room and made her way back to the terrace; she would leave the way she came—retracing her steps, covering her tracks on the way out.

Before she'd completed half the distance to the terrace, every sensor in Sigrid's system shot the warning to her. She rolled into cover, behind one of the many pillars that lined the reception area. Someone was there.

Sigrid didn't breathe; she reached out with every sensor she had, scanning the vicinity. The signals she got back were confusing. She couldn't lock anything down, but was certain of it now—someone was there, watching her. She took a chance and peered out from behind the pillar.

The reception area appeared clear and quiet. She switched to her thermal optics and scanned and—*there!* She saw them. Two men hiding behind cover, and another lay in wait on the other side. They knew she was there and were blocking her exit to the terrace. There was something odd about their scans. She was only getting a partial signal, as if something was shielding them from her.

Sigrid played back the entire operation in her mind—she couldn't think of any alarm she'd missed. How was it they knew she was there?

Sigrid moved quietly into the shadows, away from the men and back toward the elevator. But her sensors picked up more movement. More men, many more, were moving toward her from the opposite direction. It was a trap.

What was it that Rosa had always drilled into her—*the path of least resistance?* She had little choice; she had to take out the three men blocking her exit to the terrace. Sigrid grabbed two flashbangs and one of the gas grenades from her belt, rolling all three in the directions of the men lying in wait for her. The explosion shattered the silence and darkness, filling the corridor with smoke and the debilitating gas. Sigrid held her breath and rolled out from behind her cover, coming into a crouch and drawing her two pearl-handled pistols.

Finally, her pursuers revealed themselves. Three men leaned out from their positions of cover. Sigrid logged the targets and fired three shots—three perfect head-shots—that bounced harmlessly off their armored helmets.

Only then did Sigrid see that all three wore some kind of mechanized armor that covered their entire bodies. She'd never seen anything like it and there was nothing of the sort listed in her database. The armor perfectly protected them from the gas bomb she'd thrown and the ballistic rounds she'd fired.

At first she'd assumed the men to be CTF security, or possibly Marines, but their armor bore an unfamiliar insignia that didn't register with her. All three men leveled their weapons at her; two had lethal looking chain guns, the kind normally mounted on heavy vehicles; they held the bulky weapons as if they were featherweight. The third man was pointing a familiar-looking riot gun at her.

Sigrid swallowed. "Crap."

The one with the riot gun moved first; Sigrid's sensors picked up the flex of his finger on the trigger and she launched herself forward, moving directly at him. She saw the flare as the weapon discharged the restraining net at her. Sigrid hurled herself out of its path. Her pistols were back in her holster and she'd already drawn the katana from its sheath as she came back up on her feet. She was vaguely aware of the net smacking harmlessly against the wall behind her. The clanking of the two chain guns firing sounded loud in her head as the armored soldiers frantically tried to track her. All her focus was on the armored man in front of her.

Her PCM registered the weak spot in his armor, just below his helmet and above his shoulders. Her katana sliced through the composite material, relieving the man of his head. Sigrid charged onward; the terrace was just in front of her; though her path took her between the two remaining men. She could feel the explosive rounds from their chain guns nipping at her heels. Sigrid crashed through the doors, shattering the heavy glass, not daring to slow. In a second she was up and over the railing, leaping from the terrace, 222 stories above the city of Buenos Aires.

For a terrifying instant Sigrid feared she'd miscalculated and leapt too far, but she crashed down onto the next terrace three stories below. The drop was nearly fourteen meters and she hit the concrete hard, absorbing as much of the energy as possible in a desperate tuck and roll. But her momentum propelled her into the oncoming railing and she smacked her head solidly on the barrier. She screamed, fighting to keep her wits. The nanomites surged through her system, working hard to repair the damage, ease the pain and keep her conscious.

She had to keep moving. The armored soldiers were already firing down at her. Sigrid ran for the safety of cover. She fired her pistols to smash the glass doors in front of her before charging inside.

Sigrid skidded to a halt. Standing, waiting in front her, dressed in the same mechanized armor and with a rocket launcher leveled at her face, was Sara.

"Hello Sigrid," she cooed.

Chapter 15
Reunion

"Sara..." Sigrid's mouth hung open. Sara stood before her; she was older now, but it was definitely Sara. She was alive! "But...how? We thought you were..."

"Spare me the false concern."

"What are you doing here? How'd you—"

"Believe it or not, I'm here for you."

"Here for me?" Sigrid frowned. "To kill me, you mean."

"Don't be so dramatic. I'm here to help you."

"But you—you're dressed like them, like those *men*."

"Them? Don't worry about them."

Sigrid folded her arms and eyed the rocket launcher warily. "Right now, I'm more worried about you."

"If I wanted to kill you, you'd already be dead." Sara lowered the launcher. "Sigrid...what do you really know about Kimura? Do you really trust them? They left me for dead—they took us all. You don't owe them anything. I can help you."

"Help me? And were your *friends* back there trying to help me? Is that what you call it?" Sigrid had no loyalties to the corporation. But the Lady Hitomi...the woman was *not* what Sigrid had expected. Sara, on the other hand, was the last person Sigrid was willing to trust.

"We don't want to kill you, Sigrid. But make no mistake, if you choose to work against us—you, or any of the girls..." Sara took a deep breath and frowned. "The Council will try to control you. We can't let that happen."

"Is that why you're here? To stop the Council, or to get me?"

"Like I said. We can't let them take any of you. They'll use you, Sigrid. They'll use all of you."

Sigrid's hands slid down to her hips. "And this is how you want to recruit me—at gunpoint? What if I say no? What of the other girls?"

Sara shrugged. "You're either with us or against us. Now, are you going to stand down like a good little girl, or am I going to have to blow you to bits." Sara aimed down the sight of the launcher. "I'm happy either way."

Sigrid pursed her lips. There was no way in hell she trusted Sara, or would let her harm the girls from Alcyone.

Sara hadn't noticed Sigrid's hand resting casually on her belt, hadn't noticed the tiny frag grenade she rolled between finger and thumb. Sigrid popped the frag and charged straight at her. Surprised, Sara fired, straight at Sigrid's face, but Sigrid was already moving sideways, spinning, continuing her charge forward. With her shoulder down, she barged heavily into Sara, tackling her. She released the grenade; it clattered along the marble floor toward the elevator doors just ahead. The blast blew the metal doors inward sending bent and twisted shards tumbling down the long shaft.

Sigrid somersaulted right over Sara, wrenching herself from the girl's hands as Sara made a desperate grab at her. Sigrid didn't stop, and she dived, head first into the open shaft ahead of her, disappearing into the smoking darkness.

The last thing Sara saw were Sigrid's heels disappearing over the edge of the elevator shaft. She hauled herself up and ran to the charred opening, staring down into the abyss. She saw nothing. Her scans couldn't pick anything up either. It was difficult to imagine Sigrid surviving the fall, but she thumbed the comlink on her armored collar. "She's in the shaft. Check the perimeter—nobody lets her get out."

* * *

Sigrid was grateful for Hitomi's planning as she hurried to the *Starling* waiting for her on the roof. Shrouded in camouflage, it sat still and quiet, looking black as the night around them. The skin of the heavily-modified craft glimmered faintly under the torrential downpour. Had it not been for the rain washing over it, Sigrid might not have seen it at all.

She'd barely put her foot on the mounting step when the pilot gunned the thrusters, sending the craft rocketing up toward the spilling clouds overhead. Sigrid stood on the rail, one hand gripping the open doorframe above her as she stared down at the diminishing city of Buenos Aires, with its bright, colored lights blurred and muted, dimmed by a thick layer of fog and a swirling of low-lying clouds.

The Hotel wasn't far; the flight through the dismal weather was mercifully brief. The pilot circled once, dropping altitude, hardly slowing long enough for her to leap onto the roof, skidding and rolling to stop on the slick surface. Her suite was only a few floors down so Sigrid chose to scramble down the exterior to the balcony below rather than risk being spotted in the halls.

She burst through the balcony doors. The rain slanting down onto the terrace behind her splashed into the living area. She found Hitomi waiting for her; the Lady gasped at the sight of the cuts on Sigrid's hands and face, and the rips in her uniform.

"My goodness, dear. Are you quite all right?"

"There were men," Sigrid said.

Sigrid told her immediately of the armored soldiers lying in wait for her, of her narrow escape. And of Sara.

Hitomi listened in silence, never interrupting.

When she was finished, Sigrid took out the data modules filled with the stolen files.

Hitomi waved them away. "There's no time for that now, dear. It seems we've stumbled into the midst of something. I fear we are in danger as long as we remain on Earth. We must leave, and we must leave now."

What followed was a dizzying frenzy of activity. Within minutes, the Lady Hitomi had her entire entourage packed and boarding a private transport. There would be no leisurely journey back on the TGV to see the sights this night. Tonight was all about flight.

Hitomi stared through the rain-beaded window of the transport, deep in thought. "There are more things at play in this than even I imagined. Until we get off this planet, we are vulnerable."

The *Morrigan* was still locked in high orbit, prohibited from landing to pick them up, so they had little choice but to book a return passage on the system of Orbital Elevators—the principal means of ferrying passengers and cargo from the Earth's surface into space. There was an early departure scheduled from the complex in Panama City; with luck, they'd just make it there in time.

The Panama City complex was one of the largest of the Lift Centers on the planet, with four massive elevators, each over 200 meters in diameter and six stories high. The elevators could deliver tons of material and personnel far more efficiently than the shuttles. Even more impressive were the *Lift* cables. Constructed with a carbon nanotube weave, the two-meter-thick cables stretched up 700 kilometers into the exosphere, where they were tethered to the orbital docking platforms.

They received word that the *Lift* was completely booked, but the Lady Hitomi soon crushed the will of the terrified ticket agent. Within moments, they booked a passage on the *Lift*, berthed in the most opulent accommodation.

They were halfway across the concourse, moving toward the boarding area, when a booming voice sounded behind them. "Halt!"

Sigrid spun and saw a man approaching through the main gate; he wore the blue and grey uniform of CTF Security; his shoulders bore the rank insignia of a captain. He was flanked by an entire squad of soldiers, all leveling weapons at Sigrid and her companions.

Karen squealed and her hands shot up in the air—Sigrid's hands dropped lower to rest on the pearl handles of her sidearms. She felt the Lady Hitomi's cautioning hand touch her arm.

"Easy, child," she said.

Sigrid relaxed, placing her hands behind her back, but all her attention and sensors remained fixed on the squad of security officers that surrounded them.

The captain approached them, striding briskly across the polished floor of the concourse. "Lady Hitomi. I have a warrant for your arrest—you and your party. You will come with me."

Karen shot a panicked look at Sigrid, who gave her a reassuring nod, although she herself felt a certain unease.

"My good Captain," The Lady said, in a breezy tone. "Whatever is the matter? This must be some misunderstanding."

The Captain gave her as stern a look as he could; not easy, Sigrid thought, under the withering stare of the Lady Kimura. "You are wanted for questioning regarding the break-in at the CTF Offices early this morning."

"Questions? Why I'd be more than happy to answer anything you'd like, right here. There's no need to bother anyone else."

The Captain squirmed uneasily. "Please, Madame. We don't wish to make a scene."

More footsteps approached; a prim, thin-faced man pushed his way forward. He wore a formal black business suit and his hair was sharply groomed. He also wore a security ID for the Bernardino Lift Company. "What is the meaning of this?" the man barked, staring at the captain.

The captain shifted from foot to foot and Sigrid watched his face begin to redden; she could sense his blood pressure rising. "Um—I have a warrant..."

Lady Hitomi smiled up from her chair at the newcomer, extending her hand in greeting. "Ah, Mr. Gomez. How pleasing to see you again. We're so sorry for the disturbance. The Captain here just had some questions for us."

The Captain held out the pad that displayed the warrant, but the prim little man slapped it away. "I believe you're a little out of your jurisdiction here, Captain."

"Sir, my orders are quite specific. If you do not let us proceed in our duty—"

"The Bernardino Lift Company is *not* a member of your *Federated Corporations*, sir. We are an independent organization. *You* are now in BLC territory."

"Sir," the captain's voice remained firm, "I must insist you allow us to remove the Lady and her entourage."

Gomez raised his index finger as a signal. Instantly, the concourse filled with more security, this time dressed in the red outfits of the Bernardino Company. "And I too, must insist."

Sigrid studied all the men and women, now faced off against one another; the problem was that she and her friends were standing in the middle of a potentially explosive situation. Sigrid lowered her hands, resting them again on the handles of her pistols. She made a quick calculation of the rounds available in each weapon, choosing a selection of primary and secondary targets.

The Captain and Gomez stared at each other coldly. Gomez stood erect and calm. Sigrid saw the Captain scan the group of BLC Security that confronted his own men; he was outnumbered two to one. His chest rose and fell heavily, the smallest trickle of sweat escaped from below the brim of his uniform cap.

At last, the captain nodded, with some reluctance, relenting. "Very well. Stand down." He signaled his squad to lower their weapons. "I will have to report this, Lady Hitomi. I'm sure the Council will be in touch."

Hitomi gave a slight nod as answer. The captain retreated, followed by his men.

"I'm so sorry for all this fuss," Hitomi said to Mr. Gomez.

"Not at all, Milady. It is always a pleasure to have you aboard our Elevators. You must let me know if there is anything we can do to make your trip more enjoyable."

Hitomi chuckled. "I think just the fact that we *are* making the trip...I can't thank you enough, Mr. Gomez." She held out her hand; Sigrid gave a little gasp as she saw the man kiss Hitomi's gloved hand—she'd never seen such a gesture. *The Lady really is...a Lady,* she decided.

With the excitement fading behind them, the group proceeded through the waiting airlock to the *Lift.* Only once safely inside, only when she felt the giant machine start its slow climb into space, did Sigrid allow herself to relax.

The Lady Hitomi headed immediately toward their rooms down the hallway. Sigrid and Karen followed, shadowed closely by Hitomi's personal guard. "Now, let's go take a look at what you brought, Sigrid. Perhaps we'll find some of the answers there."

They reached Hitomi's suite, locked the door and Sigrid began uploading the stolen files to Hitomi's pad.

Next, Hitomi did something astonishing; Sigrid watched as Hitomi took out a data-uplink module and proceeded to insert it into the access port in the side of her head. Ever since she'd spotted the telltale port hidden behind Hitomi's ear, there had been a question Sigrid had wanted to ask.

She decided to ask it now. "Mistress—*Hitomi-san,* are you…are you like *us*?"

Hitomi put down the data-uplink and took Sigrid's hand. "No, my dear. It was my hope…but no. I am not like you. I am a failure."

"A *failure*…?"

Hitomi laughed and rubbed at the telltale slot. "This—this is nothing more than a testament to my own hubris. I had thought I could enhance myself as we have with you. But…" she looked down at her crippled legs in their mechanical harness, "…as you can see, I failed."

Sigrid looked at her worriedly; she hadn't meant to upset her.

Hitomi took up the data link again, reconnected it to the port and winked. "Don't worry, my dear. I still retain some benefits. At least I won't have to *read* through all these communiqués."

Despite having been up all night, the Lady Hitomi sat diligently working her way through the walls of security and decryption that barred her way as message after message sparked along her synapses. It was much like Gillings had said. The Council intended to appropriate, *or seize*, all materials pertaining to *Project Andraste* and take over every one of the girls' contracts, either by paying-off Kimura or by force of sanction. If necessary, military action was also listed as an option. Gillings was confident that the extreme measures would not be necessary. But the Council was resolute—they would not suffer another 'Daedalus'.

More disturbing to Sigrid were the clauses pertaining to the girls. If the girls could not be properly controlled, they were to be—how had the Council put it—*deconstructed for the purposes of reverse-engineering.*

Sigrid gasped. "How could they do that?"

"I'm afraid the Council feels they can do with you whatever they like. And more than likely, they will try." Hitomi patted her hand. "Fear not. I won't let things get that far. I have no intention of letting Gillings or any of his cronies get their hands on you or any of your sisters."

Hitomi set about repairing the partially destroyed message Sigrid had found. Sigrid watched, open-mouthed, as the Lady's fingers flew over the pad as she wrote, from scratch, a program to reconstruct the scrambled data.

"Well, isn't this interesting." Hitomi scrolled quickly through the message; her repairs working, slowly filling in the blanks. "Look, here. There's a reference to Gliese…"

"Gliese? That's the planet Selene mentioned—where Tarsus was headed."

"Indeed. And look, there's more." Hitomi highlighted a section that referred to a Dr. Joseph Farrington, but Sigrid didn't understand any of it. "Dr. Farrington is an old colleague of mine," Hitomi explained. "We worked together several years ago on your…well, on this project. He had some interesting theories, but the man was, frankly, erratic. I had to let him go."

"Is he…do you think he's behind all this?"

Hitomi laughed. "Farrington? Definitely not. The man couldn't organize his day-timer let alone a military action. No, but I have no doubt that he's working with whoever is."

Hitomi paused in her scrolling, causing Sigrid to shift uneasily in her chair; the Lady had found the same name that had captured *her* attention: *Tansho.*

"Suko…" Sigrid said. "Is it about Suko?"

Sigrid watched as more words merged into repair, filling in the sentences around the name. Hitomi shook her head. "I'm not sure. A large part of the data is still corrupted. But, Sigrid, these can't be coincidences. Tarsus, Dr. Farrington—the attacks…and now we find a link between them and one of our girls. We must consider the possibility…"

Sigrid stiffened. "No, Mistress. It's impossible. Suko's no spy, she'd never betray us." Sigrid knew Suko felt no love for Kimura, but to work with men who would attack them? Kill them? *Not Suko—never.*

"I know how you must feel, Sigrid. But someone is clearly working with them. We must consider—"

"No!" Sigrid couldn't believe it. *I have to tell her*, Sigrid thought. "Mistress…Suko and I…well, I just know it's not possible. She would never…"

Hitomi considered her words for only a moment. "Very well. If you are certain, then that is all I need to know."

Sigrid suddenly noticed the fatigue etched in Hitomi's face; the effort of deciphering the messages and the long hours had clearly taken their toll.

Hitomi seemed to realize as much herself. "It will take more time to repair the rest of the message, but for now—*sleep*. Unlike you, my child, being up all night is a little hard on me." She directed her wheelchair to the small bedroom just off the anteroom where they'd been sitting. "I suggest you do the same. The *Lift* won't reach the orbital station for at least another thirty-seven hours."

"Yes, I will, Hitomi-san. Shall I come by later?"

"No. I'll be busy here. There's little more you can do. Go enjoy yourself. Go do...whatever it is you young girls do nowadays."

Sigrid bid the Lady goodnight and headed to her own room. She felt exhausted as well. For the first time in over a month she fell asleep as soon as her head touched the pillow.

Chapter 16
The Long Fall

April 18, 2348

Alone in her room above the girls' dormitory, Suko rolled over on her bunk and took a last look at the picture of Sigrid before folding the pad back up and putting it away. She'd made up her mind and wasn't going to back down. Suko clipped on all her weapons, threw on her jacket and grabbed up the small backpack she'd prepared. The door to her room led out to a short staircase behind the dormitory. Suko carefully scanned the grounds with her optical implant. All clear. The gates would still be guarded by the mercenary squad stationed there. She was free to come and go, but Suko didn't want anyone taking note of her departure; she'd need to remain undetected if her plan was going to work.

The wall that framed the Academy was only twenty feet high, so Suko scaled it easily with the rope and small grappling hook she'd fashioned. She paused at the top to take one last look back at the Academy. She felt a moment of loss, thinking of the young girls, her students; she'd grown attached to them so quickly. She worried about what would happen to them after she was gone. But they weren't her responsibility, she told herself.

She had enough to worry about. Her plan was desperate and she didn't hold much hope, but she had to try. If she failed, if they caught her, she had no idea what they'd do with her; better not to think about that now. Suko slid down the wall, pulling the rope after her. In an instant she was trotting off into the forest. She resisted the urge to steal a transport—it would be too easy to track. Getting to the Southern Station would take weeks on foot, perhaps longer, but Kimura would find it far more difficult to hunt her down in the tangle of the bush.

She hadn't even covered two kilometers when she stopped. There was no mistaking the sound; a sonic boom...and then another...followed by a third. The distant rumbling grew louder, decibels blaring to a deafening level. Her first thought was that they were out looking for her, but as the distant rumbling grew louder, Suko realized that it wasn't atmospheric craft she was hearing; it was the sound of heavy ships coming down from orbit.

Suko tracked the sounds and scanned upwards, zooming in with her optical implants. There were few clouds, making it easy to locate the transports. Three large ships descending directly onto the Academy grounds. And they weren't Kimura, Suko could see that. They bore no markings or designation, but they were clearly troop transports, and carrying at least a battalion, by her calculations. Suko homed in on the weapons pods on the sides, manned and ready.

Someone was attacking the Academy.

"Shit."

A strange thought occurred to Suko—this might be the break she'd need to get away. The Kimura soldiers would have their hands full—too full to worry about her. She might actually get away and find Sigrid.

Her heart pounded. *I should be running. Why am I not running?*

"Shit," she said again. Suko knew she wasn't going anywhere. If they were being attacked—*her girls...*

"Dammit!"

Suko turned and tore off toward the Academy. She was on a rise, looking down at the grounds when another sound stopped her. Eyes narrowed, Suko looked up; the transports were ejecting something from the ports in their sides. Her first thought was bombs, but as she zoomed in she saw the hulking machines leaping from the drop ships. Heavily armored and carrying multiple armaments, the bipedal constructs were as big and ugly as tanks. They leapt from the drop ships, slowing themselves with retro-thrust rockets and landing solidly on thick, tri-jointed legs.

The small pistol she always carried was quickly in her hand. Suko gasped. The *Mechs* were landing right in among the Mercenaries, raking the scrambling soldiers with their chain guns and high-powered explosives. Three *Starlings* made it into the air, but the *Mechs* swiftly dispatched them, blasting the small craft from the skies with a barrage of missiles fired from their shoulder-mounted pods.

Suko was trained for combat, but what could she do against such a hail of mechanized destruction? The wall was now before her. She took a deep breath, leapt as high as she could and scrambled spider-like to the top of high wall before jumping over the side and hitting the ground running. The girls...she had to get to them first. Suko sprinted the last few yards to the dormitory, skidded inside and slammed the door closed behind her. All forty-two girls were awake, sitting up in their bunks with eyes full of terror. Khepri was already with them, gathering them up and shouting at them to get dressed.

"Where were you?" Khepri demanded, eyes mixed with anger and fear. But what could Suko say? There was no time; they could hear the explosions and cries from wounded and dying Mercenaries.

Lei-Fei came dashing in, startling both of the older girls. "Let's go! What are you guys waiting for?"

"Bunker?" Suko asked, lowering her sidearm.

Khepri nodded and pushed the group of terrified girls toward the door. A testament to the girls and their training, none of them hesitated or questioned as they ran for the door Lei-Fei held open for them.

Suko stifled a scream as the wall behind them collapsed, crushed under the weight of a giant *Mech* as it crashed through the roof of the dormitory. Khepri and the last of the girls stopped, transfixed, staring at the giant metal monster as it leveled its twin chain guns at them.

"Run!" Suko yelled. Khepri picked the last two girls up in her arms and dived for the door as a torrent of bullets rained down on them. Suko rushed forward, rolling under the hail of gunfire. The *Mech* raised a metal foot to crush her, but she leapt, clambering up its torso until she came face to face with the startled operator seated in the cramped cockpit. Suko drew her sidearm and fired, but the bullets bounced harmlessly off the protective glass. The operator grinned, but the grin vanished when Suko pulled a grenade from her belt and stuck it to the glass in front of his face.

Suko jumped, then rolled through its legs. She watched the mechanical arms trying to claw the grenade off; then it detonated, ripping through the tempered glass, and blowing the *Mech* backwards off its feet. Suko screamed, leaping out of the way to avoid being crushed. Her leap took her out through the hole where the wall had once been. Suko lay on her stomach, out of breath, shielding her head from the shower of shrapnel and debris.

As the blast subsided, she looked up, ears ringing, to find two more of the metal giants before her, flanked by a squad of soldiers in some kind of mechanized armor.

"Fuck," Suko said as the lead soldier raised his weapon and fired, point blank.

* * *

Sigrid's sensors picked up the movement and woke her from her dreams. Someone, no, several people, were in the room. Slowly, she opened her eyes, just a slit, and peered out into the darkness. The men were already on her and she felt the prick of a syringe pressing against her neck.

Before her assailant could plunge the needle into her, Sigrid's arm shot out, slapping the man's arm away. She leapt out of the bed, grabbed him by the neck and spun him about using his body as a shield while his companions fired round after panicked round in her direction. They must have been firing shock-rounds, Sigrid realized; the body of the man she held in front of her spasmed crazily as they unleashed their 300-plus kV blasts of electricity; they were still trying to trap her.

She saw now that there were four men in her room, minus the one who'd just tried to stick her with the needle. Her sensors picked up the panic they felt—*they were terrified.*

Sigrid hurled the limp body of the needle-man at one of her assailants; he collapsed under the weight, crying out and dropping his weapon. She was on the next one in an instant, grabbing his pistol from his trembling hand, blasting him, while throwing a terrific kick into the sternum of the third that sent him crashing through the small door of the bathroom, tearing it right off its hinges. The only man still conscious was pinned under the body, struggling to push it off of him. She aimed the pistol and fired off a couple of shock-rounds, rendering him unconscious as well.

She rifled quickly through his pockets until she found the man's ID. It had to be a fake. The man carried a *student* identification card. Sigrid read the embedded code. 'Hekate...' It was a planet, separated over a decade ago from the Federation. She searched the others to find all their IDs were the same. Were they real, or faked?

Sigrid dressed quickly, grabbing the camouflage gear Hitomi had given her. She was still zipping up her boots and buckling on her gun belt as she hurried down the corridor to the Lady Hitomi's room. When she got there, she froze—the door was ajar. Sigrid had assumed that the attackers were just after her. She cursed her foolishness—she hadn't even considered that the Lady might be targeted as well.

A quick thermal scan revealed three men in the Lady Hitomi's suite, as well as the Lady herself. Hitomi's four bodyguards lay dead on the ground. At least Hitomi looked to be alive; Sigrid scanned her to be sure, and breathed a relieved sigh. One of the men carried her in his arms as the other two moved toward the door. There was nowhere for her to hide in the narrow hallway so Sigrid shrouded, ducking out of the way just as the door opened. One of the men poked his head out into the corridor. He motioned his companions out, guns drawn. The last one carried the Lady Hitomi. Her hands were bound and they'd wrapped a gag around her mouth. She was awake though, and she looked directly at Sigrid—her eyes did not betray that she could see the shrouded girl.

Sigrid fired three shots from her pearl-handled pistols, catching Hitomi in her arms as the three attackers slumped to the ground, dead. She pulled the gag from her mouth and smiled.

"Mistress."

The Lady smiled, much relieved. "Now, Sigrid, you know to call me 'Hitomi-san'."

Sigrid's cheeks reddened, but her smile widened affectionately.

The noise from Sigrid's shots had caused quite a stir. Several doors opened up and down the hallway as curious passengers stuck their heads out to see what was going on. Sigrid heard several gasps and cries at the grisly sight. The loudest outburst was from Karen who ran up to them, pulling her dressing gown around her.

"Oh my goodness—are you two all right?"

Still in Sigrid's arms, Hitomi nodded. "Quite all right, my dear, although..." She looked around at the bodies at Sigrid's feet. "I suppose we should inform the Lift Administrator."

More footsteps could be heard rumbling down the corridor; Sigrid lowered Hitomi to her feet, still supporting her with an arm around her waist. She raised her pistol in the direction of the commotion. Three armed guards, dressed in the Bernardino uniforms ran up, followed by the chief of security. All four raised their hands upon seeing Sigrid's gun leveled in their direction.

Realizing there was no threat, Sigrid lowered her weapon and put it slowly back into her holster.

"Lady Hitomi!" the security chief said, alarmed. "What on earth happened here?"

"These men tried to abduct us. I'm afraid they murdered my bodyguards. Heaven knows what they intended."

He signaled to his men. "Let's get this cleaned up." To the people in the corridor, he called out, "Sorry for the disturbance—please go back into your rooms—nothing to see here."

They all heard the terrible, loud *clang* and the sounds of metal shrieking and grinding somewhere in the bowels of the *Lift*. Even with the inertial dampening systems of the elevator engaged, they could all feel the *Lift* come to a juddering halt; several passengers gasped, looking around in bewilderment.

Sigrid turned to Hitomi and Karen. "We've stopped."

* * *

Selene sighed as she pulled Rodney away from the *Morrigan's* Chief Engineer. The two had been at odds since they'd come on board. Even here in the ship's mess, their arguing was quickly spiraling out of control. Rodney *was* a brilliant engineer, and he knew far more about the ship's systems than the stuffy officer, but he still needed to learn about the chain of command. She couldn't keep intervening on his behalf. He had to learn.

Mercifully, the spat was interrupted by the chirping of the ship's intercom.

"What is it, Christian?"

"Uh, excuse me, Commander, but we've got three ships coming in."

"Mr. Lopez, we're in high Earth orbit. There are ships coming in all the time."

"Yeah, but these...I think they're headed for us."

"I'll be right there." She turned back to Rodney and the Chief. "You two—behave!"

Selene walked quickly to the bridge and slid into her seat at the helm. "All right, Mr. Lopez. Let's see what's got you so worked up." Selene called up the tactical information on her monitor. Lopez was right: three ships, not much bigger than the *Morrigan* were bearing down on them. They were already exceeding the port speed limit, and they were still accelerating. None of them were listed in the registry. *"Independents..."*

A red light on the center console flashed and series of alarms shrilled for their attention.

"What the...They've got a firing solution on us!" Christian said, more confused than alarmed.

"Dear God..." They had missile lock—and her own ship was moored and locked with the orbital platform. She was a sitting duck. "Hang on!"

Without warning, Selene sealed the airlocks and disengaged the mooring locks.

"But, Commander—we have no departure clearance," Melissa cried.

"They can fine me." Selene hit the maneuvering thrusters, blasting away from the station at maximum thrust. "General Quarters. We're under attack. This is not a drill."

"They're firing missiles!" Christian shouted.

Selene studied her monitor; all three attacking ships were braking hard as they closed to 10,000 kilometers. Her own ship was barely moving, still maneuvering with the small steering jets, trying to put some distance between themselves and the station.

She could hear the angry shouting of the station's docking master in her com. She switched it off.

"Counter measures," Selene barked. "Get our jammers up—I don't want anything getting through."

"Aye, ma'am," Christian said.

Selene saw the blast of flares from the viewport as the *Morrigan* belched out an array of defensive devices, flares, and hundreds of tiny *pods* designed to both deflect and attract incoming ordnance. The little ship even had a reasonable phalanx system; it could use the rail guns to hurl thousands of pellets into the path of oncoming missiles. The only problem was, with all the traffic in the port area, they'd most likely tear apart tens of innocent ships parked close by. *As long as they're not using nukes*, she thought. But that would be truly insane.

"Impact in ten," Christian informed them.

The *Morrigan* was still struggling to clear the station when Selene fired the massive rear thrusters, pushing them to maximum; they all winced at the horrible screeching sound as the hull met the edge of the station. No sooner had they cleared the giant docking platform when six missiles slammed into it. A huge fireball flared up, exploding silently outside the window, winking out in an instant as the oxygen was quickly consumed in the blast. The only sound was of the thousands of bits of debris peppering the hull of their ship.

"Holy shit…" Christian gasped.

* * *

The corridor was abundant with confused passengers looking about, wondering why the *Lift* had stopped. Such a thing was an extremely rare occurrence.

Still in her dressing gown, Karen came out of Hitomi's quarters with the wheelchair; Sigrid eased their mistress into it.

"What do you think the problem is?" Karen asked. "I hope it's nothing serious."

Sigrid felt her skin tingle. She was growing accustomed to the various ways her sensory modules functioned to alert her to danger. She felt something now, something familiar.

"We have to get out of here now," she said, starting down the corridor at a jog. "Everyone—back in your rooms!"

The bemused passengers looked at her in wonder as she ran by. Even the Security Chief looked confused.

"Get your men out of here, Chief," Sigrid said over her shoulder.

"Wait!" Karen said. "Where are you going?"

Sigrid stopped at the corridor junction just ahead. When Karen saw her draw both her pistols, she gasped, but instantly quickened her pace, rushing alongside Lady Hitomi. Sigrid stood with her back to the wall, hurriedly motioning them past her.

"Keep going. Run!"

Neither Karen nor Hitomi stopped to question her—probably what saved them. The corridor behind them erupted in a hail of gunfire forcing Sigrid to duck back behind the wall out of harm's way. She'd seen what she needed—three men in the same mechanized armor, just like the ones in the CTF tower the night before. The Chief and his security team weren't so fortunate. They fired back at the attacking soldiers, but their bullets bounced harmlessly off their armor—Sigrid looked on in horror as the security men were gunned down mercilessly. Passengers screamed and ran quickly back into their rooms, most of them fortunate to get out of the way. Most, but not all.

"Dammit," Sigrid said. She dialed the ordnance selector on her pistols, switching to the armor-piercing rounds she'd added to her arsenal. Taking a moment to shroud, she rolled out into the corridor, coming up firing. The thunder of the high-powered slugs was deafening; two of the soldiers stumbled and collapsed as the armor-piercing rounds ripped through the plating on their chests, bursting through the layers of composite material into the soft flesh underneath.

She missed the last one and was forced to dive aside into an open suite. Explosive rounds pierced the air, tracking dangerously close to her own head. Sigrid touched the side of her ear and her hand came back a bloodied mess.

The man—the *Mech*—she wasn't sure what to call it—was on her in an instant. She couldn't believe such bulk could move so swiftly and gracefully. His huge frame suddenly silhouetted in the doorway, and she fired, wide, as he leapt forward, crushing her with his massive weight and knocking the wind completely out of her.

Sigrid tried to raise her guns, but powerful arms, aided by some kind of servo system, pinned her back easily. The weight on her chest was too much. Sigrid couldn't breathe. Her guns were still in her hands, but even trying with all her strength she couldn't wrestle her arms or hands free of his grip. She fought for breath, already starting to feel the blackness coming. If she didn't break free in the next few seconds she knew it would be over.

The gun in her left hand was pointed at the glassed-in viewport on the suite's wall.

Sigrid fired.

The explosion and howling rush of air was deafening. Alarms sounded all over the *Lift,* but the vacuum lifted her assailant off her, pulling him quickly toward the opening and out into space. He grabbed the frame of the window and clung precariously to the edge. Sigrid was also carried across the room; her PCM had already logged every possible handhold, and she opted for the leg of the table in the center of the room; she could only hope that the bolts held where it was fastened to the floor.

The armor her attacker wore must have been pressurized; he was already clawing his way back inside. A drawer from one of the dressers flew across the room and smacked into his helmet, but he still managed to hang on with one gloved-hand. Sigrid lowered her pistol and fired; the armor-piercing round shattered his faceplate, and he cart-wheeled freely, finally, out into space.

Firing at the window had been an act of desperation, and Sigrid's predicament hadn't exactly improved. The freezing cold of space pervaded her bones, just as the torrent of air from the *Lift's* environmental systems threatened to blast her out into oblivion. She was only meters from the doorway and safety, but reaching it was like climbing up a waterfall. All the time, she had to dodge the debris that was tumbling by her from the corridor beyond.

With the last of her strength, Sigrid lunged for the doorframe and heaved herself out, sliding it closed behind her and sealing it shut. The sudden silence filled her ears, and she shivered; she was blue with cold. Her uniform was torn where the mechanized hands had held her, and she was bruised and bloodied. She had a long laceration on her right arm; she couldn't even remember how she'd gotten it, but she was alive.

Sigrid hauled herself up and started back down the corridor; she only hoped that Lady Hitomi and Ensign McTeer were still all right. She caught up to them at the next junction. It was sealed off from the breach, but she was able to override the locking system and let herself through. She collapsed in Karen's arms, sinking to her knees.

"Oh, my God!" Karen said, distress visible on her face as she held Sigrid.

Hitomi looked equally concerned. "Those men, are they...?"

Sigrid nodded. "Dead. I had a little trouble with the last one," she said, managing a grin—she didn't want them to worry about her. "But he's off touring the universe."

"Do you suppose there are any more?" Karen looked terrified.

Sigrid opened her mouth to answer, no, when they heard the sound of a far-off explosion, followed by the agonizing sound of groaning, twisting metal.

Karen screamed, clutching at Sigrid; all three of the women looked to each other. Sigrid noticed it first—the slight tilting of the floor.

"Oh no..." she said.

Even Hitomi, always so steady and strong, paled. "They cut the tether."

* * *

"Yes, Lieutenant, I see it," Selene said, leaning forward.

They'd all seen it—a massive explosion just at the top of the *Lift* that carried Sigrid and her party. The *Lift* had already reached the Earth's thermosphere, at some 135 kilometers, but the explosion had severed the tethering system that connected the elevator to the orbital platform above; the sheer weight of the massive cable, still connected to the base of the *Lift*, was already dragging the elevator back down toward the planet below.

"Holy..." Ensign Greenway said, breathlessly.

"Can you reach them on the com?" Selene asked.

Christian's hands flew over his console. He shook his head. "Too much interference, ma'am."

Selene nodded. "All right, I'll bring us in closer."

"*Closer?*" Christian asked.

"We can't very well do much good back here, now, can we." Selene pushed the thrusters harder, accelerating and moving the *Morrigan* ever closer to the massive elevator.

"Uh…Commander," Christian said, nervously.

"Watch your tactical monitor, *Lieutenant*. I want a second by second report on the course of that elevator."

He gulped. "Um—it's headed down, ma'am. And we still have those three ships on our tail."

"*I know!*" Selene said. She bit her lip. *Well, you're really in it now,* she thought and laughed.

Christian caught the laugh. "Ma'am?"

"Just keep trying to hail them—we don't have much time."

* * *

Sigrid heard the second explosion, followed by a horrible tearing sound of metal being ripped away. Karen screamed again.

Sigrid's comlink chirped on the emergency frequency and she heard Selene's voice. She quickly hushed both women, listening as Selene fed her the series of instructions. Only when Selene was finished did she turn to her companions. "We need to get down to the lowest level, and we have to hurry."

"Wait!" Hitomi said. "The data modules—I left them back in the rooms. We must go back."

Sigrid looked down the long corridor, and then at the increasing tilt of the floor. She could feel the vibrations intensify as the *Lift* accelerated in its descent.

"I don't think there's time."

Hitomi nodded and Karen looked relieved to keep going, helping the Lady's chair along.

Sigrid led them quickly down the corridor. The tilt of the floor slewed even more as they ran, making progress difficult as the three forged ahead. Sigrid stopped at each junction, checking to make sure their path was clear.

"Sigrid, wait!" Karen called out to her.

She turned back and saw the girl struggling with Lady Hitomi's wheelchair; the angle of the floor was pitched at thirty degrees and Karen could no longer manage the chair. Lady Hitomi looked thoroughly angry and embarrassed.

"You girls go ahead. I'll only slow you down."

Sigrid scanned the corridor, checking again to see that their path was clear before rushing back to the two. Holstering her weapons, she lifted Hitomi out of her chair.

"Sigrid—"

"Please don't argue," Sigrid said, starting back down the corridor. "We're not leaving you behind."

"I'd never dream of it. I was only going to tell you—it's the other way. We need to go down."

Sigrid chuckled, as she turned around and spotted the maintenance hatch at the end of the corridor.

Sigrid helped Hitomi along as fast as she could. She could feel the vibrations in the floor becoming more pronounced, and she realized they must be entering the planet's atmosphere. They heard a series of loud bangs—what sounded like entire sections of the *Lift* being torn away as the elevator shifted further on its axis. Sigrid stumbled and fell, twisting so that Hitomi landed on top of her. They all rolled from the floor onto the wall as the *Lift* dipped sharply. Sigrid tried not to think of how far or how fast they were falling as the cabling system dragged them further down into the atmosphere.

The *Lift's* stabilizing systems groaned in protest, working desperately to right the elevator. The three women were thrown back in the other direction. They landed hard on the floor; Sigrid caught Hitomi, who shook her head at Sigrid in surprise.

"Sorry about this," Sigrid said, gathering Hitomi up into her arms and carrying her the rest of the distance to the maintenance hatch. She kicked it open. "Go!" she yelled at Karen, who scuttled inside, climbing quickly down the ladder. Sigrid looked down the shaft—the ladder led down two decks below.

"I'm sorry," Hitomi said, frowning at the ladder. "I don't think I can manage that."

Sigrid examined the length of the access shaft again. "Hang on!"

Hitomi nodded bravely and Sigrid jumped, pursing her lips as she landed hard on the deck below; the pain was intense, and she felt something tear, but she'd worry about that later. Sigrid looked about her; they were at the bottom of the elevator in a small maintenance room; there was a large access panel in the floor painted with red warning signs, marked, 'Authorized Personnel Only'. The small room shook with tremendous noise and violence.

"Now what?" Karen asked.

"Stand back," Sigrid said, and slammed the emergency release on the floor panel at her feet. Explosive bolts blew the panel away, sending it twirling downwards to be whipped away by the buffeting winds. The sound of the air rushing past them thundered in their ears; Karen's light dressing gown swirled about her head until she forced it back down.

Through the open hatchway they could all see the Earth rushing up toward them, perhaps little more than six thousand meters away and closing fast; Sigrid saw the sorry, twisted shape of the lift cable coiling up beneath them.

But also there, somehow, impossibly, below, the *Morrigan* danced in time with the whipping of the cable. Sigrid thought Selene had to be completely mad as she maneuvered the ship deftly, drifting closer and closer to the plummeting elevator. She brought it as close as three meters, and Sigrid saw one of the dorsal hatches open. Christian emerged from the opening, tethered in a harness and wearing a breather. He waved to them frantically.

"Go!" Sigrid screamed to Karen above the worsening din.

Karen swallowed hard, but there was no time to debate the issue and she jumped the short distance. She landed on hands and knees, spread-eagled on the hull.

Sigrid stumbled as the lift tilted hard over, almost colliding with the *Morrigan,* but the small ship banked hard over, blasting down and away, keeping its distance from the massive *Lift* just above it. The maneuver lifted Karen back into the air off the hull—Sigrid held her breath—but Karen came crashing back down, clinging desperately to the hull some ten meters down the length of the ship.

With a tight grip on Hitomi, Sigrid leapt and hit the ship's deck next to Christian. She handed the Lady over to him and he helped her quickly inside.

"We have to go—now!" Christian shouted.

Sigrid looked down the length of the ship to where Karen still clung desperately for her life.

"Not yet."

Taking one brief look up, Sigrid gulped at the sight of the massive elevator above them—she didn't want to think about how close the Earth was beneath them. She moved quickly and carefully to where Karen clung to the top of the *Morrigan*; The ensign looked completely petrified and desperate.

"I got you," Sigrid said as she grabbed Karen by the wrist and hauled her up.

She heard Christian's voice loud in her comlink. *"Sigrid!"*

Sigrid grunted and threw Karen into the open hatch, diving in after her.

Christian sealed the hatch then thumbed the comlink on his uniform collar. "They're in!"

The ship shook beneath her as the massive thrusters fired, blasting forward. Somewhere, not too far distant, Sigrid heard the crash and explosion of the *Lift* smashing into the Earth. All of them collapsed into a sweaty, breathless heap.

"We're not out of this yet, people," Selene said over the com.

After making sure Hitomi was uninjured, Sigrid, followed by Christian, made her way to the bridge. The door was open and she could see that they were already clearing the upper atmosphere.

The tall woman rose from her seat at the helm and leaned surprisingly casually against the bulkhead. "Well, to think I worried this job might be dull."

Sigrid smiled. "Sorry."

"Look, we've got three *Independent* ships on our tail and the entire CTF Earth Defense force moving to blockade the Relay. I just thought you should know."

Sigrid ran quick calculations on the scenario—she wasn't trained in fleet tactics. "Can we run the blockade?" She was worried that Selene might protest, but the woman smiled.

"I'll do my best, ma'am."

The ship lurched in time with a deafening explosion. Selene turned to Christian. "Report."

"Torpedo—that one got a little close."

Selene cursed and slapped the com button on the arm of her chair, shouting at the men in the weapons pods. "I told you—nothing gets through. We're lucky those weren't nukes. I want a phalanx pattern on those guns."

"What is it?" Sigrid asked.

"Rookies. They couldn't hit a cow's ass with a banjo; so I've got them strictly firing a defensive pattern."

Sigrid smiled. "Maybe I can help."

* * *

Sigrid relieved the frazzled crewman manning the ship's dorsal weapons pod. Exhausted and drenched in sweat, he was more than happy to give up his post.

As she slipped into the pod, she noticed the number of physical hookups for the operator as well as the VI helmet that provided a full 360 degree view of the combat area. Sigrid pushed all these aside, preferring to interface directly with her PCM; all the operational information she needed was displayed in her HUD. Three ships, only slightly larger than her own, were bearing down on the nimble *Morrigan*. As fast as her ship was, even faster than the *Agatsuma,* the three *Independent* ships were gaining on them. Quickly.

The pursuing ships were still launching missiles. Sigrid watched them all streaking closer as the *Morrigan* continued to belch out a barrage of countermeasures. The pod's gun was set to a phalanx-mode, firing concentrated blasts of ordnance into the paths of the oncoming missiles, shredding any that got close.

Selene was putting her ship through a series of desperate evasive maneuvers, but Sigrid knew that, as their pursuers closed the distance, it would become virtually impossible to dodge the hail of ballistic rounds that they were firing from their own rail-systems. They were already within 15,000 kilometers; when they got within five, they'd be virtually defenseless.

Aiming her quad-mounted rail-gun wasn't easy with the ship moving so erratically, and her targets weren't exactly holding still. Sigrid tried for a computer lock, but of course the attacking ships were using their own countermeasures and the automated aiming-systems were completely useless.

Sigrid switched her ordnance from the defensive phalanx-rounds to fragmentation rounds and took aim at the lead ship in pursuit. The quad-mounted guns belched out a quick burst, missing her target completely as the *Morrigan* jigged to avoid yet another incoming barrage; she'd have to compensate for that, she chided herself. Tying directly into the ships navigational computer allowed her to track the ship's movements and anticipate the violent maneuvers. Her next shot tracked perfectly, ripping apart the bow of the lead ship, severing vital systems. The ship's drive shut down, and the vessel dropped quickly away as the *Morrigan* continued to accelerate at maximum thrust.

Sigrid tracked the next ship; it was veering off, possibly trying for a flanking position, but the ploy left the length of the ship exposed and Sigrid's next shot tore through it from stem to stern. Several of the fragmentation rounds connected with the ship's main engines, erupting in a tremendous explosion. The captain of the last ship must have had enough; Sigrid saw it flip over on its axis, showing the *Morrigan* its massive stern tubes. They flared brilliantly as it decelerated away, eager to put some distance between themselves and the waiting death in Sigrid's gun.

This fight was over. Sigrid was about to shut down the Pod, but then something occurred to her and she felt a coldness spreading inside herself. These men had attacked her and her friends, killed all those people on board the *Lift*. And what of the Panama Complex? The loss of life would be staggering. Sara's words rang in her head—they would continue to pursue her and all the girls. They were still a threat.

Sigrid targeted the fleeing ship. It was already at a tremendous distance and retreating fast. She took a quick moment to calculate its evasive patterns and set her ordnance for proximity detonations before firing. The ballistic rounds covered the distance between the ships quickly and Sigrid watched the flares from the series of explosions. The ship was gone. Whoever they were, whoever they had been, they would bring no harm to her or her friends again.

Safe for the moment, she pulled herself out of the pod and headed back to the bridge.

Selene turned as she came in. "Nice shooting."

"Nice flying," Sigrid said, returning the compliment.

Selene turned back to the small monitor mounted on her chair and brought the tactical display back up on the main viewer. "The next part might be a little trickier," she said.

Sigrid could see the *Morrigan's* position as it moved quickly away from the Earth toward the Warp Relay. Still millions of kilometers away, but moving to block their path, were fourteen CTF naval ships ranging in size from light Corvettes to heavy Cruisers. The wall of ordnance they could put up was far more than even a nimble ship like hers could dodge.

"Shit," Sigrid said.

Helped by Karen, Lady Hitomi emerged in the doorway of the bridge. "I might be able to help with that," she said as Karen eased her into one of the little jump seats in the back.

Selene nodded. "This might call for more of a *diplomatic* solution."

Hitomi raised an eyebrow. "Oh? I had something a little more radical in mind." She gestured to the console at her side. "With your permission...?"

"Of course," Selene said.

Hitomi's fingers danced over the console while Sigrid and Selene watched over her shoulder.

"What the hell is that?" Selene asked.

Almost embarrassed, Hitomi looked at Sigrid. "I hope you don't mind, but I had my people make a few modifications while we were on Aquarii. I meant to tell you..."

Sigrid studied the new schematics and smiled.

"This is my own design," Hitomi said. "I'm sure you'll all understand why I need you to sign a nondisclosure agreement once we're out of this pickle."

"You're joking," Selene said, laughing, but when she saw that Hitomi was serious she closed her mouth.

"Not even my Board knows about this. If this works—"

"*If?*" Selene asked.

"Well, it's never been tested."

Sigrid looked at the monitor; they'd be in weapons range in moments. "Whatever you're going to do, do it fast—Mistress..."

Hitomi chuckled and activated the new system she'd installed. It was a variation of the same stealth systems that she'd given to

Sigrid, but on a much larger scale. The *Morrigan* became virtually invisible, both to the eye and to any tracking devices the opposing ships might employ against them.

"Nice trick," Selene said, suitably impressed. "So, now we just drift through their ranks?"

"Yes—but you'd best shut down the drives. I'm not sure how the shielding will affect that."

Selene nodded and disengaged the main thrusters. The ship grew eerily silent.

Sigrid watched the CTF ships trawling this way and that, searching for her ship. "They're firing," she said.

"Do they see us?" Karen asked, worried.

Sigrid studied the pattern and shook her head. "No—they're guessing. They're just trying to cover our path, hoping to get lucky."

The stealth systems that Lady Hitomi had employed worked perfectly and within minutes the *Morrigan* had drifted safely between the blockading ships, slipping harmlessly past the plethora of mines they had laid.

"I am *so* glad I took this job," Selene declared with a jubilant smile.

When they deactivated their cloak, Sigrid saw all the CTF ships moving quickly to pursue, but it was too late; the *Morrigan* and her crew were safely away with nothing between them and the Warp Relay.

"Course?" Selene asked.

"Aquarii," Hitomi told her. "We must warn the Board of these developments. It's a shame we lost the evidence you stole from the CTF offices. I just hope they'll listen to reason."

"I still have the one partial message," Sigrid said, tapping her head. "I never deleted it."

"That's something, at least. With the facilities on Aquarii, I should be able to finish reconstructing it. With luck, we'll uncover the truth to all of this."

As they blasted toward the relay, Sigrid couldn't ignore the feeling of worry and dread she felt growing within her. They were definitely caught in the middle of a whole new war. And what of her friends on Alcyone? What of Suko? Would they be able to protect them—warn them in time—or were they already too late?

Hitomi saw the look on her face. "Don't worry, Sigrid. We'll go to Alcyone. But we'll go in strength. I will convince the Board of the need to send a sufficient force this time. I won't let anything happen to any of them."

Chapter 17
Independents

May 2, 2348

Naked, bruised and bloodied, with wrists and ankles bound, Karl Tarsus was dragged down the narrow steps into the damp corridor below. There were several puddles on the moist floor and the place stank of mildew and sweat. They hauled him into an open room at the end. Rough hands deposited him on a small wooden chair that creaked and threatened to collapse under his weight.

It took great effort, but Tarsus lifted his head, looking up at them from beneath the swollen lids of his eyes.

So, this is it, he thought. They finally got him. And then he laughed. *They.* 'They' could have been one of a hundred people or organizations. How many contracts had he taken over the years? How many people had he angered? How many people had he killed…

Of all the people who could have walked through the door, the last person he thought it would be was *Smith*, but that's exactly who it was. Tarsus would recognize that thin face, those narrow eyes anywhere.

Smith. His most generous benefactor—the man responsible for his demise. This time he had a woman with him; someone he didn't recognize. She appeared to be in her fifties, but she seemed odd, out of place; she had the look of an academic, hardly a military type. What she was doing with him, he could only guess.

"You…" Tarsus said. His voice was dry and rasped, like metal grating.

Smith nodded to the guards, who untied him and tossed him a grubby blanket. Someone handed him a cup of water which he drank from thirstily.

"Glad you could make it, Mr. Tarsus. It's been a long time."

Tarsus drained the cup and glared at him. "What's the meaning of this? Why have you brought me here?"

"I couldn't take the chance that someone could trace you here to me. Not now."

Tarsus stared at him in disbelief. "Then this…this is just…"

"I have a job for you, Karl. Whatever else would we be here to discuss."

Karl gaped at him a long moment and then laughed, a huge belly laugh. Then, the menace returned to his eyes. "Work for you? I'll *kill* you."

"That would serve neither of us. Besides, who pays you better than I do? Let's save time and dispense with the games." *Smith* threw a pad onto Tarsus' lap; displayed there were the details of a new contract, and for a staggering sum of money.

"This…this is enough to buy a ship—four ships. And not just *haulers*—the real frontline jobs."

"More than that, I'd wager."

Tarsus was tempted by the money. He was completely broke. But, he also remembered how the last job for the man had gone. *Smith* had completely failed to give him proper intel on his targets. That group of *girls* had turned out to be a highly trained group of…he wasn't even sure what to call them. They'd acted like Spec-Ops, but they were wild, fearless. They had taken apart his best men like they were a bunch of recruits. Worse, his men had let themselves be captured, killed. Evidence had been left, and his organization had been fingered in the operation. His mercenary group had been devastated by fines and sanctions from the CTF. Tarsus had been completely ostracized from the guild.

Smith had ruined him, and now the man wanted him to work for him again.

"If I remember correctly," Tarsus said. "The last job we did together didn't exactly go swimmingly."

"Granted. Things could have gone better."

"Better? We failed—we didn't retrieve any of the girls."

"Fortunately, where your organization failed…" *Smith* gestured to the woman next to him, "…Ms. Kirk here has succeeded."

Tarsus eyed the woman. He'd never heard of her. "Then you don't need me."

"You sell yourself short, Karl. I've always found your service satisfactory. I see no reason to terminate our relationship."

"You destroyed my organization, and now you want me to—"

"Rebuild it. Double it. You're going back to work, Major."

Major—now he was spouting rank...

Tarsus couldn't figure out the man's game, but the money... "If I start buying up ships now, people are going to start asking questions."

"I would imagine."

Tarsus studied him carefully and then laughed heartily as he put his thumb to the contract. "Don't you think it's time you told me your name?"

* * *

Suko woke up. Her head throbbed and it took several minutes for her vision to clear. *What had they done to her?* They'd hit her with something, but it wasn't like anything she'd felt before. The blast had thudded into her in the chest like a mallet, scrambling all her systems and frying her PCM. She searched for it now, but all access was gone. She couldn't locate any of her systems, not even her most basic bionics.

Suko surveyed her surroundings. She was lying on the cold metal floor of a small room. She didn't know where she was, but she was sure it wasn't any room in the Academy or Annex. Her wrists and ankles were bound and her clothes had been taken away, leaving her only with her underwear.

"Suko!"

Suko rolled over to discover Khepri and Lei-Fei sitting behind her with their backs up against the wall. They were also trussed at wrist and ankle.

"Thank God you're alive!" Khepri said.

Suko could see they'd both been crying. Their eyes were red, dark; half-circles lined their eyes. "You got hit so hard—we thought you were dead."

Suko hauled herself up next to Khepri as best she could. She tried to scan herself to see how badly she was hurt, but she still couldn't access any of her systems. "*My PCM...*" Suko said; her voice cracking dry as she tried to speak.

"It's fried, but it'll reboot when it resets," Lei-Fei said. "At least, it did for us."

"Where are the others?"

Khepri and Lei-Fei looked to each other. Lei-Fei spoke first. "Mei, Petra, Leia...they're dead. The others..."

"They took them," Khepri said, fear in her words. "Suko...they...*did* something to them."

Who were they? Suko wondered. "Where are we?"

Both girls shook their heads. "We don't know," Lei-Fei said. "We definitely dropped through a relay, but where..."

They listened to the footsteps coming down the corridor outside; The two girls recoiled in fear, and she, too, slunk back against the wall. A face appeared in the grated opening near the top of the door. Two eyes studied her for a moment, then the face disappeared; the footsteps diminished into the echoes until all was quiet.

Suko looked frantically about the small room looking for any means of escape. She struggled to her feet, not easy with her ankles bound and her hands tied behind her back. There was nothing in the room but a small bucket—used, from the smell of it. Suko threw her weight against the door, but it was completely solid.

"It's no use," Khepri said. "We tried."

Stubbornly, she threw herself against it repeatedly until her shoulder was bruised and sore.

The footsteps returned—more this time. And there was something about them, something familiar, the same heavy sounds she'd heard during the attack.

The door rattled and swung open. Three people stood before her. Two were soldiers, dressed in their heavy mechanized armor, leveling assault rifles. The smaller of the two removed her helmet, shaking her hair loose and staring at Suko through narrow eyes.

Suko's eyes widened in shock. It was impossible. "*Sara...*"

"Hello, Suko," she said.

Suko couldn't believe it. The girl was alive, free—and *armed*—wearing the same armor as the soldiers who had attacked them. *Sara was with them?*

Another man stood to her side. He looked to be in his late twenties, with jet-black hair. His eyes explored her carefully, strangely. He stepped toward her, but Suko recoiled from his outstretched hand, falling back against the wall away from him. *But his eyes...*Suko thought. *There was something...*

"Suko..."

"Who the fuck are you?" Her parched words came out as a croak.

"Get some water," the young man snapped at the guards. "And, godammit—bring back her clothes." His face and voice were firm and commanding. He looked back at her, apologetically. "I'm so sorry about this, Suko. But I'm glad you're here."

It seemed impossible. It had been so long...It couldn't be. *Could it?*

"Riku...?"

Riku, Suko's brother, smiled. "You do remember."

Suko stumbled back. Her older brother, Riku. She'd barely known him—he'd left when she was so young. *How is this possible? He can't be...*She couldn't believe it. "Riku...what are you doing here? Where are the girls...?"

Riku held his hands up. "I'll explain everything. I promise. You just have to trust me."

Suko gestured to her bound wrists and ankles, at Khepri and Lei-Fei, who looked so frightened. "Let us go. Then I'll trust you."

"I can't. Not yet. But I will. I promise."

Another man appeared, accompanied by two more of the armored troopers. He carried a bundle of clothes for them. Suko was given water. One by one, they were untied and allowed to dress, before their wrists were bound once more.

"Take that one," Sara said, pointing to Lei-Fei.

"*What?*" Suko cried.

"No!" Lei-Fei cried, shrinking away from them, but the bound girls were no match for the soldiers in their powered armor. They dragged Lei-Fei out, kicking and screaming. Khepri jumped on one of the hulking figures, but he easily beat her back down. Suko kicked at Sara, cracking her shin against the hard shell of her armor, and then fell backwards as Sara smacked her hard on the head with the butt of her gun.

And then Lei-Fei was gone. Khepri and Suko lay bruised and beaten on the floor of their cell.

Suko glared up at her brother and Sara, anger clouding her eyes. "Don't you hurt her."

Riku didn't respond.

Suko's heart pounded. "What are you going to do to her?"

"I'm only trying to help. You're a slave, Suko. You just don't know it."

"They've programmed you, Suko," Sara said. "They did it to us all."

"I'm going to help you," Riku said. "We're going to set you free."

"You're mad," Suko spat.

"You don't know what they're capable of. You don't know what they've done."

"I don't know what you're talking about."

Riku held up his hands, imploring. "You can't know what it's like out there, Suko. Tens of billions living in abject poverty, starving, while the Federation grows fat. With each planet the CTF opens up, with all its resources, you'd think that there would be some relief, but it just gets worse. More wealth for the rich, more crippling debt for the rest of us." Riku shook his head and laughed, the tired laugh of a cynic. "And all of us so willing, so eager to sell ourselves, our children—to the very people who created the problem."

"He's telling the truth," Sara said.

"When our parents sold you…when they took you…I knew I had to do something."

Suko couldn't believe what she was hearing. "You? You're responsible for this?"

"Not myself alone, no. There are many of us. And we're going to stop them, Suko. We can do it together. With your help…we can put an end to this. We can make some real change."

Suko turned her eyes to Khepri, bruised and bleeding, to her own bruises and the restraints on her wrists. "You attack us, you kill my friends...now you say this is to help us?"

"I'm sorry, Suko. That was...regrettable."

"Let us go," Suko pleaded.

"I can't. Not yet. But I will. When it's time."

* * *

Riku closed the door and turned to the man at his side. "Satisfied?" he asked, not hiding the disgust in his voice.

Riku stood before his compatriots, Nicola Kirk and Dr. Joseph Farrington, in Nicola's makeshift office in the hastily assembled facility. Nicola had discovered the abandoned mining operation years ago during her work in the Records Office for the CTF.

Like everyone there, Nicola bore the marks of exhaustion. Dr. Farrington was lost in his calculations, his face locked on the monitor before him.

Nicola sat on the edge of her desk. She was only in her fifties, nearing middle-age, but her duties with the movement didn't exactly lend themselves to eating right and taking care of herself. It was starting to show. Still, she had a strong face and carried herself with the confident air of command. She'd proven herself capable time and again, and had risen to become one of the principal architects of the movement against the Federation and its ruling Council.

"Dammit, Joseph—you stink," Nicola told him.

Farrington didn't bother to look up. "Find me some decent water and I'll shower."

Nicola folded her arms and turned her attention back to Riku. "You're doing the right thing, Riku. After what they did to her, your sister will be better off. I promise."

Riku paced, uneasily. "She's not what I expected."

"Of course she's not. Look what they've done to her—she's as good as grown up in a cult. Who knows what kind of crap they've subjected her to."

"No, it's not like that at all. She's like—she's just like I remember. It's my sister."

Nicola pinched the bridge of her nose. "We've discussed this. Those girls have had their genetics scrambled, mutated and reassembled. Dammit—they have a controlling chip in their brain! They're nothing but a bunch of trained assassins, programmed for a CTF murder-squad."

"And now you want to reprogram them for yourself."

She gave him a sympathetic look, but her voice remained firm. "The damage has been done."

Riku stared contemptuously at Farrington. "Well, I'm not letting *him* touch her, not after what happened to the others."

"They'll be fine," Farrington said, unimpressed, not bothering to look at him. "I'm still tweaking the program. You can't expect me to undo years of work in a day."

"We'll fix it, don't worry," Nicola assured him. "We're going to need *all* those girls for the next phase. We need you for this, Riku. You're a valuable member of the movement, but if you're having doubts..."

Riku nodded away his reticence. "I know. Don't worry. I'll be fine."

* * *

As soon as the *Morrigan* emerged through the Relay and blasted its way toward Aquarii, they could tell something was wrong. The closer they came to the planet the more the surrounding space became littered with the wrecked hulks of ships orbiting the planet, some Kimuran, some of unknown origin. Sigrid gasped at the devastation.

They landed without delay. On the tarmac, Sigrid could see more evidence of the attacks—burned wrecks of fighters and service vehicles mostly, but several buildings had been crushed under the bombardment. Cleanup crews were busy everywhere repairing and salvaging what they could, and hauling away what was beyond repair.

Sigrid stepped through the airlock. She was fully armed and dressed in her combat outfit, sporting a short pilot's jacket. She helped Hitomi onto the lift, steadying her as they were lowered to the tarmac. Selene, Karen and Christian followed close behind, climbing down the short steps.

They were greeted by Markus Emerson and Hitomi's son, Shinji, who rushed to the base of the stairs. Both men were surrounded by a squad of marines in full battle gear. Sigrid noted another man in their midst, grey-haired and thin, he wore a black suit with the Federation emblem on his collar. Her PCM confirmed him as the Federation Envoy to Aquarii.

Hitomi wheeled herself forward to meet them. "Shinji, Markus. What on earth happened?"

Markus scanned the scene of destruction. "*Independents*, from what we could tell, but...I've never seen them operate in such numbers. It happened nearly two weeks ago—soon after you left."

"We must convene an emergency meeting of the Board. We'll need to deal with this immediately. I fear it's more than just the Council that is moving against us. We'll also need to send a force to Alcyone—"

"Mother," Shinji said, distress haunting his face. "Alcyone is...gone."

"No..." Sigrid moaned.

Hitomi put a steadying hand on her arm.

"What? When?" Hitomi demanded.

"A ship came back, soon after the attacks here."

"Survivors? On Alcyone?"

Markus shook his head. "Unknown. The ship barely made it away itself. We haven't been able to launch a rescue mission—not with all the work to do here."

Sigrid felt sick. "Mistress..."

"Don't worry. We'll investigate right away." She turned to Markus and Shinji. "How many ships do we have available? We must return in force to Alcyone immediately."

Sigrid watched as Markus and Shinji looked uncomfortably at each other. Hitomi picked up on it as well.

"Markus...?"

"I'm afraid that won't be possible, Milady," the Federation Envoy said, stepping forward at last.

Hitomi shot the man a disparaging look. "Markus, what is *he* doing here?"

The envoy answered for himself. "Alcyone and all materials pertaining to the project known as *Andraste* are now property of

225

the Council for Trade and Finance." His gaze fixed on Sigrid. "*All* materials, Milady."

Hitomi's eyes hardened on Markus Emerson and her son. "I don't believe it. You took the Council's offer."

Markus cleared his throat uncomfortably. "Milady…after the attack. We had little choice."

"You always have a choice, Markus. You made the wrong one."

The envoy stepped forward, placing his hand on Sigrid's arm. "The girl must come with me, of course."

Sigrid jerked her arm from his grasp; Hitomi wheeled herself forward, putting herself between the two. "Impossible. The girl is contracted to me personally. The Council has no claim on her."

"My orders are explicit, Lady Hitomi. I am to retrieve *all* materials. Kimura has already signed the girls' contracts over to the Council."

"Not *this* contract. She has been granted special dispensation as a private operator under the Guild Act."

"A technicality, Milady. You may file a grievance with the local CTF office, of course."

"Magistrate, you *are* the local CTF office."

The envoy ignored the remark and grabbed Sigrid's arm again.

He gurgled ever so slightly as Sigrid's free hand gripped his throat, lifting him clear off the ground. His eyes bulged and he grabbed frantically at her arms, his feet kicking madly as his outstretched toes reached for the ground.

"Sigrid!" Hitomi's hand came up, half-covering her mouth in surprise.

Sigrid had as little intention of going with the envoy as she had with Sara. "I'm afraid I won't be taking that contract offer from the Council at this time," Sigrid said, her eyes locked fiercely on his. "You may file your own grievance."

"Goodness. Just don't…*kill* him."

Sigrid put him down and shoved him backward; he clawed at his throat, choking and gasping for air.

Sigrid turned to Selene behind her. The pilot had her sidearm drawn and pointed at the envoy on his knees before them. "I think we should be going now, don't you think?"

"Aye, ma'am."

Selene holstered her weapon and backed up the stairs toward the ship.

Still clutching his throat, the little envoy waved at Sigrid, calling to the troops behind him, "Stop them! Arrest them."

The squad of Marines looked to each other uncertainly and then to Markus, who nodded. The Marines stepped forward, weapons raised.

"Markus?" Hitomi exclaimed.

"I'm sorry, Milady. But this is no longer Kimura's affair. The girl must be turned over to the Council."

The envoy was back on his feet, gesturing frantically to the Marines. "Take her! Arrest her!"

Sigrid's pistols were in her hands; she was already locking her HUD on the nearest targets.

But Hitomi's reaction was just as quick, and she grabbed Sigrid's arm, pulling herself to her feet—shielding Sigrid from the oncoming squad.

"Sigrid, no!"

Sigrid stared at the woman in disbelief; her heart was pounding. "Mistress…"

Hitomi gave her a warning, cautioning look. "Sigrid, they'll kill you."

At that moment, Sigrid wasn't sure she even cared. She only knew she wasn't going to let them take her. She had to get to Alcyone—she had to know if Suko was alive, and she wasn't going to let them hand her over to the Council. She shook her head again. "No, Mistress."

"Sigrid, please. Trust me."

She looked at the soldiers surrounding her; fourteen soldiers stood just feet away from her, assault rifles leveled at her. Sigrid made the calculations, but she couldn't see how even she could defeat those odds. And then there was Hitomi, still clinging to her arm, looking to her pleadingly.

Sigrid dropped her weapons. The soldiers surged forward, moving the Lady Hitomi out of the way and stripping Sigrid of all her weapons, which wasn't an easy task. When it was over, the tarmac was littered with knives, pistols, even the tiny pinhead grenades she'd stitched into her bra. With wrists shackled, Sigrid was marched off.

She was their prisoner.

Chapter 18
Prisoner

The prison on Aquarii was modern, clean and comfortable, the inmates well taken care of. But it was still a prison.

They placed Sigrid in their maximum security facility, in solitary confinement and under constant guard, monitored by scanners and armed guards who never left the front of her cell. She'd studied the layouts for days, but not even she could calculate a method of escape.

And Sigrid knew well that she had to escape. Alcyone had been attacked, that much was obvious, but the fate of the girls and of Suko?…well, she wasn't going to find the answer to that question trapped in her cell. Sigrid studied the clear perma-glass door again. It was as solid as steel and incorporated a simple mechanical locking mechanism. There was no way for her to interface with it or tamper with it at all. The rest of the walls were of ultra-dense reinforced permacrete. There had to be a way out, but for the moment, Sigrid couldn't see one.

The door down the hall to her section rattled open and Karen burst through, pushing her way past the guard. She saw Sigrid and ran forward, pressing her hands up against the perma-glass of Sigrid's door.

"Oh, Sigrid, I'm so sorry. I can't believe they did this to you."

Sigrid frowned. "I'm learning to believe a lot of things."

"Listen. Kimura isn't going to take you to Earth. They're keeping you here until a CTF transport comes to get you. That won't be for another five days."

Five days! In another five days, where would Suko be?

"I…I just thought you should know," Karen said tearfully. "I also wanted to finally thank you. On the elevator—you were so brave. You saved us all. You saved my life."

"You would have done the same for me. I just did what any of us would have done."

Karen laughed. "Don't be silly. You were incredible. I've never seen anyone do the things you can do. You were so cool and calm."

"Please! I was terrified!"

"Well, I'd never have known it." Karen put her hand up on the glass. "They won't let me stay—I just wanted you to know. I'll try to come back tomorrow."

"Thanks."

Karen disappeared back down the corridor, prodded along by the attending guard. Sigrid suddenly felt very alone.

She had more visitors that day; Christian came by, muttering several scathing comments about Kimura and their betrayal. Sigrid cautioned him not to say anything that might get him in trouble, but he didn't seem to care.

Selene Tseng came as well. Sigrid hadn't stopped to think about her or what would happen to the *Morrigan*. She'd just assumed that Kimura would confiscate it, claiming it derelict. They had tried, but Selene had stopped them.

"You should take the ship, Selene," Sigrid said. "It doesn't look like I'll be needing it anytime soon."

Selene put her hands on her hips, considering the offer. "Tell you what, I'll take it, but only under a Stewardship. You may find yourself needing it some time in the future."

"It doesn't look like I have much of a future at all."

Selene gave her a reassuring smile. "You're a very remarkable girl, Sigrid. If anyone can figure a way out of this, you can. I'll keep the ship in good order. It will be ready and waiting for you."

The one person who did not visit her was Hitomi Kimura. *'Trust her,'* she'd said. How could the Lady Hitomi allow her to be handed over just like that? But where was she? Sigrid had a terrible thought; if Hitomi's own company had truly turned their back on her, perhaps even the Lady herself was powerless against the influence of the Federation Council. If that were the case, then Sigrid knew to trust herself alone.

She needed to effect her own escape.

They would have to remove her eventually to transfer her to the CTF transport. That's when she would make her move.

They'd be expecting it, but Sigrid was determined. She could not let them take her to Earth.

Sigrid hardly slept for the next few days; it was as if she could feel the CTF transport coming for her, looming ever-closer. The day the ship was to arrive, Sigrid was at her bleakest; she barely looked up from where she lay on her bed when Karen came to see her.

"Hello, *Sigrid*," she said.

There was something odd about the way she'd said her name; there was an urgency in her eyes. Sigrid sat up.

"I wanted to come say goodbye. And I wanted to give you something. It's not much, just a souvenir." Karen took the Ensign insignia off her collar where it was pinned. She started to hand it to Sigrid through the tiny slot in the door, but the guard in attendance rushed over to stop her.

"Wait!" the guard cautioned, grabbing for Karen's hand. "You can't do that. She's not allowed to have anything."

Karen twisted her body, holding the pin out of reach of the guard. "No, it's nothing—it's just a little pin—completely harmless. See?"

The guard glared at her. "Hand it over."

"Please…"

"*Now!*"

The guard held out her hand for the pin, her other hand rested on the handle of her sidearm.

"Oh, all right." Karen looked reluctant, then thrust the pin into the palm of the guard's hand, pressing down firmly. The guard was completely startled and began to protest, but the heavy dose of flunitrazepam entered her system and her eyes rolled back in her head.

Karen eased her to the ground, blinking frantically at Sigrid. "Well—come on!"

Sigrid glanced up at the monitors.

"They're out," Karen said. "We've got two minutes, but we must hurry."

Sigrid tried the door—to her surprise, it slid open for her.

"Lady Hitomi…" Karen breathed in explanation. She was already busy unzipping the guards uniform and pulling it off her.

"Ah…what are you doing?"

Karen looked confused. "I thought…I thought you could wear her clothes as a disguise…"

Sigrid laughed. "I've got something better." She stripped off the paper coverall she wore, even taking off her socks and underwear.

Karen started with embarrassment as Sigrid stood naked before her. "Um…what are you…?" And then she gasped as Sigrid shimmered and disappeared. "Oh my!"

"Come on," Sigrid said, suddenly right next to her, causing Karen to squeal in astonishment.

"Well, aren't you full of surprises." Karen reached out with her hands, touching Sigrid, as if to make sure she was still there for real.

"I could say the same of you. *Careful!* That tickles."

"Sorry."

"You're taking an awful risk doing this."

"You saved my life. I can't stand by and let them do this to you."

Karen led her out into the guard room. There were three security personnel there; two at monitoring stations and one man, a corporal, who appeared to be supervising. Sigrid noticed the younger of the two guards give Karen a subtle, knowing look.

"One moment, Ensign," the corporal's voice boomed out, stopping Karen cold.

She turned, lashes fluttering an innocent *who me?* look. Sigrid rolled her eyes.

"You need to sign out," he explained, extending a pad to her and unfolding it.

"Oh—right."

Karen was about to put her thumb to the pad when one of the guards at the monitor called out, "Sir! She's gone!"

"What?" The corporal turned and headed for the monitor.

Sigrid knew she'd only have a moment before they keyed the alarm. She hurled herself at the corporal, grabbed him by the neck and clocked him hard on the back of the head. He collapsed sack-like to the ground. Sigrid had lost the shrouding effect and the two guards stared in shock at the abrupt sight of the wild, naked girl appearing in front of them. One of the guards rose from his chair, hand moving to his sidearm; Sigrid kicked him in the throat, sending him sprawling. She was on him quickly, jabbing him with her fist, applying pressure exactly as Rosa had drilled into her. He made a gurgling sound and his shoulders drooped. He was out.

The last guard had his hands raised, but Sigrid already knew he'd been the one who had helped them. She walked slowly to him. "Sorry, but this is for your own good."

"No—wait!"

Sigrid sent a measured punch to his mouth; his knees buckled, threatening to give way.

"Ow!" he cried. "Thanks a bunch." He wiped the blood from his torn and swelling lip with the back of his hand

"It'll leave a nice mark, but there'll be no lasting damage—and you still have your teeth…"

"I'll *try* to remember that…"

Karen tossed a set of binders to Sigrid.

The guard, still holding his jaw, looked imploringly at Sigrid. "Oh, *man?*"

"Sorry. But there'll be fewer questions for you."

Karen quickly bound the other two guards and the two girls ran outside, where a large, black ground-car was waiting for them. Sigrid and Karen piled in the back.

"You!" Sigrid cried, staring across at Hitomi Kimura seated opposite them.

"I told you to trust me," Hitomi said, with a broad smile. She tapped the glass that separated them from the driver, and he gunned the car forward. "*No one* harms my girls."

"Here, put these on," Karen said, handing Sigrid a bundle of new clothes.

Sigrid took them; it was a Kimura naval uniform. "Only an *ensign?*" Sigrid said with a wink.

"You're a little young for Captain," Hitomi said, amused.

"Hey—I'm an ensign," Karen protested.

Sigrid chuckled as she dressed quickly in the new Naval uniform while Karen helped tidy her hair, knotting it quickly into a neat bun. She'd just finished buttoning up her collar when the car came to a stop at the security checkpoint off the aerodrome.

"Shhh!" Hitomi cautioned both girls as they saw the fully-armed guard approach the driver-side window. Another guard stood a few feet back, also holding a rifle.

Hitomi lowered her window. "Good evening, Corporal."

"I'm sorry, Lady Hitomi, but the port is closed."

"Closed? Then how on Earth will I get to my ship. I'm due on Crucis in days."

"I'm sorry, Milady. You'll be informed as soon as we return to normal status."

Hitomi pouted her disappointment, causing Sigrid to stifle a laugh.

"Oh—that just won't do. Certainly there must be something you can do. Perhaps if we could contact your superiors. I'm sure Major Grayson would permit us."

"I can make the call, Milady," Sigrid said, opening the door beside her.

The corporal put his hand on the door, slamming it shut again. "Please stay in the car, ma'am. I'm sorry, Lady Hitomi, but you'll have to turn back."

Hitomi looked at him more sternly now. "Now, Corporal—it is *Corporal*, isn't it?" Sigrid saw the color drain from his face. "I have a *very* important engagement on Crucis. You will either allow us to pass or we *will* contact Major Grayson. Certainly whatever orders you have don't pertain to myself or my staff."

The corporal squirmed, considering his options. "Very well—you may contact the Major."

"Of course."

The corporal stepped back and allowed Sigrid to exit the vehicle, then followed her into the little guard booth.

"Oh, my…" Karen said. From her seat she could just make out the muffled sounds of a brief struggle and see a pair of booted-feet fly up into the air. The gate before them clanged open, rolling out of their way.

Sigrid came back and let herself into the car, straightening her hair and tunic. Karen couldn't suppress a snicker. Sigrid gave the girl a wink.

Hitomi tapped the glass and the car sped forward again, speeding across the tarmac past the rows of parked ships. They came to a screeching halt at the pad that held her ship, the

Morrigan; Sigrid felt a strange tingling sensation at seeing the ship again. Her ship.

The first of the alarms sounded as she opened the car door. She glanced back at her two companions. She felt overwhelmed; there was so much she wanted to say to both of them, but there was no time.

"I can't thank either of you enough. You've taken an awful risk in helping me like this. I don't know how you'll be able to explain any of it."

Hitomi laughed. "My dear, this isn't *goodbye.* We're coming with you. Now, help me out of here. They'll be here in a moment."

Karen chuckled at the expression on Sigrid's face, then both girls helped the Lady Hitomi from the car. Hitomi took a moment to thank the driver before he sped quickly off.

"Will he be all right?" Sigrid asked, as they helped Hitomi up the stairs to the ship. They could already hear the sounds of vehicles speeding toward them.

"Oh, they won't give him too much trouble. They can hardly fault a chauffeur for driving his Lady to her ship now, can they?"

Sigrid sealed the ship behind them and they hastened to the bridge; the thrusters were already firing. The *Morrigan* tilted back on its tail before blasting skywards.

Selene greeted them as they helped Hitomi into one of the jump-seats. "Nice to see you again."

Sigrid stared at her companions. She knew she must look ridiculous, but she felt completely overwhelmed. "I—I can't believe you've all done this for me." She thumbed a stray tear from the corner of her eye.

Karen laughed. "Now don't you start or you'll get me going."

"But your career—*your life.* You can't go back."

"Oh, it was just a job." Karen paused, suddenly flustered, and looked quickly to Hitomi. "Sorry, Milady...that came out all wrong."

"That's quite all right. I understand, and you may dispense with the ridiculous title. My Board has relieved me of it. I am merely Kimura by name now."

Sigrid wasn't sure if she'd heard correctly. "Milady...?"

Hitomi frowned. "Yes, it appears I've been *sacked.* It seems the shareholders blame me for the recent attacks. And after our extracurricular activities on Earth...they've seen fit to strip me of my office. My son will head the company now."

"Mistress, I'm so sorry."

"Bah! Think nothing of it. We'll have time enough to lament that later."

Despite her easy dismissal, Sigrid could tell Hitomi was quite annoyed with the firing. It was a betrayal; nothing less than a coup.

The bridge door slid open and Lieutenant Lopez stepped in. Sigrid threw her arms around him. "Christian!"

Her tight embrace winded him; he grunted, exhaling hard.

Sigrid stepped back, embarrassed. "Sorry."

Christian flexed, probing his bruised ribs. "It's okay."

"I still say you're all crazy."

"I think you misunderstand," Hitomi said. "This isn't a *rescue* mission. Sigrid, I need your help."

Sigrid gaped at Hitomi, clueless as to what she was talking about. "Mistress...?"

"I need your help—the help of all of you. I have no intention of letting the Council, or anyone else, take my girls from me. Sigrid, we have to save them."

Chapter 19
Search & Rescue

May 11, 2348

Sigrid stood in the center of what had once been the Academy grounds on Alcyone. Now, all that remained were the burned and collapsed remnants of the school and dormitories. Smoke still wisped up from the blackened piles of lumber and debris. The stench was raw and acrid, threatening to overwhelm Sigrid's sensors.

"Whatever happened here, we missed it," Christian said, waving the small scanner in a horizontal arc. "I can't find any life signs or any energy readings. I'm sorry, Sigrid."

"Thank you, Christian."

The Academy had been attacked, there was little doubt. Dead Kimura Marines lay everywhere, but there was still no sign of the girls, not Suko or any of the young ones. And where was Dr. Garrett? Where was Rosa? If they were hiding, they should be able to get them on the comlink, but Sigrid's only answer was faint static.

"Chesna…" She bent over the woman's body, that still clutched a heavy rifle. Her face was black and caked with blood around her nose and mouth, her eyes open and staring skyward. The macabre sight fed Sigrid's growing sense of dread.

"This was no snatch and grab," Christian said. He picked up a discarded, broken assault rifle from the ground. "They had heavy equipment. Look." He pointed to the tracks on the ground.

Sigrid saw the tracks, but they didn't make any sense; they weren't vehicle tracks, at least none like any she'd ever seen before. These were more like giant foot prints.

"*Mechs*," Christian said. "They had bloody *Mechs*." He tossed the broken rifle to the ground.

Sigrid scanned her database; as far as she could see only Diego Systems were developing prototypes for such a weapon, but those had been little more than walking, armored shells. Her records revealed some scathing reports about the technology; while Diego's claims of the weapon's potential was grand, the project had so far been a disaster; only a few malfunctioning prototypes existed.

"There's no way *Independents* did this," Christian said grimly. "It looks like a whole battalion landed here."

Sigrid nodded. "Come on. We have to keep looking."

She led him through the ruins, out of the Academy grounds and into the woods. The place she sought was a little less than half a kilometer away. This was where the bunker was located, built by the Kimura Engineering Corps during the expansion. If the girls were alive, if they hadn't fled into the woods or been captured or killed, this was the only place they could be. The bunker was perfectly hidden amongst a dense copse of trees with the entrance buried under a deep pile of dirt and leaves.

Sigrid went straight to where the hatch was and stopped dead in her tracks. The camouflage had been cleared away leaving the hatch clearly visible. Like all the girls, she knew the codes, and she tried them now. The door refused to open. She tried several more times, to no avail.

"What is it?" Christian asked. "Is it broken?"

"I'm not sure." Sigrid scanned the hatch mechanism and drew in a sharp breath. Someone, *something,* had completely fused the locking mechanisms. Sigrid pounded her fists on the metal seal. "*Shit!*"

"What?"

"It's been sabotaged! The lock's totally melted away."

"They're not...they're not trapped inside?"

"No. They sealed them *out.*" Frantic, Sigrid scanned the area again, searching desperately for signs of any of them, but nothing turned up in her sensory modes. She tried calling out with her comlink. If the girls were in range, they'd pick up the signal. But there was still nothing. Not even the orbital satellites showed any sign of the girls, or survivors for that matter. Whoever had done this had been brutal and thorough.

Sigrid knew she would kill them.

She tried to remind herself that all wasn't lost—twenty-one of the girls had gotten off the planet before the attacks. They were already well on their way to the assignments that Hitomi had arranged for them. Hitomi had sent word through the Mercenary Guild to Marylyn Lawther to warn them of the danger. She had also asked her to personally look out for the girls who had been assigned to the Naval Academy.

But that didn't change the fact that Suko, seven other girls, forty-two little ones, Dr. Garrett and her staff, were all still missing. Killed or taken from Alcyone? Sigrid could only guess.

Her comlink chimed for her attention, followed by Selene's urgent voice. "*Sigrid, we just spotted four ships coming through the Relay. They're Kimura, and they're on their way.*"

"How long?"

"*Four days, best speed, as far as I can determine.*"

"All right. Thank you, Selene."

"That still gives us time to keep searching," Christian said. "There could still be survivors."

Sigrid wanted to believe him. She scanned for any signs of life, desperate to turn something up, but there was nothing. "They're gone. Everyone here is dead. Selene, you better come pick us up. I'll send you our coordinates."

"*On our way.*"

Within minutes, Selene returned with the *Morrigan*. Their search of the Annex had turned up virtually the same results: death and destruction, but no sign of the girls, and no evidence of who had perpetrated the attack. Not only were the girls gone, but they'd cleaned out the facility; all the servers had been wiped clean of all information pertaining to *Project Andraste*. There was still no sign of Dr. Garrett or her staff.

"Where could they have taken them?" Karen asked.

"We don't even know who took them," Christian said. "There's no way the CTF did this."

"It's Sara," Sigrid said. "At least, it's the people she's with. I'm sure of it."

"But where?" Karen asked.

Sigrid didn't know. But perhaps there was someone who did. Sigrid thought back to the partial message she'd recovered from the CTF offices.

"Tarsus."

Selene looked at her skeptically. "I'm sorry, Sigrid, but I doubt Karl could have organized anything on this scale."

"No, but he knows who did."

Hitomi's eyes lit up. "*Gliese.*"

"What? What is it?" Karen asked.

"It's a message we found," Sigrid said. "It mentioned Tarsus, among other people, Alcyone and…Gliese. This can't be a coincidence. There has to be a connection."

Selene's eyes narrowed. "That *is* where Karl was headed. But would they take your girls there?"

"I don't know, but I think that's where we'll find some answers."

"Gliese it is, then," Selene said, pushing the thrusters to their maximum.

They still had to deal with the four Kimura warships headed their way, standing between them and the Warp Relay. Crewed only by the six of them, the *Morrigan* was in no position to go into battle against such a superior force. Sigrid had assumed they'd employ the ship's new stealth system again, but it hadn't been necessary. Hitomi simply contacted the commander of the task force and explained the situation to him.

"Thank you, Admiral," she said, addressing the officer. "I hope this won't cause too many problems for you back on Aquarii."

The Admiral scoffed at the suggestion. "I have no direct orders instructing me to either detain your ship or apprehend you or your crew, Milady. We were only dispatched to Alcyone to investigate and bring back any survivors. Frankly, I don't think they wanted to put any of us in the position where they'd have to test our loyalties in this matter. You must know the Board's move against you was not greeted with enthusiasm among the Admiralty."

"You are most gracious, Admiral. I must tell you, we found no survivors on Alcyone. But we were a bit pressed for time. I do hope you have better luck than we did."

"Milady—if I may. It's not just the Admiralty…I believe that you may find that there are many still loyal to you back on

Aquarii. Your family helped build that planet. People won't soon forget your many contributions."

Sigrid could hardly believe what she was hearing. She knew that what the Admiral was saying bordered on insurrection.

Hitomi, for her part, brushed it off. "You are more than kind, Admiral. I thank you for the kind thoughts, but for the near future, I fear my path will take me away from Aquarii."

"We will all be looking forward to your return. Good luck in your journeys."

"And to you, Admiral."

Hitomi signed off, and indeed, the Kimura task force allowed them to pass through their ranks and onward to the Warp Relay. In less than four days, the *Morrigan* dropped through the relay to Gliese.

* * *

May 17, 2348

Christian Lopez sat back in his chair in the ship's Mess; his heels rested on the table and he was busy observing Karen as she presented her latest creation to Sigrid.

"It's pink," Christian said.

"It's not *pink*, it's magenta," Karen corrected as she helped Sigrid into her new uniform. Karen had spent the last few days altering Sigrid's special camouflage outfit. The old Kimura colors were gone; the one-piece suit was still largely black, but she'd replaced the Kimura red with a mix of white and *pink* trim. "I think it looks much more flattering—*sporty,* even." Karen seemed quite pleased with her creation.

"It's girly," Christian added.

Sigrid finished pulling the stretchy fabric over herself and fastened her gun belt to her waist.

"Well, as you can see," she said, sweeping an arm before Sigrid, "our ship's Master is indeed a girl." She put her arm through Sigrid's. "And *quite* a girl, at that."

Christian raised a brow. "Well, as long as you're not planning to dress us all in the same colors."

"Well, *I* like it," Sigrid said, pulling a short jacket over her shoulders. "Thank you, Karen."

"You're quite welcome," she said, sticking her tongue out at a bemused Christian.

Selene called them all to the bridge. They were coming up on Gliese fast. Despite its Earth-like appearance, Gliese 581g was more than three times the mass of Earth and much higher in gravity. Its few inhabitants were forced to spend most of their time in the gravity-controlled habitat structures scattered across the surface. Being one of the very first Earth-type planets ever discovered, Gliese had been a curiosity. Pioneers had quickly settled in, but after the discovery of other new planets, all with more forgiving gravities, the planet had largely been abandoned.

"Take us down to the main complex," Sigrid said. "And let's drop a spy-sat, I don't want anyone slipping away without us knowing."

"Aye, ma'am," Selene said, nosing the ship down into the atmosphere; behind them, a tiny satellite, not much bigger than a pea, slipped from the ventral rack mounted on the bottom of the *Morrigan*. The tiny device would monitor all incoming and outgoing traffic from the system, keeping them informed.

Gliese was an ugly, squat-looking world. The trees and vegetation were Earth-like to a degree, but everything seemed stunted, huddled close to the ground. Or so it seemed. As they closed with the surface, Sigrid discovered that the trees she'd thought to be short were massive; like giant mushrooms with stalks ten meters in diameter.

"My God, they're huge!" Karen cried in delight.

Sigrid noticed the huge patches of clear-cut scarring the surface. Her database confirmed, not surprisingly, that logging was Gliese's primary resource and export.

"Just one of those can go for over a million and a half at auction," Hitomi said, pointing at one of the giant trees.

"No doubt," Sigrid gasped. Any type of wood was an extreme rarity on Earth. It was more prized than diamonds.

They descended steadily and landed at the small port using full retro-thrust as a precaution. There was no traffic and there were only three other ships parked on the tarmac. The scene was oddly quiet compared to the few other ports Sigrid had seen.

"At least it shouldn't be hard to find the people we're looking for," Sigrid said as she opened the outer hatch. A strange little vehicle approached from the spaceport and parked next to the ship. A hydraulic lift raised it up to the level of the *Morrigan's* outer hatch where it extended a small gangway. The door opened and a bored-looking man stared out at them.

"Twelve-hundred a head for the lift," he said in greeting, barely acknowledging them.

"Your sales-pitch leaves something to be desired," Hitomi said.

The man shrugged. "You're free to walk—if you don't mind the extra Gs."

"Twelve-hundred!" Sigrid couldn't believe such an outrageous sum. "We're not paying that! It's only 1.4 Gs. We'll walk, thank you very much."

"Speak for yourself," Karen said, and pressed her thumb to the proffered pad. "I'm not as strong as you." She climbed on board. "Come on. It's on me."

Sigrid shot the driver a disapproving look. "Very well."

Selene smiled lightly at the Lady Hitomi. "Begging your pardon, Milady, but it might be best if you remain on board."

"Oh?"

"We might attract less attention without, well…you."

Hitomi considered her words and nodded. "Very well. Young Rodney and I will stay and *guard* the ship."

"Call us if you see anyone snooping around," Sigrid said, stepping into the now crowded little vehicle. The man released the locks and the cab lowered itself jerkily back to ground level and lurched off toward the spaceport.

"It's so empty," Sigrid observed as they walked from the port into the gravity-controlled warrens. There was evidence of what used to be a bustling port town, but those days were long gone.

"And quite filthy," Karen said, scraping something dubious from her shoe. "Urghh, what was that?"

Christian negotiated a rental car. It wasn't much more than an electric cart, but the transportation was welcome. The city was small by planetary standards, but the chain of complexes still covered several hectares.

"So, where do we go?" Christian asked, seated at the controls.

Sigrid chewed on her thumbnail. Her plan had been to get here, but after that—she was so desperate, she had to admit she hadn't thought it through. "There must be some kind of registration office—immigration, or something."

Selene barked a laugh. "Not here, sister."

Sigrid slumped. *What then—drive around?*

"Why not start at the most obvious spots?" Selene suggested. She eyed the man who'd just rented them the transport. "Hey, buddy. Know where a girl can get a drink?"

Once Sigrid had adequately greased the merchant's pad, he directed them to several establishments. They went from pub to pub, each seeming to outdo the previous in seediness and decrepitness as they moved further away from the port. All the while, Sigrid gently charmed or bribed the clientele for information. Her meager funds were growing short and they'd still found no one with any information on the whereabouts of either Tarsus or the girls, but some of the barflies *had* heard about the girls.

"You! You're one of them," the man Sigrid was currently interviewing said.

"And just how is it that you know about them?" Christian asked; he was losing his patience now. He grabbed the man by the collar.

"Me? I know nothing. I only know what Karl told me." Terror had taken residence in the little man's eyes. He looked at Christian, then at Sigrid. "Please! I'm telling you everything. He was here—but he left weeks ago."

"*Weeks?*" Sigrid couldn't believe it. *They'd been so close…*

"Two—maybe three," he wheezed, clutching at Christian's hands.

"Alone?"

"No—there were men. They took him."

"Took him? You mean, he left with them?"

The man gulped. "If by that you mean at gunpoint, then yes."

"What men?" Christian asked. "Where did they go?" He tightened his grip momentarily.

"I—don't know. I never saw them before. They came in on a ship. Please…"

Sigrid put her hand on Christian's. "It's all right. He's telling the truth. He doesn't know." Sigrid cursed silently; she still couldn't believe they'd missed Tarsus by so little time.

Christian frowned. "With all due respect, how can you tell he's not lying?"

Selene chuckled. "Oh—she knows..."

It wasn't much help, but it was their first lead. The frightened little man was also able to direct them to Tarsus' favorite watering hole—a peeler bar out on the farthest edge of the complex. The pink, painted walls of the modular habitat structure stood out like a beacon as they approached, with its gaudy neon postures of women and men in various states of undress glowing above the darkness.

"I should have known," Selene said as they parked.

Sigrid had to give more funds to the doorman. "Welcome to Paradise," he said, handing them over to a bubbly hostess who escorted them to a table.

"Well, at least we know where everyone is," Christian shouted over the din as he looked around the crowded bar. The *Paradise* was packed with patrons, waitresses, dancers female and male. There had to be close to 400 people there.

Sigrid scanned the room, taking stock of the many patrons. None stood out. She was struck by the dull, complacent looks of the men who sat passively as women, and sometimes men, danced for them at their tables and private booths. The mood was markedly subdued and quite in contrast to the driving music that came from the sound system.

Everything Sigrid heard was seemingly performed by a single, lone woman on a small stage. She was seated before what looked like a piano and surrounded by banks of computers. Sigrid couldn't believe such a powerful voice could come from such a small package; her presence pervaded the room as she sang out, resting one of her heels on the edge of the keyboard. She was clad in little more than a transparent plastic bikini and knee-high boots with preposterous heels. Her long, full hair had to be a wig; a bright yellow affair topped with a tall hat in the shape of a—Sigrid zoomed in to make sure—yes, a unicorn.

"Goodness."

The dancers and hostesses mingled freely, their skimpy outfits providing the patrons with a plethora of exposed flesh. Sigrid wondered how many of them were working under indentured contracts like herself, well, as she had been. She wasn't really sure what her status was anymore.

"Oh, my..." Karen gasped as their waiter approached. He wore no shirt, and the thin fabric of his tight pants highlighted his *manly* attributes handsomely.

"Ladies—gentleman," he offered in warm greeting. "What will be your pleasure?"

Karen burbled out their drink orders, making a point of stuffing an actual paper credit note in his trousers.

"Where did you get that?" Sigrid said. She'd never seen paper money.

Karen pointed to a dispenser by the door. "They sell them! Here..." she handed a stack to Sigrid, and more to Selene. "You'll want some. Trust me."

Christian frowned. "I thought we were here for information, not to ogle men."

Selene chuckled and leaned close, rasping into his ear over the noise, "In a place like this, who do you think we'll be talking to? If Tarsus was here, it's the dancers who'll know."

"Good point," Christian conceded, taking a stack of bills from Karen.

They had no trouble soliciting attention from the array of dancers who trawled each and every table. Once word got out they were asking about Tarsus—and paying—they all made a point of stopping by.

Sigrid showed a picture of Tarsus to a young dancer who went by the name of Cherry Bomb. She had dark, wavy hair that fell all the way down to the small of her back. Like all the dancers, she wore the flimsiest of outfits, the gossamer material of her bikini left little to the dullest of imaginations. Sigrid stuffed another bill into her bra.

"I remember Karl," Cherry said.

Sigrid felt her cheeks flush hot as Cherry melted onto her lap and wrapped her arms around her neck. The girl's voice was soft and low, and she kept her lips close to Sigrid's ear, taking care not to shout.

"Karl never came in here with anyone, but there were always people here looking for him."

"These people—would he meet with them?"

Nodding to Sigrid's question, her hair fell forward, brushing against her cheek. "From time to time. I don't think he liked them very much though. He was always...tense afterward."

"And you know the names of these men?"

Cherry's only answer was another sway of her hips and a sweet bat of her long lashes. Sigrid sighed and stuffed another credit note into her bra. "No, but I bet I know someone who does."

Sigrid didn't wait, stuffing more credits into her panties this time.

Cherry gestured toward the stage. "Talk to Honey Dew. Tarsus was always hanging out over there. I think he liked her music."

Christian snorted. "I'll bet."

"No, I mean it. I think he really was a fan. *Everyone* knows Honey. Trust me. Hang out here long enough, and Honey gets to everyone."

The song ended and Cherry extracted herself from Sigrid's lap. "Don't be a stranger," she said, giving her a wink and blowing her a kiss before retreating into the darkened bar.

"Is it wrong that I found that hot?" Christian asked.

Karen swatted him on the shoulder. "Come on," she said, taking Sigrid's hand and leading her through the crowd.

The four of them made their way to the stage just as Honey finished one of her songs. Sigrid waved and called out, "Honey!"

Honey smiled down at them from the stage. "One sec, sweetie." Honey made some quick adjustments to one of her computers, queuing up a particularly raunchy tune. She sat down at the edge of the stage, swinging her legs over the side. "There. That should keep them happy for a while. Now, what can I do for you?"

"We were looking for Karl Tarsus. We heard you knew him."

Honey stiffened at the mention of Tarsus' name; the color drained from her face. She took a quick look around before leaning close. "Karl's gone. You should leave now."

Honey stood up abruptly, but Sigrid reached out and grabbed her hand. "Please. It's very important. We're just trying to find our friends."

"I have to go. My shift is over." Honey pulled at Sigrid's hand, but Sigrid held tight. Seeing the distress on Honey's face, Sigrid suddenly felt a pang of guilt. It wasn't her intention to frighten the girl.

Sigrid felt a meaty hand on her shoulder. She turned to face the large bouncer behind her.

"Don't touch the talent, Miss."

Sigrid let go of Honey and watched her scurry off backstage.

The bouncer folded his thick arms across his chest. "I'm afraid you'll have to leave now, you and your party."

"But—"

Sigrid's protests were greeted by the arrival of two more bouncers.

"We'd better go," Selene cautioned.

Sigrid didn't bother to resist; there was no point in starting a brawl. They had definitely struck a chord with Honey. The question now, was how to get the girl to talk.

Chapter 20
Robots

May 17, 2348

Suko and Khepri looked up as the door to their cell rattled open.

"Lei-Fei!" Suko said, scrambling to her feet. She would have given the girl a hug had her hands not still been bound behind her back. Suko sensed something was wrong and stopped cold. Lei-Fei regarded her with a blank stare. There was no warmth in her eyes, no recognition. She was now dressed in a grey coverall and she was *armed*. "Lei-Fei...?"

Lei-Fei pushed her roughly, making Suko stumble backward against the wall.

"Please stay back. I don't want to hurt you."

Suko looked down in confusion at Khepri.

"They did it to her too," Khepri said, tearfully. "Tara, Christi...they did it to all of them."

"Did what?" She had no idea what Khepri meant.

"Freed them," Riku said as he entered the cell; Riku was followed by his guards in their mechanized armor.

Suko's PCM and some of her sensory modules were functioning again and she scanned Lei-Fei, but it was all wrong. "Lei-Fei? Are you...Lei-Fei!"

But Lei-Fei merely stared back vacantly; the girl she knew was gone. Suko turned to her brother, seething. "I'll kill you for this."

Riku raised his hands in a calming gesture. "It's not what you think. I can explain everything Suko. I'll show you. Come with me."

Suko backed away, looking fearfully at Lei-Fei.

Lei-Fei extended her hand to her. "We mean you no harm."

The voice was hers, but the inflection was all wrong, *and her eyes… no way was she going to let them do that to her…*

"Suko, it will be all right. I promise."

With her hands bound behind her back, Suko could put up little fight as the two soldiers dragged her out of the cell. They carried her up several levels to a brightly lit room that looked to have been set up as a makeshift medical facility. An operating table was set up in the middle of the room, complete with restraints. Banks of monitors surrounded the table, and several technicians were seated there, making preparations. Suko noticed the older woman sitting on the edge of a table in the corner, observing from lowered eyes. She didn't know who she was, but it was clear—this was the woman in charge.

Suko dug her heels into the ground, struggling against the metal hands that gripped her. "No…" she screamed. The soldiers picked her up bodily and dumped her on the table, face down, while they cut the binders from her. Suko struggled in vain as they flipped her over and fastened her into the restraints.

Riku watched the doctor warily. There was a warning chill in his eyes. "You can't fuck this one up, Farrington. This is my sister."

The woman in the corner stood up. "She's not your sister anymore. She's a drone."

Riku glared at her. "And this will bring her back?"

Dr. Farrington looked at him, not bothering to disguise his anger. "If you don't trust me, then get Doctor Garrett in here. Or can she walk yet?"

Suko felt the panic well up in her. "Riku, don't do this…"

Farrington moved toward her with a long metal wire, reaching toward the access port behind her ear. He smoothed her hair out of the way and moved the wire closer, but Suko jerked her head back.

"Dammit—hold her," Farrington hissed at the guards.

Suko felt the tears on her cheeks. "Riku, please…"

Riku grabbed Farrington by the arm. "I want your assurances this time."

Farrington looked at the hand on his arm and then to the woman in the corner.

Nicola sighed, heavily. "Dammit, Riku. Let him do his job."

Before Riku could respond, the door burst open and a frazzled-looking woman came running in. "Sir—ma'am...!" she gasped, trying to catch her breath.

"What?" Nicola barked, irritated at yet another interruption.

"We're...we're under attack," she said. "It's the CTF."

All of them froze.

"Mother fu..." Nicola was on her feet in an instant, running toward the door. She turned back, shouting a command to the guards. "Take the girl back to her cell. We'll take care of her later."

"I can *handle this*," Farrington said, annoyed.

"*Later*, Joseph. Not till I get back. Come on, Riku. We've got work to do."

* * *

"I can't believe it," Sigrid said as she continued pacing around the small hotel room they'd rented.

"She knows something," Karen said. "She's scared."

"Maybe scared of us," Christian suggested.

"We're not done yet," Selene said, leaning forward on her chair. "Trust me. A lot of people saw us asking questions today. This is a small settlement; people will talk."

"So, we wait?" Sigrid asked.

"At least a day or so. Tomorrow, we should split up. We can cover more ground."

"I want to stay on that girl," Sigrid said. "I don't think we should let her out of our sight."

Christian sat up. "I'm happy to go back to the club."

Karen swatted him again.

"I'm just saying..."

"What about the other complexes?" Karen said. "Maybe one of us should take the ship?"

Selene shook her head. "No. Tarsus was here, and this is where the port is. If anyone came for him, this is where they got him."

Sigrid grabbed her coat from the bed and headed for the door.

"Where are you going?" Karen asked, sitting up.

"Out. You guys stay here and get some rest."

Christian leapt up. "I'm coming with you. You're not going out alone. It's too dangerous."

Sigrid had to smile at his protectiveness but knew he'd only get in the way. "I'll be all right. I want to make a visit to the port's records office. I want to check the transit logs."

Karen glanced at her watch. "But—they'll be closed!... Oh...right."

"I highly doubt that whoever took Tarsus left an accurate flight plan," Selene said.

Sigrid knew Selene was probably right, but she had to check. She desperately needed a lead. Mostly, she wanted to get out and at least feel like she was doing something. "I won't be long."

Sigrid opened the door—the two girls leaning against it from the other side stumbled forward.

"Honey! Cherry!" Sigrid said, catching both of them in a neat sweep of her arms.

Even in their street clothes, and without the outlandish costumes, Sigrid recognized the women from the *Paradise*. They were breathing heavily and seemed quite panicked.

"You totally fucked my gig," Honey said, shooting a frightened glance over her shoulder. Sigrid pulled them inside and closed the door.

"It was my fault," Cherry said, clutching Honey's arm. "I never should have said anything. I was scared—"

Honey put a reassuring hand on the girl's cheek. "Don't blame yourself, Cherry. You didn't know."

"What happened?" Sigrid asked.

Honey's eyes darted nervously over the other people in the room before she answered. "Your little *question and answer* session got quite a bit of attention today. You got us fired."

"Oh, my...I'm so sorry," Sigrid said.

"Save the sympathy," Honey said. "The men you're looking for—the ones who took Karl...they're not nice men."

Sigrid helped them both to a chair and Karen brought glasses of water for the two performers.

"Do you have anything stronger?" Honey asked.

Karen shook her head, but Christian took a hip flask from his pocket and handed it to her. She clutched it in both her hands and took several gulps before handing it to Cherry, who stared at it skeptically.

"Thanks," Honey said, starting to level out.

"The men...?" Sigrid urged.

"I'll tell you what I know, but you have to promise to take me with you."

"And me! We want out of this hellhole," Cherry said.

"Of course," Karen said. "We'll take you anywhere you like." She turned to Sigrid and winked. "We will, won't we?"

Sigrid nodded.

"All right—I saw three of them. They came by after you were gone...I remembered the one because he had this thing..." Honey pointed to the top of her head.

"He was bald—and there was this mole," Cherry added. Honey glared at her. "Sorry—you tell it."

"Karl met with them several times. I could always tell...these were not fun meetings..."

"Who were they?" Sigrid asked, frustration setting in. "Did you get their names?"

Honey shook her head.

Cherry sat up. "Ooo! There was one. Karl used to talk about him a lot."

"Who?"

"I don't think he liked him very much. He always got quite angry when he talked about him."

"*Who!*"

"Sorry—ah, I think he called him *Sven*, or something."

Honey swatted her on the arm. "It was *Smith*. That's who he was always bitching about."

Selene and Sigrid looked to each other.

"*Smith,* are you sure? Did you see him?" Selene asked.

Honey shook her head. "Sorry. But I'm sure that's who Karl said they worked for."

Cherry nodded agreement. "Definitely."

Sigrid looked at them intently. "Do you know where they took him?"

"They were asking questions. I told them I didn't tell you anything. Karl...he only hung out there. He liked to talk—he tipped well."

"*Really* well," Cherry added.

"*Where?*" Sigrid asked, more urgently. "Honey, please. It's very important. You have to tell us where they took Major Tarsus."

"*I don't know!* I told them the same thing, but they didn't believe me. They were waiting outside our apartment. I think they followed us here."

Cherry's eyes went wide. "They're going to kill us."

Sigrid's pistol was in her hand, and she moved quickly toward the door.

Selene stood up, gathering her few things. "We should get out of here quickly."

Sigrid nodded. "You guys get to the ship. I'll be there shortly."

Karen gasped. "Us? What about you?"

Sigrid studied Honey for a second. "We're about the same size, don't you think?"

* * *

Honey wasn't that much bigger than Sigrid, but she still had to keep tugging up on the girl's skirt to keep it from slipping down over her waist. The jacket and shirt were a bit baggy, but anyone spying from a distance shouldn't notice, especially with Honey's wig and dark glasses. Karen had done a masterful job making her up in such short order. Unless someone got up close, they should think Sigrid was Honey Dew—she hoped.

Sigrid made her way back toward the habitat section of the Port Complex, all the while scanning the streets for the men that had followed Cherry and Honey. She'd picked them up almost instantly as she left the hotel, much to her relief. *Odd to feel relieved about being stalked,* Sigrid thought, stifling a laugh. The men kept their distance, spread out behind her and across the street. They weren't doing much to conceal themselves, causing a moment of doubt, perhaps she wasn't being followed. *Could they really be this obvious?* She changed her course several times, crossing the street and cutting through a narrow lane, but the men stayed with her. She was definitely being tailed.

She was almost outside Honey and Cherry's apartment, wondering when the men would make their move, if at all, when the man in the lead picked up his pace, getting closer. His two companions remained further back about 25 meters away. Sigrid frowned; it would be simple enough to take them all out, but the plan wasn't to kill them. She needed them alive enough to answer questions, and that would be difficult with them all spread out. Honey's apartment presented the answer. It was just across the transit lane and Sigrid picked up her pace, not quite running across the street, but stepping lively in Honey's high-heeled boots.

The man behind her ran to keep up, crossing behind Sigrid just as she slipped through the doors to the apartment complex. She hurried up the stairs to the second level and let herself into the girls' room. The place was a royal mess, with clothing strewn and hung everywhere, some looking more like decorations than outfits. Sigrid spent a moment taking a quick look around, but apart from a selection of rather daring undergarments and empty food wrappers, Sigrid found nothing.

Now it was up to her pursuers. Sigrid flipped off the lights and lay down on the lone bed, pulling the blankets around her. Minutes went by and she decided she might have miscalculated. She'd been expecting the men to follow her up to the unit, but they seemed to be waiting. If they doubled-back, then this ruse had all been for naught. Sigrid cursed. She should have tried to take them in the street. She started to get up when she sensed the movement outside; her thermal optics picked up the shapes of the three men moving toward the door. Sigrid heard one of them working the hacking device in the lock. She lay her head back down, leaving her eyes open barely a slit.

The door opened and she listened, breathless, as they crept toward the bed. Sigrid saw the gloved hand reach down to cover her mouth. She screamed and struggled against the arms that reached out to restrain her—not too hard she hoped, just enough to be convincing.

"Keep her quiet!" one of the men whispered urgently.

"I'm trying…"

Sigrid eased her struggles, staring at the three men with what she hoped was the right amount of fear in her eyes, all the while studying them, ascertaining their intent.

What she saw surprised her immensely. In her years at the Academy, and in her short time as Mercenary with Kimura, Sigrid had been a little awed by the professionalism and training of her instructors and the men and women who served in the Kimura forces. But these men looked about as frightened as she was pretending to be.

"We're not going to hurt you," the first man said. "We just need to know who those people are, the ones you were with. You tell us—we go."

Sigrid shook her head frantically, letting the tears flow from her eyes.

"You're still holding her mouth, idiot. How's she supposed to answer?" the one in the back said; Sigrid decided to label him *Target Three*.

"If I let her go, she'll scream."

Target Two thrust his hands into his pockets. "This is ridiculous. Why the fuck did they leave us here for this? I told them I wasn't going to hurt anyone."

Target Three punched him in the shoulder. "Don't tell her that, you numnut."

"Will you two shut up!" *Target One* hissed through gritted teeth.

Sigrid saw *Two's* eyes narrow, looking at her more closely. "Hey...are you sure we got the right girl?"

"What the...?" *Target One* mouthed as he looked more closely at Sigrid.

Sigrid knew her disguise wasn't sufficient to stand up to close scrutiny; it had worked so far because they'd kept the lights off. It didn't matter. She'd heard enough.

As they leaned closer to her, Sigrid pulled her hand out of her pocket and thumbed the little gas grenade she held between her fingers.

* * *

Sigrid and Karen stared at the three new prisoners in the *Morrigan's* brig. They painted a miserable picture, sitting there in their boxer-briefs as they continued to scowl at Sigrid. But Sigrid wanted more information, and it was time to find out where they'd taken Tarsus, who had taken Suko, and why.

"We've answered your questions," *One* said. "Now will you give us our clothes back, or what?"

"Not quite," Sigrid said. "These men, the ones who left you on Gliese—"

"We told you. We never met them before."

"And yet, you followed their orders?" Sigrid asked, skeptically.

"Nicola—Kirk…she told us to," *Two* pleaded.

"And this woman, Kirk, she's your leader?"

"Nicola's a great woman," *Two* said. Sigrid could see him begin to unravel. "This is crap. This whole thing's out of hand. This was supposed to be a nonviolent movement. It's not her fault. Everything was fine until *he* came."

Three glared at his companions. "Will you *stop* talking! Don't say anything else. They're nothing but a bunch of Federation stooges."

Sigrid raised an eyebrow. "Federation? You think we're with the CTF?"

"If you're not, then you're working for them," *Three* said.

"We could say the same of you," Karen said, wagging her finger at them.

Three laughed. "You Feds are all the same, nothing but a bunch of butchers."

"We're not with the CTF…or anyone," Sigrid assured them. "I'm just trying to find my friends."

Three eyed her warily. "You're one of *them,* aren't you. He warned us about you."

Karen poked her head out from behind Sigrid, scowling hard. "You tell us who you're working with…or…or we'll throw you out the airlock!"

Sigrid smiled. "That's not a bad idea."

Karen looked surprised. "Really?"

Sigrid drew one of her pistols, motioning the three of them to exit. "Come on. All of you."

Karen opened her mouth and raised a correcting finger. "But, we're still—"

Sigrid elbowed her in the side.

Karen grunted, but she seemed to get Sigrid's meaning. She did her best to look menacing and pointed toward the lower airlock. "Come on, you...*you*."

Two shook visibly and had a wild glaze in his eyes. "You can't be serious."

Sigrid shoved him down the corridor, putting her boot to the others.

Three gave her a defiant look. "I told you. You're all butchers." He looked to his companions as Sigrid opened the inner door to the airlock and shoved him inside. "Don't tell her anything!"

"This is your last chance," Sigrid said. "Tell me where they took my friends and I let you go."

Three spat defiantly. "The Federation is doomed. You're fucked. You won't get away with this!"

Sigrid cycled the lock, sealing him in. There was a frantic pounding on the door until Sigrid opened the outer door. *One* fainted and slithered to the floor in a heap.

Two stood blinking at Sigrid, completely terrified. "Scorpii! They're on Scorpii. I don't know much more, but that's where the base is. I don't even know if that's where they took Tarsus. You have to believe me!"

Sigrid grabbed him by the collar, moving him toward the lock. "*Who* are *they*? Why did they take them?"

He shook his head. "I don't know. This was a peaceful movement but the Federation...the embargoes are killing us. Then *they* came—"

"*Who?*"

"I thought they were Mercs, but I don't know. They had ships, weapons; the technology..." He shook his head. "I've never seen anything like it."

"How many ships?"

"*I don't know!* They don't tell us anything anymore. I told Nicola she was making a mistake. There's a man—I don't know his name—he came to us a few years ago. He's the one you want."

Sigrid knew he was telling the truth. He was scared witless and he'd wet himself. She felt a fleeting pang of guilt for what she'd done, but she had the information she needed. She keyed her comlink. "It's Scorpii, Selene. I want to be underway as soon as possible."

The airlock opened and Christian came through holding a very angry-looking *Three* by the arm. "I found this guy outside. Who the hell let him out?"

Two gaped at his companion. "You...you're alive!"

"We're still on the ground, idiot."

Karen covered her mouth with her hand but couldn't hold back her laughter.

Once *Two*, whose real name turned out to be Gene Wehr, started talking, he didn't seem to know how to stop. Sigrid let him clean himself up and gave him his clothes back, before taking him to the Mess for some food and coffee. He'd met the woman, Nicola Kirk, five years ago on his home planet of Hekate. As a student growing up on the impoverished world, he'd been frustrated by the Federation's treatment of his home planet. He'd met Nicola and eagerly joined her movement. But what had once been a peaceful protest movement had grown exponentially into what was quickly becoming a full-scale rebellion.

"And the bombings?" Sigrid asked; she remembered the terrorist attack she'd witnessed on Earth, and the ones that were so much in the news.

Gene scoffed. "Terrorists! We're not terrorists. Ask the Council about the so-called terrorist attacks."

"What do you mean?"

"It's an old tactic, Miss..."

"Sigrid."

"It's an old tactic, Sigrid. They bomb their own people, blame us and garner sympathy. We're not killers."

Sigrid wasn't impressed. "I saw the bodies on Alcyone. You might want to tell them that."

Gene frowned. "This is all so out of hand."

"And you *are* kidnappers."

"I don't know anything about that. I'm not exactly in the 'loop' anymore. That's why they stuck me on Gliese. I—*we*—were just supposed to watch for anyone snooping around and report."

Sigrid rose, putting her mug back in the recycler.

"If you're really not with the CTF, then what will you do with us?"

Sigrid hadn't thought that part through. "I suppose we'll let you go. As soon as we make port somewhere."

"Let us go? Just like that?"

Sigrid didn't answer.

"We could be allies in this. If you're telling the truth, if you're really not with the CTF."

"I only care about my friends, Mr. Wehr."

Sigrid left him there and headed toward the bridge. She was shocked to find the Lady Hitomi working her chair onto the airlock lift; she had a small suitcase balanced on her lap.

"Mistress?"

"Ah, Sigrid—I was going to send for you."

"Where are you going?"

"I'm afraid I have some urgent business to attend to."

"Here? We're not leaving you on Gliese."

"I'll be quite all right—and I'm not staying here. I've arranged for transport."

"Where?"

Hitomi gave her a reassuring smile. "Don't you worry about that. There is little I can do for you on Scorpii. You'll be fine. I'll be of far more use to you where I am headed. There are still the other girls to think of."

"I can't let you go off on your own!"

Hitomi chuckled. "I'll be quite all right, dear."

"But—" Sigrid found herself dreading the idea of Hitomi leaving her.

"Go to Scorpii, Sigrid. Save our girls. Save your sisters. They need you. *I* need you to do that."

Sigrid swallowed and nodded. "Of course, Hitomi-san."

"When you get them, I need you to take them here." Hitomi handed her a pad, detailing the coordinates she wanted Sigrid to jump to. "It's very important. No matter what happens, whether you succeed or not. You *must* travel to these coordinates."

"Of course, Mistress."

"And Sigrid, if you can, as a personal favor to me—please find Dr. Garrett. She's…Lisa…she's very dear to me."

"I'll do everything I can, Hitomi-san."

"That's all I can ask. Good luck, Sigrid. And whatever happens, I just want you to know how proud I am of you, and how glad I am that we met."

Sigrid wasn't sure how to respond so she remained silent as she watched Hitomi exit the airlock and lower herself on the lift to the tarmac. And then she was gone. Sigrid was still considering Hitomi's words as she sealed the lock and keyed her comlink to the bridge. "Take us up, Ms. Tseng."

Chapter 21
Scorpii

Nicola Kirk stood in the monitoring station of the abandoned mining facility. She was surrounded by a strange mix of soldiers in their mechanized armor and some very *non-military-looking* types, manning the assemblage of consoles.

One large monitor had been mounted on a stand in one of the corners. Nicola stared at it now, worrying a well-chewed thumbnail. She couldn't take her eyes off the task force of four CTF Naval ships that were marked and moving across the screen.

"I don't think they've seen us," the young woman seated before her at her station said.

The task force had just entered the system and was headed toward Scorpii IV; it would take them the better part of four days to reach the planet. The once-habitable world had been stripped clean of all things valuable by overeager corporations long ago. The planet had been bled-dry and then laid to waste during the first of the Corporate Wars as the giant multinationals had fought to seize control of the planet's riches. That had been decades ago, before the Federation and the Council had decided to extend their reach to planets further afield. They'd used 'peace' as an excuse, but Nicola knew it was all a question of control, of commerce, of power and profit.

Scorpii was a fitting location for her movement, she thought.

The CTF forces would find their old facilities on Scorpii, but she'd anticipated that and moved virtually everything out to one of the larger asteroids that orbited between Scorpii V and VI months ago.

"Let me know if their status changes," she told the young woman.

A major in full combat gear approached her, helmet clutched under his arm. "All our ships are in position. Say the word and we'll move in. They won't know what hit them."

Nicola winced; these military-types were always so eager for a scrap. There was a good chance the CTF ships would simply leave after finding their old base abandoned. The task force would most likely turn around and leave without the need to fire a shot. On the other hand, she had twelve ships at her disposal, and a mercenary force that was spoiling for some action. *Should she order them to attack?* Nicola laughed to herself. Farrington had said she was a closet-general. Perhaps he was right.

"Very well, Major. You may engage them. Just…we can't let even a single pod escape. I don't want anyone reporting on our position."

The major nodded and smiled broadly, eager for the chance to engage the enemy. "Yes, ma'am. We'll take care of them."

* * *

From the bridge of the *Morrigan*, Sigrid looked out at the giant Warp Relay before them; they were still decelerating hard, the distance closing quickly. Selene transmitted the navigational codes to the Relay Monitor. Sigrid watched quietly as the giant construct aligned itself.

"We're clear to jump once the transaction is complete," Selene said.

No one could travel through the Relay without first paying the huge tolls charged by Daedalus. Sigrid leaned forward to key in her account access; it would take a sizable portion of the money Lady Hitomi had transferred to her.

"And don't you think you should take your seat?" Karen asked, eyeing the empty command chair.

Sigrid still felt uncomfortable with the idea of sitting in it; her crew were looking at her expectantly. *What was she afraid of?* Scorpii lay ahead on the other side of the Relay. The girls were there. Suko was there.

Sigrid slid slowly into the chair; it felt surprisingly comfortable.

"It looks good on you," Karen said brightly.

Sigrid felt her cheeks glow warmer; she shook her head and smiled at the lively ensign.

"Begging your pardon, Sig...*Captain*..." Selene said. "But do we have a plan for this? We don't exactly know what we're flying into here."

A plan? So far, she'd been propelled along, either by the wishes of her masters or by the inertia of events unfolding around her. Did she have a plan?

Gene had told them much of Scorpii; his group had a base on one of the larger asteroids, nestling in an old mining facility. There were only a few hundred people there, mostly workers and students from Hekate, but they had been joined by a paramilitary group backed by a wealthy friend and patron of Nicola Kirk's. His involvement had been the catalyst that had seen their protest movement move from peaceful demonstrations to full-scale military engagements.

It had to be *Smith.*

As for having a plan...? Sigrid closed her eyes and thought for a moment. "What will happen if we engage the stealth systems going through the Relay?"

"It shouldn't affect anything," Christian said. "Travel through the Relays is more contingent on mass, inertia, velocity and our entrance vector. I don't see how the cloak will affect that."

Selene let out a long breath. "It does expend a tremendous amount of energy. If it causes some kind of feedback as we enter the effect..."

Christian did some quick calculations on his console. "I see only a small chance of that being a possibility."

"Small? How small is small?" Selene asked, furrowing her brow.

"A little over four percent."

Karen swallowed hard. "But...what would happen—"

"We could end up on the wrong side of the Galaxy," Selene said.

Christian stroked his chin. "More likely, any energy discharge would simply disrupt the Relay."

"You mean, we might break it?" Sigrid asked.

He nodded. "Quite likely."

Selene laughed. "So, either we get trapped somewhere across the galaxy or we get trapped here."

Sigrid considered her options. "Wehr told us how many ships they have there. He figures they'll have between fourteen and twenty ships guarding that base. If we fly straight in, they'll see us. We can't take on an entire fleet."

Christian plunked an elbow down on his console, leaning heavily on his hand. "Well, isn't this fun."

Sigrid sat quietly, calculating the different scenarios. "Either way, it's a gamble, but we have to make the best of the cards we hold. Engage the stealth, Lieutenant Lopez. Ms. Tseng…take us to Scorpii."

* * *

Captain Samson Potter stood on the bridge of his ship, the flagship of the large task force that was currently pursuing the four CTF Naval ships inbound for Scorpii IV. They'd been accelerating toward the force for nearly three days, coming in on a vector that had completely cut the CTF ships off from the Relay behind them. They were cornered and trapped. He'd been somewhat surprised when the CTF ships had not turned to engage; they were still hanging there in orbit around the dead planet. He'd expected them at the very least to bring their ships up to speed to try to match the velocity of his attacking force. But instead they'd remained parked in orbit. *They were sitting ducks.*

Knowing that didn't make Captain Potter feel any better; he'd learned long ago that when an enemy, especially a cornered one, didn't do the expected, then there was a good chance that *he* was the one who was being cornered. Right now, Potter could feel all the hairs on his neck bristling.

"Break off," Captain Potter, said to his helm. "All ships disengage."

"Sir?" his XO asked. She shook her head in complete disbelief. "We have them!"

"Break off. All ships, 180 degrees about. Maximum acceleration."

His XO took a deep breath, but acknowledged the command.

"Sir!" the tactical officer cut in. "We've got ships in system—coming in from the Relay."

And so the trap was sprung. "How many?"

The face of his tactical officer turned white as a sheet. "Thirty-two."

Potter laughed.

"Sir?"

"They played us," he said. "They drew us out, and we took the bait. We showed them *exactly* where the base is." Potter slammed his hand on the arm of his chair. "What's the vector on those ships? Are they attacking?"

"They're splitting into two groups, sir. Some heading for the mining facility, the rest look to be engaging us."

"How many?"

"Twenty-eight, sir—headed toward us. Four moving to engage the base."

Thirty-two ships against his task force of twelve. Now he was the one surrounded. It was a goddamn ambush.

Captain Potter sighed grimly. "Get the crews to their Pods. Let's prepare for battle."

* * *

"How many?" Sigrid asked. What she'd heard didn't seem possible.

"Thirty-two in total," Christian said. "They came through the Relay right behind us."

"But how?" Karen asked. "How could they have followed us?"

"They didn't," Selene said. "There were no ships in-system at Gliese. Their exit vector doesn't match ours either. Wherever they came from, they didn't follow us."

"So, we just walked into a full scale invasion?" Christian said.

"It would appear so."

Sigrid peered over Christian's shoulder at the tactical monitor; four of the ships from the CTF forces had peeled off from the main force and seemed to be following them in. "Do they see us? Is our cloak still engaged?"

Selene nodded. "Yes. I don't think they see us—but the harder we push our engines the more the cloak drains us. If we're not careful we won't have enough in reserve to get back through the Relay."

Sigrid opened a channel to her engineer. "Rodney, how long can we maintain the stealth field?"

"As long as you're not planning any crazy maneuvers, I should be able to hold it. It would be great if we could ease off though. I don't like some of these readings."

Sigrid grimaced. "And if we slow, those ships behind us will overtake us. How far behind us are they?"

Selene checked her readouts. "They exited the Relay about two-point-four hours behind us. We're still faster. If we keep accelerating at this pace, we should increase that gap to nearly five hours by the time we reach the facility."

"What kind of ships are those?"

"Two troop carriers with destroyer escort."

Two troop carriers against her crew of five...? Sigrid had a thought. "How many mines do we have aboard?"

Christian's eyes lit up. He smiled. "Six, ma'am."

"Well, let's see if we can even the odds somewhat."

"Yes, ma'am."

Christian and Selene worked diligently to coordinate the mine-laying, dropping five into the paths of the oncoming CTF ships that were so close on their tail. Then it was just a matter of waiting the few hours for the ships to catch up. With luck, the four pursuing vessels would be snared, much in the same way that the *Agatsuma* had been.

While they waited, Sigrid spent her time grilling Gene Wehr on everything he knew about the mining facility, piecing together a map and committing everything to her PCM. It wouldn't be accurate, but it would hopefully save her some time once they landed. That wouldn't be for another two days.

At least the main CTF Force was engaged with the...Sigrid laughed to herself. What should she call them? The Hekatians? The Scorpions? *The Rebels?*

It didn't matter. This was a rescue mission.

They gathered on the bridge again to monitor their mine-laying efforts. Three of the mines attached themselves to their targets. Needles of piercing light radiated outwards as the mines detonated, completely obliterating one of the transports and disabling two of the oncoming destroyers. One mine drifted off harmlessly and the fifth suffered a malfunction, allowing the second transport to continue unscathed.

"We still have one mine," Christian said.

"No, I want to keep that in reserve," Sigrid said. "I have something in mind for that one."

Now, all she needed to do was deal with a single company of CTF Marines and whatever they had down on the Scorpii base. *Piece of Cake.*

They neared the base just as the CTF forces began clashing with the Scorpii ships. The smaller task force put up an admirable fight, taking out eight of the CTF Naval ships, but their defenses were overwhelmed by the sheer weight and numbers of incoming ordnance thrown at them. Their smaller force was quickly obliterated.

Sigrid and her crew observed the surviving CTF ships wheeling away from the battle area, changing course and accelerating in their direction.

Karen's eyes went wide. "They're heading this way."

"Let's just make sure we're not here when they arrive," Sigrid said.

The *Morrigan* decelerated, pushing its maximum Gs as it slewed into orbit around the large asteroid. Christian kept close monitor over the station's defensive activity. With the programs Hitomi had provided them, Sigrid had masterfully hacked into their communications and they'd been monitoring the chatter coming from the station for some time.

The base still had a sizable defensive force of soldiers, who were bracing for the invasion that was certain to come.

The crew of the *Morrigan* held their collective breath as six large fighters launched from the base. But the fighters headed straight for the troop transport and its trailing escort ships; the *Morrigan's* stealth systems were doing their job.

"Take us in, Ms. Tseng," Sigrid said. She pointed to a spot on the navigational map, two kilometers north of the base. "Put us down there, just on the other side of that ridge." She hoped that would keep her ship hidden from prying eyes.

"Aye, ma'am."

While Selene directed the landing, Sigrid made for the airlock, gathering her weapons and pulling on the EVA gear she'd need to make it across the surface of the asteroid to the base. She looked up in surprise as Karen squeezed in next to her and started gearing herself up.

"Just what do you think you're doing?" Sigrid asked.

"If you think I'm letting you go in there alone, you're crazy."

The girl's sentiment was sweet, but Sigrid knew she'd only slow her down. "Karen, I want you to stay here."

Karen stood up straight, clipping the ammunitions belt around her waist. "I'm not just an Orientations Officer," she said, primly. "I've had full weapons training. I'm checked out on all of these." She held up one of the heavy assault rifles—upside down, Sigrid noted.

"Karen—"

"Don't argue," Karen said fiercely. "I'm helping you whether you like it or not."

Before she could muster her voice, Christian ran up, clutching similar gear.

"Not you too!" Sigrid said.

Christian grinned. "Of course…"

"No, you have to stay here with Selene. I need you at Tactical to monitor the station—troop movements, com-chatter, everything. If they detect us, I need you to let me know."

"But—"

"That's an *order*."

Christian nodded. "Very well. But you call us the moment you need extraction."

"That's the plan."

Sigrid fastened her helmet, gathering all the ordnance she could carry into a duffel, while Christian helped Karen into the rest of her gear. Christian heaved the bag up and handed it to Sigrid, who took it easily in one hand.

"Get the ship to a safe distance and stay on the comlink," Sigrid said. "We'll signal when we're ready."

"Aye, ma'am." Christian saluted and went about sealing the airlock after them.

Sigrid opened the outer airlock door as soon as the *Morrigan* shuddered down on the surface of the asteroid. She leapt out. There was no point in trying to walk across the surface. The gravity was so low it wouldn't take much for her to bounce off the terrain at escape velocity.

Karen floated down beside her, arms waving an unlikely flight pattern. Sigrid hooked a tether into the belt on Karen's suit. "Hang on!"

Using the maneuvering jets on the EVA thruster pack, Sigrid blasted toward the Scorpii mining facility; she heard Karen's tinny squeal over the comlink as the tether took hold and yanked her forward. Keeping low, she skimmed over the surface, taking care that Karen was trailing obediently behind her and not hitting the rocks that jutted out here and there.

The mining facility was buried deep in the rock of the asteroid. The only evidence of the facility was a large landing pad and an airlock used to deliver heavy machinery and ore from the bowels of the mines. Sigrid had another entrance in mind; a few light boosts later they arrived at the small access shaft Gene had told her about. She found the hatch to be just as Gene had described it; the grey metal door of the airlock, jutting out from a pile of dusty rocks.

"We're in," Sigrid said over her comlink. She pulled off her helmet, quickly stripping off the EVA gear before helping Karen out of hers. Within a minute, Sigrid was armed with her twin pistols, katana, a load-out of grenades and shuriken belted to her waist; Karen was furnished with a compact eSMG—light, easy to aim and capable of spitting out an incredible number of rounds per second. "Try not to shoot me with it," Sigrid said with a wink.

Sigrid keyed her comlink; if the girls were here, if she could reach them, she could locate them that much quicker. She called several times on all the channels, but only static hissed back. *Dammit.* She reminded herself that it didn't mean anything—*they were here. They had to be.*

A quick scan with her thermals showed the corridor beyond the airlock was clear and the two girls headed quickly out. The complex was massive, spanning nearly 20 square kilometers—there wasn't enough time to go searching blindly through the maze of twisting tunnels, not with the CTF invasion force closing in behind them. There was only one place large enough to house all the girls—Ore Processing. It was at the lowest level, deep beneath the surface. She could only hope the girls were there, and not scattered throughout the facility.

Up ahead, Sigrid sensed movement and signaled Karen to stop and move back. Three people were coming down the corridor toward them. Karen backed into the shadows around a corner. Sigrid shrouded.

Two people in civilian clothing approached; they were accompanied by a man in what looked like a military uniform, but it wasn't CTF or any of the Mercenary clan colors that Sigrid was familiar with. There would be time for questions later.

Sigrid drew her pistols, taking care to dial them to their *silenced* modes. She fired two quick shots, felling the soldier and one of the civilians. She grabbed the last woman from behind and covered her mouth.

Karen came out from her hiding place and stared at the two bodies. "You...you *killed them*..."

Sigrid ignored the remark as she dragged her captive back around the corner. "The girls—where are they?" she demanded.

The terrified woman shook her head. Sigrid jerked her neck back, tightening her grip. *"Where?"*

Slowly, Sigrid eased her hand away from the woman's mouth. "They're...they're in the habitat. Lower level. Tier 3."

Sigrid smacked her on the back of the head and eased the unconscious woman to the floor.

Karen, who had gathered her wits, was already struggling to drag the other two bodies into the dark passage. "I'm sorry. I...suppose I should have been expecting this." She took a deep breath. "That won't happen again."

Sigrid squeezed her arm. "It's all right. But I won't let them stop me."

"Of course. I know—I remember what they did on the *Elevator*...all those people. I'll do whatever it takes."

Moving smartly, the two girls padded down level after level without having to eliminate anyone else. Most of the people were gathered near the surface, preparing for the station's defense, with only the occasional group flitting through the lower parts. Sigrid checked her watch again. They had a little more than three hours before the CTF troop transport arrived, unless the station's defense systems managed to take care of them.

They avoided two more squads of patrolling soldiers before finally reaching the lowest level, which looked more like a storage facility for the habitat—just a narrow corridor lined with large lockers, by the looks of it. Sigrid spotted the three armed guards.

Karen gasped at the sight of the soldiers in their mechanized armor. "Oh-my-God..."

"Stay here."

Karen nodded vigorously, slinking back into the shadows as Sigrid shrouded herself again.

"I'm not sure I'll ever get used to that," Karen whispered.

The soldiers carried motion trackers—as soon as Sigrid entered the corridor they turned, searching, trying to locate her. In slow motion, Sigrid drew her pistols and selected the armor-piercing rounds. She focused on the weak spots in their armor: neck, joints, faceplates. One of them raised a hulking chain gun to his shoulder. Sigrid leapt forward, fast as light. She fired two shots, shattering the faceplate of one soldier; the second shot glanced harmlessly off the next as he turned, his composite armor deflecting the blast. He was still turning, still trying to track her. Drawing her katana, she charged at him full-on before diving and slicing his leg clean off below the knee. He fell backward—the slugs from his chain gun chattering up and ripping a pattern on the ceiling before his finger slackened on the trigger.

Sigrid leapt cat-like onto the chest of her last target. She let her momentum carry them both back. He stumbled, dropping his weapon as he fell backward onto the floor. Sigrid was quickly upon him and brought her sword straight down with all her strength, piercing the mirrored faceplate. His body shuddered under her as his arms clanged limply to the floor.

Sigrid stood and grabbed for the hilt of the katana, but the blade had penetrated deep into the floor. She tugged again, but the sword held fast. With her foot planted solidly on the soldier's metal breastplate, Sigrid heaved and twisted the blade free.

"*Uhchh...*" Karen said from behind as Sigrid wiped the gore from her blade.

"Sorry."

They hurried to open the lockers. Most of them held little more than supplies, then Karen called out as she opened one of the locked doors at the end. "Sigrid!"

Sigrid raced over; her heart pounding loudly as she entered the room. Huddled in the corner, disheveled, starved and filthy, with hands and feet bound, were Khepri and—

"Suko!" Sigrid screamed. She dropped the katana from her hands and threw herself at Suko, gathering her into her arms and placing kisses on her face and lips.

Karen carefully cut the bindings from Khepri's wrists and ankles, then set about liberating Suko. All three girls were weeping softly—even Karen joined in with a tearful wail of emotion.

"What took you so long?" Suko said, still trying to pay back all of Sigrid's sweet kisses.

Sigrid laughed. "You didn't exactly leave a forwarding address."

"I knew you'd come."

"I'll never leave you again. I promise." Sigrid said, wriggling out of Suko's warm, koala embrace with some reluctance.

Suko's eyes fell on Karen. "Who's this?"

"This is Ensign—er—Karen McTeer."

Suko's eyes narrowed at the girl somewhat suspiciously.

Sigrid swatted her on the shoulder. "She's a *friend.*"

"Ooh! I'm so pleased to meet you both," Karen chirped.

Sigrid shook herself out of her euphoria; she'd found Suko, but they were hardly out of trouble. "Where are the others? I tried to reach you on the comlink, but I couldn't. I feared the worst."

"They deactivated most of our implants," Suko said. "What they couldn't switch off..." she shivered, "...they removed. The others—"

"Mei, Petra and Leia are dead," Khepri said.

"Lei-Fei, Tara...?" Sigrid asked, fearful of what the answer might be.

"And Christi," Suko said. "They...did something to them. I saw what they did to Lei-Fei. They can access the Control Program. I don't know how, but they changed her."

"*Changed*—how?"

"They programmed them," Khepri spat.

Suko looked downcast. "There's more. Sigrid—my brother, he's here."

"Your brother?" Sigrid instantly recalled the message and the name—*Tansho.*

"He...he said *we* were the ones who were programmed. He said Kimura did it to us. He said they'd fix us."

"That's bullshit," Khepri said.

Sigrid frowned. She thought about Lady Hitomi. Despite her feelings toward Kimura, she trusted the woman; she *liked* Hitomi. She couldn't believe she would do such a thing. And Hitomi, she was like *them.* She'd helped her to escape and provided means to rescue Suko and the girls. She shook her head. "No way. I don't believe it."

"How can we be sure?"

"*I'm* sure." Sigrid helped Suko to her feet. "I can't explain now. We have to get out of here before the invasion force arrives. We need to find the young ones."

"*Invasion?*" Khepri asked.

"Later." Sigrid gathered the weapons from the fallen soldiers and handed them to Khepri and Suko.

"What about Lei-Fei and the others?" Suko asked. "We can't leave them."

"They're with *them* now," Khepri said. "The people who took us."

"We'll get the young ones first," Sigrid decided. "We'll get them to the ship. Then we'll see about the rest."

Following Sigrid's lead, the four of them sped off toward the ore-processing facility. Mercifully, their path took them further away from the operations center, where most of the activity was. Sigrid only had to take care of two patrols on the way. Suko and Khepri looked on in amazement as Sigrid shrouded herself and took out the first batch of guards.

"No *way.*" Suko said as Sigrid shimmered and reappeared before them.

"I didn't know we could do that!" Khepri said.

Sigrid winked. "I'll get you the program."

The processing room was a cavernous facility, filled with the massive earth-moving machines and separators that used to load the containers with their precious minerals. All the machinery lay in rusting heaps, some the victims of weapons' fire, others from decades of neglect. Looking down from a catwalk, high above, they spotted the forty-two girls gathered in an empty ore container. The huge container had been sandblasted clean and outfitted with bedding and portable toilet facilities. The young girls were assembled in a miserable huddle. A squad of soldiers guarded them; Sigrid was relieved that they wore regular fatigues rather than the composite armor the others had worn. Unfortunately, one of the giant *Mechs* patrolled nearby, manned and ready. It clanked back and forth, scanning the surrounding area.

Karen let out a breathless squeak.

"What the *hell* is that?" Sigrid asked

"They used those on Alcyone," Khepri said. "They took out the entire company of Marines."

"*I* bagged one," Suko said, mildly.

"How?" Sigrid was transfixed by the walking tank.

"Oh ye of little faith."

"Suko—"

"No worries. I got this one." Suko plucked one of the grenades from Sigrid's belt and rolled off the catwalk, sliding silently down one of the supporting pillars.

"*Suko!*" Sigrid hissed after her, but it was too late.

The girls watched anxiously as Suko crept along, flitting from cover to cover behind the huge piles of ore and lumps of decaying machinery. The whole time, Sigrid kept a watchful eye over the squad of soldiers. At least they looked bored, switched off, and unaware of the girl who was busy skirting around them as she crept ever closer to the walking tank.

Suko reached the last piece of cover, but there was still fifty meters of clear ground between her and the tank.

Khepri stiffened. "She's going to get herself killed."

"Stay here," Sigrid said to the other girls.

"Not you too!" Karen implored.

Sigrid winked. "I'll be right back."Sigrid engaged her shroud, rolled over the side and slid quietly down the cold metal pillar. She used her limited invisibility to venture closer to the squad of soldiers until she was safely behind the cover of the container.

Sigrid de-shrouded and breathed a deep sigh; the process was still terribly exhausting.

Sigrid could see Suko now; she lay hidden behind a hydraulic prop, but she wasn't yet close enough to the *Mech*—it would rip Suko apart if she made a run for it.

Sigrid keyed her comlink, cursing as she remembered that Suko's had been deactivated. But, she knew Suko; they'd trained so much together and she trusted her more than anything. Suko would understand her signal.

Sigrid plucked three grenades from her belt, braced to roll out from her cover when a voice from behind stopped her.

"I know you!" the girl's voice called.

Sigrid spun, completely stunned. Behind her stood an eleven-year-old girl. Two more of them were scrambling over the wall of the container. *How the hell were they getting out...?*

"Look! It's her!" another girl called.

Sigrid cringed and shot a finger up to her lips. "*Shhh!*"

But the damage had been done. The soldiers had heard the commotion and were heading quickly toward her position—and so was the *Mech*.

"Get back!" Sigrid yelled as she rolled the grenades toward the oncoming soldiers. She dived, shielding the girls from the explosions and falling debris and the burst of gunfire that erupted behind her. More gunfire came from above. Sigrid looked up to see Karen and Khepri firing at the fleeing soldiers. The *Mech* had also spotted them.

"Oh, shit..." Sigrid said. With her pistol in one hand, Sigrid threw three more smoke grenades out followed by a series of flashbangs. Thick black smoke swirled around them as the shockwaves of the flashbangs echoed around the facility. All hell was breaking loose—and more of the girls were scrambling out of the container.

How on earth...?

Only three of the soldiers were still alive. Sigrid picked them up with her thermal optics and targeted them through the smoke. Three *shuriken* spun in swift succession from her fingers. The soldiers fell dead to the ground. The fight wasn't over yet; the chunking of a chain gun sent her diving to ground. There was a deafening explosion followed by the protests of groaning metal and a series of loud bangs. And then it went quiet.

Sigrid was still holding her breath when the smoke finally started to clear. She had to laugh at the sight before her—Suko, standing on top of the wrecked hulk of the *Mech*, one hand on her hip, the other holding the gun Sigrid had given her.

"That's *two*," Suko said.

A rousing cheer ensued; the young escapees stampeded past Sigrid and crowded around the valiant Suko. Khepri received a similar greeting when she climbed down from the catwalk. They'd obviously bonded in their short time together at the Academy. Even Karen was mobbed by the excited girls.

Sigrid heaved open the heavy metal door of the container; there were still over twenty girls inside. Sigrid had to appreciate how they'd built a teetering pyramid using their bedding and three porta potties to effect their escape.

The girls gathered quickly around, shouting questions at her—was Sigrid there to save them and take them home?

She raised her hands and the girls fell silent. "I'm getting you *all* out of here. But you're going to have to do *exactly* what I say—*when* I say it. Do you understand?" To a girl, each nodded in affirmative silence. Sigrid smiled. "Good. I have a ship—it's going to be a little crowded." Sigrid scratched her head, wondering if she could actually get them all aboard. "But we're all getting out of here now."

"You've become very *masterful* since you've been gone," Suko teased, coming up behind her.

"Sorry—it's just that we don't have much time."

Suko gave her a light kiss on the cheek. "No worries. I *like* it."

* * *

Nicola Kirk slumped over the desk in the monitoring station. The defense force assigned to her was gone. Twelve ships and their crews...

The CTF troop carrier would be there soon, carrying an entire battalion of soldiers. And what did she have left? Less than half of a company for defense against so many. She had two transport shuttles in the loading bay—not enough to evacuate everyone.

She pounded her fist on the desk. And where the fuck was Tansho? The man was always disappearing. "Has anyone seen Riku?"

No one answered her. Seemed they didn't even want to look at her.

Fuck. He was gone. She knew it. If he took that girl with him...

But she had even bigger problems.

Nicola could sense the latent panic. Things had spiraled out of control—long ago, long before the CTF had found them and ambushed their forces. Her forces were devastated. Riku was gone. And so was *he*. They'd all abandoned her. A cynical laugh escaped from her.

"Ma'am?" the major asked.

Nicola shook her head and composed herself. There was only one reasonable course of action, but she wasn't sure how it would be received. "I need you to gather the girls and get them to the shuttles."

"Uh...ma'am?"

"They're the reason this facility exists, Major. We have to get them out, or all this...all this has been for nothing."

The major shifted uneasily. "Uh...I'm not sure that will go over well with the troops. They'll want a chance at those shuttles."

Did she have to ward off a mutiny as well? "Major—"

Nicola screamed as the shot ripped a ghastly exit wound in the major's face. He slumped to the floor looking as shocked as a dead man can.

Sara stood behind him with her gun still raised, and wearing her full suit of composite armor. "He was going to cause trouble."

Nicola gagged at the gore covering her chest and her arms. She could feel the beads of his blood on her lips.

Sara calmly re-holstered her sidearm. "We have a new problem, ma'am. We're under attack."

"I know we're under bloody attack. Don't be stupid."

Sara shook her head. "No. Not the CTF. It's *them*—the other girls from Alcyone. They're here. I suggest you get your people to the shuttles while there's still time. I'll take care of the girls."

Nicola nodded slowly. This girl—she was so strange. They all were. "Very well. I'll wait as long as I can. Just get them all. I'll get Farrington and that other doctor. We still need her."

Sara turned. "I'll be there. Just don't be late."

* * *

Sigrid led the girls back up the corridor, retracing their steps to the airlock. She would have thought it nearly impossible for forty-two girls to proceed up the corridor without causing a racket, but to their credit, they all kept remarkably silent. She'd already received word from Christian that the CTF troops were landing and entering the base through the main loading bay. The two crippled destroyers were trailing slightly behind, with the larger force still days away. But their little fracas in ore-processing had clearly raised the alarm.

"*Whatever you're doing, do it fast,*" Christian urged over the comlink.

"We're on our way back to the airlock, just be ready when we get there."

"*Aye, ma'am.*"

Sigrid heard a combination of screams and gunfire behind her. She desperately wanted to run back to investigate but she had to keep leading the girls forward; Suko and Khepri were back there. She had to trust them to handle whatever trouble had transpired.

Finally, they arrived at the airlock door where they'd come in. "We're here!" she said through her comlink. Christian acknowledged; he was already on his way. "Clear a path," Sigrid called to the girls, waving them against the wall. The girls did as they were told. Sigrid ran back to find out what had happened. The fight was already over. None of the young ones had been injured but Khepri was dragging Karen along while Suko kept watch.

Sigrid ran to her. "Karen!" Her chest was bloody and her face ashen, but her eyes were open—though not sparkling like they usually did.

"He got me," she said, sounding more surprised than hurt. But Sigrid could see that the wound was serious.

"Christian, we're going to need some medical assistance," she said over the comlink.

"Affirmative. We're already here—I've got Rodney fixing the emergency collar. But Sigrid..." Christian's pause made her nerves tingle. *"We can't keep the cloak up with the collar on. They'll know we're here."*

"I understand. We'll do this quickly." She looked down worriedly at Karen, and Khepri who was still tending to her. "Take care of her."

Turning, Sigrid ran back to the airlock. Through the window, she could see Rodney, clad in an environmental suit, working to affix the flexible collar to the outer door. She could also see her ship; *not good*. Everyone would know they were there. She drummed her fingers in time to the minutes dragging on as Rodney did what he did best; there was nothing Sigrid could do to speed up the process.

"Got it!" Rodney signaled.

Sigrid had the door open and was already hoisting the first of the girls into the short, flexible tube that extended to her ship. One by one, the girls scurried through the tunnel. Dragging Karen through was a bit more awkward, but Khepri took as much care as she could.

"Go on," Sigrid said to Suko, who was holding up the rear.

"What do you mean, *go on*?"

"The other girls—we can't just leave them. And...I made a promise. I have to find Dr. Garrett."

"Sigrid, they're not...*themselves* anymore. I saw what they did to Lei-Fei. You can't rescue them. They'll only try to kill you."

Sigrid's jaw tightened. "I have to try."

"All right, then I'm coming with you."

"Suko, you're hurt—half your implants are deactivated."

Suko sealed the airlock as she stepped clear. "And you're wasting time."

Sigrid sighed and keyed her comlink. "Christian...get the ship out of here."

"What? Sigrid, we're not leaving without you."

Sigrid couldn't contain her frustration. "Will everyone stop arguing with me! I'm not asking you to abandon me—just get the ship safe. I can't leave yet."

"Sigrid..." It was Selene's voice this time. *"That base is crawling with CTF troops. I—we just thought you should know."*

"Thanks. We'll be careful. And don't go too far. I'll want you on station when we're ready."

"We'll be there before you can sign off. Don't worry. And, Sigrid...good luck."

"What's that?" Suko asked, not having heard the exchange.

"We're going to have some more company."

Suko winked. "Brilliant."

Sigrid watched the collar retract as her ship blasted away from the asteroid's surface. She suddenly felt very, very alone. Suko grabbed her arm and gave it a squeeze. "Come on. We've got work to do."

"One sec," Sigrid said, bending and rummaging through the bag she'd brought; it still lay on the ground in the airlock. She pulled out the bulky weapon and slung it over her back.

"That's a little *inelegant*, don't you think?" Suko said, eyeing the hulking rocket launcher.

Sigrid laughed. "I also have a little something for you." She bent down and pulled an auto-loading-grenade launcher from the bag. She handed it to Suko. "I think the time for *quiet* has passed."

"No kidding."

With no one to slow them down, they made swift and silent headway toward the habitat—to the one place Suko had seen Dr. Garret: the Medical Facility. The deeper they went into the base, the more they could hear of the battle being waged—growing louder, ever closer.

"At least it's keeping them occupied," Suko said.

"For the moment."

The medical center was three levels below. The two girls leapt down the metal stairs as fast as they could. They burst through the doors, startling the three medical technicians cowering there. Sigrid's pistols were in her hands and two quick shots went into the legs of two of the men. The technicians howled in pain, falling to the floor. The last one, a woman, raised her hands and screamed.

"Dr. Garrett," Sigrid demanded. "Where is she?"

Terrified, the woman pointed; Sigrid grabbed her by the collar and pushed her to the front to lead the way. The frightened woman led them down two more corridors before she pointed again. "There! She should be there."

Sigrid clouted her on the back of the neck and eased her smoothly to the floor.

Suko looked at her with wide eyes. "You don't mess around, do you."

Sigrid snorted.

The door the woman had indicated was locked so Sigrid kicked it in rather than slowing to hack the electronic lock.

An astonished Dr. Garrett looked up at her rescue party. "Girls!" She ran to them, wrapping them in her arms.

Sigrid had only ever seen Dr. Garrett when perfectly put together; she was always neatly groomed and dressed. But the woman Sigrid saw before her was almost unrecognizable. They'd taken her clothes and dressed her in the same grey coveralls that they'd given to Suko and Khepri. Her hair was matted, and she looked exhausted and filthy.

"How did you find me? When did you get here?"

"Later," Sigrid said. "Dr. Garrett...Lei-Fei, Tara, Christi...we still need to find them."

Dr. Garrett grabbed Sigrid's arm. "I know where they are, but...Sigrid, I don't know if they...I'm not sure if we can save them."

"Why? What happened? Do you know what they did?" Sigrid asked.

"Yes, they..." Dr. Garrett studied the floor, ashamed. "They...*I*... altered their Control Program. I didn't want to...they made me. I was afraid if I didn't—I thought it would be worse."

"It's all right, Doctor."

Suko fixed her eyes on Dr. Garrett. "Sara said you did the same to us. Is it true?"

Dr. Garrett looked up. "What? No!"

"But it's possible, isn't it," Suko said. "You *could* program us."

Dr. Garrett nodded slowly. "It was part of the...contingency. It was a mistake. I'm sorry."

"We can discuss this later," Sigrid said, with some urgency. "Doctor, you have to take us to the girls. We have to try."

"Of course. Follow me—quickly."

Dr. Garrett led them through the twisting corridors to another room. This one held several beds, all of them hooked up to banks of monitors and computers. Suko recognized the room—the same one where she had been brought—but now it looked abandoned.

"They were here," Dr. Garrett said. "This is where they were treating them...It's where they worked on the girls. I saw—"

"Wait!" Suko said, and Sigrid saw it too—the one bed, in the far corner held a shape, almost hidden under the sheet draped over it.

Sigrid pulled back the covering. It was Tara. Her eyes were closed and there was no color in her face. She was dead.

"Bastards!" Dr. Garrett cried. "I warned them. I told them, but they wouldn't listen."

Sigrid squeezed her shoulder. "Come on. We still need to find the others."

She nodded, steadying herself. "Of course. They must be in the programming facility. Come, I'll take you there."

Dr. Garrett hurried out into the hall just as Sigrid's sensors exploded in alarm.

"Wait, Doctor!"

Dr. Garrett looked back over her shoulder. Sigrid grabbed her arm, pulling her back from the hall just as she felt the concussive surge of a blast. The ground exploded before them, sending them all flying backwards. Sigrid hit the wall hard, shielding her face from the falling debris. Suko landed on top of her—both girls coughed, wiping at their stinging eyes.

Dr. Garrett lay beside them, bloodied, but still, somehow, alive. "I'm okay," she assured them.

Sigrid and Suko were both on their feet, grabbing up their dropped weapons. Sigrid's scanners showed a platoon of fifteen soldiers moving toward them down the hall. She signaled to Suko, indicating the number and direction. Suko nodded, hefting the grenade launcher. She fired three times, bouncing the little grenades off the wall and out into the corridor. In an instant it was awash with searing flame and falling debris and charred body parts.

Sigrid launched herself into the fray, charging into the corridor. Even through the smoke, her targets were displayed and locked in her HUD. Sigrid fired quickly, shot after shot from her pistols, never stopping, always moving. Her programming functioned optimally, anticipating and logging each threat, reacting before any threat could be brought to bear on her. Ducking, rolling and diving, she came up in the midst of the surviving soldiers and drew the katana. In her hands, it became a spinning whirlwind of death. The cries of the dying gave way to silence, and as the smoke cleared, Sigrid counted the bodies of the fallen CTF soldiers at her feet. All accounted for.

Dr. Garrett was still reeling from the concussive effects of the blast; she let Suko help her along.

"You're shot!" Suko cried as they approached.

Sigrid looked down and saw the wounds; her leg had a deep gash where it had been grazed by a bullet. There was a long, bloody tear below her breast in the fabric of her outfit. Another bullet had penetrated her forearm, passing clean through. She could already feel the nano-swarms moving to repair the damage, even shielding her from the pain.

Suko steadied her, trembling as she scanned Sigrid for further injuries.

"I'm all right," Sigrid assured her. "I'll be okay."

Their brief respite was broken by the sounds of more troops heading toward them—many more.

"We're not getting out that way," Sigrid said.

There had to be another option. Wehr had given her as much information as he was able, but they were hardly detailed schematics.

"Back," Sigrid said, gesturing to the stairwell at the other end of the corridor.

Suko frowned. "Back?"

"We need to head down. We'll go through the mines."

"Whatever you say, boss."

The two girls hoisted Dr. Garrett off the ground and set off at a searing pace. Down the levels they went, back to the depths of the mining facility, slowing only when Sigrid was sure there was no more sign of pursuit. They found themselves in one of the many access tunnels that led even further into the belly of the asteroid. Ahead, it was completely black, the tunnel having long been vacated by the miners.

"I think we lost them," Sigrid said.

"Well, yeah! That's because there's no way out this way."

Switching to her night-vision, Sigrid scanned the blackness ahead. It was cold, empty and creepy. "There's got to be a way out. A ventilation or maintenance shaft, or *something*."

"How's that?" Suko asked.

"Because there's still air. It has to lead somewhere."

"Yes. It leads *down*."

Sigrid shrugged and chuckled. "It's an asteroid—if we go down long enough, we'll eventually be going up."

* * *

Selene looked over her shoulder as Christian came into the bridge. "How is it back there?"

"Crowded," Christian said, settling into his seat. "Karen's hurt, but I think she'll be okay."

Rodney's voice came over the com. *"Hey, guys. I think we have a problem."*

Selene hit the com. "What is it, Rodney?"

"Uh...it's this whole stealth thingy..."

"I believe that's the technical term," Christian muttered.

"Uh—I don't think it was ever meant to be used this long."

"What's the problem?" Selene asked.

"I think..."

"Rodney!" Selene said, in earnest. "Get to the point."

"I think it just broke."

* * *

Sigrid jumped, startled, as she heard her comlink buzz for her attention. Someone from the *Morrigan* was trying to get through, but the signal was weak, blocked by hundreds of meters of rock.

"Christian?"

"Sigrid..." She could hardly hear his voice. *"We have a problem. We've lost the stealth field. Rodney's trying to fix it, but*

he says it's fried. We've put the asteroid between us and those CTF destroyers, but...."

Shit. There was nothing her small ship could do against a pair of destroyers—even a crippled one. And the remainder of the task force would be arriving soon. "Get clear, Christian. Get the girls through the Relay."

"No way—not going to happen."

"Christian—stop arguing with me. There's nothing more you can do. Just get yourselves to safety."

"What about you?" Selene demanded.

Indeed, Sigrid wondered. "You worry about the ship. I'll worry about us."

Seconds went by, and all Sigrid heard was static, and then she heard Christian's glum voice, *"Aye, ma'am. Good luck."*

Suko leaned close, whispering in her ear. "I guess we just lost our transportation."

"We'll find a way," Sigrid said—with more conviction than she felt.

There was still the matter of finding their way out of the mines. Sigrid started ahead, leading both of them by the hand. Suko's optics had been disabled, so neither she nor Dr. Garrett could see anything in the pitch blackness of the mine. They walked in silence for close to ten minutes; even Sigrid was starting to question her choice of direction. She had to find a way out and find it soon. *Please.*

Sigrid was still scanning ahead, searching through the darkness for a way out when she sensed something. She came to a sudden stop, squeezing Suko's hand. Neither woman made a sound. Sigrid was sure she'd seen something...

Very quietly, she helped Dr. Garrett and Suko to the side of the shaft. The rocky walls were jagged and uneven, providing plenty of cover for them—but also for whoever lurked further ahead.

"What is it?" Suko whispered.

"Trouble. Stay here."

Sigrid eased ahead, keeping close to the wall, searching through the darkness. She couldn't see anything, but the hairs on her neck bristled. She nearly leapt out of her boots when she felt Suko's hand on her shoulder.

286

"What are you *doing?*" Sigrid asked.

"Helping you."

Sigrid sighed—there was no point in arguing with her. "There's something up ahead. At least, I could have sworn…"

"I felt it too. I guess it's good news in a way."

"How's *that* good news?"

"Well, if they're here, then there really must be another way out—or in. You know what I mean."

"I see your point."

They crept further along the sloping tunnel, but Sigrid couldn't scan anything. She was starting to wonder if she'd imagined it.

"Close your eyes," Sigrid said, taking a flashbang from her belt. She rolled the grenade forward; the pebble-sized grenade bounced along the floor of the tunnel. Sigrid shielded her eyes as the grenade went off. A combination of the flashes, squeals and smoke pervaded the darkness—Lei-Fei, Christi and *Sara,* stumbled out from their cover, eyes still full of green neon from the burning flare of the flashbang. Sigrid's guns were in her hands, but she hesitated. She hadn't come all this way to *kill* them.

"Sara!" Sigrid called. "I have a ship. I can get us all out of here."

Sara's reply was a torrent of bullets unleashed in their direction, but Sigrid had already dragged Suko into the cover of the rocky outcroppings along the wall.

"I heard your little conversation. You just sent your ship away. You're trapped."

"So are you," Sigrid countered. "Those Federation troops aren't here to rescue you."

"I'm not worried about them. They're far more afraid of us, trust me. Don't fight me, Sigrid. We're on the same side."

"So what about Mei, Leia and Petra?" Suko called out. "We saw what they did to Tara. Are you on their side as well? They're too dead to care, of course."

"They're dead because Dr. Garrett wouldn't help them," Sara called out, louder. "Isn't that right, Doctor? You could have saved them."

Dr. Garrett came out from her cover and felt her way forward. "It's not that simple, Sara. I warned them of the dangers."

"But you didn't warn us."

"No…we didn't. I'm sorry for that."

Sigrid could feel the regret thrumming in Dr. Garrett's voice.

"Too late, Doctor."

"Let us go," Sigrid said. "Better still, come with us. We can get out of here together."

Sigrid endured the uneasy silence until Sara said, "All right—throw out your weapons first. No tricks."

Sigrid began unfastening her holster; she felt Suko's hand grab her arm.

"*No!* Sigrid…it's a trick. She's lying. Please don't…"

Sigrid hesitated, but she patted Suko's hand. "It's okay."

She tossed the belt with her pistols out onto the floor of the shaft, slowly emerging with her hands out wide. With her optics, she could easily see the three girls up ahead of her, about twenty meters down the tunnel; Sara, in the powered-armor, with Lei-Fei and Christi flanking her. They held weapons, raised and aimed at her, but the faces of the two girls were set blank and lifeless. And their vital signs seemed oddly low.

"Suko too," Sara said.

"No," Sigrid said, motioning Suko back into cover. "'Together' was the deal. We'll not go as prisoners."

"If we're getting out of here, we're going to need weapons," Sara said.

"Yes—but not aimed at us."

"All right!" Annoyed, Sara lowered her weapon. "Now tell Suko to come out where we can see her—and Dr. Garrett."

"What about them?" Sigrid asked, looking at Lei-Fei and Christi, who still had their weapons raised.

"Them?" Sara laughed. "They'll do whatever I tell them."

"Then *tell* them."

Sara seemed to consider this, and finally nodded. "Stand down. Don't fire on them."

Sigrid held her ground. "Now, tell them they're not to harm us."

Sara looked to the two girls at her side. "You are not to attack them. You hear me?"

Lei-Fei and Christi obediently lowered their rifles.

"Now let's go," Sara said.

"Wait," Sigrid said. "I have your word? You won't harm us or try to turn us over?"

Sara sighed impatiently. "Yes. *I promise.* We won't try anything. Satisfied?"

"Very," Sigrid said.

Without warning, Sigrid launched herself at Sara, who grunted in surprise and brought her gun up, but Sigrid was already diving out of the way. Her hands reached into her boots, drawing a pair of knives as she rolled to her feet; the deadly blades blurring in rotation as they rushed to greet Sara.

Sara ducked the throws easily, but was thrown off her aim and her shots went high.

Sigrid dived on her, tackled her, pounded her face with angry fists.

Sara grabbed her; her already genetically modified strength was magnified by the powered-armor she wore. She threw Sigrid off easily, roaring with rage as she grabbed for her rifle. She leapt on top of Sigrid and pinned her to the ground, pressing the muzzle of the rifle up against her neck.

"You crazy fucking bitch! I told you I wasn't going to hurt you."

Sigrid fought for breath under the crushing weight of the girl's armor. She stared up at her; the familiar glow of hatred had returned to her hawk-like eyes.

"You *lied.*"

Sigrid had monitored their conversation closely. She knew Sara had no intention of cooperating with them. None of that mattered now. She could see Sara's knuckle, white, on the trigger of her rifle. Sigrid had gambled and lost.

Sara's eyes flared. "I should have killed you in the CTF Tower. I should have killed you on Alcyone. I always hated you, you stupid little bitch."

"I told you to leave her alone," Suko said from somewhere in the shadows.

Sara looked up in surprise.

A shot rang out. Sara's head jerked back, blood poured from the hole in her forehead as she slumped on top of her. Sigrid groaned under the dead weight of the girl in her armor.

It took all of her strength, and Suko's, to roll Sara off her.

"She always was a lying bitch," Suko said, helping Sigrid up.

Sigrid studied her in the dark. "I didn't think you could see anything."

"I can't—I just followed her voice."

"You might have hit me!"

Suko feigned a hurt expression. "Never. Now come on."

Sigrid grabbed a flare from Sara's belt and lit it. Lei-Fei and Christi still stood there silently.

Suko reached out a cautious hand and touched Christi; the girls were like cold, stone statues. "Are they going to be all right? I mean, you don't think they'll attack us, do you?"

"I don't know. They seem to be obeying Sara's orders."

"Let's just hope they obey ours."

Sigrid nodded.

They quickly gathered their weapons up and retrieved Dr. Garrett. Mercifully, Lei-Fei and Christi seemed just as willing to follow their orders in place of Sara's, but Sigrid took the precaution of removing their weapons from them—just in case.

They found the maintenance shaft Sara had used, and proceeded to haul Dr. Garrett up the 300 meter length of it until they reached the top. The sounds of battle raged louder here. The sound of death; the CTF soldiers were already mopping-up the remainder of the routed Scorpii forces.

"The hangar should be this way," Sigrid said, leading them cautiously down another corridor.

There was a monitoring station just above the hangar, occupied by a squad of Marines; Suko made quick work of them with one of the tiny gas grenades, plucked from the seam of Sigrid's bra. Two large windows gave a clear view of the loading bay below. It was bristling with CTF troops. Evidence of the fierce battle was strewn everywhere—the destroyed, burning hulks of *Mechs* and bodies, scattered, twisted, over the floor of the bay.

The shuttles were gone, but the bay was full of the CTF Naval drop ships used to ferry the soldiers back and forth from the carrier.

"Now what?" Suko asked.

"We take one of those," Sigrid said. "That one." She pointed to the drop ship nearest to the hangar doors.

"I'll take the one next to it," Suko said.

"What?"

Suko shrugged. "Why just steal one when you can steal two for the same price?"

"All right, but let me go first. You take the others—I'll get the guards attention."

"You? Why do you get the dangerous assignment?"

"Because, I can do this, silly." Sigrid winked and shrouded herself, disappearing from view.

"When we get out of here, you're showing me how to do that."

"I promise," Sigrid said, delivering a moist kiss to Suko's lips.

Suko wriggled from Sigrid's invisible embrace. "Now, that's just weird."

Sigrid snorted and lowered herself from the open window. She padded silently toward the waiting drop ship. The soldiers were mostly concentrating on the main entrance to the mining facility, but even the soldiers facing her failed to notice as she slipped by them and climbed carefully into the small ship.

She took quick stock of the craft and its controls. The ship wasn't much different from the *Kingfishers* they'd used on Alcyone. Sigrid hoped the controls were similar—she couldn't find any of the specs for the craft in her database.

"Here goes nothing," Sigrid muttered as she eased the power up, lifting the craft off the ground.

The alarms shrieked out a hooting cacophony, and all around her she could see the CTF soldiers running toward her, raising their weapons.

"Uh-oh," Sigrid said. She blasted upward, bouncing into the ceiling-netting. "Whoops!" The controls were extremely sensitive. She throttled back, and promptly crashed back down to the floor. Soldiers and personnel dived out of the way, pointing and screaming up at her. "Sorry!" Sigrid called out.

More troops were pouring in through the main entrance; Sigrid wheeled the ship hard about, releasing the safeties on the missile pods mounted on the ship's side. She hit the trigger and watched four missiles arc out. The explosions ripped through the doors and into the corridor beyond, sending men and machinery flying in every direction. Switching to the chain gun mounted in the nose, Sigrid spun the ship in a circle, spraying the ground around her with a chattering burst of fire.

All the attention was focused on her. No one saw the four women at the far end running for the other drop ship. Once they were in, Sigrid aimed her ship at the hangar doors and unleashed another barrage of missiles. The high-yield warheads ripped the metal doors apart, the rush of escaping atmosphere whisking away what was left of them. It took all the drop ship's power to keep it from sailing out of the bay, out of control, but Sigrid's frantic adjustments held the craft in place. Once the turbulence had abated, she pushed the power forward, easing the craft out through the narrow opening, and out into space.

Sigrid slipped her headset on. "You with me?"

"*I-firmative,*" Suko responded.

Sigrid breathed a sigh.

Now what? They were free of the base, but the drop ships were only designed for short hops. They'd never make it to the Relay, let alone have the power to push through it. At each stage, Sigrid had been thinking on her feet, moving from one obstacle to the next, but this one was different. *How could she break the intrinsic laws of physics?*

The answer lay ahead of her. Sigrid set a course toward the hulking troop carrier before her, still in orbit around the asteroid.

"*Uh, Sigrid...*" Suko's voice crackled over the com. "*You're going toward that? Shouldn't we be going away?*"

"I have an idea," Sigrid said. She pushed forward on the power, accelerating to maximum.

The commander of the carrier had different ideas; the giant ship opened up with all its armaments, firing wildly at her small drop ship.

"Maybe that wasn't such a good idea," she said, arcing her ship over, and out of the larger ship's weapons range. She had hoped to get much closer to the carrier, maybe even get aboard before they'd realized who was piloting the craft. But clearly, someone aboard the carrier was far more diligent in their duties than she'd expected.

"*They're launching fighters!*" Suko warned her.

"Shit." Her slow moving transport was no match for even one of them, and by her calculations they'd be on her in a matter of minutes. "Get clear, Suko. Run."

Sigrid rolled her ship over on its axis and accelerated toward the oncoming fighters.

"*Sigrid! Don't you dare.*"

Sigrid quickly calculated the trajectories of the fighters, pushing her craft forward onto a collision course with the lead ship. She swept an arc across all their paths with the chain gun in the nose of the ship. It was desperate, but she knew the small slugs were still capable of holing the fighters—*if* she scored several lucky hits, *if* they failed to maneuver out of the path of her desperate attack.

With so many 'ifs' she wasn't expecting them to explode—which was what each of them did, in quick succession.

"What the…?"

The proximity alarm bleated a warning on the control console; Sigrid jerked the controls hard over, narrowly avoiding a collision with a ship that clipped across her path in a blur.

It was the *Morrigan.*

Sigrid heard Selene's voice over her comlink. "*Just what kind of crazy stunt were you trying to pull?*"

"Erm…well…" Sigrid replied, too stunned and elated to expand further.

"*Get yourself clear, missy,*" Selene chided.

"Yes, ma'am!" Sigrid said, doing exactly that.

She watched on her screen as the *Morrigan* swung around in an easy curve toward the CTF troop transport. The bulky ship was firing all its thrusters, desperately trying to maneuver, but it was too big, too slow, built for hauling and not combat. The *Morrigan* raked it stem to stern with tens of thousands of rounds from its twin rail-guns and a full spread of torpedoes.

Burning chunks of the carrier broke off amid several explosions as the ship started venting atmosphere from its compartments. The *coup de gras* was delivered as the rail guns reached the stern of the ship and tore apart the main engines. One moment Sigrid was looking at a ship, the next it became a grenade of debris and wreckage exploding outward; she was forced to employ some fancy maneuvering to avoid the hail of shrapnel.

"Thanks, Selene," Sigrid said, blowing a deep sigh.

"Our pleasure—Stay there. We'll swing back around and pick you up."

Within minutes, both drop ships had docked and transferred to the *Morrigan*. Sigrid stared in amazement at the interior of her ship; it was so incredibly crowded. Every centimeter was jam-packed with the young girls from Alcyone, along with her crew and friends. Sigrid weaved quickly and carefully through the swell of bodies as she made her way to the bridge.

Suko was already there—waiting. She swept Sigrid into her arms, smothering her with a long, deep kiss. "Don't you ever try that again."

"Never. I promise."

"Glad to have you back in one piece," Selene said over her shoulder.

"What's the status?"

"Other than the stealth system, we're fully functional and clear to maneuver. I've got us on a wide trajectory back to the Warp Relay. That should keep us clear of those destroyers."

"What about the other ships?" Sigrid asked.

Selene shook her head. "They're moving to cut us off, but they're still too far out. They committed all their ships to the attack on the Scorpii forces. I don't think they were expecting us to be in the mix."

"Well, that's something, I suppose. Very well. Take us to the Relay." Sigrid leaned over her and keyed a series of numbers into the navigational array. "I want you to warp to these coordinates."

Selene studied the numbers and frowned at Sigrid. "Uh—begging your pardon, but those...those don't go anywhere."

Suko squeezed her arm. "Sigrid?"

"There's no Relay listed in the database there," Selene explained. "If we go there, if there's no Relay, there's no way back."

Sigrid felt the familiar doubt growing inside her again. *Would Hitomi lie? Is this why she left—to trap them?* No. She couldn't believe that. Whatever Sigrid thought of Kimura, she trusted Lady Hitomi. She was one of them.

"That's the heading, Ms. Tseng. That's where we're going."

Selene let out a breath and shrugged. "Okie dokie."

Sigrid caught Suko's stare as she held her hand. "It's all right. I know what I'm doing."

She hoped.

It took three days for them to reach the Relay—more than enough time for doubt to creep further into Sigrid's thoughts. Where was Hitomi sending them? And what would they find on the other side?

Sigrid spent most of her time caring for the young girls. She warmed to the actions of Cherry and Honey, who took to caring for all the girls, making sure that each of them got enough to eat, even working a schedule so they could all make use of the ship's limited bathroom facilities.

As they closed on the Relay, there was little more to do than wait. The crippled CTF destroyers, ever present on their tail, were drifting further and further behind. When time allowed, Sigrid visited Karen in the cramped infirmary; she was recuperating well, and in good spirits. In engineering, Rodney and Christian continued to wrestle with Hitomi's stealth system, but neither of them were able to figure the thing out. As far as Rodney was concerned, the whole thing was voodoo.

Sigrid was having a rare moment to herself in the ship's head, when she felt someone pushing the door open.

"Occupied!" she cried, alarmed and covering herself. Her one-piece outfit was down around her ankles—it clearly hadn't been designed with latrines in mind, she thought. The door pushed open and Suko slipped in.

Sigrid laughed her relief. "I thought it was one of the little ones again. They certainly ask a lot of questions."

Suko closed the door and grinned. "Bloody ankle-biters."

Sigrid flushed the loo and stood up, struggling to pull her suit up in the cramped space of the head. Her eyes fell on Suko; she'd forgone the grey coverall and now wore a pair of Sigrid's shorts and a T-Shirt. The shirt was clearly too small, leaving a portion of her midriff exposed, and the shorts, were a little snug; Sigrid couldn't help but admire how the outfit highlighted her long, slender form in a much more flattering fashion than the awful prison garb had.

Suko's hands fell self-consciously over the clingy clothes. "They're a little tight, I know."

Sigrid winked. "I hope that's not a knock at my size."

"Not at all. I'm quite fond of your *sizes*."

Sigrid tilted her head up, standing slightly on her toes, putting her face close to Suko's. "You know, I've been wondering how to get you alone, all this time. I never considered *the head*."

"Well, don't get any ideas now. I only came in to tell you they need you on the bridge."

Sigrid ignored her, pressing up against her and kissing her with such a passion that it took them both by surprise.

But when Sigrid's hands slid under her shirt, Suko pulled back, taking a deep breath. "Wow. I…can't believe I'm saying this…but they *really* do need you."

Sigrid straightened, surprised. "What—really?"

Suko pointed at the door. "Selene says we're almost at the Relay. You better get up there." She laughed. "Sorry."

Sigrid zipped her suit up the rest of the way and quickly straightened her hair. "Oh, you are *seriously* trying to get me in trouble."

"Me! I only came in to deliver the news. You know what they say—don't kiss the messenger."

"I think that's *kill*. We'll finish this later."

"I'll hold you to that."

Slipping as casually as possible out of the head, and carefully negotiating the girls sitting in the hall outside, Sigrid led Suko by the hand toward the bridge.

Selene and Christian looked over their shoulders as they came in.

"Glad you finally found her," Selene said with a smirk. "I was about to send the search party."

"Sorry," Sigrid said taking her seat in the command chair, with Suko at her side.

Selene had already sent the navigational commands to the Relay; Sigrid watched the towering halo-like structure as it turned on its axis, powering up and aligning itself.

"We're set," Selene said. "You sure about these coordinates?"

"I'm sure," Sigrid said; but her palms were sweaty, and she knew that Suko could feel the doubt in her. And there was one thing she needed to take care of—something she'd been thinking of since they'd left the base. "Lieutenant Lopez, do we still have any of those mines?"

Christian nodded. "Just the one."

"Very well. I want you to set it for a two-minute delay. I want you to launch it before we drop."

Christian swallowed and nodded. "Yes, ma'am."

Suko squeezed her hand, looked at her intently. "Sigrid? Are you sure about this?"

"I'm not letting any of them come after us. I'm through being hunted. Whatever they started—it ends here."

Selene chuckled. "Daedalus won't be very happy with you."

"They can send me a bill."

"Thirty-seconds to drop," Selene said.

Sigrid signaled to Christian and nodded. "Drop the mine, Lieutenant."

"Yes, ma'am."

They could hear the distant *thunk* of the mine dropping from the mounting rack in the stern. The ship was closing fast on the Relay, accelerating forward, making its final course corrections. They passed quickly through the warp field and the stars became needles of light; then came the familiar long, white flash, followed by the glittering of the stars as they coalesced again before them.

The huddle of observers gasped as they gazed through the viewport, craning their necks to look more closely. Warp jumps were always performed outside of stellar systems, both incoming and outgoing. The risk of even the slightest gravitational anomalies, or collisions with debris, let alone planetary bodies, was far too great to attempt within the confines of a solar system. But the *Morrigan* had emerged from warp space directly in the orbit of a massive gas giant surrounded by countless moons, several of them much larger than Earth. Sigrid knew it was a miracle that they hadn't suffered a collision, or been pulled off-course. And then she had a horrible thought—*perhaps they had.*

"Dear God," Selene said.

"Where the hell are we?" Christian asked.

Selene's hands flew over the navigational controls, scanning quickly for any indication of their location. "Pegasi—it's Pegasi."

"Uh-oh..." Christian said, peering closely at his own monitors. "There's...there's no Relay..."

Sigrid felt the knot in her stomach again. If there was no Relay...*why did Hitomi tell us to come here?* Frantically, Sigrid checked and double-checked the coordinates, but they were correct. They were exactly where Hitomi had told them go. *To go through all this...*

"I trusted her..."

Chapter 22
Medea

With no sign of a Warp Relay, Sigrid's focus shifted away from Hitomi and why she'd directed them there, to the simple matter of survival. They wouldn't survive for long on the small scout vessel. The environmental controls were already being pushed beyond their limits and soon the food stores would run out.

The Pegasi system held several earth-type planets, three of them in orbit around the gas-giant that loomed so close to them.

"This can't be a coincidence," Sigrid said. "Hitomi must have known we could survive here."

"Survive? But we're prisoners," Suko said, bleakness in her voice. "Is this just to get rid of us?"

"I don't know."

After studying the options, they picked the planet that promised to be the most hospitable. From what they could tell, it was a veritable paradise, lush and green, with a mild, temperate climate. It was largely covered in blue oceans, but there were several sizable islands dotting its surface.

"Incredible," Christian said. "I've...I've never seen anything like it."

Sigrid took a deep breath. "Take us in, Selene. I suppose we should go investigate. It appears this is our new home."

Selene nodded silently, angling the ship down and breaking through the wispy atmosphere.

Suko gave Sigrid's hand a squeeze as they cast their eyes over the blue oceans. "It'll be okay," she said, looking bravely at Sigrid.

"Where do you want to set down?" Selene asked.

"Anywhere—pick your favorite—pilot's discretion."

Selene chuckled and nodded. "How about somewhere hot? I think we could all use a nice relaxing vacation on a beach somewhere."

"Not too hot," Christian said. "I burn easily."

The easy banter relieved some of Sigrid's stress; she felt responsible for them all being trapped here. No, *she was* responsible.

Her mood lightened further when Karen joined them on the bridge, easing gingerly into one of the empty seats. "Where are we?" she asked.

Sigrid couldn't bring herself to answer.

Christian spoke up. "We're at Pegasi."

"Pegasi!" Karen said. "But there's no Relay at Pegasi." Karen looked at all of them, at the grim look on their faces. She sank back in her seat. "Oh."

"Uh…wait a minute," Selene said. "I think I found our island."

Sigrid sat up straighter. "Where?"

Selene swiveled around in her seat, eyes wide with excitement. "There!" she said, pointing out the window.

Sigrid leaned forward and stared at the sight before her. There, down below, on one of the larger islands, was a settlement of sorts. It was small—only a few buildings, but it was definitely a settlement. "There are people!"

"I *know!*" Selene exclaimed.

"Who—what?" Suko asked.

The com squawked for their attention, causing them all to jump. Christian leapt for the button to open the channel, but Sigrid beat him to it. "Hello?"

"Hello, yourself," Lady Hitomi Kimura said. "Welcome to Medea. What took you so long?"

Chapter 23
New Home

June 21, 2348

Lady Hitomi Kimura stared up into the sky at Medea's newest satellite. Construction on the new Warp Relay was nearly complete, and the 400 meter-wide structure could clearly be seen through the pair of binoculars she carried. She watched for a few minutes as the Daedalus crews began maneuvering the last of the sections into position before handing the binoculars back to the man at her side.

"Thank you, Joffrey," she said. "Just think. In a few more days, you'll be free of this place. Although I can't imagine why you'd be in such a rush to leave." Hitomi looked down the beach at the group of girls cavorting in the shallow surf, while others languished on the shore under the warm sun.

Joffrey grunted, not letting his eyes linger.

"Why, Joffrey, I do believe you're blushing."

"Perhaps you might arrange for some bathing costumes for the girls..."

Hitomi let out a sympathetic laugh at the man's discomfort. His name was Joffrey Deschamps, CEO of the Daedalus Corporation. Hitomi had always found him handsome, in a rather dashing sort of way. She didn't think he looked at all out of place in the paradisiacal setting, standing there, barefoot on the soft, sandy beach. She knew that he was not at all happy having to be there, but Hitomi hadn't given him much choice.

It had taken time, but she had finally repaired the message Sigrid had found, and the message had revealed a great deal. What they had found turned out not to be a letter, but a file detailing all of Daedalus' payments to the Dalair Mercenary Group. Daedalus had been behind the attempt on the *Agatsuma*.

They had forged the Permit for Seizure, and worse, they had taken bribes to divulge information on traffic through the relay system. It was an understatement to say that the Federated Corporations would not be at all pleased with Daedalus—should they find out.

No one would tolerate anything less than complete neutrality from Daedalus. Learning of their attempt against Kimura would be the excuse many corporations were looking for to finally move against the giant company and break its hold over the relay technology. Learning of the bribes and payoffs would be their undoing.

"This makes us even, you realize," Joffrey said, looking up in the direction of the Relay. "My debt to your father is repaid after this."

"Of course. But let us not forget our agreement..."

"Yes, yes—no one will know of this Relay. Not our Board, not the shareholders."

Hitomi looked up at him slyly. "No one *can ever* know, Joffrey. Unless you wish to see how widely and how quickly I can make copies of that file available. People would *not* be pleased with you."

"You have my *word*, Hitomi. No one will find out about the Pegasi Relay."

She patted his hand. "That's all I can ask."

"You know, I *could* have just left you here," he said with mock indignation.

"Ah, but that's why I insisted you come along. Now, let's enjoy this wonderful sunshine. I may even arrange to take a dip. Perhaps with your assistance..." Hitomi held her hand up to him.

* * *

Five of the young ones raced along the beach, leaping over Sigrid and Suko, who lay basking in the afternoon sun. All five girls cleared them easily, but kicked up a good amount of sand, spraying Sigrid for the most part.

"Hey!" Sigrid was still dripping wet from her swim and the sand stuck to her bare skin. "Oh, look, they got sand everywhere." Sigrid brushed the sand from her stomach and

302

thighs, aided a great deal more than was necessary by Suko, whose hands seemed to linger on various parts of Sigrid's exposed flesh.

Sigrid laughed. "Not here," she protested, but no one seemed to be taking any notice.

"Come on. Let's go wash that sand off."

Hand-in-hand, the two girls walked back toward the water.

After more than a month on Medea, Suko still claimed she was unable to swim, but Sigrid knew she was only pretending.

"No! You have to save me," she said, splashing Sigrid and diving into her arms. "See. I'm sinking." Suko kicked and splashed and Sigrid held her in her arms, floating easily in the salty water.

It had taken a while to adjust to life on Medea—strange to have to adjust to the idea that no one was trying to kill them—but the last month had been the most pleasant and peaceful of Sigrid's life. And no one seemed eager to leave once the new Relay was complete—not even Honey and Cherry. Sigrid had discovered their real names were Stefani and Katherine, and they were content to stay, at least for a while. They were further down the beach, the surf washing over their toes as they collected the little shells that washed up in the sand. Rodney was eagerly pointing out various aspects of the marine life to the two girls, who were rapt with fascination. Like most of them, Honey and Cherry had probably never even seen an ocean up close before.

"Hello!" Karen called from the beach, arms waving.

Both girls waved back and swam toward the shore. As they strolled back through the surf, another splashing group of girls ran giggling by.

"Oh my," Karen said, jumping out of the way. Always well-dressed, Karen had on a little bikini, in deep burnt-orange and red. It was daringly cut and very brief, but still she blushed at the sight of the two girls before her who wore nothing at all. "Why is it I suddenly feel a tad overdressed?"

Sigrid and Suko laughed.

Suko said, "Sorry. We didn't exactly get a chance to pack our togs."

Karen blinked back her confusion.

Sigrid translated for her. "She means our swimsuits."

"Oh...Well, when in Rome," Karen said. Steeling her nerves, she slipped out of her bathing suit, still feeling a little self-conscious. "Well—that's actually quite exhilarating!"

"We're just glad you're finally up and about," Suko said.

"Dr. Garrett worked wonders. Look, you can't even see where the bullets went in."

A loud rumbling emanated from somewhere above followed by a telltale sonic boom; a ship had just entered the atmosphere. Sigrid froze and her head jerked up, scanning the heavens for the source.

She felt Suko's hand tighten around her own. "They found us."

"They couldn't have," Karen said.

"No, wait. Look!" Sigrid pointed up at the ship as it feathered its way down, circling ever lower. Zooming in, she could see now that it was just a shuttle, definitely a mercenary vessel. She could clearly make out the markings of the Athena Corp. "That's one of Ms. Lawther's ships."

Sigrid grabbed both their hands and towed them quickly in the direction of the landing pads, stopping briefly to gather up their clothes.

"Gah!" Karen said, reaching for her discarded bathing suit, before hurrying after them.

They arrived in time to see the shuttle settling in on its landing struts. All the young ones from the beach had run up to witness the spectacle, even Hitomi and Joffrey had joined them on the rise. Sigrid was just pulling her shirt back on when the lower airlock opened and a very familiar redheaded girl leapt out.

"Leta!" Sigrid and Suko screamed, jumping forward and gathering her in a rib-crushing hug. "We've been so worried about you. Thank God you're okay." Leta looked sharp in her Mercenary Naval Cadet uniform.

"Us?" Leta said. "What about you! We all heard about Scorpii."

"We? Who's with you?" Suko asked.

"Why—all of us!"

Leta stepped out of the way, and sure enough, the rest of the girls from Alcyone began to emerge from the ship, each of them staring in wonder at the stretch of sandy beach and inviting waters, framed by swaying palms and tall grass.

"Holy..." one of them said, gaping, while the girl behind her shoved her along.

Marylyn Lawther stepped out of the airlock. "Marylyn!" Hitomi cried, wheeling herself forward and extending her hand to her friend.

She wore a ship's uniform in her clan's colors of red and gold. Sigrid noted the rank insignia of admiral on her collar. She also wore a large black sidearm on her hip. Sigrid expected she'd be quite capable of using it, as well. She was even more of a commanding presence than she'd been on Crucis.

Marylyn took Hitomi's hands in her own. "Hitomi. What a wonderful spot you've chosen."

"I've had my eye on it for some time. You remember Sigrid, of course."

"Sigrid, so nice to see you again."

Marylyn Lawther held out her hand to Sigrid who bowed deeply instead. "Lady Lawther."

Marylyn chuckled. "Oh, you and your manners."

"I can't thank you enough for this," Hitomi said. "I trust you didn't have too much trouble with the authorities."

"Oh, posh. We girls must stick together. And no, we intercepted the transport exactly where you said. I'd like to claim that I *rescued* them, but by the time we arrived your girls had the situation well in hand. I don't think those CTF soldiers knew what they were taking on. The only problem we had was trying to convince the girls we weren't there to harm them as well. Your girl here..." she said, nodding to Leta, "...proved invaluable. Without her I think they may very well have destroyed us! I'm just glad you decided to place some of them in our care at the Naval Academy."

"I knew you'd take good care of them."

"You should be very proud of them, Hitomi. The things I've seen...it's no wonder they've caused such a stir."

"I am proud. Very. I owe them my life," she said, looking directly at Sigrid. "Now, come. We have much to discuss. I've prepared a delicious dinner for all of us. I think you'll be quite pleased."

"Wonderful. I'm absolutely ravenous."

The two ladies headed off toward the larger of the two buildings that had been completed, while Sigrid led the others to their new quarters. Like the Annex, each of the girls would have their own accommodations; Hitomi was busy building a sprawling new complex to house all of them, with room for many, many more.

It was difficult to get them all settled. None of them would leave Sigrid's side, demanding to know what had happened on Alcyone and Scorpii.

Sigrid gave in. She gathered everyone in the large common room so she could tell them all at once instead of over and over again. They'd heard of the attacks, but knew very few of the details. Sigrid told them everything—all of them listened without saying a word, although there were several gasps when Sigrid told them of her encounter with Sara, and more when she described the destruction of the elevator over Panama and their narrow escape. All the while she spoke, Suko held her hand, especially when Sigrid described the rescue of her and Khepri and the new girls from Scorpii.

The girls were extremely angry to hear of Mei and the others who were killed in the attempts to reprogram them, even more so to find that Lei-Fei and Christi still suffered. Dr. Garrett was confident she could restore them, but it would take time. Dr. Farrington's work had been invasive and thorough, but also incredibly careless.

"We can't let this ever happen again," Leta said.

There was a murmuring of assent.

"But aren't we prisoners still?" another girl asked. "We're here—we may be safe—but will they ever let us leave?"

"Leave?" Khepri asked. "Where would we go? Anywhere we go they'll hunt us down and kill us. Or worse. I saw what they did to the others. That's not going to happen to me."

The girls started talking all at once, arguing over whether to stay or go, or whether they even had a choice in the matter.

Sigrid listened for a few minutes before raising her hands, asking for silence. "You're all free to go." A hush fell over the room at that. "You're also more than welcome to stay. You won't be safe on Earth, or anywhere else right now. But I promise, whatever you choose, it will be *your* choice. No one will tell you what you can or can't do anymore."

"What about school?" one of the younger ones asked. Her name was Lilith and she was nearly twelve. "Do we still have to study?"

Sigrid smiled. "Yes. You still need to keep to your studies. Now more than ever. But you're all free." Sigrid glanced at Suko who was still holding onto her hand. "This is my home now. I know I'm staying right here, and I hope you all will too."

Lilith looked up at her. "Can we really go home?"

"I can answer that."

The gathering of girls turned to see Lady Hitomi enter the room, accompanied by Marylyn Lawther.

"Medea was never meant to be a prison. I'd rather hoped you'd find it a haven, a sanctuary. You will always be welcome here, regardless of whether you chose to leave or stay. When the Relay is complete we will take any of you that wish to back to Earth. But Sigrid is correct in her estimation of the danger. If you leave here, you will be hunted, and I fear I will not be able to protect you."

"You will also be welcome on Crucis," Marylyn offered. "The Guild can offer some protection."

"I want to go home!" one girl called out, and there were more rumblings of the same vein.

Sigrid felt her heart sink—*what if they all left? What would happen to them?*

"I'll stay," Suko said.

"Me too," Leta said.

Khepri stepped forward. "Think about what you're saying. If you leave, what kind of life will you have? Go see Lei-Fei, see what they did to Christi. Then tell me you still want to leave. Sigrid saved my life. I say we stay."

"I'll stay," Lilith said, putting her hand in Sigrid's.

Sigrid gave it a little squeeze, feeling her spirits rise.

One of the girls in the back stood up. Her name was Una, and like Leta, she wore one of the Naval Cadet uniforms. "Sod it. I say we stay. What do we have to go back to anyway? We're with you, Sigrid!"

A cheer rose from their ranks, and Sigrid was nearly crushed under the surge as the animated young ones crowded around her.

Suko laughed. "I don't think any of the little ones will ever leave you."

Sigrid smiled and raised her hands. The girls grew silent again. "Some of you may change your minds when you find out what I have in mind. Alcyone is gone, and it won't be safe for any of us on Earth—not as long as there are men out there who want to dominate us…and girls *like us*."

"Like us?" Suko asked.

Sigrid nodded. "We know we're not the only ones. The Council knows it, and clearly others do as well. They failed trying to capture us, but now they know what to look for. It's only a matter of time before they look for the others like us. With your help, I plan to stop them. We'll need to be ready. We'll need to train. The young ones will need to be taught. And I'll need volunteers to help bring any girls we find back here."

Hitomi looked up at her, intrigued and very impressed.

"Forgive me, Mistress, I know I haven't discussed any of this with you."

"By all means, Sigrid. I think it's a marvelous idea. All my resources will be at your disposal, of course."

"Thank you, Mistress."

"And for the last time, call me Hitomi."

Sigrid laughed. "Yes, Hitomi."

* * *

"You've changed," Suko said. She lay sideways on their bed, covered only by the edge of one of the soft white sheets. The windows were open—they were always open, as no glassed enclosures seemed to be necessary on Medea. Even at night, the cooler temperatures were still quite comfortable.

Sigrid stood and stretched, then wandered to the window, where she breathed deep of the salty air and let the cool breeze caress her body. The light of three of Medea's sister-moons shone down, bathing her skin in a pale glow of light.

"Well, I don't feel very different. I see the girls and the way they look at me. I'm never sure what to say. I only know I don't want to let them down."

Suko laughed. "But don't you see—they *do* look to you. Even Hitomi. We all see how she listens to you."

"I never meant to tell anyone what to do."

"And you don't. You just say what needs to be said."

"It wasn't my intention to take charge."

"Sigrid, we trust you. You *lead* by example."

Suko rose from the bed and moved slowly to Sigrid, slipping her arms around her waist and holding her close. Her eyes were playful as she made a show of looking her up and down.

"What?" Sigrid asked, blushing.

"My new sensory modules must be out of sync—I was sure you'd grown taller."

"Oh!" Sigrid laughed and pinched the soft area of Suko's bottom.

"Hey!"

Sigrid leaned back against the low ledge, pulling Suko closer to her, absorbing the softness of her skin and the warmth of her body. "You shouldn't tease. I'm far too fragile right now." She tilted her head back, letting Suko's lips fall against hers, only coming up for air after a few minutes.

"They say the Relay will be done in days. Will you be leaving then?"

Sigrid nodded. "I have to. I'm not going to sit back wondering what the Council is up to. The next time someone moves against us I plan on knowing well in advance."

"See! You even think like a general."

"If I do, it's just the programming."

Suko shook her head. "If that were true, then we'd all be thinking the same thing. I think it's wonderful. I feel safe knowing you're looking out for us."

Suko leaned forward to kiss her again, but Sigrid pulled her head back and flashed a sly smile. "You do! Then who's looking out for me?"

"Who do you think? Now shut up and kiss me already."

"Now who's being commanding?"

Epilogue
Silver Linings

June 22, 2348

It had been a very good day.

Randal Gillings sat back in the comfortable chair behind his desk as he scanned the report his attaché had just brought to him. Outrage over the attack and destruction of the Panama Lift facility, combined with news of the apparent 'rebellion' on Scorpii, had fueled calls for increased defense spending. And with the loss of the thirty-six ships at Scorpii, those calls had been upgraded to demands for immediate action.

Coran Industries had personally signed a contract to deliver seventy-eight new front line ships, with options for hundreds more. His shareholders would be rich, and Coran stood to surpass even Daedalus as the single most powerful company in the Federation. His position as Chairman of the Council would not be challenged for decades to come. There would be a Draft to recruit new personnel for the CTF forces, and Coran's own workforce would also need to be increased tenfold. He was already being hailed as the architect for the *New Society* by the news readers. Of course, Coran had supplied the services with the appropriate copy to read.

Yes, it had been a very good day.

So why didn't he feel better? Gillings frowned and poured another whiskey from the decanter on his desk. He neglected to offer one to his attaché who sat before him. The man was efficient, but he was excessively timid, and Gillings wondered why he hadn't yet fired the man. *Relatives.*

He brooded again on why his mood was so foul. The answer was simple. *Andraste.* Those little girls had thwarted his latest attempt to appropriate Hitomi's technology. Twenty-one girls had been delivered personally by the Kimura Forces, and yet those girls had escaped. But not on their own—they had been aided.

Gillings stared hard at his attaché. "You're sure it was her—Lawther."

His aide squirmed uncomfortably. "I can't say if it was her personally, sir, but it seems they were definitely aided by the Mercenary Guild."

"Which clan?"

"Uh—all of them, sir."

"And you have no idea where they've gone?"

"No, sir. Daedalus has so far refused to divulge any information regarding their destination. We even offered double the usual amount of the bribes."

"*Compensation*," Gillings reminded him. "Bribes are illegal." He took another gulp of the whiskey and refilled the glass. That news was somewhat disturbing. It wasn't like Daedalus to refuse him information. He'd have to have words with Joffrey, and soon.

"Triple it. Quadruple it," Gillings said. "Someone in that blasted organization is bound to know something. I want to know where they've gone. And perhaps you should add some of this business with the Mercenary Guild to the news feeds. It might not be a bad idea to implicate them along with the Hekatians in this rebellion."

His attaché made a quick note on his pad. "Of course, sir. Might I say, early reports show the stories are playing very well with the public. Seventy-eight-percent of people polled are calling for a military strike on Hekate."

"Seventy-eight? Change it to ninety-two and run that story."

"Very good, sir. With those numbers, you might actually be able to persuade the Council to move against the Mercenary Guild now."

Gillings dismissed the idea. "No. Not just yet. With the losses on Scorpii, I'm afraid we'll still need to suffer the Mercenary clans, at least for the short term. We still need to retain them under contract to maintain order." He drained his glass. "Soon, though. Let's just deal with the news campaign first. We'll need full public support to move against the Guild."

Gillings' attaché bowed and headed immediately down the elevator to the parking level where his car was already waiting for him. The chauffeur held the door for him and he slipped inside. Unlike Gillings, the man who waited for him in the car *did* offer him a drink, and he took it, raising the glass politely.

"Thank you, Karl. Might I say, you're looking much better than the last time I saw you."

Karl Tarsus snorted a laugh, nodding to the man he'd only known as *Smith* until very recently. His real name, he now knew, was Harry Jones, Special Attaché to the Council Chair, and Personal Aide to Randal Gillings. He still didn't trust him, but the money and resources he could get his hands on were staggering. Tarsus still hadn't been able to trace the source, but it was *not* the Council or Coran Industries. More investigating would be required.

Thanks to Harry Jones, Karl Tarsus was now a man on the move—a new player in Mercenary Services. But he was operating as an *Independent* now. The Mercenary Guild would not take him back, but that was just as Mr. Jones wanted.

"Have you arranged for the new ships?" Jones asked.

"Crewed and ready." Tarsus took a case out from under his seat and opened it. "And I got your package—CTF Naval transponders. Not easy to get your hands on."

Both men knew that to be true. Tarsus held out one of the tiny devices in his hand; all CTF ships carried the transponders that would confirm their identity to other ships."

"Have them installed right away. I have your first target. Crucis Prime."

Tarsus closed the case and looked up. "Crucis! You can't be serious. Six ships against that facility...Perhaps with fifty ships..."

Harry Jones chuckled and poured two more glasses of whiskey. "Don't worry. We only need to poke the hornets' nest, not destroy it. I want you to get in, cause as much trouble as possible, and get out. Just make sure you've got *these* installed." He patted the case with the transponders. "I want every Mercenary on that station to know who attacked them."

"I don't suppose they'll be too happy with the Council."

"No, I don't suppose they will."

"This might actually galvanize the clans against them."

"I would imagine that's a possibility."

"They may even chose to move against the Council in force."

"I would be surprised if they didn't."

Tarsus studied him for a long while, then shook his head. "Harry Jones, you're an interesting man. I don't suppose you'd care to tell me the rest of your little game? What this is all about. Is it Power? Money? *Women?*"

"Why not all three?"

Tarsus's grin was bordering on leering. "Forgive me, but you don't seem the type—at least, not for such *mundane* pursuits. Now, do tell."

Harry Jones opened his mouth to answer, but then closed it and raised his glass instead. "To possibilities, Mr. Tarsus."

The End

<<<<>>>>

Visit Cary Caffrey at carycaffrey.com

Follow Cary on twitter @CaryCaffrey

Made in the USA
San Bernardino, CA
05 December 2013